Way to Go

By the same author

Stories
Its Colours They Are Fine
Stone Garden

Novel
The Magic Flute

Poetry
ah!
Glasgow Zen

Playscripts
Sailmaker
Space Invaders
Changed Days

Way to Go

Alan Spence

Phoenix House
LONDON

First published in Great Britain
in 1998 by Phoenix House

A CIP catalogue record for this book is available
from the British Library.

ISBN 1 897580 48 7 (cased)

Typeset at The Spartan Press Ltd
Lymington, Hants
Printed by Butler & Tanner Ltd,
Frome and London.

Phoenix House
The Orion Publishing Group Ltd
Orion House
5 Upper Saint Martin's Lane
London, WC2H 9EA

To the memory of

Charlotte Spence
(1920-1959)
and
Alexander Spence
(1915-1979)

Thanks

to Jim Patterson of West Linton and Audrey
Antoniuk of Leith for kindly talking to me
about the business.

to Ven Begamudre, Adarsha and Snatak
for some of the jokes.

1

I sat up in the coffin, reading a comic and eating a sherbet fountain. Bit the tip off the licorice, sucked the sherbet through it. Mix of the two tastes, that was the thing. The sticky sweet licorice, a dark taste, flat. Then the rush of sherbet, sharp and tart. Wersh. The word my father would use, screwing up his face.

Wersh. You could taste the word in your mouth.

My father had gone out to the pub, put me down here in the basement, among the coffins. Locked the door. Told me I had to learn. I was used to it now, the punishment. This time it was for losing my school cap.

You have to learn.

I had learned, not to cry. I had learned to plank a stash under a floorboard in the far corner, sweeties and comics, to keep me going.

And down here at least I liked the smells. Fresh wood and polish. The ground floor smelled too much of the business, flowers and air-freshener drowning out the harshness of chemicals, metallic, all of it covering up the sick sweet smell of death. And the first floor, where we lived, smelled too much of my father. Staleness of fags and booze, dull male-smell.

My father must have had a drink or two in the afternoon. Or three. A tipple. A snifter. A dram. A wee refreshment. The drink could tip him either way, turn him maudlin or mean. And no way of telling which it would be. This time it was mean.

You have to learn. Losing my stupid cap. Must have fallen out of my pocket, crossing the wasteground on the way home from school.

D'ye think these things grow on trees?

A whole orchard of them, specially cultivated, its branches weighed down with clusters of navy blue school caps.

No.

Right then.

I finished the sherbet, poured the last of it down my throat, chucked the empty tube over the side. I slid further down into

3

the coffin, got comfortable. I'd picked one that was finished, not just a bare box. A heavy oak job, big so I had space. The inside was padded, covered in shiny white satin. My stocking soles slipped when I tried to bring my knees up, so I kept my legs straight out. When I got tired sitting up, I slid right down and lay on my back, held the comic up above me. But after a while it made my arms ache and I let the comic drop. I'd read the whole thing anyway, was just flicking through it again, passing the time.

With a bit of luck my father might not be too late back. Might even be in a good mood, bring me something from the pub, bottle of lemonade, packet of crisps. Show some remorse for being mean. That was usually the way.

I shivered, beginning to feel the cold. Nights fair drawing in. Would need to stash a blanket down here, with all the rest of the stuff.

The sudden crash made me sit up. My father, at the front door upstairs. I climbed out of the coffin, jumped down from the bench it was resting on. Pulled on my sandshoes and tied the laces quick. Picked up the cardboard tube from the floor where I'd dropped it, its paper wrapper pale yellow with a chalky dusting of sherbet. Bent and crumpled it, stuffed it in my pocket. Put the comic back in its place.

The footsteps down the stairs. Key turning in the lock. He stood swaying in the doorway, a packet of crisps in one hand, bottle of American cream soda in the other.

'Ach son.'

Not too far gone. Slurred and muddled, but a kind of smug contentment in the eyes. What he called happy.

The one time he'd caught me actually slouched in the coffin, he'd skelped me on the side of the head, told me it was sacrilege, I had no respect. So now I made a point of being up on my feet, ready, facing the door when my father came in.

'Here, Neil.' Arms outstretched, holding out the peace offering, the crisps and cream soda. 'Time to let you out the jail, eh? Done your time. Paid your debt to society. Time off for good behaviour. Crisps and a bottle of skoosh thrown in. Ach aye. Wee carry-out. Friday night. But you had to learn your lesson. Am I right?'

4

Aye. Sure.

Back upstairs I ate the crisps, slugged the soda straight from the bottle. The bubbles came back up my nose, made me snort, made my eyes water.

'Good stuff,' said my father. 'Eh?'

Reached into his inside pocket for his own carry-out, half bottle of Bell's, poured himself a glass. Not a good sign. More drink could push him over, kill the good mood.

He switched on the TV. It took time to warm up. The sound came on before the picture. I recognised the voices as Steptoe and Son. Rag-and-bone men, living in their own junkyard.

'Used to be a rag man came round the street,' I said. 'Remember?'

'Toys for rags.'

'Gave you a balloon, or a crappy windmill. Or if you were really lucky and gave him a pile of woollens, you got a skittery wee plastic mouth-organ.'

'Way of the world, son.' My father knocked back the whisky, poured himself more. When the picture cleared on the TV, he laughed out loud, more astonished than amused – the shock of recognition, a crazy coincidence. The Steptoe house was chock-a-block with coffins.

We'd missed the first half of the programme, would only see the last ten, fifteen minutes, but the story wasn't hard to work out. Harold had bought a job lot, going cheap, thought he'd be able to unload them, sell them off. The old man, Albert, was having none of it, didn't want to be in the same house, they gave him the creeps. He stomped off in the huff, to sleep in the shed across the yard. And of course there was a storm, like Hammer horror, a howling wind, thunder and lightning, rain battering on the roof. And the old man slept through it like a baby, and Harold was up half the night, couldn't sleep, scared shitless. Had to get up and go out to the shed, wake the old man, pretend he was worried about him, he'd just sleep here to keep him company. Ended with the old man's gumsy smirk.

'Typical,' said my father. 'Terrified out his mind by a pile of wooden boxes. But that's the thing. That is the thing. People *are*. Scared of the box. Scared of the whole business. Scared of

5

me. I walk into the pub for a quiet drink, it puts the fear of death in folk. They turn away, or make wee jokes. A dying trade. Last man to let you down. Not the cough that carries you off.' He drained his glass again. '*Timor mortis*, son. *Timor mortis conturbat me.*'

This was another road the drink could take him down. Beyond maudlin and mean, could end up morbid. It went with the job.

'Ach!' He glared at the TV. After Steptoe there was just the news, and nothing on the other side, a play. I switched it off. The black-and-white picture pinged and shrunk to a single bright dot. We sat and stared at it till it faded, disappeared.

'The thing is,' he said. 'End of the day it comes to us all. Know what I'm saying? The coffin they carry you off in. Saw this poem on an old grave up the Necropolis. Never forgot it.

> *Ah me I gravel am and dust*
> *And to the earth descend I must*
> *Thou painted piece of living clay*
> *Man be not proud of thy short stay.*'

Great. Cheery stuff for a Friday night.

'And don't you forget it either,' said my father. And the grimness was there again, in the eyes, in the voice, another sudden shift in the mood. The bitterness that was never far away. Just had to wait for it to pass.

The half bottle was empty. He heaved himself up onto his feet, stood unsteady, struggling to keep things in focus. 'I'm fine,' he said, and pitched forward full length, crashed to the floor.

I tried to get him up, at least to his knees, but I couldn't do it. He was dead weight, inert. Wouldn't budge. All I could do was cover him with a blanket, put a pillow under his head, leave him to stew, sleep it off.

In bed, I laughed at the thought of what I'd really like to do, if I had the strength. I'd drag the old man right downstairs to the basement, lay him out in one of the coffins, let him wake up there in the morning. Shock of his life. Sober him up for good. Now that would give him *timor mortis*, good style!

6

In the morning my father was up early, washed and shaved, spruce in his sober suit, collar and tie, hair Brylcreemed flat. Only the greyness of his face gave him away, the slight shake in the hands as he dragged on his cigarette, poured a cup of tea. He glanced across as I came in to the kitchen, still in my pyjamas, yawning, tousled from sleep.

'All right?'

I recognised this as the nearest I'd get to an apology. I rubbed my eyes, scratched my head. 'Aye. Fine.'

'Tea?'

'Thanks, aye.'

He poured another cup, the milk in first after sniffing the bottle to make sure it hadn't gone off, two sugars from the blue and white bag, stirred in. Clink of the teaspoon on the sides of the cup. An apology, as good as.

'Can make yourself a bit of toast if you like. I didn't bother.'

'Couldn't face it?'

'Didn't feel like it.'

Subject closed. He stubbed out the end of his cigarette, ground it into the over-full ashtray. He called the fag-end a doubt. Smoking his doubt. Nipping a doubt. I took two slices of pan bread from their greaseproof wrapper, shoved them under the grill, lit the gas and jumped back as it caught with a whoosh.

'Smell be all right? Won't make you queasy?'

'I'm fine.'

'Cup of tea and a fag.'

'All I need.'

'What is it this morning?'

'Cremation. Old Mrs McAllister. Are you wanting to come along?'

'I canny.' I checked the toast, turned it. Sliding the grill pan made a scraping noise I felt in my teeth.

'I thought with you being off school the day.'

'I'm playing football.'

'Aye.' A silence. Hush of the gas grill. 'It's just that you're never too young to start learning the trade. Getting the feel of it.'

7

'It's Saturday, Da. I want to play football.'

'Right. Fine.' He checked the time on his old fob watch. Been in the family for three generations, passed on from father to son. He flipped it shut, put it in his waistcoat pocket. 'I'll see you later then.'

'Aye.'

I listened as he clumped downstairs to take charge of another funeral. Just a job of work. A living.

A living from the dead!

The smell of burning wrinkled my nose. I whipped out the toast but it was burnt black, brittle. Cremated! I laughed, made the sign of the cross over the charred remains. 'Ashes to ashes!'

I chucked them in the bucket, slid in two more slices, made a fresh pot of tea.

When I'd eaten, I had a quick wash at the sink, changed into my t-shirt and jeans, the old blue jersey I liked. Rubbed dubbin into my boots, packed them in the knapsack with my strip, the red and white striped top, black shorts, red socks. Flash.

I heard voices in the yard, looked out the window and saw my father by the parked hearse, its back door raised, open. He was talking to Andy the driver, the pair of them serious in their black suits, black ties. They disappeared inside, came out again a few minutes later, the front end of the coffin up on their shoulders. Andy's two sons were at the back, taking the rest of the weight. The boys were big and gawky, had both left school. They came in to help with the lifting and carrying, got paid a few quid on the side.

Even though the old woman was small, the casket itself was heavy, and they grunted as they heaved it into the hearse, slid it into place. My father said something to the two boys and they went back inside the building, came back out looking awkward with their arms full of flowers, a shock of colour in the grey day, the wreaths and posies that people had sent. Usually with a cremation it was no flowers by request, but the old woman's family must have wanted this specially. After the ceremony they'd likely be sent to a hospital.

My father arranged the flowers round the coffin, adjusted a wreath here, a spray there, gave a nod when he was satisfied

8

with the effect. Andy closed down the back door. The boys said cheerio, went out the gate nudging and shoving each other, free.

Andy looked up then and saw me at the window, gave me the thumbs up, shouted to me. 'Mind and score a couple of goals the day!' He mimed a glancing header. 'Do a Denis Law. Use the auld noddle!'

My father looked up, face blank.

'Sound advice, that, I'm giving your boy,' said Andy. 'Use the noddle!'

My father managed a smile across that face. Watery sunlight in a grey sky.

'Right!' said Andy, and he gave me a wave, climbed in to the driver's seat. My father got in the other side. The engine started first time and the hearse moved off, eased away. In the back, the flowers blazed.

The road to the crematorium passed by the pitches. As I jostled in the penalty box, waiting for a corner kick to be taken, I caught sight of the hearse, the little convoy of cars tucked in behind, moving slowly through traffic. It was just enough to distract me as the ball swung over. Just enough, eye off the ball, and I mistimed my jump, didn't connect. The big centre half stepped in and blootered it clear.

A howl from the touchline, four or five boys from my class who hadn't made the team.

'What a diddy!'

'Dig a hole and bury him!'

They laughed at that, harsh, fake laughter that strained their throats.

'He should have buried that one anyway! Stuck it in the back of the net!'

What net? Did they think this was Hampden?

They sounded like animals, jackals. As I jogged back up the field, they did the music from *The Addams Family*, clapped together on the double beat. *Diddly-dum, clap clap.*

One of them shouted, 'Hey, should you no be in the box?' And that set them off again, cackling.

'Aye, a wooden box!'

I did nothing after that. Ran about daft, chasing the game. I'd lost my touch. As I came off at the end, another one called out, 'Died a death out there, eh?'

Bastards.

The next week I was dropped from the team. Competition for places, said the PE teacher. Give somebody else a chance. Keep you on your toes. Meant I had a free Saturday, no excuse. So I came along with my father. Felt like a miniature version with the suit, the shirt too big, the black tie, the polished shoes. Something creepy about it, a wee man. Like a midget, a ventriloquist's dummy. Jimmy Clitheroe or Archie Andrews. But it kept my father happy.

It was a Catholic house, on the second floor of a tenement, and the body had been laid out in the front room for a wake. The old man had lived alone, but his children and grandchildren had gathered round to see him off. They had prayed, lit candles for the dead man, told stories about him. Now it was time.

My father took charge, and the men of the family lifted the coffin, shuffled with it towards the door. I looked round the room the old man was leaving for the last time. A few holy pictures on the wall. Couple of ornaments, a glass swan, china boxer dog. And lying on the mantelpiece, the old man's glasses, a pipe on its side in the ashtray. Maybe nobody could bear to throw them away. But something about them lying there, as if the old man had just laid them down, gone out of the room for a minute.

The old man's dog had been whining out in the hall. When they opened the door to take the coffin out, the dog rushed in. A scraggy black mongrel, it ran berserk in circles round the room, yelping and howling, its ears flat back against its head. Then it started squirting piss, and got itself tangled among the legs of the pall-bearers. The man nearest the front swung a kick at it, lost his balance and stumbled. The others lurched and almost dropped the coffin, just managed to right it as it skewed to the side.

That was when I laughed. I couldn't help myself. The whole thing was mad, like a crazy scene from a film. All it needed was

Norman Wisdom clowning about, chasing the dog, the coffin clattering down the stairs and shooting out across the street. I could picture it. My shoulders shook as I tried to contain it. One of the young women caught my eye, gave me a quick half-smile then straightened her face again, looked away. My father tweaked me by the ear, hard. Told me I'd get what for.

So here I was, back down in the basement, locked in.

My father had raged at me, bawled me out. 'You think death's a big joke? You think it's a laughing matter?'

It wasn't like that. Not what I meant.

'When I think about it. What these poor people were going through. And then for that to happen.'

Please God, don't make me laugh, not again.

'And for you to find it hilarious!'

I couldn't hold it in, burst out laughing all over again.

'Right!' My father smacked me one to the back of the head. 'That's it!' Smacked me again. 'Give me a showing up, would you? Didn't know where to put my face!' One last sore smack, then he slammed the door shut. Locked it. Went upstairs and left me.

I subsided, calmed down. Not really funny at all. Just at the time. I'd been in that strange mood. Something to do with the place, the house. Not the family and their grief. I saw that all the time. No. It was the old man's room, his things. Those pictures on the wall. The ornaments. The specs. The pipe. This was somebody that had been alive, had been sitting there just a couple of days ago. Reading his paper. Drinking tea. Now it was finished. Like that. The dog whining. Christ.

It was all so matter of fact. Sad and ordinary. I had felt something rising in my chest, a huge emotion. The madness with the dog had broken it. The laughing had been a release.

Upstairs the front door banged, my father going out. Familiar sound of being left alone. Another Saturday night.

That was a song. Another Saturday night and I ain't got nobody. Sam Cooke.

Ain't got no body! That was good. There were two of them in the cold back room upstairs. All we had space for at any one time. Limited the amount of business.

The small family firm of McGraw and Son has been serving the people of Glasgow for generations.

My father had left in the *and Son*, hoping I would follow him into the business. The thought of it made me sick.

We offer a service that is second to none in terms of dignity, understanding and quiet efficiency. Each and every client receives individual personalised attention. Our pledge is in our motto: Rest Assured.

My great-grandfather had come up with that. Rest Assured. Had a ring to it. Like *Aye Ready*. Or *Sure and Stedfast*. The same kind of dour strength. But clever too, the double meaning.

My father had told me about an undertaker called Barkis, back in the old days, before the War. Barkis had stood for election to the town council, put a sign in his window that read *Vote for Barkis – he'll bury your carcass!* And another time he'd put *You may pass this way but once, but we'll get you in the end. Join our Christmas club.*

My father had been appalled, but I had laughed, found it funny. In the midst of life we are in death. They were always saying that at the funerals. So in the midst of death there should be some life. Made sense, but it wasn't my father's way. Not at all. The word for my father was *dour*.

My father's face that morning when I'd laughed at the daft dog, the stumble, the falling coffin. The feeling I'd had, just before it, was coming again, rising in my chest. The sense of that old man's life, in the sad room, the few pathetic possessions. One day it would come to that, for my father, for me, for everybody.

It seemed stupid to put it into words. Of course everybody died. But somehow I'd never thought it applied to me. I was a special case. An exception would be made. But now, just suddenly, like that, I saw it clear. The decision was final. There was no appeal. I was going to die. Pass this way but once. We'll get you in the end. Vote for Barkis!

There was a Barkis in Dickens. Barkis is willing. *David Copperfield*. I'd read the comic. Classics illustrated. Seen the serial on TV. And at Christmas I'd had a hardback comicbook of *Oliver Twist*. The story in pictures with words underneath.

Some of it had made me uncomfortable, right in my stomach. Young Oliver apprenticed to an undertaker, sleeping among the coffins. And the bit at the beginning where his mother died.

I'd never known my own mother, only seen photos. Cracked black-and-white Box Brownie snaps. Young woman in a WACS uniform during the War, posing in a party frock at a dance, eating an ice cream on a day trip to Ayr.

I remembered asking my father, when I was wee. What happened to her? And he'd struggled with how to answer, what to say, had finally come out with it.

'She died in childbirth. The child in question being you.'

The child in question. I'd never asked too much about her after that, just the odd time when my father's mood was up, when he seemed approachable. Now and again, at a certain stage after the drink, he might look at me, tell me, 'Ach son. You're awful like your mother.'

And the look on his face would be one I couldn't read, the emotions too confused, too raw.

Now in this new mood that was on me, I saw that he hadn't coped with that one death right at his door. Had never coped. Wasn't coping still. I shivered. Somebody walking on my grave. I didn't feel like climbing into a coffin. I lifted the floorboard in the corner, but I'd finished off the sherbet, gone through the stash of sweeties, had nothing left. And the comic I'd folded up and stuffed underneath was the same one I'd read last week. *Creepy Worlds*. I hadn't got round to changing it. I turned the pages, but it didn't scare me or make me laugh, seemed childish. No joy in it any more.

What happens when you die?

I asked auld Jack, the joiner who made the coffins. His name was Jack Auld, and he'd been called Auld Jack even as a boy at school. 'Soon as they read out the register,' he said. 'That was me. And it stuck. Auld when I was young, eh? Auld before my time!'

Aye.

'But what happens?'

Jack stopped what he was doing, sanding down a hardwood

panel. 'Ask me something simple, why don't you?! Like who won the Scottish Cup in 1898? Vale of Leven actually. Or what's the capital of Albania?'

'Tirana.'

'Very good.'

'But.'

'What happens when you die? You think I should know? I suppose I've kitted out plenty folk with these.' He indicated the coffins in the workshop, in various stages of completion. 'Made to measure. Seen enough dead folk in my time.' He rubbed the stubble on his jaw. 'Well I'll tell you this. By the time they're laid out in one of these, they're gone. Offski. They're well out of it. What gets buried or burnt is not the person. It's just stuff. Like this.' He knocked the piece of wood he was working on. 'Or this!' He knocked my head, made a clicking sound with his tongue.

'But what happens to the person then? Where does the person go?'

'Now you're asking! All I know is, we'll all find out soon enough.' He showed me the panel of wood again. 'See this? Just about your size, eh? It's for a young lassie, maybe a year older than you. So this is it. You never know the minute.'

Great. Thanks.

I asked the teacher, Miss McCurdie. What happens when you die?

'Is everything all right at home?' she said. 'It can't be easy for your father, bringing you up on his own. And I suppose the nature of his work might tend to make you a wee bit . . . morbid.'

Glad I asked.

I tried Andy the driver, the one who told me to use the noddle. What happens when you die?

'The big one, eh? The sixty-four-thousand-dollar question! Course, in a job like this you think about it a lot. Only natural. Comes down to what you believe, doesn't it? Like, is it just darkness when you die? Oblivion sort of thing. Nothingness. Only good thing about that is you wouldn't know anything about it. Nothing to know and nobody to know it. Or is there

14

really some kind of afterlife? Heaven and Hell sort of thing. Saint Peter at the pearly gates.' He grinned. 'Here, have you heard this one? Saint Peter's feeling tired one day, so Christ comes along and offers to take over for a bit, give him a wee break. Fine, says Peter, and away he goes, leaves him to it. So Christ's sitting there, and after a while this old boy comes doddering up to the gates, asks if he can get in. Well Christ goes through the procedure like, asks him about his life. And the more the old boy tells him, the more interested Christ gets.

I grew up in a small town, he says. *I was a carpenter.*

Oh aye? says Christ.

I only had the one son, and I wanted him to follow me into the business.

Uh huh?

But God had other plans for him. My son left home and went out into the world.

Aye?

He became very famous.

And by this time Christ is so excited, he can't keep it in any longer. He shouts out *Father!*

And the old boy looks at him, says *Pinocchio?'*

That made me laugh out loud. But it still didn't answer the question. What happens when you die?

Finally I asked my father, one night in the kitchen when we'd finished our tea. At first my father said nothing, sat smoking his cigarette down to the doubt. (Miss McCurdie said the word was *dowp*, said it was slang and I shouldn't use it). My father flicked ash, brushed it off his trousers, stubbed the doubt. (Stuff Miss McCurdie). Crushed it into the plate congealed with egg yolk, bits of bacon rind, tomato skin. Then he started, his voice quiet and flat.

'First thing that happens, right away when the person dies, all the muscles relax and go loose. All the wrinkles on the face smooth out, like the struggle's finally over. The person looks years younger.' He rubbed his own tired face, the slack cheeks, furrows across the forehead.

'After an hour these red patches come up all over the body. After three hours the muscles start to stiffen up and go hard.

That's what they call rigor mortis. It's good if you can get to it before that, for removal like. If somebody dies sitting up in a chair, it's not easy laying them out on a stretcher with any kind of dignity.'

I wanted to laugh at that, stifled it.

'Year or two back,' my father went on, 'had to deal with this old boy that had slipped right under the table, got himself tangled up with the chairlegs. Had a hell of a job getting him out.'

I snorted, tried to turn it into a cough. My father glared at me, raised his voice just a fraction, just enough.

'After a day, the body cools down to room temperature. The skin on the face and the hands shrinks back, tightens. If there's any flies around they'll have laid their eggs between the lips and eyelids. Maggots.'

I looked away, the urge to laugh gone.

'After two days the rigor mortis starts to go and the body begins to decompose. There's these enzymes getting to work, attacking the tissues, making them soft and moist. Then the bacteria get going, turning the body into fluid and gas. That's when it really starts to smell a bit choice.'

For a moment I felt sick, slight catch of nausea in the throat, but it passed.

'If the body's not been dealt with by that stage,' said my father, 'if it's not embalmed or put in cold storage, things get pretty unpleasant. After a week it's changed colour, turned purple and green. The skin's that loose you could rub it off. After two weeks the gases in the gut make the stomach swell up. Stuff gets forced out the nose and mouth.'

I stared straight ahead. The queasiness came up again. The fry-up I'd eaten sat heavy. I could taste it. Still my father went on.

'After three or four weeks the body's really decayed. The hair and nails are falling out. The whole thing's bloated. The tongue's swollen up and sticks out the lips.'

The greasy plate, smear of egg and baconfat, puckered scrap of tomato skin. I put my hand to my mouth, stood up and rushed to the bathroom, made it just in time, spewed the lot down the

16

toilet. When it was finished, when I'd retched and gagged and had nothing left to bring up, my eyes watered and my hands shook. I splashed my face with cold water, rinsed out my mouth. Went back through.

My father had lit another cigarette. Picked up where he'd left off.

'If it's buried it just keeps rotting, into the earth. Feeds the plants. Pushing up the daisies right enough. If it's burned it goes into the air. The bones get ground down to ash. Scattered. Either way there's nothing left.'

He looked across at me sitting there, still shaky.

'You did ask.'

My father said if I was going to run the business some day, I would have to get over my squeamishness. Learn to live with death. Face it. See it as something natural.

'I mean how can you be an undertaker if you throw up at the first whiff of decay? It won't do, son. It won't do at all.'

'But what if I don't want to be an undertaker?'

'Don't be daft. It's the family firm. It gets handed on. You're the son and heir.'

One day all this will be yours.

The hearse, the van, the yard, the workshop, the office and waiting room, calendar with views of the Trossachs, the black suit black coat black shoes black tie black hat.

Rest Assured.

'But what if I just don't want it?'

'Think you're too good for it?'

'It's not that. It's just, I might fancy doing something else.'

'Such as?'

Be an artist. Play for Scotland. See the world. Walk on the moon.

'Don't know. Just . . . something else.'

Anything else.

'Ach!' said my father. 'Your heid's full o mince.'

Next day he said it was time I started helping out a bit more. Learning the ropes. The sooner the better.

'I want you to come and give me a hand with a chesting.'

This was it. What I'd been dreading. Going with him to lay out a body. Clean it and dress it. Put it in the box. Meant having to touch it, deal with God knows what kind of mess.

All the way there in the van I sat numbed, stared straight ahead. Under sentence. No reprieve. The house was a semi-detached in one of the older schemes. The next-door neighbour had the key, let us in. The dead man was in the bedroom, she told us, through to the back. The widow had gone to stay with a daughter. Probably for the best, the neighbour thought. Better off out of it.

'Indeed,' said my father, and he looked at his watch.

'A fine man,' the neighbour said. 'Never a day's illness. Out the blue, just like that.'

'It's often the way,' my father said. He flipped the watch shut, tucked it back in his waistcoat pocket. Made a point of saying nothing else, let the silence hang in the room.

'At least it was quick,' said the neighbour. 'He didn't suffer. Best way to go, if you ask me.'

My father didn't ask her, thanks all the same. Gave a nod that said as much, deepened the silence.

'Well,' said the neighbour at last. 'Better leave you to it.' She flicked a glance at the bedroom door, tugged her cardigan tight across her throat, shivered though it wasn't cold.

'Yes,' said my father. 'Thank you.' And he nodded again, businesslike.

'Thought she'd never leave,' he said when she'd gone. 'Let's get on with it.'

He opened up a holdall he'd placed on the floor, handed me a green overall and a pair of rubber gloves, took out a set for himself and put them on, nodded to me to do the same.

The fear came back at that, sick emptiness in the gut. But at the same time I felt ridiculous. The overall was too big, hung down past my knees, and I had to fold up the sleeves. I pulled on the gloves with a squeak and a smack. They made my hands huge. I waved them in front of me. Al Jolson singing *Mammy!* I wanted to laugh but I caught my father's eye. Maybe not.

'Right,' he said, and he pushed open the door.

In. To the room. All my senses suddenly sharp. Dark with the curtains closed, but an old couple's room by the smell, fusty mix of stale and cloying sweet, talc and naphthalene, old mothballed clothes. Then a dull undertone, faint shit smell, and all of it overlaid with air freshener. My father switched on the light. I brought myself to look. The shape on the bed, covered over with a sheet, a pink candlewick bedspread folded down. Then my father was turning back the sheet, and I was staring at the body, the dead man lying there, skinny and pale, dressed only in underpants. The face was gaunt and drawn, waxy. White stubble on the cheeks, wisps of soft white hair standing up round the head. And the thing that stopped me short, the look on the face. The corners of the mouth turned down, contorted in a last grimace of pain.

He didn't suffer.

Not what the face said.

At least it was quick.

'Heart attack,' my father said. 'Not too messy.' He was blunt and functional, the way to deal with it. 'The wife must have cleaned things up a bit. Got rid of the bedding, the pyjamas. That's something to be grateful for, eh? Small mercies.'

He sent me to the kitchen to boil up water, bring it through in a bucket. 'I know this is hard for you,' he said. 'But believe me, you'll get used to it.'

'Don't know if I want to.'

'Ach.'

Already he had slipped a plastic sheet under the body, peeled off the pants and dropped them in a rubbish bag. 'Like changing nappies!' he said.

He washed the body down with the hot water. Then he took little wads of cotton wool, smeared them with vaseline and plugged up all the openings. 'To stop the seepage.'

Did the nostrils first. Then the throat, prising open the mouth. Last the rectum, getting me to hold the old man's legs. This was me touching a dead body. I watched with a kind of detached amazement as my father did his work with a quick, brisk efficiency, and yet with a gentleness that surprised me. Carefully he closed the mouth, held it shut with a cord looped round the top of the head and knotted under the chin. Then he took a white sheet, and nodded at me to help again. Slipped it under the body and wrapped it round, with a few deft folds, a nip and tuck, made it look like a smock.

Finally we brought in the coffin, basic cheap pine job, lightweight for transport. Laid the body in it, so light, like nothing. Took it back to our place and left it in the cold room smelling of formaldehyde. My father would deal with the business in the morning, talk to the widow about the details, the style of the thing, the cost.

He smiled at me, hopeful. 'There you are. That wasn't too bad, was it?'

I went upstairs and ran a bath. But even after I'd soaked in it, soaped myself with carbolic, washed my hair with medicated shampoo, scrubbed under my nails with Dettol, I still felt as if I stank of death.

That old man's face, twisted in its last spasm of shock and pain. I saw it when I shut my eyes. Lay awake half the night, staring. And when I did sleep it was there again, and the same look was on my father's face, then on my own, and I woke up shouting out.

The same bunch of meatheads who'd barracked me from the touchline sat behind me in class. Deans was the worst, led the others on. Made the sign of the cross at me, as if I was a vampire. Called me Pugsley, Thing, Cousin It. Spoke in a deep voice like Lurch the butler. *You rang?*

When I sat down, Deans went into convulsions, holding his nose, clutching his throat, pretending to choke. 'Had a bath in disinfectant?' he said. 'I think the BO was better!'

I rounded on him, spat out, 'Shut it!'

Miss McCurdie was in a bad mood. 'Right!' she shouted. 'The two of you, out here!'

She belted us both, twice. Uncurled the strap and lashed it down. Left hand on top, then right. Sent us back stinging. As we sat down, Deans hissed at me, 'That's it. Outside at four o'clock. You're claimed, pal. You're dead meat.'

What we all were, sooner or later.

Deans was waiting for me in the playground, end of the day, his cronies backing him up. One of them started shouting, *Fight! Fight!* and the others joined in. The noise brought a crowd that made a ring round about us. No way out of it. A square go.

Deans started it, shoved me. I swung a wild punch and missed. Before I could right myself, Deans thumped me one hard in the stomach. A sickener. Knocked the breath out of me. I doubled up and Deans caught me again, a stunner right in the face. I lunged at him and we grappled, fell to the ground. It was all unreal, the noise, the crowd of boys closing in, yelling, howling for blood. Then the noise was subsiding, the crowd breaking up as Miss McCurdie waded in, grabbed the pair of us. Marched us to the headmaster's office.

'Animals,' she said. 'I'm disgusted.'

The headmaster was disgusted too. The Heedie. Deperate Dan. He gave us another four of the belt. Made the two from McCurdie seem a joke, a wee slap. Every stroke from Dan was brutal. He swung from the shoulder, put his whole beef into it. My hands felt flayed, bruised to the bone.

Then to make it worse, rub salt in it, Dan ordered us to shake hands. We did it, in bad grace, grudging, barely able to grip. Went out the room with our heads down. Outside, Deans blew on his fingers, his palms. I tucked my hands under my armpits, gritted my teeth. Christ it hurt.

We said nothing to each other, went our separate ways. I looked down, saw a rip in the knee of my trousers. My nose had bled, spattered the front of my shirt. Fuck it. I would have to face my father. Another night in the basement.

Shite.

In the dinner school next day it was the usual rammy. I took my tray to a table in the far corner, out of the way. Dinner was meatballs in a brown sludge of gravy, two scoops of dry grey mash, a dollop of pale soggy cabbage. For pudding it was a square of plain sponge covered in bright yellow custard. If I didn't eat it I would go hungry. Nothing else for it.

'Do you mind if I sit here?'

I looked up, saw the Indian girl from my class. Her name was Padma. She had only been at the school a few weeks and I hadn't spoken to her. She was quiet, kept to herself. Her black hair hung in a long shiny pigtail halfway down her back. A tiny jewel glinted in her right nostril. I realised I was staring.

'Eh, sure,' I said, awkward. 'Aye. No bother.'

'Thank you.'

She sat down opposite, placed a red plastic box in front of her, saw me looking at it.

'I'm vegetarian,' she said. 'Means I can't eat most of the food.'

'I know the feeling.'

'They let me eat in here, but I just bring my own.'

'Sounds like a great idea!' The gravy was coagulating on my plate. I cut into one of the meatballs and the smell wafted stronger.

She put her hand to her nose. 'Not too appetising.'

'The last time we had these,' I said, 'I dropped one on the floor. I mean, it was an accident like.'

'I believe you!'

'I just kind of stumbled and it rolled off the plate. But see when it hit the floor, honest to God, it bounced!'

She laughed, covered her mouth with her hand.

'I'm not kidding,' I said. I looked round to check nobody was watching. Picked up the other meatball, held it out and let it drop. When it hit the ground, sure enough it bounced, three, maybe four inches, rolled under the table.

Padma laughed even more, put her hands over her eyes. I fished up the meatball off the floor, dumped it back on my plate.

'Well you certainly can't eat it now.'

'Too bad, eh?'

'Would you like some of mine?' She peeled back the lid of the box, showed me. Two little triangular pasties, gold-brown. I was suddenly awkward again, unsure.

'Is there enough? I mean, can you spare it?'

'Please,' she said. 'Take.'

I leaned across and took one. It still felt slightly warm. It smelled like the Indian grocer's.

'Kind of Indian bridie.'

She smiled. 'Kind of. It's called a samosa. You can get them with meat, but this one's filled with potatoes and peas. Some spices.' She stopped, hesitant. 'Oh!'

'What?'

'I just thought. Do you like curry?'

'I don't know. I'm not sure.' Again I was flustered, self-conscious. 'I've never tasted it.' I felt myself blush. This was ridiculous.

'Oh well.' She shrugged. 'One way to find out.'

I bit into it. Soft pastry then explosion of tastes, burning but good, left my whole mouth tingling.

'Woh!' I breathed out, fanned with my hand.

'Too hot for you?'

'No! I mean it is nippy, but it's great, it's brilliant. Never tasted anything like it.' To show I meant it, I ate the rest, scoffed it down. Padma finished hers more delicately, handed me a paper napkin to wipe my fingers.

'Are you going to eat the pudding?' she asked.

The glazed custard had formed a skin. 'Don't think so.'

'Fine.' She unwrapped a square of what looked like tablet or fudge, milky white flecked with lime green. 'We can share this.' She broke it with her thin fingers, gave me half. Again it was like nothing I'd ever tasted, intense sweetness overlaid with a fragrance that lingered far back.

'God, it's incredible!'

She looked pleased. 'It's a sweetmeat made with curds and condensed milk. A little rosewater, cardamom, pistachio.'

She was talking a foreign language to me. I shrugged. 'Whatever it is, it tastes magic!'

She looked up behind me, wary. I turned round, saw Deans and his pals heading towards us. They must have made a detour on their way out, come over to annoy me.

'Found yourself a wee friend?' said Deans, that sneer in his voice. 'Right enough, she's just about your level. Couple of untouchables. Don't know who smells the worst!'

I started to stand up, ready for another go. But Padma reached across and touched my arm. 'No, Neil. Don't.' And the way she said it, quiet, made me stop and sit down.

'Hiding behind lassies now?' said Deans. 'That's really sad!'

For the moment it was enough of a victory. As they moved away Deans raised his voice, highpitched, mimicking Padma. *No Neil, don't!* And they all laughed.

'They're not worth it,' said Padma.

'I know. It's just hard.'

'They're mean and stupid,' she said. 'I've heard some of the things they say to you and it's not fair. But they do the same to me. Call me names. Darkie and Paki. Tell me I stink.'

'Bastards.'

'My father says they're afraid. Frightened of anyone that's different.'

'That's it. They're cowards. Fearties.'

She smiled at the word. 'My father also says karma will take care of them.'

'Who's Karma?' A big brother maybe. Six foot two and built like a wrestler.

She laughed. 'It's not a *who*, it's a *what*!'

'Well what is it then?

'It's hard to explain. It's a kind of law. Means everybody gets what's coming to them, one way or another.'

I tried to take that in, think about what it meant, but then the bell was clanging, end of the dinner hour, clatter of plates and cutlery, scraping of chairs. I walked back with her to the classroom, along crowded corridors, not saying much.

I didn't even look at Deans the whole afternoon. Ignored him. There was more to life. The tastes were still in my mouth. Spices. Sweetness and fragrance. Tasted magic.

The church was cold and gloomy and smelled of polish and dust. The minister's voice was a tired drone, intoned the same old words for a dead man he hadn't known. *A good man. A kind and loving husband and father.*

The old boy we'd washed and laid out, plugged and wrapped and put in his box. *In my father's house there are many mansions. Sure and certain hope. Our Lord Jesus Christ.*

The hymns that always got to me, no matter what. *Rock of Ages. Abide with Me.* The family all in black, crying.

The old boy's face, that grimace of pain. He didn't suffer. Something to be grateful for. Small mercies.

I felt the air of the place press down on me, its atmosphere oppressive, heavy with the weight of its own seriousness. It made me want to jump up and run screaming down the aisle and out the door. But I didn't. I sat through it. I had no choice.

I got into the habit of looking out for Padma, on the way home from school, or in the morning coming in. Noticed what time she passed the end of my street. Fell in behind her as if by chance. Acted casual. Hello there.

I wanted to ask her things, find out more about this karma business.

'According to my father,' she said, 'everything's karma.'

'Everything?'

'The way things work out.'

'Like what?'

'Like, if you do something good, then good follows. If you do something bad, it catches up with you.'

'So how come people get away with things?'

'They don't. Not in the long run. Everything has consequences. And everything's connected.'

'So it's karma that we're walking along here talking?'

We were crossing the wasteground, where old tenements had been ripped down to make way for a road that was never built.

'Yes,' she said. 'It's all meant.'

'Like fate?'

'Kind of. And it carries on from life to life.'

I stopped. Stood there. Felt on the edge of something, opening out, almost understanding. 'So you're saying we live again and again?'

'That's right. Over and over, until we get it right.'

I held the top of my head with both hands, as if to keep it in place. I asked her the big one.

'So what happens when you die?'

'That depends on your karma too. The soul leaves the body and takes a rest. My father says there's a verse from the Gita about it. That's like our Bible. It says it's like casting off an old worn-out coat.'

'Then you come back and start again?'

'In another body.'

'It never ends?'

'No!' She laughed. 'It goes on and on. Forever!'

For a moment I felt I'd had this conversation before, in another time, like rereading an old book, half remembered. The wind stirred the weeds growing on the wasteground, scattered ash from a dumped plastic rubbish bag. Cloud scudded overhead and the sun glinted on dented tin cans, bits of broken glass. It flashed a moment on the tiny jewel in Padma's nostril, on the thin bangles that jingled as she raised her hand to push a wisp of hair back from her face.

'Forever!' I said, amazed.

'See you're getting quite pally wi that wee Paki lassie,' said my father. 'Walking her down the road and that.'

'Her name's Padma and she's Indian.'

'Same difference.'

The way he said it made me want to punch him, hit his stupid smug dour face. Instead I went out to the yard, scuffed my heels, kicked the gate.

Andy startled me, stuck his head out the back of the hearse. 'Hey!' he said. 'How about this one? Two maggots were fighting in dead earnest!'

A beat while I got it.

Dead Ernest!

Made me laugh.

The end of term was coming up. I worked up the courage and came out with it, asked Padma to the school dance.

'I'm sorry,' she said. 'It's very nice of you to ask, but I can't.'

It was dinner time. We sat at the same table where we'd first spoken, weeks ago, the same rammy in the background, some other sludge on my plate.

'Why not?' I'd gone this far, might as well push it.

She looked down and blushed, her dark skin darker. 'My father wouldn't let me.'

'It's only a dance. What's the harm?'

'The thing is, I'm promised to somebody.'

'Like, somebody's already asked you?' I couldn't think who.

She shook her head. 'No, I mean I'm promised to be married. I'm engaged.'

'But . . .' I couldn't get any words out, couldn't think.

'It won't be for a while yet,' she said. 'Not till I'm sixteen. But it's all set up.'

She was wearing a long chiffon scarf, a deep rose colour with flower patterns picked out in gold. She pulled it through and through her fingers. I sat and watched, finally managed to ask. 'One of these arranged marriages sort of thing?'

She nodded. 'That's right. Our families know each other.'

'And what's he like, the guy?'

'I haven't actually met him yet. But my mother says he's very nice. He lives in Bradford.'

'You're signed up to marry a guy you haven't met? In Bradford!'

'He's a good bit older than me. I'll meet him later.'

'But, what if you don't like him?'

'It'll work out.'

'Karma again?'

'That's right.'

'Just have to accept your fate?'

'Yes.'

'But don't you sometimes have to fight? Tell your fate to fuck off?'

She flinched a little, tensed her shoulders. 'Maybe sometimes, it might be your karma to do that.'

I pressed the palm of my hand to my forehead. 'You're nipping my heid!'

She laughed at that, relaxed, almost.

'But how are you supposed to know?' I said. 'How do you know if you're doing the right thing?'

'Just have to trust. See what happens.'

I mimicked my father. 'What's for ye will no go by ye.'

'That's it.'

I shrugged. 'Oh well.'

At the end of the long drag of an afternoon I walked her home. All part of the great scheme of things. The sun warmed the weathered grey stone of the tenement, made it even shabbier. Initials, slogans, were chalked on the wall. RFC. FTP. AJ LOVES PK TRUE.

Padma's two wee sisters played peever on the pavement, hop and skip, skite a puck – the lid off a tin of shoe polish. They stopped and looked up at me, spoke to Padma in their own language. She'd said it was Bengali, and it sounded like singing. The wee girls shouted something, ran laughing into the close.

'Monkeys!' said Padma.

'What did they say?'

'It doesn't matter.' She shook her head. 'Listen. I'm sorry about the dance. You understand?'

'Kind of.'

'We can still be friends.'

'I'd like that.'

'Good.' She touched my arm. 'See you.'

'Aye.'

She turned away into the dingy close where the dank smell of bad drains couldn't quite drown out the sharp tang of spices. I watched her go, swish of bright colours disappearing round the turn of the stair.

'Ach son.'

Not drunk really, he'd only had one or two, but a strange mood on him.

'Comes to us all, you know what I'm saying?'

Aye.

'You pass on. Pass away. Sing your swansong. Breathe your last. Shuffle off the mortal coil. Give up the ghost. Meet your maker. Go to a better place.'

All these ways of saying it, of not saying it.

'Snuff it. Croak. Kick the bucket. Pop your clogs. Hang up your boots. Take an early bath. Jack it in. Cash your chips. Final curtain. Finito. Kaput.'

He shrugged, hunched his shoulders. 'Whatever way you look at it, it's a long walk off a short plank. And the long and short of it is, we die. End of story. Bottom line. We die.'

He spread his hands, palms out, accepting and warding it off at the same time. Looked at me. Shook his head.

'Ach.'

This time I hadn't been banished, sent downstairs. The door wasn't locked behind me. I had chosen to come down, of my own free will. No comics or sweeties either. I wanted to imagine it, the real thing.

What happens when you die?

I kicked off my sandshoes, peeled off the socks as well, smelled them, dropped them on the floor. Climbed into the coffin and lay down flat on my back, my arms down by my sides.

Close my eyes. Feel the breathing, the heartbeat. They would stop, like that. I'd be stiff and cold. I shivered. Only I wouldn't feel it, wouldn't know. Hard to imagine nothing. Always something imagining it.

He looks dead . . . He looks dead . . . He looks dead . . .

A game we used to play at school, to make somebody levitate. Mind over matter, raise them up.

He is dead . . . He is dead . . . He is dead . . .

Four of us lifting with only the fingertips, raising the person with ease so they seemed to float weightless. Try it now, tell myself, *I am dead.*

I'd see nothing, not even this red behind my eyelids. I'd be deaf and dumb, taste and smell nothing. Feel nothing. Not be this body. Then I'd think nothing, know nothing. No mind. I would *be* nothing.

It only seemed a moment, but it happened. Not a dream, it was real. I was suddenly floating above myself, disembodied, looking down. Saw the wee figure in the coffin stretched out, the jeans and t-shirt, the bare feet. That was me. But so was this up here flying free. I rose higher, up to the ceiling, took in the whole room with its half-finished caskets and lids, its slabs and planks of wood, auld Jack's workbench in the corner. I looked down again at myself still lying there, saw my sandshoes and socks where I'd dropped them on the floor, and it all seemed wonderfully funny, a joke. And just as quick I was back down inside the wee body, back in this me.

I sat up laughing, astonished. Looked at my hands, wiggled my toes. *Ha!* Something in me was not this, was more.

The bit in Tom Sawyer *where Tom and Huck and Joe turn up at their own funeral, sneak in at the back of the church and listen to the speeches. The congregation singing hymns to their memory. The minister reading the text. I am the Resurrection and the life. Then telling stories about the boys, their graces and winning ways, their rare promise. Moving the whole congregation to tears and himself breaking down and sobbing. Then the rustling from the gallery, the door creaking open. The three dead boys marching up the aisle.*

What I always thought of when my father said I'd be late for my own funeral.

2

Senior Secondary school was a zone of hell, and the situation at home turned me in on myself, made me solitary. Friendships didn't come easy.

Want to come round to our house for your tea? Listen to some records? This is the old man by the way. Doctor Death getting bevvied out his skull. Yes, the basement is full of coffins and there's bound to be at least one dead body. The smell is formaldehyde, but don't let it put you off your spam. Or maybe you'd prefer some potted heid?

Fucking Addams Family right enough. Diddly-dum. What chance did I have? Even worse with girls. Padma had moved away. To Bradford. Part of the great scheme of things. Karma. What's for you will no go by you.

I hadn't met anybody else I could talk to like that. *What happens when you die?* Pretty duff as a chat-up line. Just confirmed what they thought anyway – I was weird. Diddly-dum.

Deans had gone to the Junior Secondary, must have found other victims. I heard he'd left school as soon as he could, the day of his fifteenth birthday. Got a job in a garage. Greasemonkey. I hardly ever saw him, just now and again in the street or hanging about the corner. And even then I'd cross the road, keep out of his way. But then things changed, the way they do.

Towards the end of fourth year, I was up in my room, pretending to revise for the O-levels.

'Auf Wiedersehen!' sagte der Kleine, aber er erhielt keine Antwort.
Why was the boy at home? Which room did he go to and what did he find there?

What were the main proposals made by John Knox in his First Book of Discipline?

Areas X, Y and Z on the map of Scotland are faced with

problems of industrial decline as well as possibilities of industrial development. Describe and account for both the problems and the possibilities.

Calculate the area of triangle ABC correct to the nearest square centimetre.

Which character in a book you have studied would you like to have as a friend? Justify your choice.

Fuck it. I switched on the recordplayer, put on *Paint it Black*. That was the mood. No colours any more. I strutted and posed, punched the air. A banging at the door cut across the beat. The old man. I hadn't heard him come in. Turned the volume right down.

'Thought you were supposed to be studying?' An accusation.

'I was. I am. Just taking a break.'

'Aye. Well.'

'So. Is that it?'

'No. I came up to tell you something. I just picked up a body from the mortuary.'

So what else is new?

'Bloke that worked in the yards. A welder. Dropped dead last night in the pub. Took a heart attack, in the middle of a singsong.'

And?

'Thing is, I spoke to the widow, and it turns out you were at school with their boy. Name of Deans.'

Small world.

'I just thought it might help if you came to the funeral. Might help the boy, I mean.'

'Maybe. Only we never really got on. In fact he always gave me a hard time.'

'What does that matter at a time like this?'

'No, but . . .'

'Try thinking about other people for a change.'

'Fine.'

'And don't get smart with me either.'

'I wasn't.'

'Well don't.'

The way most of our conversations ended up these days. He banged the door shut, clumped downstairs. I played the Stones again. *Paint it paint it paint it paint it black.*

I spoke to Deans when it was all over, outside the crematorium.

'Sorry about your da.'

'Aye.' He nodded. 'Thanks.'

What to say. 'At least it was quick.' One of the old man's stock responses. Christ.

'Right,' said Deans. 'Suppose it's the way he'd have wanted to go. Pie-eyed. Giving it laldy, belting out *Ten Guitars*. Fucking embarrassing when you think about it. Still.' He looked round, at the mourners filing out, his mother weeping as she shook everyone's hand. 'Makes you wonder all the same. What it's all about.'

'This is it.'

'Ten Guitars.' He shook his head. 'I don't know.'

Another hearse had drawn up, another convoy, the next funeral party waiting to go in.

'Know the really sad part?' said Deans. 'I never really liked the cunt. Never got on with him. He was a cantankerous old bastard. Used to batter fuck out me, till I got too big for him to get away with it. And he always gave my ma dog's abuse. So it's like we're well rid of him. But still there's this feeling, you know? Like he can't have been all bad. Like it's just a shame the way things turned out.'

'A waste.'

'That's it.'

'And now it's too late.'

'Right.' He looked at me. 'Listen. I know we used to take the piss out you at school and that. But you're all right.'

'Gee, thanks!'

'Naw, but you know what I mean, ya cunt. You know what I'm saying.'

'Aye. Sure.'

He held out his hand, bigger than mine and grimed, engrained with oil from his work. 'No hard feelings.'

We shook on it.

'Embalming,' said my father. He was the closest I'd seen him to being excited.

'It's the latest thing,' he said. 'The Yanks have been big on it for years. But it's really just coming in here.'

'Didn't the Egyptians do it? Mummification and that?'

'That was the fullblown thing. Permanent job. Lasted forever. This is much simpler. I've been reading about it.' I swear to God he actually rubbed his hands together.

'It's really straightforward. Basically just a blood transfusion. Drain it all out and replace it with formaldehyde. Tint it with a drop of pink dye, and bingo. Puts a bit of colour back in the cheeks.'

'But why?'

'Preserves the body.'

'But why the pink dye?'

'It's cosmetic. Makes it less distressing for the family, the loved ones. Looks more like the person they knew.'

'Well I think it's ghoulish.'

'Ach! You'll see.'

'What do you mean?'

'There's a guy in Kirkcaldy travels around doing it.'

'And nobody's arrested him?'

My father ignored me. 'He's trained and he's got the equipment.'

'Have formaldehyde, will travel.'

'He's coming here to do a job for us, try it out.'

'It's too weird,' I said. 'An embalmer fae Kirkcaldy. Hey, they should call him the Wraith Rover!'

He fixed me with that look, distaste and total lack of comprehension. 'You've got to treat everything as a joke, haven't you?'

'I do my best!'

He took a step towards me, drew back his hand to smack me one. My arms came up, a reflex, to ward off the blow. But he changed his mind, thought better of it. Dropped his hand and glared at me again. 'Ach!'

The Wraith Rover came round a few nights later. Not what I'd expected – a spooky cross between Christopher Lee and John Laurie. Instead he was small and slick, dressed in a sports jacket and black knitted tie. Came across like a salesman, easy and glib. Brought with him a hard black case, a small electrical machine, a metal drum with a lid.

'There's three main aspects to this,' he said. 'Three main advantages.' He counted them off on his thumb and first two fingers. 'Sanitation. Preservation. Appearance.' He flashed a smile at us, reassuring and benign. For the first time he addressed himself to the body laid out on the steel slab. 'I understand the family of the deceased want the proceedings delayed for a few days.'

'That's right,' said my father. 'His son's in Canada, can't get back till then.'

'And they plumped for embalming?'

Plumped.

'They'd read about it,' said my father.

The Rover nodded, pleased. 'Perfect solution in a case like this. Maintains the dignity of the deceased and gives everybody a chance to come and pay their respects.' He looked again at the dead man. 'So, shall we begin?'

He clicked open his case, took out a green overall and rubber gloves, put them on. Made him look like a surgeon. He laid out his instruments on a steel tray, flexed his fingers in the gloves, got to work. The whole way through, he kept up a running commentary, to explain what he was doing, and to make it sound normal, matter of fact.

What's the recipe today, Jim?

'One point injection. Raise the common carotid artery, here in the neck. Inject into the heart while we're draining the jugular.'

I looked away. He switched on his machine, a pump. Thick liquid trickled into the metal drum.

'Could you pass me that?' he asked, pointing at a long sharp three-sided blade. I handed it to him, at arm's length.

39

'It's called a trocar,' he said. 'We use it to go in to the upper abdominal cavity. Aspirate any fluids that have accumulated. Replace it all with cavity filler. That preserves and sanitises the internal organs. The whole thing's neat, clean, hygienic.'

When he'd finished, I sneaked a look at the dead man. The features had filled out, looked firm and smooth, faint blush of the pink dye under the skin. A waxwork model. Painted clay.

'Just needs made up for the viewing,' said the Rover. 'Bit of cosmetology. Put the teeth in. Comb the hair. Dress him up in his good suit, and there you are.'

Here's one I prepared earlier.

For days it was all my father talked about. 'I should learn how to do it,' he said. 'Buy the equipment. If it really is the coming thing, we could save a few bob in the long run.'

'We?'

'I thought I could teach you as well. Be a big help.'

'Oh great. That's just how I want to spend my weekends. Pumping corpses full of pink stuff so they look like something out of Madame Tussaud's.'

'I thought the effect was quite tasteful,' he said. 'Sort of rosy glow. Looked quite healthy.'

'Healthy? The guy's dead!'

'So we shouldn't make him look nice for the family?'

'Nice, aye. But no like a waxwork. It's totally artificial. It's creepy.'

'Well according to that embalmer, there's more and more people wanting it.'

I mimicked the Wraith Rover. 'Sanitation. Preservation. Appearance.'

'Know what he told me?' said my father.

'What?'

'He said a lot of folk have a terror of being buried alive. Or waking up in the coffin as it slides into the flames.'

'That's horrible!' I said, a real fear twisting my guts.

'So the thing is, embalming does away with that.'

'Eh?'

'Well, you know for sure the person's really dead.'

40

I let it sink in. 'Let me get this straight. They're scared of premature burial, but they're not worried about having all the blood vampired out of them and replaced with pink gunge?'

'That's one way of putting it.'

'Weird.'

The problem was, my father still wanted me to learn the trade, keep it in the family. Rest assured. But I just wanted out. Get through the O-levels, maybe stay on another year for the Highers, then take off. No clear idea what I wanted, but not this.

Not this.

At least for the moment I had the exams to hide in. It was all I had going for me, his vague faith in a good education. A few qualifications under your belt, he said, do no harm. Might even be useful when it came to running the business. So that was the line, keep the head down, too busy studying to think about anything else.

As if.

The last exam was Geography, a Friday afternoon. I came out of it dazed, filled with the bursting urge to do something freakish and joyous, I didn't know what. I went to a café near the school, an oldfashioned Italian place, unchanged since the fifties – darkwood seats in booths, mirror-glass along the wall. Current pop on the jukebox, mixed in with old Italian standards, *Volare* playing as I came in. I ordered a lime icecream float, sat in the corner booth. *Volare . . . oh . . . oh.* Meant to fly. *Cantare . . . oh . . . oh . . . oh . . . oh.* To sing. Worked it out from the Latin. To fly and to sing. I sipped my ice drink. The coffee machine spurted, hissed. This was me sitting here, not with the sense of freedom I'd expected, just a tired emptiness, let-down. I ate the ice cream from the bottom of my glass with a long spoon, noisily slurped up the dregs through my straw.

Heading home I took the long way round, through a scrap of park where kids ran and screamed and fought over a couple of swings on rusty chains, a sticky chute, a roundabout that thudded and clanked as it turned. Two young mothers passed by, pushing prams. Not much older than me, they both had short-cropped hair, one bleached, one dyed-black. They both wore short skirts and skinny-rib tops. The dark one caught my eye, kind of smiled. I got hard, had to shift my briefcase in front of me to hide it. Stumbled awkward and blushing to the nearest bench, sat with the case on my lap till I'd subsided. The dark girl glanced back, said something to her friend and they laughed. I stared straight ahead, burned.

When I could stand up, I went out of the park, down along the canal bank. Looking at the water, listening to it, brought a kind of ease. Although it was a turgid greybrown, it flowed, lapped the bank, rippled round the rusted hulk of an old wrecked car dumped there years back. I picked up a stone and chucked it at the hulk, threw it too hard and missed. Tried again, not hard enough, the second stone fell short. If at first. One more time. Could see myself standing here till dark, getting more and more frenzied. Third time. Lucky. Hit the frame bang on, made a deeply satisfying clunk.

I raised my arms, fists clenched. 'Beauty!'

Nearing home, I cut across the wasteground, saw Deans coming the other way. First thought was to avoid him, but he made a point of stopping, gave a kind of gruff nod of the head.

'OK?'

'Fine,' I said. 'Just finished my exams.'

'Oh aye?'

'Felt like doing something mental to celebrate. So here I am going home for my tea!'

'Aye. Right.'

I hadn't seen him since the funeral, hadn't got used to him not being the enemy. So he caught me by surprise.

'Wee bird I know's having a party the night. Come if you like.'

I heard myself say 'Aye. Great. Thanks.'

'Meeting a couple of the boys at the corner. Eight o'clock. Get a carry-out and that.'

Wee bird. A party. A carry-out. This was more like it. This was more like the thing.

I waited for the right moment. We'd finished our tea, the usual fry-up. My father wiped his mouth with the back of his hand.

Then he lit a cigarette, inhaled, held, blew out, screwing up his eyes as the smoke curled about his face.

'Ach aye,' he said, and he checked the time on his pocket watch. Half past opening time. 'I'll bring you something back,' he said. 'Bottle of ginger or that.'

'It's OK,' I said. 'I'm going out as well. To a party.'

'Party?' The word sounded strange in his mouth. He held the idea of it, wriggling, at arm's length. 'Who with?'

'Remember that boy Deans? The one I was at Primary with?'

'Deans?' He knew the name, couldn't quite place it.

'You cremated his old man, month or two back.'

'Right! Big chap. Welder. Collapsed in the pub.'

'Ten Guitars.'

'Eh?'

'That's what he was singing.'

He tried to make sense of the information, couldn't. 'So it's his boy that's having the party?'

'Pal of his,' I said. Pal sounded safer than wee bird.

'But I thought you didn't like this Deans character? Didn't get on with him at school?'

I could feel the irritation rising. 'Make up your mind. I thought you wanted me to make friends with him. You said it would help.'

'I meant at the funeral and that. Somebody his own age to talk to. Somebody he knew.'

'Just part of the job?'

'Has to be done. Put folk at their ease.'

'Switch it on and off, just like that.'

'Listen, son.' The patient voice, infuriating. 'In this game you've got to learn a kind of professional detachment. Like being a doctor. If you let yourself get too involved with people's suffering, it'll drive you right up the wall.'

I was about to bat back some smart reply, but the look in his eyes stopped me. He'd been through it, been drawn into that unremitting grief, again and again, had learned to deal with it. Professional detachment. His eyes glazed over again. The look had passed, a glimpse in. It made me feel tense in my stomach.

'So I talked to the guy at his da's funeral,' I said, dragging the

43

conversation back on track. 'And he was different, like he'd changed.'

'Bereavement can do that,' he said. 'Open folk's eyes. For a while.'

'So anyway.' The tension was there again, in my guts. 'I met Deans today, got blethering about this and that, he said he was going to a party, I could come if I want, end of story, OK?'

I was winding myself up, my voice getting louder, higher in pitch. My father flipped back into his usual mode, talking me down.

'Did I say it wasn't OK?'

Deep breath. 'No.'

'Right then.'

'Fine.'

I calmed down once he'd gone. I had plenty of time, a couple of hours before I had to meet Deans. Put on the immerser to heat up water for a bath. Ran it as hot as I could take, filled the bathroom with steam. Eased myself down into the water inch by inch feeling scalded and lightheaded, the blood thudding a pulse to my brain. At last lay full length, immersed up to the chin.

I had tuned my transistor in its white plastic case to Radio One, propped it on the windowledge where it crackled and whined. Reception wasn't good, but now and again the signal came through sharp, in focus, for minutes at a time. I plugged my fingers in my ears, sank right down with my head under the water, bobbed up again, surfaced to Simon and Garfunkel's *Sound of Silence*, pure and clear. *Hello darkness my old friend*.

I lay back enjoying it, buoyed up. I remembered the time I'd stretched out in the coffin, had felt disembodied, floating free. It had never happened again, but now I felt on the edge of it, ready to let go. *Echoing the sound of silence*. The voices hung, thin and tinny. The steam swirled. The warmth of the water surrounding held and numbed me, blurred my boundaries. I shut my eyes and it felt like merging, flowing away. The music disappeared again, lost in a rush of static, interference.

I opened my eyes, looked at my pale wee body under the

water, foreshortened, the legs tapering away, the bellybutton breaking the surface, the fuzz of hair and the wee cock puckered and limp.

Me.

I became aware of the sides of the bath enclosing me, its enamel surface patched and flaking. The wallpaper was grimy, peeling away in the top corner. On the single line of tiles above the bath, the grouting was mouldy, black. Decay and rot.

This.

I soaped myself, lathered shampoo into my hair and ducked under one last time to rinse it. Climbed out dripping and pulled out the heavy brass plug. The bath drained out slowly, belched and gurgled through clogged-up pipes. Dried myself quick before I cooled down. The towel smelled a bit from lying too long damp. No matter. A swift rub-down, brisk tousle of the hair – starting to get long so the old man complained, said it needed a trim, short back and sides. Cropped in to the wood. No thanks.

The underpants were clean on today so they'd do. Give them a sniff to make sure. Fine. Pull on the hipster jeans with the two-inch belt. Checked shirt with the button-down collar. Cord jerkin. Last the white socks and tan suede shoes. Wipe the steamed-up mirror and check the effect. Not too bad. Had problems with the hair but. The fringe wouldn't lie flat. I wanted it straight like Brian Jones, but mine had a curl, turned up at the ends. I'd read an article in *Rave* magazine, said what girls did was stick down the fringe with sellotape while it was still wet. Going to the party, it might be a good time to try it.

I found a roll of tape in the kitchen, picked and picked at the end till a strip came away. Peeled it off and snagged it with my teeth, tore it. Held both ends and stuck the fringe in place across my forehead.

I laughed at myself in the mirror. I'd have to remember to take off the tape before going out. Imagine what Deans and the boys would make of it. Call me a weirdo, a poofter, arse bandit. No party for me, they'd tell me to fuck off. No uncertain terms. I felt my face burn at the thought of it, the sweat prickle my neck.

45

When my hair felt dry to the touch, I eased off the strip of tape, left the fringe neat and flat. Looked good. Cool. I squinted at myself, laughed again.

I was the first to arrive at the corner, hung about waiting for Deans and the others. Seemed a long time, but probably no more than ten, fifteen minutes. Deans looked sharp in a high-button mod suit. Gave me a nod, a gruff *Aye*. Dragged at a stub of cigarette between his thumb and first finger. Flicked the dowp into the gutter.

'Aye,' I said, and tensed, untensed my shoulders.

I didn't know anybody at the party except Deans.

The name's Rab, by the way,' he said.

'Deans, Robert.'

'Fucking register. Fucking school.'

'Right,' I said. 'Rab it is. I'm Neil.'

'I know.'

I had a memory of him in the dinner-hall, taking the piss, mimicking Padma. *No Neil, don't*. But that was long ago and things had changed. Now he was Rab.

Rab's wee bird was called Helen, and her parents were away – enough reason for a party. She came over and took Rab's arm, made me ache. Small and dark, pretty face and hard eyes. Sleek black hair bobbed short at the neck, hanging long at the front and sides. Red mini-dress with thin straps at the shoulders, showed her bare arms and neck.

'Neil,' said Rab. 'Helen.'

I cleared my throat. 'Pleased to meet you.' I heard my voice, like it didn't belong to me. Boring. Helen smiled, looked through me. Her perfume was too strong, cloyed, but I found it intoxicating. Deans – Rab – was a lucky bastard.

'Enjoy the party,' he said over his shoulder as Helen tugged his sleeve, led him away.

The place was filling up with more people I didn't know. Mostly the boys stood around in groups and the girls crowded together on the couch and chairs. One couple were already going at it, winching on the floor in the corner. There was a lot of loud laughing and the volume on the recordplayer was turned up full, a stack of 45s playing, all upbeat thumping party stuff to dance to, though nobody was. *Uptight. Twist and Shout. Not fade away.*

I couldn't see the other two boys, Rab's friends Ian and Doug. And I'd chipped in to the kitty for the carry-out, couple of cans of lager, bottle of *Lanliq*, bottle of cider. I'd paid my whack and I wanted my share.

I tracked them down in the kitchen. Ian had poured half he wine into a huge jug, Doug was topping it up with the cider.

'Punch,' said Doug.

'Packs one as well,' said Ian, and he punched me on the arm, just a bit too hard.

Doug stirred the cocktail with a wooden spoon. 'Nothing like mixing your drinks.'

'Something you should never do,' said Ian. 'Bet your old man's told you that.'

'No,' I said, trying to imagine the old man saying any such thing. *Man to man, son, a word of advice – don't mix your drinks.*

No.

Ian laughed at me. Doug poured the mixture into three mugs, handed me one. 'Cheers.'

'Cheers,' I said, and knocked it back.

With the cider it didn't taste too bad, a bit sticky-sweet but it went down easy. Doug filled our mugs again, mixed another batch in the jug, and we slugged it down till we'd finished the lot.

Then I was back through in the front room again, laughing at nothing, at everything. A few people were up dancing now, bopping in the cramped space as the music beat and thumped. *I can't explain.*

I looked about the room, noticed things in precise detail. The wallpaper pattern, vertical red and grey stripes divided by thin gold lines. The circular mirror framed in curlicues of gilt metal. Veneered fireplace with a coal-effect electric fire, red light flickering behind moulded plastic coals. Clock on the mantelpiece, brass works rotating under a clear glass dome.

'The living room!' I heard myself say to nobody in particular. 'Opposite of the dying room. Where I live, eh?'

'You're pissed ya bastard!' Deans – no, Rab – had loomed up in front of me, one arm still round Helen.

'Du bist half pissed,' I said, dazzled by my own wit.

'Mental,' said Rab.

'I'm a poet and I fucking know it!' This was wonderful. I had never been so lucid in my life. Another girl had come over to talk to Helen. Pale lips and big dark eyes mascara'd, razorcut red hair, black skinny top and lowcut hipsters.

'Aren't you going to introduce me?' I demanded. Oh yes, the fucking bold boy now, not shy any more.

'This is Jeannie,' said Rab. 'This bampot is Neil.'

'Bampot schmampot!' I said. 'There, that proves I'm not pished if I can say schmampot.'

'Daft cunt,' said Rab, and he was suddenly gone again with Helen, and I was asking Jeannie to dance.

'Sure,' she said. Shrugged. 'Why not?'

Why not!

The space was even more tight now so we danced close, jerking mostly from the waist up. The Who were still playing, or playing again. *Dizzy in the head and I feel bad.* But I didn't, felt great, flying, and Jeannie moving in front of me, head bobbing, thin shoulders twitching, dancing with *me*, yes this was it. *I know what it means but . . . can't explain.* Swung my arm in an arc like Pete Townshend, nearly gubbed some big guy dancing behind me.

Easy pal.

Sure. Sure. Sorry.

Can't explain, think it's love.

And the wall of feedback jangling frazzled buzzing the nerves raw. BAM. Yes.

The next song was softer. *Groovy kind of love.* Jeannie leaned closer. 'Is your old man really an undertaker?'

I put my hand on my heart. 'As I live and breathe. A dying trade.'

'Must be strange,' she said.

'A-dirty-job-but-somebody's-got-to-do-it. Otherwise what?

Bodies would just get left out in the street, eh? Dumped like rubbish.'

'That's horrible,' she said, and gave a wee shudder. But something else was there in her eyes, a kind of eagerness, a wanting to know.

'So what do you reckon?' I said. 'What d'you think happens when you die?'

'Fucked if I know!' she said.

'And fucked if you don't!'

I laughed again and so did Jeannie and my hands were on her waist her arms round my neck and dancing I pressed hard against her kissed her ear breathed in her scent couldn't get enough of her. But fuck it I needed to pee.

'Back in a minute,' I managed to say, but it was all going wrong, she swam away from me, out of focus like the rest of the room, and when I did get a fix on anything, hold it steady, everything else pulsed and swirled round about it. Nothing would stay still in its place. Everything had its own sickening rhythm – the coal-effect fire throbbed and glowed the glinting brass innards of the clock kept up their endless irritating birl the wallpaper stripes clashed and flickered against each other seared my eyes started nausea rising in waves and I caught sight of a grey face my own in the mirror with the gilt metal writhing around it had to shut my eyes shut it all out but no good too late the damage done it was all inside welling up the vertical hold gone the room flicking up and up and my legs buckling out the door and everything narrowed to this corridor and me falling down it trying to get to the toilet or out to the street or anywhere found myself pushing through bodies to the kitchen shouldering shoving my way in racked and heaved and threw up in the sink. Watched it spatter the stainless steel, swill round a cup a glass a teaspoon, silt up the plughole, and the stink made me retch again, shudder and heave till nothing was left just the dry acid taste like heartburn tearing at my raw throat.

'Fucksake,' said a voice behind me. Ian. 'You better clean that up. It's stinking the place out.'

He was right. I ran the tap, did my best to sluice away the mess, unclogged the plughole with my fingers, made me gag again the dry boke. I rinsed the cup, glass, spoon, splashed my face with the cold water, shivered, wanted to curl up in a corner and die, get home and crawl into one of the coffins. The living dead for fucksake.

I dragged myself into another room, a big bed in the middle heaped with jackets and coats. All I wanted was oblivion. I lay down on the floor, pulled a coat over me to keep warm, went out like I'd been switched off. Half woke sometime, God knows when, heard noises I didn't want to hear, from the bed, giggling and shooshing and Rab's voice, low, saying *Never mind him he's out the game dead to the fucking world.* A shriek of a laugh stifled, then rustling and moaning, Rab and Helen going hard at it under the covers on the bed piled with coats three feet away from me. My eyes were stuck shut, I couldn't open them even if I wanted to, and I didn't, listening was bad enough, was torture, and maybe it was just a sick dream and I couldn't open my eyes because I was asleep, or maybe I really had died and this was hell, listening to other people shagging for all eternity. But no, it had an end, they finished, bucked and shook the bed, knocked another couple of coats off on top of me. They subsided and I lay still and didn't move. And at some point they got up and went, and I still couldn't open my eyes and I must have gone back into deep sleep, was dazzled awake by the light switched on, so bright it hurt, and people were loud, crowding in to the room, grabbing their coats, the cover whipped off me. Ian and Doug looking down at me, looking down on me.

'Party's over,' said Doug.

'Told you not to mix your drinks,' said Ian, prodding me with the tip of his chisel-toe. Then we were outside and the cold air shocked me awake, my legs still unsteady as I lurched towards home, trailing behind Ian and Doug. As we crossed the swing-park, Rab caught up with us.

'Sobered up yet, bampot?'

I groaned, held my head. 'Feel like shit.'

'Great party, eh?'

'All right for some.'

'So you *were* listening!'

'Never had much choice.'

'Manky bastard!' But the way he said it, he was kind of pleased he'd had an audience.

'If you could hold your drink,' he said, 'you could have been right in there wi wee Jeannie.'

'Aye, sure.' I didn't want to think about it.

'No, I mean it. She's kind of weird. I think she liked you.'

'Thanks.'

'Naw, you know what I mean.'

'Makes it even worse.'

'How?'

'I'm in wi a shout and I fuck off and leave her, spew my ring and end up paralytic on the floor.'

He shrugged. 'Nothing to worry about. She probably thinks you're mental.'

'You reckon?'

'I'll ask Helen.'

Ian and Doug were spinning round slow on the roundabout that clanked as it turned. Ian unzipped himself and pissed over the edge, the stream of his piss dispersing as he spun. I sang the theme tune from *Sunday Night at the London Palladium*, the one that played at the end as the stars of the show spun round on a carousel.

Rab laughed and slapped me on the back. 'That's funny. That is fucking funny!'

Back home, the house was quiet, no noise from the old man, probably out the game himself, blootered. Heard myself saying *Ssshhh* to nobody, finger to my lips, admonishing the door, the floorboards. Caught myself doing it and laughed, stopped myself. *Ssshhh!* Made it up the stairs and into my room. Bent to untie my shoelaces and keeled over onto the floor, lay flat on my back laughing. Still not a sound from the old man, must be dead to the world. A sudden image of him laid out in one of the coffins. Push it away. I laughed again. Maybe things weren't too bad right enough. Maybe Jeannie did like me, thought I was mental or fucking funny. Maybe I was still in with a chance. And tomorrow I would feel I'd been through an initiation, got drunk for the first time. I would talk to the boys about it, shake my head and be rueful and agree it was a hell of a night.

Hungover. The way I'd seen my father. Fragile, raw, pushed over into nausea by the banging shut of a drawer, the rattle of cutlery, smell of toast or a stubbed-out cigarette, acrid. Dowp. Doubt. Sickness and the pain thudding right inside my skull. Brain-ache.

Now I knew.

He looked across at me, saw how I was. 'You must have got in late last night.'

'Back of twelve.'

'Twelve going on two or three.'

'Maybe it was one. What does it matter?'

He lit another cigarette. The grate of the match scraped my nerve ends. 'If I didn't know better, I'd say you'd been drinking.'

'Couple of glasses of cider, that's all.'

'That's how it starts. A mug's game.'

'You should know.'

'I do. And you're too young.'

This was going nowhere. 'Ach!' My answer to it all.

Ach.

He peered at me between drags. 'Sure you don't want any breakfast?'

'Cup of tea'll do me fine.'

An almost-smile. He was enjoying this, winding me up. 'By the way,' he said. 'That embalmer's coming over this afternoon. Doing another job for us.'

Us.

'Thought you might want to sit in on the session again. See what you can learn.'

'Great. Just what I need. Watching somebody drain the blood out a corpse.'

Even the thought of the smell of formaldehyde made me feel sick. I took a sip of the stewed, bitter tea. 'Need some air,' I said, and went out into the yard, screwed up my eyes against the daylight.

Andy looked up from under the bonnet of the hearse. 'You look terrible,' he said. 'Death warmed up.'

'Thanks.'

'Rough night?'

'Sort of.'

'Want to talk about it?'

I gave a kind of shrug, casual. 'Nothing to talk about. I went to a party. Met a wee bird.'

He gave me an encouraging leer. 'Get off wi her, did ye?'

I shook my head. 'I could have. I mean I had a chance. I think. But I blew it.'

'Made an arse of yourself?'

'Got bevvied. Threw up in the sink.'

'It happens.'

'I mixed my drinks.'

'Worst thing you can do.'

'Lanny and cider. God knows what else.'

He grimaced. 'Lethal.'

I still felt uneasy in my guts, but it helped, it definitely helped, this talking things out.

'So what's the next move?' said Andy. 'Head in the oven? Throw yourself under a bus?'

I laughed and it made my head hurt, but not as much as before.

'Listen.' I wanted to ask something, wasn't sure what.

'I'm listening.'

'Did you always want to do what you're doing?'

'You go in for the big questions, don't you! Are you still asking folk what happens when you die?'

I remembered the party, asking Jeannie. *Fucked if I know.*

'I live in hope,' I said.

'So. You're asking did I choose the life I'm living?'

'I meant your job and everything.'

'Well, I wasn't sitting when I was your age thinking wouldn't it be great to drive a hearse and lug coffins about.'

'No.'

'But things could be worse. It's a decent job. Steady. And let's face it, death isn't gonnae go out of fashion.'

'So what did you want to do?'

'Went into the army. Thought I'd make a career out of that. Had a few good years. Saw a bit of the world. Germany, Cyprus,

Aden. Learned a trade, came out a motor mechanic and driver. By the time I chucked it I had that to fall back on. Good qualifications for this.' He indicated the hearse, the yard. 'And of course there's my dignified military bearing. Perfect for the job.' He stood to attention, saluted. 'Sir!'

'At ease!' I said.

'I suppose you're making choices all the time,' he said. 'Things don't always work out, but you make the best of it, right?'

'Suppose so.'

'So what's all this about? It's not just the hangover or the party or the wee bird.'

'No.'

'So what is it?'

I didn't know, couldn't say. 'Just everything.'

'Bad as that?'

'Ach, I suppose it's the old man. He's got this embalmer coming round again.'

'The Wraith Rover!'

'That's the one. But my da wants me to work with him. All part of learning the trade so I can run the business some-day.'

'And you don't want that.'

'I've tried telling him, but he won't listen.'

'Is there something else you want to do?'

'*Anything* else!'

He nodded. 'Problem is, you don't want to end up like him.'

I stared at him. He was absolutely, totally right.

'It's natural,' he said. 'My two are the same wi me. I canny talk to them. They just don't want to know. So don't be too hard on your da. He's toiling as well.'

'Has he always been . . . the way he is?'

'He was always a bit dour. But there wasn't so much darkness about him when your mother was alive. He took that hard, her going so young.'

'I know.' The child in question.

'Can't have been easy,'

'No.'

54

'He had to get somebody else in to handle the arrangements. Couldn't face it. Might have been better if he had.'

I couldn't imagine that, felt uncomfortable, out of my depth.

'Listen to me!' said Andy. 'What do I know? Talk's cheap, eh?'

'Aye.'

'And as far as the job goes, you could do a lot worse. I mean, put it this way, you'd never be out of work, eh? Nothing surer than death.'

'Sure,' I said, the bleakness closing in again.

'Tell you what,' he said. 'See when they carry me out that door? I'm going for a solid oak lead-lined coffin, shouldered to the furthest cemetery I can think of. Give they boys of mine something to moan about!'

Auld Jack looked tired. He had started talking about retiring.

'Been at this game all my life,' he said. 'Came into it straight out the school. Left school on the Friday, started here on the Monday. That was it.'

All his life. The same job. Stuck in this basement. I felt a kind of panic.

'Course in those days it was your grandfather's firm,' said Jack. 'You'll no remember him.'

'Died before I was born.'

'A hard hard man he was. Stickler for discipline.'

'Just like my da.'

Jack laughed, a dry cackle. 'God, no! Your da's all sweetness and light compared to his da.'

'You're kidding.'

'Not at all. I've seen him send your da in when he was just a lad, get him to scrape a body off the floor it was rotted that bad.'

'God.'

'Or make him clean up after a suicide. Guy that had blown his brains out. I mind once he sent him in to collect a guy's head from Central Station!'

'Eh?'

'The guy had walked in front of a train. His body had been left at the side of the tracks, but his head had got caught on the engine, ended up at the terminus! Your da had to bring it back in a box, inside a canvas bag. Hell of a thing for a young boy. But the old man reckoned it would toughen him up. I mean it's no an easy line of work.'

'You're telling me! So what made you choose the job in the first place?'

'Choose?' Jack laughed again. 'Choice never came into it. The job was there, you took it. Never thought twice. Glad of the chance. Yous youngsters the day . . .'

You don't know you're living.

'Don't know you're living.'

Luxury. When I were a lad we worked a forty-hour day, eight days a week, for tuppence ha'penny a year.

'No, it was a good job,' said Jack. 'A trade. In those days the firm was McGraw and Sons, Undertakers and Joiners.'

'Makes sense, I suppose. Doubling up.'

'I could have went in to the undertaking side as well,' said Jack. 'Could have done the training. But ach, I wasnae really up to it.'

'In what way?'

'All the business of consoling people. Keeping up that front all the time. It's just no me. Oh, I used to help out a bit in the early days. Do some of the lifting and laying, cleaning the bodies, that sort of thing. But to tell you the truth, I never had the stomach for it. Decided the joinery would do me fine. And here I am.'

'Here you are.'

'I've even built my own casket. Your old man said I could. Perks of the job sort of thing. Kind of golden handshake.'

Christ.

'Never charged me for the materials. Let me work away on it when times were quiet.'

'Right. Aye.' All heart.

Jack stood up, stretched and creaked, his hands on the small of his back. 'I'll show you.'

It was against the far wall, covered by a dustsheet. He unveiled it, stood smiling down at it, proud. 'Top of the range. Like I said, it's a casket and no a coffin. Technically like. Least that's what the Yanks cry it. The box shape and that. Coffin's your standard tapered job. Course here everything just gets called a coffin. But if you want to be accurate, this is a casket.'

'It's, eh, a beautiful bit of work.'

'Craftsmanship,' he said, stroking the polished wood, touching the brass handles. 'You wouldn't believe what gets passed off these days. Veneered chipboard. Glued together. Can you imagine? Might as well use a cardboard box! Still, it's the way the world's going, isn't it? Mass-produced. Standard size. They'll end up selling flatpacks in the do-it-yourself shop!'

'Not a bad idea.'

'Except it would put us out of business.'

'And that would be terrible, eh?'

He gave me a baffled look, not quite sure what I was saying. Closed the lid of his coffin, his casket, draped it again with the cloth.

'Hello again, Neil.' The embalmer shook my hand. His was clammy, the way I'd expected. He smelled of the chemicals he used, overlaid with the tang of too much pungent aftershave. His cheeks were red, as if he'd been using his own products, injecting dye into his veins, bit of colour, touch of cosmetology. 'Glad you'll be helping me out today.'

'Aye.' I said it flat, uninterested. Here under protest, didn't want to know. My father was busy in the office, had left me to it.

The body was, had been, an old woman. She had died in her sleep. Slipped away. The look on the face wasn't agonised, or even startled. It was more a kind of blank acceptance – Right, so that was it, a life, oh well.

The Rover went through all the same procedures as before, but this time he asked me to do more of the work. Held the point of the trocar against the abdomen, just below the ribs, told me to push, make the insertion.

I froze, couldn't move. 'I can't,' I said, my voice shaky.

'It's not a person,' he said. 'It's just a carcass. Dead stuff. The old woman's long gone. You can't hurt her.'

'I know that. But it still gives me the creeps.'

'Just have to face that,' he said. 'Get over it.'

He guided the point of the blade again, pierced the skin. 'Now. For God's sake just do it.'

I gripped the handle and shoved and it was done.

'Good,' he said, encouraging but matter of fact. And he pulled the blade out again, set it to one side. 'Aspirate the gases.' He pressed down on the abdomen, there was a noise like the old woman's stomach gurgling and a smell that knocked me back, made me gag.

'You get used to it,' he said. And I knew it was true, I could harden myself to any of this, the way my father had done. End up exactly like him. Just a job. The Rover worked quickly, without fuss. He asked me to mix in the dye to the formaldehyde, a few drops from a bottle labelled Safranine Pink.

'A nice warm tone,' he said. 'A comfortable pink. Friendly.'

He showed me where to make the injection, into the heart. And I did it. I moved into the same detached functional mode that always took over when I helped my father with a chesting. Distanced and clinical, outside myself.

The blood drained into the metal drum. 'We use a coagulant,' he said. 'Thickens it. Gives it a consistency like strawberry jam. Makes it easier to dispose of.' He chuckled. 'You can always offer your pals a piece and jam!'

Made me feel ill again.

When the job was done and I'd helped the Rover clean up, my father made an appearance, his work in the office conveniently finished. 'Everything go all right?' he asked.

I gave him a look, turned away.

'Fine,' said the Rover. 'A good boy you've got there. Found it tough but he did it just the same.'

'That's what it's all about,' said my father, turning to me. 'And let's face it, you'll have to deal with a lot worse in this job.'

'I know,' I said. 'That's the problem.'

My father shook his head. The embalmer smiled. The old woman lay there, dead stuff pumped full of preservative. The look on her face was the same blank acceptance. The waxy cheeks glowed a warm friendly comfortable pink.

*

I met Rab in the street again, on his way home from work.

'By the way,' he said. 'That wee bird Jeannie was asking Helen about you.'

'Oh aye?' I felt my face hot.

'I was right. She did like you.'

'Except I messed it up.'

'I don't think she's bothered. I think she'd go out with you if you asked.'

'You reckon?'

'Pretty sure. Listen, me and Helen are going to the pictures on Friday night. There's one of these horror pictures on at the Vogue. I'll get Helen to ask Jeannie if she fancies coming, making up a foursome.'

'That would be brilliant. What's the picture?'

'*Premature Burial.*'

I held my head. 'That's all I fucking need!'

'Should be a laugh.'

Jeannie said yes and I couldn't think about anything else the rest of the week. Even the old man couldn't touch me. Inside me was a fire, exhilaration he couldn't reach. School term was over. I had no excuse for not helping out and he gave me jobs to do, kept me busy, involved. But with the good mood that was on me, I just got on with it and didn't care. Whatever my father thought, this wasn't my life.

On the Friday night as I washed and got ready, straightened the tie, flattened down the hair, I was overwhelmed at the thought that Jeannie was getting ready too. She'd be choosing what to wear, and putting on make-up, and brushing her hair, checking herself in the mirror. And she was doing all this to come and meet me. It made me feel good.

Rab and I arrived outside the Vogue at the same time, had to wait a few minutes for the girls. I saw them in the distance, arm in arm, giggling as they crossed the road. Jeannie looked great. Jeans and a denim jacket, black t-shirt underneath. Her short red hair looked soft, framed her pale face with the big dark-lined eyes. I looked at her with a kind of amazement. She was really here, we were going out together.

59

She smiled. 'Hiya.'

No drink this time to boost the confidence. But just seeing her made me elated. I felt an idiot grin on my face, not at all cool.

'Hi.' My hand waved in front of me, of its own volition. 'Eh, you look nice.'

'Thanks.' That smile again. 'Sticking to the Kia-Ora the night?'

'Eh? Oh aye. Unless I go for the hard stuff. A drink on a stick.'

We queued for the tickets. I bought mine and Jeannie's. Again that good feeling, this was real. Two for the stalls. We sat in the back row, Rab, Helen, Jeannie, me. We'd come in halfway through the wee picture, some black and white thing about zombies. A few people shouted things out in the dark, daft things like *I'll get ye!* and *Watch yer back!* Some of them just shrieked or screamed. The usherette kept raking with her torchbeam, telling them to keep quiet or they'd be out the door. But you could tell she didn't mean it, didn't care.

At the break the lights came up and the usual music filled the hall, Mantovani strings. But it didn't bother me, was all part of the atmosphere. I loved the warm orange light, the colours and shapes of the curtains, a rippling satin wall like red and gold waves. They shifted and changed as you looked at them – one minute the sections looked concave like long troughs, the next they seemed to curve out in 3-D, endless crests. I tried pointing it out to Jeannie, but she couldn't see what I meant.

'Sort of optical illusion,' I said. 'One way every section goes in, like a trench. The other way it comes out, like a tree trunk. See?'

She looked hard. Shook her head. No. Couldn't see it. 'Just looks like material to me. Bunched. Hanging there.'

'Oh well.'

The lights changed, dimmed. The curtains went up on the big picture.

Rab had his arm round Helen from the start and they kissed a few times. I kept glancing across when the action was flagging on screen. With Ray Milland cracking up, going mental, they were necking good style and Rab was busy with his hand up under her jersey. I casually stretched my arm along the back of Jeannie's chair, let my hand rest on her shoulder. And she didn't flinch, didn't shrug me off. In fact she moved a little closer, snuggled. I leaned and kissed her cheek. She turned and looked at me, amused, gave a wee chuckle, kissed me on the mouth hard and quick, and again, and we were kissing for real, lingering, soft and moist and warm, me and Jeannie winching, and I wanted it not to stop. But she broke the clinch, turned, left me slobbering her cheek.

'I want to see this bit,' she said.

I came up for air, grateful the dark hid the bulge in my trousers, like a tent-pole. 'Right,' I said.

On screen a coffin lid was ripped open, revealed the corpse of a woman, hair matted and wild, flesh rotted to the bone, nails grown long on skeletal fingers fixed in the act of clawing at the lid.

She was placed alive in the tomb.

A scream.

Jeannie hid her face in my shoulder, cooried in. I kissed the top of her head. She looked up at the screen. A long close-up of the corpse with its gnarled fingers faded out and we locked mouths again.

Outside there was still a late halflight, yellow streetlamps bright against a gunmetal blue sky. Everything looked intense and clear, sharply defined. I didn't know the next move. Rab was walking Helen home, left me to it. I looked at Jeannie.

'See you home?'

'Sure.'

She lived in a scheme about a mile away. I waited with her at the bus stop, not saying much. *Great picture, eh! Dead horrible. A good laugh.*

In the pictures, in the dark, it had been easy. No need to talk. Now, out here in the real street, I had lost it again, felt separate, shut up inside myself. Sitting together on the bus made it easier again, touching. Off the bus and down her street, through the close to the back. Leaning together, pressing, up against the wall. Why they called it a close. Kissing hard, her arms round my neck, my hands on her back, inside the denim jacket. Where we'd reached at the party. Before. Then I brushed her left breast with the right hand, tentative, through the t-shirt, and she didn't shove me away, smiled, and I pressed it, felt it soft and flattening out, and my hands were under the t-shirt, feel of warm skin and the shiny stuff of the bra, and something instinctual kicking in, like a memory, how did I know what to do here? Moving against each other, grinding, dry riding, and me not used to it, never got so far, starting to come, Christ, and Jeannie suddenly tensing, heavy footsteps in the close, a man's drunk voice, singing. *The old home town looks the same.* Dear God I couldn't stop if I wanted to not now don't let him see us or say anything. But he didn't, he dragged himself up the stairs, stumbled and cursed, *Ya bastard!* Righted himself and sang more. *Hair of gold and lips like cherries.* Shouted again. *Cunt!* And Jeannie relaxed, laughed into my shoulder, and I jerked and spurted, finished, clung to her.

'Got excited there, eh?' She smiled, enjoying the power of what she could do to me.

'Aye,' I said. 'Sorry.'

'Nothing to be sorry about.' She touched me there, felt it wilting, dying. 'It's natural.'

'Know what the French call it? When you come?'

'What?'

A boy in my class had found it in the dictionary, passed it round the library, sniggering.

'*Petit mort*,' I said. 'Means little death.'

'Weird,' she said.

'Isn't it.'

And so it was. And so was everything. The night sky darker now, flare of the streetlamps more vivid. And the lights on in kitchens and living rooms, all the wee lives. The buildings here gritty pebbledash. Shabby scheme of things. Street where you live. My fair lady. The pavement stayed beneath my feet as I walked the mile and a half home.

'I think you're right in there,' said Rab. 'Take her out another couple of times. Get her back to your place when your old man's out. You're away.'

He was hanging about the corner, waiting for Helen. I'd crossed the road to talk to him.

'I'm seeing her again the night,' I said.

'There you are then. Where are you going?'

'Don't know. Dancing maybe.'

'Great. Might see you up there.'

'Right.'

'And mind, I'm telling you, you're in wi a shout.'

The Drifters were singing in my head. *Friday night has finally come around.* I waited for Jeannie at the bus stop, waved as she got off. She looked great, smiling at me that way. I couldn't get used to it.

'So where d'you fancy going?' I asked, taking her arm.

'I'm no bothered,' she said, shrugging those thin shoulders.

'Pictures? Dancing?'

'Whatever you like.'

'We could just go back to my place. Listen to records and that.'

'And that!' She laughed. 'No, that's fine.'

And I heard it in her voice, the fascination, the curiosity, the wanting to see for herself how we lived.

They're creepy and they're cooky. Mysterious and spooky. Diddly-dum.

'Will your old man no mind?'

'He's out at the pub.'

'Fine.'

The way she looked round the house made me see how shabby and grubby it was. Not squalor, the place wasn't a pigsty. Just cluttered and run-down and not exactly clean. Surfaces dusty. Dust to dust. The staleness we lived with and ignored. I became aware of the kitchen table, formica top sticky, gritty with crumbs, a spill of granulated sugar, ashtray full of stubbed-out dog ends. I picked up an empty milk bottle that hadn't been rinsed out. Swilled it under the tap, but it had stood too long, wouldn't come clean. I filled it with water, left it to stand in the sink beside a stack of dishes we hadn't washed.

Jeannie shivered, hugged herself, rubbed her arms. 'Kind of

cold in here.' Meant the emptiness maybe, the drab bleakness she brought into focus just by being here.

'I'll show you my room,' I said.

She nodded. 'Can I see downstairs first?'

I showed her the office and reception area. Framed paintings of highland landscapes – mountains and lochs, supposed to be calming and reassuring, ease the mind.

'The back room's through here,' I said. 'And that *is* cold.'

'Is there any . . . bodies?' She had that look I'd seen before, part fear, part excitement.

'No,' I said. 'Nothing. Ain't got no body!'

I showed her the room anyway, the slab, the table, the big stainless steel sinks. The bright striplights buzzed.

'Creepy.'

'It's where we lay the bodies out. Wash them, dress them. We've started doing embalmings. A guy comes in and I help him.'

'Embalmings? Like mummies and that?'

'It's different. Just temporary. Basically you drain out the blood and replace it with preservative.'

'Yuch!'

I had never done this before – showed somebody round – and I found myself taking a pride in it, in the place and in Jeannie's reaction to it. I could see the creepiness excited her, and her excitement worked on me, roused me towards her as I followed her downstairs to the basement.

'God!' she said, as I switched on the light in the workshop and she looked round at all the coffins, some half built, some complete, on the floor, on benches, standing on end against the wall. 'It's incredible. Like something out a horror picture.'

'Tales from the Crypt sort of thing. Can just see one of the lids opening, and Vincent Price sits up and leers out at you.'

'Don't!' She covered her eyes.

'Then another one opens, and it's Christopher Lee. And they both start to climb out and come after you.'

I held my arms out straight in front of me, did a zombie-walk towards her.

'No!' She gave a wee scream that had a laugh at the heart of it,

64

and she pushed me away but not too hard. And I put my arms round her and she hugged me back and we were kissing and pressing against each other in amongst the coffins.

'You're mad!' she said.

In a Boris Karloff voice, I said 'It's living here. It's made me . . . strange.'

'Chuck it!' she said, laughing again.

'I'll tell you what, though.' I spoke in my own voice. 'When I was wee, my old man used to lock me in here. As a punishment sort of thing. If he thought I was being bad.'

'You're kidding!'

'No. Straight up.'

'That's horrible!'

'Suppose it was. Just got used to it but. I used to plank sweeties and comics. Got settled down in one of the coffins. Was quite comfy really, specially if it was one of these fancy plush padded jobs.'

'Like this one here.' She ran her hand along the shiny oak surface of Jack's customised casket.

'That one's really special. It's auld Jack's. I mean he's making it for himself.'

'Building his own coffin? Now that's too weird.'

'Makes him happy,' I said. 'And you have to admit, it's a beautiful job.'

'Sure.'

The lid was open, hinged back, and she looked inside, stroked the satin lining, felt the quilted padding.

'It does look comfy right enough,' she said, and gave me a sideways look, a half smile. 'Can I try it out?'

I laughed, a bit nervous. 'Why not? As long as you take your shoes off.'

She kicked off one shoe, then the other. Stepped up on the bench. Climbed in the coffin. Sat down.

'This is dead strange.' She tensed her shoulders, giggled.

'Oh right. *Dead* strange.'

'You know what I mean!'

And I did. It was exhilaration, and a kind of guilt, like this was almost sacrilege.

65

'You won't shut the lid on me, will you?' she asked, leaning back on her elbows. 'I mean, I'd just die.'

'You'd be in the right place then. Be quite handy.'

'No, but promise!'

'Cross my heart,' I said. 'Hope to die!'

Now we were both laughing, like little kids, a bit manic. Jeannie lay right back, stretched out in the coffin. Tensed a moment, and let out a breath, said quietly, 'This is pure mental. Like it's so spooky.'

'You look like a vampire.'

She bared her teeth, made a noise in the back of her throat, like a cat. I got hard again looking at her, leaned in to the coffin and kissed her on the mouth.

'Come on in,' she said. 'This is pure fucking kinky.'

And I was prising off my shoes, and climbing in on top of her, lying on her with my full weight and she was rising to meet me, pushing up against me and we were fumbling and groping, my hand down between her legs feeling it soft and warm and opening up and her hand kneading me through the jeans unzipping me flipping it out and both of us getting frantic sliding around on the satin bumping the sides of the coffin as we made each other come and lay there clinging, spent and damp.

I don't know how long we lay there. Seemed like no time. I was absolutely content, breathing in the smell of her, listening to her heartbeat, aware of the utter strangeness of us being there. Then I heard it, a noise over by the door. Everything clenched in me. The old man's voice.

'What in the name of God is going on?'

This couldn't be happening. He never came home this early. But he had. It was real. He was here. And I hadn't even heard him come in, been too far gone.

We disentangled ourselves, me zipping up, Jeannie pulling up her tights and smoothing down her skirt, and we climbed out of the coffin not knowing where to look. I had never seen my father so angry, a cold rage.

'Ya dirty wee bugger,' he said. 'You want to be ashamed.' He turned on Jeannie. 'As for you, madam, there's a word for what you are, and you know fine what it is.'

Jeannie got her head down, rushed past him out the door and up the stairs.

He shouted after her. 'That's right, ya wee hoor! Get out and don't come back!'

'Now wait a minute,' I said. I heard the outside door open, bang shut.

He pointed at me. 'I don't ever want to see her face around here again, right?'

I knew I shouldn't have said it, but the words formed, came out. 'I didn't think it was her face that was bothering you.'

And I felt myself say it with a smirk, and that was it, one thing too many. He stepped forward and swung a punch, but I was quick enough, brought up my left arm to ward it off, followed through with a straight right, hit him in the centre of the chest. He staggered back, winded and shocked. Then before I realised what he was doing he was out the door and had slammed it shut, locked me in.

'You'll stay in there till you learn respect!'

I heard his footsteps receding, going up the stairs. I threw myself at the door and battered it, battered it.

'Ya bastard!' I shouted. 'Let me out!'

The first hour I stamped around cursing, kicking coffins, punching the wall. Then I forced myself to calm down. No point in going crazy. I kept thinking he would come down and let me out, but he didn't. Another hour went by. Another. He was going to leave me here all night. The bastard was mad. I figured I wouldn't get much sleep, but thought I might as well try. I climbed into Jack's coffin again, the most comfortable place.

I could still smell Jeannie, her perfume on the satin lining, the smell of her on my hand. I put my fingers in my mouth, tasted her. I kept re-running the whole scene. The old man standing there outraged and righteous, Jeannie rushing out the door. It was a long night. My body was tired but my mind wouldn't stop. I twisted and turned, this way and that, couldn't rest. The few times I did drift off I slid into bad dreams, being buried alive, or not knowing who I was but knowing if I moved so much as a muscle I would die, and I'd have to break it by sitting up, thrashing around.

Eventually I couldn't take it. I got up cramped and stiff and shivery, eyes gritty, an ache in my shoulder. I paced up and down, trying to get warm, shouted once or twice, made noise, banged on lids, hoped it would get to him. And somewhere around eight I heard him moving about upstairs, and coming down, and the key turning in the lock.

He walked right past me, looked inside Jack's coffin. 'You can get some stain-remover,' he said. 'Clean this thoroughly. I want it spotless.' Then he turned again and went out the door, not locking it this time.

He didn't say another word to me the whole day. Didn't answer when I spoke to him. Ignored me completely, as if I didn't exist.

I went out and walked the streets, went and knocked at Jeannie's door but she wasn't home. Saturday. She had probably gone into town, would be going round the shops, trying on clothes, listening to records. Simple stupid things I wanted to be doing with her. Making a day. Instead I was standing here in her close looking out at the miserable street. Two wee boys kicked a red vinyl football back and forward. The ball was burst and didn't bounce, just scuffed along the ground. A scabby pack of dogs prowled the pavement, snuffled in the rubbish dumped in the doorway of a boarded-up shop. A bunch of men hung about the corner, waiting for the pub to open. You could smell Saturday.

I went home in the afternoon, couldn't settle. Horse racing on the TV. Lay on my bed and played the Who and the Stones. Can't explain. Paint it black.

The old man was out at a cremation, came back at tea-time, still not talking to me. He clumped about the kitchen, made a pot of tea, didn't offer me any. Then he disappeared into his room, changed out of his funeral clothes into his old suit.

Finally he spoke. 'There's nothing in for the tea. I'll get a pie and a pint down the pub. You can get chips or something. Whatever you want. Do what you like.' He turned to me as he said it. 'That's your style now anyway, isn't it? Do what you like.' And he was out the door.

I did go out for chips. Stood and ate them outside the shop. Crumpled up the paper and blootered it into a close. Volleyed it off the instep. Denis Law. Last-minute winner. Top corner. Beauty.

I walked about the streets again, aimless. Passed the pictures. Always something there to remind me. Thought about going round to Jeannie's but didn't think she'd want to know. And Rab would be out with Helen. Fuck it. Back home.

The old man came home late and drunker than I'd seen him. Pie-eyed. Legless. Out the game. Still mad at me but incoherent. Then his eyes fixed on me, held. And he brought it all into focus, all of it, the venom and resentment gathered into one word and the way he spat it out.

'You!'

The child in question.

He flapped a fist past me, an attempt at a punch but with no weight behind it, and the effort threw him off balance and he fell over, thudded to the floor. What they say about drunks and babies, they don't tense when they fall, roll with it, don't hurt themselves. He lay there, cursing, not moving. I left him to it, made myself tea and drank it, hot and sweet. Came back and he was still lying, out of it, unconscious. I tried to shake him awake but all he did was moan and snort, turn over.

I thought about leaving him there, what I usually did. Chuck a blanket over him, let him sleep it off. Then I decided. What I'd been wanting to do all these years, but I hadn't been big enough or strong enough, hadn't had the nerve.

I got my hands under his arms and dragged him across the floor. It wasn't easy, the sheer dead weight of him. I had to keep stopping to rest. But I got him to the stairs, and down to the basement, bumping his heels on every step. I sweated, head and neck prickling, breathing heavy, heart hammering against my ribs. But I made it, got him down there, and into the workshop. Stopped to get my breath back, work up the strength for one last push. And I gripped him, heaved him up and into the nearest coffin, stretched him out in it, flat on his back.

I stood looking down at him. Show the bastard once and for all. I had gone through some kind of barrier, felt elated and awed by it. I laughed and it sounded strange to me. The room was quiet, except for the noise of his breathing and mine. Just for a moment I thought about closing the lid over him. I watched the thought rise, let it go.

He stirred, moved, shouted out 'Ructions!' Settled again, lay still.

On the way out, I switched off the light. Then as an afterthought I turned the key, locked him in.

Famous last words, supposed to be.

Goethe, asking for More Light.

Somerset Maugham, saying, Dying is a dull, dreary affair. My advice to you is to have nothing whatever to do with it.

Stan Laurel, saying, I'd rather be ski-ing.

WC Fields, I'd rather be in Philadelphia.

Oscar Wilde, looking round the room. Either the wallpaper goes, or I do.

3

I got out as soon as I could. The week after I left school. Withdrew what I had in the bank, not much, closed the account. Savings from the basic wage the old man had paid me for helping him out. But I just couldn't do it any more, couldn't stay. Packed a few things in a rucksack. Left a note.

Took the overnight bus to London, nine hours of restless no-sleep. Climbed down at Victoria in the hard early morning light, stiff and shivery, head aching from breathing the stale air, the driver's cigarette smoke. Stood on the pavement looking about me. Watched the rest of the passengers disperse into their lives, to purposes of their own. Me left there standing. What now? I shouldered my pack. What the fuck now?

Round the corner was a Lyon's tearoom, open. I sat at a corner table, my pack on the chair beside me. Ordered a pot of tea, would do me fine for now. I wasn't really hungry yet, too early and my guts still knotted with the tension and strangeness, fear and excitement both. And anyway I had to watch the money, knew it wouldn't last.

The waitress brought the tea, in a stainless steel pot, set it down with a little reflex twitch of a smile. She looked no older than me, neat in her uniform, dark hair tucked up and pinned under her cap. I wanted to say something but couldn't think what. Her eyes glazed over, dull and bored. As she turned away I caught a whiff of her scent, a hint of sweat, felt a hard-on bulge my jeans. At least the table hid it. I shifted in my chair, picked up the teapot and poured. But the lid didn't fit tight, and a trickle of tea overflowed into my saucer, made a little puddle on the table. I sopped it up with a napkin, drained the saucer into the cup. Finally got the milk in, and the two white cubes of sugar, stirred a while and took a sip, felt better. This was me, in London, in a café drinking tea.

I relaxed a bit, took it all in. Smell of coffee and sticky pastry and fagsmoke. Not many customers this early. An old man in an overcoat, eking out a pot of tea, like me. Young woman, pert secretary in a white blouse and short skirt, sitting not smoking the cigarette she held between her fingers burning away, the line of smoke rising.

I looked round at the man sitting across from me at the next table, and the way he caught my eye I knew he'd been watching me. Long frizzy hair starting to grey. Could be Middle-Eastern, the skin a little dark, the hooked nose. Indian shirt and embroidered waistcoat.

He smiled across, nodded at my backpack. 'Travelling?'

'Aye,' I said. 'Yes.'

'Course we're all on a journey, aren't we?' The accent was indeterminate, could be a touch of American.

'Suppose so,' I said.

'No two ways about it. We're all going nowhere fast. Down that road to Oblivion.'

He picked up his cup, moved across and joined me. 'Have you noticed, if you take the word *nowhere*, and look at it different, it says *now here*?'

'Can't say I had.'

'Well there you are then. I've taught you something already.'

'Right,' I said, thinking I should humour him. I lifted the teapot to pour myself another cup.

'Couldn't help noticing,' he said, 'you had a spot of bother there.' He pointed at the soggy napkin. 'The problem is, the lids don't fit. The trick is to press it down tight as you're pouring.'

I tried it, spilled only a few drops. 'Ha!' He clapped his hands. 'Now we're getting somewhere. Which is better than nowhere, right?'

'Right.'

'But not as good as now here.'

'No.' I was winging this.

'A Zen master was asked what there is to do after you've leapt the void, embraced the ten thousand worlds. Know what he said?'

'No.'

'*Have a cup of tea!*' He laughed, lifted his own cup. 'So, cheers!'

'Cheers.'

76

'To the here and now. Which is all we've got. Right? Life is short. Then we die.'

'That's it.' This much I knew.

'We give birth astride the grave. The light gleams an instant, then it's night once more.'

I couldn't respond. The power of the words made me dumb.

'Sam Beckett,' the man said. 'Powerful stuff.'

'Amazing,' I said, the word inadequate.

'Astride of a grave and a difficult birth,' he continued. 'Down in the hole, lingeringly, the grave-digger puts on forceps.'

The words made a taste, like iron in my mouth.

'So what do you think?' I asked him. 'What happens when you die?'

'Aha!' he said. 'I knew it. A man after my own heart. A philosopher! As soon as you start asking questions like that, you're on the right road. Where do we come from? Why are we here? Where are we going? What's the purpose of life?' He answered himself. 'The purpose of life is to ask the question, What's the purpose of life?'

'And death?'

'Just is. Brute fact.'

'And that's it? No more to it?'

'Maybe what happens when you die depends on what happens when you live. Maybe that's the important thing.'

'Like karma?' I said, dredging up the word from years back. Padma in the school dinner-hall. Indian spice and sweet.

'See!' said the man. 'You are a philosopher!'

The waitress came over and asked if we'd finished. Cleared away our dishes, brought our separate bills. The man insisted on paying for my tea. 'Least I can do for a fellow truth-seeker.'

Outside, he held out his hand. 'The name's Abe.'

'Neil,' I said.

His hand was big and bony, crushed mine. 'So what's your plans now?'

'Don't really have any.'

'Free spirit, eh? Go with the flow.'

'Sort of.'

The uncertainty was there again, the chill, reasserting itself. What now? Nowhere to go. Now here.

'Listen,' said Abe. 'If you need somewhere to crash for a bit, there's floor space at the place I'm staying. I mean, like tons of people use it.'

'And they wouldn't mind?'

'Nah. Everybody's cool.'

'Well, maybe just for a wee while. Till I find my feet.'

He laughed, looked down. 'I think you'll find they're still on the ends of your legs!'

'On the ground,' I said.

'Cool.'

This was the hippy trip I'd read about. Crash pads and communes. Mindblowing peace and love. Cool.

'Of course none of this is accidental,' said Abe as we butted our way out through the crowds at Notting Hill Gate, up through the underpass out of the tube station. 'You running into me in the café when you'd only just arrived. Me just happening to go in there for a cup of tea. Somehow it's all meant.'

'You reckon?' I asked, shifting my pack to stop it digging in to my shoulder.

'For sure,' he said. 'The Sufis have this notion of *karass*. Means your group. And it's like, everybody you meet is connected to you in some way. You've got something to work out through them. Even somebody you just end up sitting next to on a bus. Somebody that asks you directions in the street. They're all part of your karass. Your group. So there's people you might have to connect with for a moment. And there's other people, like family, or lovers, that you're heavily involved with. Maybe for a lifetime, or more.'

'So there's no such thing as chance,' I said.

'That's right. No chance. Although chance is how it works!'

'I don't understand.'

'Well that's a good place to start.' He stopped. 'We're here.'

I looked up. We were outside a rundown brickbuilt terrace house on two floors, all the curtains drawn, black sacks of rubbish dumped outside the door.

'The garbage gets collected today,' he explained, stepping past it to turn his key, push open the door. The long narrow hall was dim and cluttered, a bike against the wall, boots and shoes, couple of cardboard boxes. The atmosphere was close and stale, smelled of cigarettes and onions, old clothes and some sweet musky scent I couldn't place.

I thought about changing my mind and backing out, saying I'd just remembered I had somewhere else to go, but I felt foolish. Abe was heading up the stairs.

'Nobody else is up yet,' he said. 'Too early. Best thing is to leave your stuff in my room in the meantime.'

'Fine,' I said, feeling numb.

The room didn't look too bad, had a kind of shabby warmth, raffia mats on the floor, Indian bedspreads over a bed, a couch, an old armchair. I sat down on the couch, sank, suddenly exhausted. The journey, everything, had caught up with me.

'You look knackered,' said Abe. 'Maybe you should crash out for an hour or two.'

'Sounds good,' I said, the words slurring. I prised off my shoes, the laces still tied. Stretched out on the couch and was gone, conked.

I was back home in the basement, lying in a coffin again, flat on my back. Not sleeping but not awake, some limbo zone between. Could hear noises, voices, people moving about. But I couldn't move, sheer dead drag of bodyweight down. And someone I couldn't see was close, bending over me almost touching, and I knew I'd be all right if only I could move, come awake. Then I knew without seeing the figure had become a bird, huge crow with a vicious curved beak. It flapped its wings and hovered above me. I was no longer in the coffin, no longer in my father's house. I'd been left out on a hillside, exposed. The bird circled in the sky. I had to move. I couldn't. Called up all my willpower and forced my eyes open, cried out with the effort of it and sat up.

But where was this? I was in another dream, nowhere I knew. A tent with a line of light coming in through a flap in the doorway. Matting on the floor. Seats, a divan, draped in rich colours, patterned cloth. Then I recognised, remembered it. Where I was. London. Daylight through the chink between sagging curtains.

First thought was to check my pockets. My money, all of it, folded in an envelope. Still there. And the rucksack where I'd left it on the floor. Fine.

I stood up groggy, mind heavy and dull. Somewhere, in another room, somebody laughed. A radio played. The noises and voices I'd heard in my dream.

I pulled on my shoes, went out to the landing. Bare lino and floorboards that creaked. The noise was from two doors down, smell of toast wafting out, Joni Mitchell on the radio singing *Chelsea Morning*. I knocked and went in.

They turned to look at me. A girl and a boy, the girl small and thin, mousy hair long and straight, the boy with a mass of muddy brown curls, a scraggy moustache.

Turned to look at me.

'Hi,' I said.

'Hi,' said the girl, and smiled.

'Another one of Abe's wee pals?' said the boy, his accent Glasgow.

'Pity,' said the girl, and she sipped her coffee.

I didn't understand. 'I met Abe this morning. He let me kip on his couch.'

'You're Scottish!' said the boy.

'Glasgow,' I said.

He shook his head. 'So where'd he pick you up? Euston or Victoria?'

'What d'you mean pick me up? I met him in a tearoom. He bought me a cup of tea.'

'I'll bet he did,' said the girl.

'What is this? What are you saying?'

The boy smiled. 'Did he tell you there's no such thing as chance? Everything's meant and you must be part of his karass?'

'Something like that, aye. Are you trying to tell me he's one of them?'

'An arse-bandit,' he said. 'A raving poof.'

'Fucksake.'

'You mean you're not?'

'No!'

He laughed. 'He will be disappointed!'

I remembered the figure in my dream, leaning over me. 'Where is he?'

'Out to the shops.'

'I'll get my stuff,' I said. 'Be away before he gets back.'

'Have you got somewhere else to go?' asked the girl.

'No really,' I said. 'I just arrived.'

'Just off the boat!' said the boy. 'Welcome to fucking swinging London!'

'At least stay and have a cup of tea,' said the girl.

'Ach aye,' said the boy. 'Abe'll no bother you. Just tell him the score and he'll back off.'

'You sure?'

'Positive. He takes no for an answer.'

'Well. Maybe a coffee then.'

The girl rinsed a mug in the sink, lit the gas under the kettle to reheat. 'I'm Vikki, by the way.'

'Neil.'

'Des.'

We heard the front door open and close, footsteps up the stairs. Abe came in to the kitchen carrying a pint of milk, smoking a roll-up.

'Abey baby!' said Des. 'Sorry man, the game's up. We've went and queered your pitch, if you'll pardon the expression!'

Abe saw the situation, took it in. Flashed me a look. 'So you're not?'

I shook my head. 'No.'

'Oh well.' He shrugged. 'Win some, lose some.'

'More philosophy?'

'Ha!'

Joni sang on the radio. *Won't you stay, we'll put on the day and we'll talk in present tenses.*

Here. Now.

The first week I just wandered, buzzing with the freedom of

being there, nothing I had to do and nowhere I had to go. Abe had loaned me a book on Zen, a peace offering, full of stories about living the timeless life, entering the gateless gate, hearing the soundless sound. I didn't understand much of it, but I caught the odd glimmer. I would come to myself, only way to describe it, find myself sitting in a café in Charing Cross Road, or walking along Oxford Street, or sitting on a bench in Hyde Park, watching the ducks on the Serpentine, and I'd laugh, feel a rush of sheer exhilaration. Life could be as simple as this. And at night I'd go back to the house in Notting Hill.

Des and Vikki weren't a couple as I'd first thought. Des had a girlfriend called Jess, shared a room with her. Jess was small and dark, Jewish, the only one of them that had a real fulltime job, working in a boutique off King's Road. So the house was rented in her name. The others signed on, drew social security. Des was a painter, had dropped out of art school. Vikki made jewellery, sold it on Portobello Road at weekends. When I asked Abe what he did, he said, 'This and that.' Grinned.

As well as the four of them, there was a floating population, a steady flow of visitors passing through. Open house. I ended up sleeping in a big room on the ground floor, what would once have been a parlour, in another age. A couple of Des's canvases hung on the walls, a few more were stacked in a corner. They all showed fantastic landscapes, deserts, forests, seashores, done in searing colours that clashed and pulsed. And areas of sky or sea, the random fluid shapes of wave or cloud, merged into geometric patterns. I found the paintings disturbing in a way I couldn't define, a tenseness in my stomach when I looked at them. The room was where Des worked on them, and it smelled of paints and turps and linseed oil.

The room was a clutter of other stuff too. Guitar without any strings. A stuffed owl with one eye. A piece of driftwood carved to look like a dragon. A tailor's dummy, just the torso mounted on a base. An orange traffic cone. A single iron dumbell. I cleared a space for myself amongst it all at the far end of the room, furthest away from the window and the streetnoise. More than once I was woken in the night by other visitors clattering in, dumping their backpacks, crashing out in their sleeping bags. Some of them I didn't meet. They'd still be asleep in the morning when I went out, were gone by the time I got back. One or two I spoke to in the kitchen. A thin, fey Dutchman called Simon who said he was from Andromeda Nebula. A big bearded American who called himself Gandalf.

The week I'd stayed felt long. Home was another country, another world.

One night Des stuck his head round the door, said they wanted a word, in the kitchen. The four of them sat at the table, Des and Jess, Vikki, Abe. A tribunal. This was it. I'd overstayed the welcome. Bum's rush. Out the door.

'Cup of tea?' said Abe, twinkling at me.

'No, thanks,' I said. 'I'm fine.'

'Fine?' he said. 'Good. It's good to be fine.'

'With this cunt,' said Des, 'you don't know if he's coming the Zen master, or if he's just offering you a fucking cup of tea.'

'And what's the difference?' said Abe.

'Ach!' said Des, having none of it.

Abe poured himself a cup. The pot was old and beat up, dulled aluminium dented and bashed. The handle, the loose knob on the lid, were red plastic. He held the lid in place with a dishtowel.

'Voila!' he said. 'Another tea ceremony.'

'Anyway,' said Jess, smiling at me. 'We wanted to talk.'

The smile was good, as far as I could tell. 'Sure.' I nodded, smiled. Keen.

'The thing is,' she said, 'we don't mind you staying here.'

Here it came. *But.*

'Got to be kind,' said Vikki. 'Help people out.'

I was with her, all the way. 'Absolutely. Yes. Right on.'

'He's learning the language,' said Des.

Jess ignored him. 'What we're saying is, you're no problem. It's just that if people stay more than a few days, we ask them to chip in, you know?'

They weren't throwing me out. She was saying I could stay. I loved them all, wanted to hug them. Didn't.

'Definitely. I can give you something right away. And I'll sign on, get a job, whatever.'

'Whatever,' said Abe. 'Good philosophy. Right attitude.'

'We're not talking much,' said Des. 'Few quid to cover the basics.'

'No problem.'

'So that's it settled,' said Jess.

Vikki came over and kissed me on the cheek, her arms round my neck. Surprised, I hugged her, crushed her thin body against me.

'You're nice,' she said, popped a quick friendly kiss on my mouth.

Des laughed, gave me the thumbs up.

'Party time!' said Abe, holding his arms out. 'My room. Fifteen minutes. Be there!'

I hadn't been in Abe's room since that first morning. I'd avoided going in there, didn't want to give him the wrong idea. But with all of us piled in it felt safe. A couple of table-lamps threw a soft warm light, mellowed the atmosphere. Abe had lit incense. 'Frangipani,' he said. And he'd put on a record of sitar music. It shimmered around us, the sound sharp and clear from good speakers. Filled the room and made it a different place.

Abe held up a long roll-up he'd just made, the paper at one end screwed to a point. 'A sublime spliff. Pure Moroccan grass. Fresh in this morning from my man in Marrakesh.'

'You scored it off Mad Mick down Brick Lane,' said Des.

'Nevertheless,' said Abe, intoning the word like a priest. 'Never. The. Less. There are two kinds of truth. The literal and the poetic. And I know which I prefer.'

'Right,' said Vikki. 'Me too.'

Abe picked up a slim silver lighter, flicked it into flame, lit up. He held the spliff between the first two fingers of his right hand, cupped it to his mouth. Inhaled long and deep, held, blew out with a big sigh. Passed on to Des who did the same. On to Vikki. To me. I gulped in the hot smoke, half choked but held it down. Spluttered a bit as I let it out. Handed it to Abe who was grinning at me. And I grinned back, laughed as my head filled with light.

By the time the joint had been round again, and Abe had lit another and we'd smoked that too, the five of us were flying, laughing at everything, all of it. I just had to look at the others and it set me off. They all had the same stupid grins, eyes puffy and half closed. And what was even funnier was I knew I looked the same. Zonked out. Mellowed. Blown away.

'God!' I said, as a strange thought came to me.

'Yes?' said Abe in his incantatory mode, from far away, on high. And that was funnier still.

'No,' I said, controlling it with effort. 'I was trying to imagine my old man on this stuff!'

'Blow his head off,' said Abe.

'Imagine the kind of funerals he'd conduct,' said Des. He held up his right hand in a two-finger peace sign, put on a voice that was hip-talk in a dour Scottish accent. 'OK man, so the guy's like dead. But hey! Stay cool! I mean it had to happen, right? Just a matter of when. Could be you tomorrow. Or me. So hang loose, OK? Ashes to ashes. Chill out.'

I was laughing so much it was hurting, tears in my eyes. Laugh till you cry. Split your sides. Fit to bust. All the things people said, all just like the thing.

'Then he'd go to his turntable,' said Abe. 'Put on some really heavy sounds.'

'Hendrix,' said Jess.

'Lift the fucking roof off!' said Des.

'The Floyd,' said Vikki. 'With a light show.'

'Floyd!' said Abe. 'That's what we need now!'

The sitar music had played out. He shook another record from its sleeve, put it on the turntable, carefully set down the needle between tracks.

'Here,' he said, passing me a set of headphones. 'You've got to hear this right. Let it blast you.'

I'd never listened through headphones before. This was new, made me laugh again. The soft pads fitting over the ears, shutting off outside noise, closing you in. Soft electronic hum, hiss of the needle in the groove. Then the track beginning, deep thud of drum hypnotic, bass coming in with the same rhythm, riff that became the melody. And this unbelievable sensation that the music was inside my head, swooshing from phone to phone through my brain.

'Wow!' I shouted, and couldn't hear myself. But the others laughed. Des covered his ears. Vikki put a finger to her mouth, shooshing me.

Then the words of the song kicked in and the whole thing built. I closed my eyes and was moving out, interstellar. *Set the controls for the heart of the sun.* Felt disembodied, pure spirit. Flying.

When the track was finished, I took off the headphones, gave them back to Abe. 'Good stuff,' I said, the words sounding ridiculous.

'Cosmic,' he said, which sounded even more ridiculous, set me laughing again.

Des and Jess were entangled on the couch, all over each other, mouths locked, hands stroking, groping. I wondered if they'd do it right there in the room. Watching them made me hard. I looked across at Vikki and she was lost in the music, eyes closed, swaying. Abe was flat on his back on the floor, the headphones on. I wanted/didn't want to look at Des and Jess. Was disappointed and relieved when they got up and left, waving vaguely as they went.

I shut my eyes again, tried not to think about anything. But now I felt agitated, edgy. Lost. *Verloren.* Forlorn.

I felt something touch my knee. Looked and it was Vikki sitting at my feet, leaning her head in my lap. I touched her hair and she smiled up at me, eyes still bleary. The hard-on bulged my jeans again and she laughed, outlined it with her thumb and finger, leaned and kissed it. Then she slid up beside me on the chair, kissed me on the mouth, said in my ear, 'My room.'

We managed to stand up and she took my hand, led me. Abe was still on his back, away in deep space. He looked up at us, waved. A benediction.

It was too quick, my first time. Everything heightened from the dope, we couldn't wait, felt ready to explode. I struggled out of the t-shirt, the jeans caught on my feet. Her long dress pulled off over her head. Never before with anyone, this nakedness amazing, touch an electric charge. Her skinny body wrapped around me, tiny breasts flattened out. Licking the little nipples, my hand down feeling her, warm and wet. Her hand pulling, guiding me up and in with the tip as we stood there swaying. Almost came right then, couldn't hold back much more. Down onto her mattress in a tangle of covers and all the way in, the shock of it, pushing in and in, grinding, no stopping, the surge and thrill, release of coming into sweet nowhere. Now here.

Somewhere, in the middle of the night, we woke and looked at each other.

'Oh fuck!' she said.

'Afraid we did,' I said. And inside I was punching the air in triumph, taking a lap of honour. Yes, I'd done it. I'd scored, got a ride, had my hole. Then the darker thoughts came in. I hadn't used anything. Been too far gone to even think of it. What about consequences? Diseases. Pregnancy.

Vikki must have read my face, said quietly, 'It's OK.'

'What is?'

'I'm clean,' she said. 'And I'm on the pill. Have been for six months.'

Yes! Wave to the main stand.

'Thank fuck!'

'Funny thing to thank!' she said.

Then the next question. 'How come you're on the pill?'

'Well I have to keep taking it, even when Gus is away.'

'Gus?'

'My boyfriend.'

'Jesus Fuck!'

My boyfriend's back and there's gonna be trouble.

I could see him, psychopathic Hell's Angel with tattoos and no neck. He would rip my face off.

'Don't look so worried,' she said. 'I told you it's OK. It's cool.'

'What does he do?'

'Plays in a rock band. Bass guitar. And he tours a lot.'

'Plays away.'

'Right. So he couldn't say anything, even if he did find out. Which he won't.'

'When's he due back?'

Any minute now. He'd kick in the door. Six foot lanky streak of misery. He'd beat me about the head with his amp.

'Not for another couple of weeks,' she said. 'So relax.'

She kissed me, her hair falling over my face. She moved on top of me, guided me in again, and this time it wasn't so rushed, she controlled it, came first and cried out, then shuddered in some kind of aftershock as I shot up into her. And I lay there, a sense of wellbeing right through me, and I never wanted to do anything else ever again.

What happens when you die?

Who the fuck cares?

Nothing was forever. Not this not anything. This time with Vikki was no time really. No time at all. And passing so fast. The word was *bittersweet*.

The songs defined it, fixed it in the memory. Ray Davies singing *Waterloo Sunset* and *Thank you for the days*. Lines rang like mantras, like prayers against time and change and death. *You're with me every single day. / I won't be afraid. / I am in Paradise.* And Joni sang *We are stardust we are golden.*

That summer.

'I'm counting the days!' said Abe, hands on hips, pouting and doing a Mick Jagger strut round the kitchen to *Brown Sugar* on the radio.

'To what?' I asked, innocent.

'Jesus Christ, man!' he said. 'What planet you on?'

'Only the fucking Stones,' said Des. 'Only a fucking free concert in Hyde Park.'

'It's good they're still doing it,' said Jess, 'with Brian dying and all.'

Face down in a swimming pool. Couldn't get no satisfaction.

'Oh yeah,' said Des, 'like they're going to cancel the biggest publicity stunt ever.'

'I think it's beautiful,' said Vikki. 'They're sort of dedicating it to his memory.'

She looked sad. 'Cheer up,' I said. 'Life's too short.'

'I know,' she said. 'Way too short.'

'Hey!' I put my hand on her shoulder. 'What is it?'

She took in a breath, looked at me, looked away. 'It's Gus.'

'What?'

'He said he'd definitely be back for the concert.'

It felt like being punched. I'd known it had to happen. Sometime. But not now, so soon.

'Tough shit,' said Des.

'All things must pass,' said Abe. 'I mean, in the light of eternity . . .'

'Abe,' I said. 'Give it a fucking rest.'

The day of the concert we all got toked up again on Abe's Brick Lane Moroccan. 'Got to be in tune,' he said.

Gus hadn't showed up yet. Vikki thought he'd go straight to the concert, come back to the house later. 'Can't wait,' I said, and she placed a small soft kiss on my mouth, full of sweet sad affection.

We walked to the park, and the state we were in, it seemed a long way.

'Imagine how all this would look from above,' said Abe. 'All these people, *converging*!'

'So many,' I said.

'Now you're quoting Dante,' he said. 'Or Eliot.'

'Am I?'

'So many. So many. I had not thought death had undone so many.'

'Death?'

'Dante's talking about the number of people streaming in to Hell. Eliot quotes it watching the crowds on London Bridge.'

'So he saw London as Hell?'

'It can be pretty infernal,' he said, clouding over. 'Wrong place, wrong time.' Then he shook off whatever it was. 'But not today, ha? Look at them all! So *many*!'

A helicopter whirred and circled overhead. 'God's-eye view,' I said, pointing up.

'That's what I want,' said Abe. 'To see it all, from on high!' And he spread his arms, spun like a dervish till he was dizzy.

Vikki sang, her voice piercing sweet.

And I dreamed I saw the bombers
Riding shotgun in the sky
Turning into butterflies above our nation.

'Yes!' Abe shouted, still staggering. 'Our nation. That's what this is. Freak nation! I'm putting my queer shoulder to the wheel!'

I laughed and threw my head back. The helicopter was a dragonfly, buzzing and turning. I stood gaping up at it, was jostled from behind.

'Come on mate,' said a hard voice. 'Move it.'

'Hey,' I said. 'Take it easy.' And somebody clipped my heels and I was down in the dust, avoiding feet. By the time I got up again, a helping hand under my arm, the others were gone, lost in the crowd, and I felt a sudden rush of paranoia.

The memory came vivid. Six years old, at a football match with my father, the terracing at Ibrox. Heading for the exits at full time I'd been caught up in the crowd, swept along, the crush so tight my feet were off the ground, too wee to do anything about it. Then hands had held, steadied me, and my father had reached me, picked me up.

I stopped again, stood still, hit by the force of the remembered moment. My father taking me to the game. My father picking me up and carrying me. What had happened to all that?

Then I was being shoved again, jolted from the back, and I felt a momentary panic at being closed in. I got my head down and pushed through to where there was more space, a clearing. Breathed deep and the tension eased.

It was miles back from the stage but it would do fine. No way I was going to try and shove up closer to the front. A lot of the people around me had settled, were sitting down, and I did the same. And the pressure lifted altogether. I laughed, lay back on the grass looking up again at the sky.

The roars made me sit up, brought me to my feet. A jangled guitar chord struck, sudden wham, amped up, screeched into feedback, cut. The band, these tiny figures so far away, moving around on stage, and Mick all in white at the microphone.

All right!

And the crowd noise rising again, drowning him out, and Mick, petulant, wanting a bit of hush so he could read something.

Are you going to cool it?

And they did. Enough so he could be heard. A poem for Brian.

> *Peace, peace! He is not dead, he doth not sleep –*
> *He hath awakened from the dream of life –*
> *'Tis we, who lost in stony visions, keep*
> *With phantoms an unprofitable strife,*
> *And in mad trance, strike with our spirit's knife*
> *Invulnerable nothings. We decay*
> *Like corpses in a charnel; fear and grief*
> *Convulse us and consume us day by day*
> *And cold hopes swarm like worms within our living clay*

In front of me, two girls were sobbing, holding each other. Mick read on.

> *The One remains, the many change and pass*
> *Heaven's light forever shines, Earth's shadows fly;*
> *Life, like a dome of many-coloured glass*
> *Stains the white radiance of Eternity*
> *Until Death tramples it to fragments – Die,*
> *If thou wouldst be with that which thou dost seek!*
> *Follow where all is fled! – Rome's azure sky,*
> *Flowers, ruins, statues, music, words, are weak*
> *The glory they transfuse with fitting truth to speak.*

Then something else was happening, a flurry on stage, more roaring from the people in front.

'It's butterflies!' a girl shouted. 'Hundreds, thousands of them!'

White clouds of them, dispersed into the air, set free.

All right!

And the ceremony was over. The intro to *Honky Tonk Woman* raunched, ground out.

And I was jumping up and down, caught up in it all, dancing with the rest, stoned free out of my head.

But at some point I began to feel distanced from everything, away inside myself. Coming down from the high I was separate, apart. The day was dreamlike, unreal. Drift of incense, hashish in the air. All these people.

So many.

I heard a noise behind me, shouting. Turned and saw a mob of skinheads stomping round the perimeter. Shoving, butting, kicking anyone who got in their way. *Fuck off the lot of you. Fuckin hippy bastards.*

And just as quick they were gone again, moved on, casually vicious in their endless search for bother.

The music blasted out. The crowd rocked on.

The others got back to the house late. They'd gone to the pub, The Sun in Splendour, just down the road.

'Thought you might have showed,' said Vikki.

'Just a bit skint,' I said. I hadn't got round to looking for work.

'You signing on yet?' asked Jess, not insistent but definitely interested.

'Monday morning,' I said.

'Cool.'

'Give the boy a break,' said Abe. 'He's got to breathe!'

'Sorry we lost you at the park,' said Des. 'Some gig but, eh?'

'It was good.'

'Good?' said Abe. 'It was divine! Mick is an angel!'

'I thought the Brian Jones thing was a bit offhand,' said Jess. 'Kind of perfunctory, you know?' She gruffed her voice, got Jagger's hip cockney exact. 'Cheers Brian, sorry you croaked and that, but let's rock.'

'But that was the beauty of it!' said Abe, waving his hands. 'Keep on trucking! On with the show! And as for the Shelley, and the whole thing with the butterflies, it was exquisite!'

'I liked it too,' said Vikki. 'It was nice.'

Abe smiled at her. 'Butterflies above our nation. It all fits!'

'I guess you're still out your head,' said Des.

'Sheer exhilaration,' said Abe. 'Butterflies!' He held his head. 'Chuang Tsu!'

'Bless you!' said Des.

'Chuang Tsu,' said Abe again, ignoring him. 'He said a man once fell asleep and dreamed he was a butterfly. And the rest of his life he could never be sure if he was a man who'd dreamed he was a butterfly, or a butterfly dreaming he was a man. Isn't that great?'

'Makes your head nip,' I said.

'It's this life we're living,' he said. 'A dream within a dream.'

There was a loud battering at the front door.

'It's a bust!' said Des. 'Drug squad rounding up every known dope fiend!'

Just for a second, Abe looked anxious, glanced at the door. But Vikki put a hand on his arm. 'I'll get it. I've a good idea who it'll be.'

I heard her open the door, and a man's voice, loud. *Vikki! Baby!* And Vikki's laugh, and the two of them coming in, the man with his arm round her. He was tall, a haze of frizzed-out dyed-black hair held with a red bandana. Beads round his neck, leather thongs at his wrists.

'Gus, man!' said Abe. As if I didn't know.

'Yo!' said Gus, giving a lazy wave that included everyone. Then he looked at me. 'Don't think I know you, man.'

'Neil,' I said.

'He's just down from Scotland,' said Des.

'Not another one!' He turned to Abe. 'One of your boys?'

'Regrettably, no,' said Abe.

'Neil's just staying for a few days,' said Jess quickly. 'Till he gets fixed up.'

'Cool,' said Gus, pulling Vikki close to him, an arm round her shoulders. He was stoned, expansive. 'What a fuckin day! Fuckin Stones, what?'

'Glorious,' said Abe.

Gus nuzzled Vikki's neck, whispered something in her ear. Then he was guiding her out the door, towards her room. 'See you guys. Me and Vikks have got some catching up to do.'

I felt sick, empty. Abe saw it, put a hand on my shoulder. 'If it doesn't break you, it'll make you strong.'

Next night I was sitting on my own in the big groundfloor room. Gus's bass guitar, his amp, his kitbag, added to the clutter. I felt abandoned there, like so much jetsam myself. Nothing to do and nowhere to go. Evening sun streaking in through the grimy windows, the gap in the dusty curtains. *Such a sad light and fading.* What was that from? Some song. It would come back to me. I lay back on my sleeping bag, stared up at the flaking ceiling. *A little brought down in London.* That was it. Donovan. Brought down. Young girl blues.

Abe knocked the door, came in. 'Got it bad, eh?'

'Ach,' I said. All I could manage in the way of explanation.

'I might have just the thing,' he said. 'Guaranteed to take you out of yourself!' He laughed, his eyes shining, held out a little yellow tablet.

'What is it?'

'Pure sunshine, he said, and leaned over, conspiratorial. 'This is very very good acid.' Then it was as if he'd caught himself being serious, laughed again. 'Guaranteed!'

'Are you on this just now?' I asked, as he crinkled his eyes at me.

'This?' He examined the word, quizzical. Then he focused on the pill again, realised what I was asking. 'This! Yeah! I dropped a tab about . . .' He looked at a non-existent watch. 'Who knows? A while ago. Two hairs past a freckle! And what's time anyway? A joke!' He steadied his concentration. 'This really is good stuff.'

'Listen,' I said. 'I'm skint. Can't afford it.'

'This,' he said, holding up the pill, 'is beyond price. It's a sacrament. Consider it a gift. On the house.'

'Are you sure?'

'Take it,' he said. 'And take it!'

I did. I took the pill, worked up saliva and swallowed it down. 'There.'

'Where?' he said. 'Here!'

'We have lift-off.'

'Set the controls for the heart of the sun!'

How much time had passed? I had no idea. Anyway time was a joke.

Some joke.

The things in the room looked funny. Took up space. Full of themselves! The sad old owl with its one eye. The carved dragon. The absurd torso on its base. The stringless guitar. For playing the soundless sound. Dance to my Zen guitars! Rab Deans. His old man had keeled over in the pub, in the middle of singing. As good a way as any. Came to us all. But didn't want to think about that. Push it away. Be here now. Here in this strange room full of objects just sitting there. The traffic cone, assertive. The dumbell. Dumb bell. Bell that never rang. Another soundless sound!

The dragon breathed, moved when I wasn't looking. The owl fixed me with its one eye. Dedicated to the one eye love. *His eye is single and his body is filled with light.* Stringband. Incredible! *Everything's fine right now.* We'd listened to that, up in her room. That feeling in the guts again. Not wanting to know. What I couldn't face.

Vikki.

And that stuff dumped there, that black stack of equipment, had something to do with it. Gus. His bass and amp. *My boyfriend's back.*

Fuck.

But what did it matter? What did anything? The dragon winked at me, was suddenly covered with scales of shimmering metal. And every surface I looked at in the room was patterned with fine traceries, like intricate ivory carving, like three-dimensional lace. The owl was golden, heraldic. Its single eye burned, a jewel. The cone and the dumbell were astonishing shapes, things in themselves, intensely there. A landscape by Dali brought to life. I stood up and walked towards a huge rectangle, pulsing and flowing with colours, a window through to another dimension. All I wanted was to stand and look at this unbelievable world.

For a moment I lost it, jarred by some noise outside. There

was a realignment of perception, and this was me standing in front of one of Des's paintings. Yes. But now it didn't make me feel uneasy. I could see. Des had been here, in this space. The painting was what he'd seen. Then the whole thing shifted again, I was no longer looking at a surface, but through to a different realm, drawn in.

I came out of a dense dank forest into a clearing, and beyond that, spiky grass, sand dunes, a beach, then the sea, vast and shining, going on forever. The ripples of the waves, the shapes of clouds in the sky, all resolved themselves into regular patterns endlessly repeated. Again I just wanted to stand and stare, lose myself in it. But I was aware of something behind me, turned and glimpsed a dark figure. And whatever way I turned, it seemed to move, stay just out of my range of vision, so I kept just catching it out the corner of my eye. Then I found myself in front of a wooden structure, a boat that had been washed up on the shore, half buried in the sand, its ribs and spars sticking up. I crawled inside it, lay down on my back, was aware of my own ribs, my skeleton, cage of bone containing me. Felt myself abandoned there, washed up, bones picked clean, the wind blowing through. What happens when you die. Skull filled with sand.

I sat up, was myself again, not dead. I pressed my head with my hands, felt the skull beneath the skin. I was laughing/crying. This wee body. Me. I lay down again, curled up. Felt the thud of my heart, pulse beating through me, lifeblood. I wanted to drift again, float, but I was closed in, constricted, pressure crushing me. My head and body were gripped, stuck. A long time trapped. No way out. I had to get out, I couldn't move. I had to get out, push through. I remembered this. Darkness and pain. A taste like metal, like blood.

I came to myself in the room, kneeling, pressing my head into the floor. Sat up, my face covered in tears. This was important. I had to get it down so I wouldn't forget. Beside the painting I'd wandered into was a little table with Des's paints and brushes, his turps and cleaning rags, a sketchpad with a pencil. I tore out a blank page from the back of the pad. The pencil was a soft 2B, its black lead blunt. But it would do. I roughed in the hulk of the boat, its frame of ribs, extended it and turned it into a human ribcage, a whole skeleton. Inside it I drew a baby, curled up. I tried to draw the patterns I'd seen in the sea and sky, and right at the edge of the picture I found myself filling in a black shape, the dark figure I'd kept not seeing.

I knew who the figure was. I had realised some important truth here. I had to write it down so I wouldn't forget. I took the pencil, wrote carefully along the bottom of the page, a message to myself.

I'd come down from the real high. Or up from the real low. Whatever. I'd re-entered this time, this place. A manky room full of other people's things, in a run-down house in London. Seen clear for what it was. It was like listening to that stereo for the first time. I was seeing in stereo. Stereoscopic. Everything sharp in focus, 3D, defined. But the things had lost their cartoon quality. *That's all, folks!* Just sat there, stolid and a little sad. The painting was a painting again, colour on a surface. But now I knew what art was about, what it could do.

I wanted to hear music. That had been missing all night. Sounds. Might have made a different trip altogether.

There was a radio upstairs in the kitchen.

I took a deep breath, steadied myself for embarking on the great quest.

And now some other need was asserting itself. I felt an emptiness, an ache that was somehow familar, centred in my stomach.

I was hungry!

That was it. Out the door. I knew I could do it. Up the stairs. Take it easy. No panic. One-step-at-a-time.

There. Made it to the landing. But a light on in the kitchen. Somebody in there moving around. Sudden shortness of breath, tremor in the nerves. Stopped. Ready for fight or flight.

Then the door flying open, this huge presence standing there.

Abe, smiling at me. Smiling *at* me.

'Hey! It's the night tripper!'

And in to the room, engulfed by the light and warmth, over-whelmed by the sheer goodwill emanating from this other, this fellow traveller. Humankind. A universe in himself.

'Abe!' I felt tears in my eyes, hugged him.

'Steady there,' he said.

'Sorry,' I said. 'I was just . . .' I searched for the words. 'Glad to see you.'

'But not in a Mae West sense!'

'Mae West?'

He put on a movie-vamp voice, was almost a woman but not. 'Is that a gun in your pocket, or are you just glad to see me?' I must have looked confused, and he laughed. 'It's OK, man, relax. I've just spent the whole night dealing with this desire thing. And it's fucking endless. Endless fucking! A serpent chasing its own tail.'

Another pang, emptiness at the thought of Vikki lying next door. Through the wall. A world away, as good as.

'It's crazy,' I said, agreeing with him. 'Drive you round the twist.'

'Round the twist!' he said, savouring, delighting in the words. 'That's it! So maybe the monastics have got it right. Maybe celibacy's the thing. Channel the energies. Get beyond it all. No polarities. All one. Ha! It's all one to me!'

He could see he was losing me again. 'Sorry, man. You're looking a bit fragile, like it's been a long night.'

'Yes,' I said. That was it exactly. A long night.

'What you need,' he said, 'is a cup of tea!'

'God!' I said. 'Yes!'

Simple as that.

'Something to eat?'

'That was what I came up for,' I said, remembering. 'Food. Music.'

'Got your priorities right, then! Some French philosopher said the four great human needs are food, clothing, shelter and music. Didn't mention the other. But still, four out of five's not bad, eh? A reasonable percentage. One of the thieves was saved. Vladimir said that. Or was it Estragon? Who cares? I'm raving. Four out of five. Can't always get what you want, but sometimes, you just might find, you get what you need.'

'Stones,' I said.

'Indeed. The wisdom of the great Mick. Shaman supreme. Showman supreme.'

He had managed to put the kettle on, and he fished a couple of mugs out of the sink, rinsed them, chucked a teabag in each one. Looked in the cupboard.

'The food situation is not great,' he said.

'Oh.' A slump. Disappointment. I was hungry.

'But fear not. We can have a beggar's banquet.' With great formality he placed on the table a sliced loaf. Reached into the cupboard again and brought out a jar of peanut butter.

'Crunchy,' he announced, with a solemnity that made me laugh again. Everything was absurd and funny. He made two sandwiches, the bread folded over, handed me one.

'Cheers.'

'The pinnacle of Western civilisation,' he said. 'Crunchy peanut butter!'

I bit into it, felt it gunge up my whole mouth. I mumbled through it. 'Fucksake. *It's* eating *me*!'

'Cosmic!' he said.

When we'd eaten the stuff, swilled it down with tea, I switched on the radio, heard a rush of static, interference.

'Nothing much on at this time,' he said.

'What time is it?'

He looked again at his non-existent watch, shook his wrist and held it to his ear.

'Eternity!' Then as if remembering, he raised his index finger, an exclamation mark. 'Sounds! Can listen to my stereo, on the headphones.'

At the door to his room, he must have seen me hesitate. 'Hey,' he said. 'No strings.'

'Like the guitar downstairs.' I recited my joke. 'No strings. It's a Zen guitar.'

'You really have been out there!'

I sang it. 'Dance Dance Dance to my Zen guitar!'

He joined in. 'And very soon you'll know just who you are!'

'That's it!' I said. 'I'd forgotten. Those really are the words!'

'Isn't it great?' he said. 'Everything's telling us, all the time.'

'Even Engelbert fucking Humperdinck!'

In the room he asked what I'd like to hear.

'Stringband,' I said.

'Or Stringless Band!' He handed me the headphones. 'Good call.'

He put on the music and I lay back on the couch, eased into it, let it fill my head.

How sweet to be a cloud, floating in the blue.

Then there was a song sung chilling and clear, the words speaking directly to me, telling me.

My name is Death cannot you see
All life must turn to me.

When the song was finished, I pulled off the headphones, sat up.

'You OK man?' Abe took of his own headphones, put them aside.

'That's what I saw,' I said. 'The dark figure.'

'Easy, man,' he said. 'You're still tripping, remember?'

'I know. This was part of it. In the painting downstairs.'

'Saw the old GR, did you?'

'The what?'

'Grim Reaper. He often shows up on trips. Really freaks people out! Hey, did you ask him your big question? Yo, Reap! What happens when you die?'

'Didn't get a chance. It wasn't like that. I could just see him and no more.'

'Oh well,' said Abe. 'Guess the time wasn't right.' And he clapped me on the shoulder, put his headphones back on.

I looked at him leaning back with his eyes closed, suddenly remembered that first morning I'd come here, just off the bus. Seemed so long ago, was just a matter of weeks. I'd slept on this couch, dreamed a dark figure leaning over me. Had it really been Abe, checking me out? Or had it been the Reaper, waiting to answer my question? It had turned into a black bird, hovering.

I shivered, stood up. I remembered I'd left a note to myself, a message. I had to go back downstairs and read it, rediscover the great truth I'd seen.

I stepped out on to the landing, shut the door quietly. Started going down the stairs. One foot. The other. Halfway down got stuck, stopped. Couldn't move. Sat down huddled on the step. Couldn't face what was waiting for me down there.

You have to learn.

He was forcing me downstairs to lock me in with the coffins. To learn. To learn what? I was the child in question. The foetus curled in the skeleton's womb. That taste like metal like blood. Astride of the grave and a difficult birth. I had killed my mother.

No!

What he'd thought, deep down. What he'd made me feel.

But I didn't ask to be born.

Was his own guilt. He'd fathered me, made her pregnant. The birth had killed her. Sex equalled death.

I felt a sudden unexpected rush of sympathy towards him. What he'd lived with all these years, turned in on himself, that awful grimness. I wanted to tell him, *Och Da, it's OK.*

I carried on down to the foot of the stairs, pushed through into the now familiar room. Where I'd spent the long night. Curled there on the floor I'd had some sense of what was before birth, even before conception, patterns of energy, pure undifferentiated being. World without end.

The message was important. I'd written it so I wouldn't forget. I found the piece of paper, scrawled all over in black pencil. It was all there, the skeleton ship, the baby. The shapes I'd seen in the sea and sky. The dark figure, almost out of the picture. And the message, in big childish printing. *My mother is dead. I will die.*

Things were changing too fast, I couldn't keep up.

The day after my trip I spent a long time in the park, just wanted to sit quiet, do nothing, take it all in.

Watched the astonishing shimmer of leaves on a huge tree, I didn't know what kind, didn't care. Each individual leaf shone, the whole thing rustled and billowed as it caught the wind.

Ducks on the Serpentine bobbed and weaved on the sparkling

water, traced patterns on its surface, their feathers iridescent. One would sprint a yard, wee feet going like the clappers, paddling. Then it would stop, duck under. Duck under! Come up again sleek, shake itself. Water off a duck's back. Sun glinted in a single drop of water, dripped from its beak.

I kept thinking there was something else I should be doing, somewhere else I should be.

But no. I was here. This was it.

Two swallows dipped and soared. Making a summer!

On the way back home (*home!*) I went in to a little hippy café I'd been to with Vikki. Sanded wood floors scuffed from walking, the varnish worn. Half a dozen mismatched tables picked up at jumble sales or pillaged from skips, a job lot of folding kitchen chairs. Batik hangings on the rough plastered walls. The food was cheap and basic, vegetarian without being finicky, eclectic mishmash dolloped up in big portions. Soup and bread. Bean stew with brown rice or couscous. Good filling stuff. What my old man would call a tightener. Stick to your ribs.

I went for the soup, a thick broth, could be the stew watered down. Took my time over it, blew on each spoonful to cool, dunked the slab of heavy homemade bread. I looked about as I ate. The place was busy enough, half full in the middle of the afternoon. Or half empty.

The woman who ran it looked harassed, overheated. Her thin blonde hair was tugged back, held with elastic at the nape. A wisp of it kept working free, getting in her face, and she'd have to blow it away from her nose, brush it out of her eyes.

'Busy,' I said, filled with post-acid compassion for all humanity.

'You don't know the half of it,' she said, and she was right. I didn't. But at least I knew I didn't know the half of it. Abe would say that was a start.

'Oh well,' I said. 'Hard work's no easy.'

Did I really say that? Something else the old man would come out with. His voice in my head.

'You're right,' the woman said, unfazed. 'And it doesn't help when people drop you in the shit.'

'No.'

'Staff not turning up,' she said. 'Bloody Aussie backpacker. Been here a month. Thought we could rely on him and he goes and buggers off, just like that.'

'Tough.'

'Tell me about it.' She flicked at the stray hair again, irritated. 'Don't suppose you're looking for a job?'

This must be meant to happen. These people must be part of my karass. This was the something else I should be doing, earning a living.

I was out with it before I could stop myself. 'Well, I am actually. Kind of. For a while anyway.'

'A while's fine.'

'What's involved?'

'Basic kitchen work. Washing up. Doing tables. Help with the preparation, chopping and that. The usual.'

'Sounds OK.'

'Get paid the going rate. Cash in your hand at the end of the week. No questions asked. And meals thrown in when you're working.'

'So, when do you want me to start?'

'No rush. You can finish your soup first!'

This was mad. But so was everything else. The thing was to go with it, for now. Now here.

The woman led me through a swing door into the kitchen, told me her name was Annie.

'Neil,' I said.

The heat was intense, whumped you in the face when you stepped in. Like opening an oven. There was only the one man working there, the cook, in a yellow vest. He was frying up a pan of onions and garlic in spitting hot oil, the metallic tang filling the air, clinging.

'This is Zen,' said Annie.

I was used to this kind of thing from Abe, thought I should respond.

'What is?' I said.

I was leaning with my hands on the edge of an old wooden table, palms flat, fingers spread. Before I knew it, the cook had

103

turned and picked up a carving knife, stabbed it into the table between my hands.

'This,' he said. 'And it's not a what, it's a who.'

It was so unexpected, unreal, I hadn't moved an inch, hadn't even twitched. I stared at the knife, stuck there. I moved my hands.

'Zen's his name,' said Annie. 'Short for Xenon. And he's mental.'

'Good reaction,' said the man, nodding. 'Didn't flinch.' He pulled out the knife, turned back to the frying pan, shook and banged it on the gas, stirred the contents round.

'I think that was some kind of test,' said Annie. 'And you seem to have passed.'

'If you can't stand the heat,' he said, 'stay out of the kitchen.'

'You'll get used to him,' she said. 'I'll leave you to it. Let him show you the ropes.'

And she was gone, back through the swing doors, leaving me here with this madman. He was small and wiry with black curly hair, intense dark eyes. The right eye looked normal, even benign. The left had a manic glint, crazy. He fixed me with it, staring.

'Welcome to the madhouse.'

'Thanks.'

'You are what you eat, right?'

'So they say.'

'So, if you eat a bag of chips, you're a bag of chips?'

'Doesn't sound quite right, does it?'

'Ditto if you eat a pink blancmange. You turn into a pink blancmange.'

'Maybe not.'

'No.' The mad eye glinted at me. 'But maybe you have the *consciousness* of a bag of chips.'

'Or a pink blancmange.'

'Right.'

'In Glasgow, if you're talking shite, they'll say Your heid's full o broken biscuits.'

He laughed. 'That's it!'

By jove he's got it, I think he's got it.

'Or Your heid's full o mince.'

'Even better! The stuff you take into your system when you eat meat. All these heavy animal vibes. Plus when the beast gets slaughtered, it's shot through with adrenalin, from the fear. So you take all that in as well.'

'Sounds bad, right enough.'

'Oh it is.' He beckoned me over, pointed to a piece of paper tacked up on the wall, the one word printed on it in block capitals.

EAT

To either side of the word were little squares of paper, stuck on, hinged at the top with Sellotape. He raised the squares with his thumbs, revealed two more letters underneath, changed the word.

DEATH

'See?' he said. And he let the little squares flap down again, changed it back.

EAT

'Cheery thing to have in a restaurant.'

'A reminder,' he said.

Annie bashed open the swing door with her hip, carried in a stack of dirty dishes, set them down on the draining board. The sink was already full, the backlog piling up.

'Two fruit crumbles, two grain coffees,' she called out. 'And Neil, if he's quite finished with the initiation, maybe you could start with the dishes, we're running short.'

'Aye, right,' I said. 'Sure thing.'

I unblocked the sink, got to work.

I was anxious to tell everybody when I got back. I'd found a job. Or a job had found me. Abe would read some cosmic significance into it. Jess would be happy I'd be paying my way.

Vikki would be pleased she'd taken me to the café in the first place. Des would make some smart remark, a put-down.

But the atmosphere was strange when I came in, everybody sitting in the kitchen, a heaviness in the air, a tension. Vikki was leaning her head on Jess's shoulder, and Jess was stroking her hair, soothing her. When Vikki looked up I could see she'd been crying. The left side of her face was swollen, starting to bruise, her eye puffed up.

'What the fuck?' I said. 'What happened?'

'Gus,' said Des. 'Mister cool. Mister fucking laidback.'

'He hit you?'

She nodded, covered her face again. I moved towards her, to put my arm round her, but she waved me away.

'Not what she needs right now,' said Jess.

'Was this because of me?' I said to Vikki, and she managed a sob of a laugh.

'There was other stuff,' she said. 'He just flipped out, went mental.'

'Bastard,' said Des. 'I just wish he'd tried it when we were here, that's all.'

'Oh yeah,' said Jess. 'Then you could have beat the shit out of him. Would really have sorted things out.'

'Sorted him out anyway,' said Des.

'What is it with guys?' she spat back. 'Why do they want to solve everything using their fists?'

'Now that's not fair,' he said, tensing up, his mouth a tight line.

'Don't you two start,' said Vikki, her voice pathetic.

'Yeah,' said Abe, standing up. 'Come on, we're like family here. Let's stay cool. Vikki's been hurt and we're all upset, that's all. Now why don't we go down the pub and have a drink? On me.'

'Thanks Abe,' said Vikki. 'I'm not in the mood.'

'I'll stay and keep her company,' said Jess, calming down, a note of truce in her voice. 'But you guys go out, if you want.'

'You sure?' said Des.

'Might be for the best,' she said.

'How about you, Vikki?' I asked. 'You OK with that?'

She nodded again, just about holding it together. 'Fine.'

'Fair enough,' said Abe. 'Makes it a cheap round!'

In the pub, Des was quiet. 'Sorry about that,' he said.

'Understandable,' I said. 'I felt the same.'

'Jess had some problems when she was a kid,' he said. 'Her old man knocking her about and that. So she hates it more than anything.'

'Welcome to the real world,' said Abe, setting down our pints.

'Hard to come back down to,' I said.

'Isn't it?' said Abe. 'That's the trick to master. Now, tell me about this job of yours.'

When I'd told him the whole story, he said, 'Sounds like just the thing. Right livelihood.'

'Just the job!'

'Right! Mind you, part of me goes for the Jerry Rubin line. Full unemployment for all!'

'Gainful unemployment!'

'I'll drink to that!' said Des.

Zen the cook was a madman, had probably done too much acid, blown a few circuits. From that one trip I'd seen how it could happen. Could imagine being stuck out there, no way back.

The one thing that kept him grounded was the work. He moved round the kitchen like a dancer, like a juggler, kept half a dozen things on the go at once. Moving in a haze of steam from a bubbling pot, smoke from hot oil, chucking in a pinch of this, a handful of that, he'd pull it all together, time it right. I'd never cooked in my life, except for fry-ups, stuff from packets and tins. I found it miraculous.

'You're a magician,' I said.

He shrugged. 'Nothing to it.'

'You should write a cookbook, call it *Cooking with Zen*!'

He didn't smile. 'It can't be written down.'

'Could you teach me?'

'What's to teach?'

'All the stuff you do.'

'You learn by watching,' he said. 'Paying attention. Then you do it. Simple.'

'Sure.'

'Here!' He took the sharp knife, the same one he'd stabbed in the table, and he threw it towards me, spinning in the air. I stepped back, made a grab at the handle, but I didn't get a grip and the knife clattered to the floor.

I picked it up. 'You've seen too many fucking Samurai movies!'

But over the next few days I did what he said. In between washing up and clearing tables, I chopped the vegetables the way he wanted. Watched what he was doing and learned.

I asked him how he cooked the rice.

'It cooks itself,' he said. 'Right amount of water, boil it, salt it, let it simmer.'

'And what's the right amount?'

'Two to one,' he said, grudging. And as if to make up for actually giving away a secret, he rapped me on the head with a wooden spoon. 'The important thing is to leave it be. Don't keep lifting the lid and sticking your fucking nose in. Trust in the process, right?'

'Right.'

I asked how much of the different spices he put in his curry sauce.

'Some,' he said. 'A bunch. Taste and see.'

And gradually he trusted me with some of the stages. Fry the onions. Cook the rice. Mix the batter for buckwheat pancakes.

'Cooking's great!' I said.

'It's a job.' He flipped a pancake in the air, caught it. 'A living.'

One day he didn't show up, phoned in sick.

'He gets these depressions,' said Annie. 'Real black dog stuff.'

'So what do you do? I mean here?'

'Simplify the menu,' she said. 'Do what we can. You up for it?'

'The cooking?'

'Sure.'

'Fuck!'

'Come on,' she said. 'You can do it.'

And I did, somehow got through it, the moments of sheer panic at doing too many things at once, the heat and not being able to breathe, the fumbling and dropping things, spilling oil on the floor, a slick left to slip on even when I'd wiped it with newspaper. But moments too when it all came right and I moved with certainty through the chaos. Dancing, juggling.

Maybe I really could do this, be a cook. Could see myself. A living.

Annie gave me a hug at the end of the day, laughed, told me I was great.

Just the job.

This life I was living. These people. This time.

I got home late from the café, ran a bath, soaped and scrubbed the smell of the kitchen off me. Pulled on my jeans and t-shirt, stood barefoot on the landing. The house was so quiet. Nobody home. Abe had been away a couple of nights, staying over with a new boyfriend in Camden. The others must be out at the pub. I'd go if I had the energy, but the tiredness sat on me, complete exhaustion. I wasn't used to work. Dull ache in my arms and back, calf muscles tight. I stood listening to nothing. Street-noise outside, a car passing, squawl of a cat. Silence again, then a girl's voice shouting out *Why*? And a boy answering *Why not*?

Good questions both.

Then the notion took hold of me, to go in to Vikki's room. No reason. Just to look, remember. Take in the smell of her. I pushed open the door, was about to switch on the light when I heard a movement from the bed. Stopped. Froze.

A thin line of light seeped in through the gap in the curtains, took the edge off the darkness. As my eyes got used to it, I could make out shapes. The single bed and what looked like two figures lying in it, two heads on the pillow.

First thought was it might be Gus. He'd come back and she'd taken him in again. But that didn't feel right. I'd have heard him, seen his stuff downstairs. Then a worse thought, it could be Des, taking his chance. Could even be someone she'd just met, picked up.

A car started up outside, choked, revved. The beam from its headlights cut in to the room through the gap, moved slowly across and up. Floodlit the bed just long enough to pick out

Vikki and Jess wrapped up in each other, long enough for me to see Vikki open her eyes and look at me, give me a sad stoned faraway smile.

Back downstairs I couldn't sleep, body dead mind buzzing unable to stop.

Why?

Why not?

At some point I heard what I took to be Jess, padding back to her own room. And later Des coming in, banging the front door shut, shouting *Bastard!* as he stumbled over something in the hall.

This time. This place. These people.

What next? What the fuck next?

I thought I hadn't slept at all, but I must have dozed, drifted off. Woke to hammering.

Batter.

Somebody at the door. Middle of the night. The loud official knock.

Batter.

By the time I'd struggled out of my sleeping bag, thrown on clothes, Des was already downstairs, had got to the door, opened it.

A young policeman standing there, stonefaced.

And the whole thing suddenly a tableau. Freeze-frame. Myself coming out into the hall. Des holding the door open. Jess a couple of steps behind him, clutching her dressing gown shut at the throat. Vikki halfway down the stairs in a thin cheesecloth dress. All of us barefoot, staring out at the policeman on the doorstep.

'Abraham Morris's residence?'

Ridiculous the formality, pompous.

'Abe?' said Des. 'Yeah, he lives here. What's the problem?'

'Can I come in a minute, sir?'

This was it. The drug bust Abe had dreaded.

'He's not here,' said Des, stalling.

'I know that, sir.' He took off his hat, looked excessively solemn, like a policeman in a play. 'I'm afraid there's been an accident.'

Vikki came down the last few stairs, stood beside Jess.

'Has Abe been hurt?' said Des, and the question sounded feeble, all of us knowing, pretending not to know, it must be something bad, for this, the knock at the door, middle of the night. Policeman with his hat in his hand.

'I'm afraid Mr Morris is dead.'

'No!' It was Vikki that cried out, denied it, voiced what we all felt. This couldn't be. Jess put her arms round her, held her.

The policeman told us what had happened. Sat incongruous in our kitchen. Out in the street there were slogans on the walls. *Police State. Kill the Pigs.* And here we were making tea for this young man, this specific individual, sitting awkward, his hat in his lap. I made the tea in the battered aluminium teapot, held the lid in place with a dishtowel the way Abe did. Had done.

He'd been out with his friend, both of them stoned, smashed, out of their heads. Walking back to the friend's place, Abe had wandered into the road in front of traffic. Been hit by a car, thrown in the air. Cracked his skull on landing. Never regained consciousness.

When the policeman had gone, we all sat, stunned.

'It's so fucking stupid,' said Des. 'Senseless.'

Vikki pulled her hair back, held it with her hands behind her neck. 'I keep thinking if I go back to bed I'll wake up in the morning and it won't have happened.'

I knew what she meant exactly. I'd even wondered if I was still tripping, if everything since the acid had just been part of it, continuing hallucination. Illusion within illusion and one day I'd wake up. Butterfly dreaming I was a man.

Abe would come dancing in the door, hit us with some daft Zen punchline, tell us it was all a joke.

But no. Abe was dead. Brute fact. No joke.

There was no getting away from funerals, from death.

Jess identified the body, made all the arrangements. She had known him longest. He had no family that she knew of.

'It's just like they say.' She was trying hard to explain. 'It wasn't him. Not Abe. It was what he'd left behind. But still.'

'I know,' I said.

'Course you do. You've seen this hundreds of times. Was my first. First time I'd seen a dead person.'

'It shakes you.'

'Especially when it's somebody you know. Knew.'

Talk in present tenses.

We were in Abe's room, the four of us. We'd opened the curtains wide, let unaccustomed daylight stream in. We'd sampled Abe's stash of best Moroccan.

'It's what he'd have wanted,' said Des.

'Absolutely,' I said.

'Respect.'

'Homage.'

And we both chuckled, the first time since the bad news.

Vikki smiled. 'We've got to make the funeral special. Make it beautiful.'

'Right,' said Des. 'Give the daft bastard a send-off!'

It was agreed. I took the last of Abe's stash, made hash pancakes for the reception. Annie and Zen let me use the kitchen at the café to cook them up in bulk, on condition they could try them.

'Should put these on the menu,' said Annie through a mouthful. 'Keep the customers happy.'

'They're not bad,' said Zen, chewing, swallowing. 'Batter could have been a bit lighter. Still.' He took another. 'Should make the funeral go with a swing.'

Jess had ordered a simple white pine coffin and Des had been inspired to paint it, bright symbols on a pale blue background. Yin-Yang circle, Sanskrit aum sign, red lotus, sun and moon, a celtic knot, a white bird.

Vikki cried when she saw it, gave Des a hug. 'You!' she said. 'That is *so* nice!'

'Abe would love it,' I said.

'Give him a laugh, anyway,' said Des.

Instead of using a church, Jess had booked a local hall that was used as a theatre space, art gallery, community centre. They'd been good about it, hadn't charged rent.

'Not that money's a problem,' said Jess. 'I found a wad of fivers stuffed in a plastic bag in Abe's room.'

'From this and that.'

'Nuff said.' She smiled. 'But it means we can do it right.'

Vikki had decorated the hall, made it look like a temple. Incense burning. Flowers everywhere. Indian drapes hung over the windows. 'Looks like Abe's room!' said Des.

The undertaker who delivered Abe's body in its painted coffin looked in shock, caught between duty and inclination, between professional concern and total incomprehension. The way my father would be. Agitation in the eyes, but the voice calm, in control.

'I'll be outside if you need me,' he said. Left us to it.

Six of us had carried Abe in, placed the coffin on a table Vikki had covered in white satin. She had chosen the music that was playing, the Stones, *Going Home*. There were fifty or sixty people gathered, a congregation of the weird. Abe's nation.

Jess stood up, smoothed the front of her green velvet dress. 'It's just great to see so many people here,' she said. 'Abe would be pleased. No.' She looked up. 'Abe *is* pleased.'

A murmur of approval round the room.

'There's no ministers here,' she said. 'No rabbis. No priests. That wasn't Abe's style. He had no truck with religion in that sense. But in his way, he was one of the most spiritual men I ever met. He was always asking the big questions. And coming up with some weird and wonderful answers! In fact he's probably having a good chinwag with God right now, setting him straight about a few things! So anyway, I don't want to turn this into a long drag of a speech. I just want to say Abe was a great guy. One of a kind. And we'll miss him. That's all.'

There was a sense that people wanted to clap, but some residual restraint held them back. A funeral, after all. Only one big man in a buckskin jacket shouted out, 'Yeah! Right!' And when people looked at him he said, 'What?'

Abe would have approved.

Des was next up, stood beside the coffin he'd painted. 'No speeches from me either. Just this. Abe was a mad bastard.'

'Ha!' shouted Buckskin, in full agreement.

'But I'll tell you,' Des continued, 'when you look at what all the sane bastards are doing to the planet, you think maybe a wee touch of that madness wouldn't go amiss.'

'No madness amiss!' shouted Buckskin.

'I never understood the half of what Abe came out with,' said Des. 'And I'm not sure about this God business. But see, if Jess is right, and Abe is up there bending God's ear, I hope he's demanding an explanation about how come he's been whipped upstairs so soon. Makes no sense to me. But then what do I know?' He patted the coffin. 'Cheers, man.'

'Cheers!' shouted Buckskin.

Des nodded to me and I stood up, felt suddenly nervous and exposed, couldn't keep the shake out of my voice.

'I only met Abe a few weeks ago,' I said. 'Seems incredible. But that's what he was like. Just treated you like an old friend right off. And I'm like Des, I didn't understand half of what he was trying to tell me. But the other day I picked up one of the books he'd given me to read, a book of Zen stories. And a bit of paper fell out the book.' I unfolded the piece of paper, held it up. 'It's a story Abe had written out. And I'd just like to read it.'

A Zen master was asked by one of his students, If nothing is permanent in this life, if everything is fleeting and subject to change and decay, if existence is suffering and we are born to die, how can there be any happiness?

Good question.

The master answered by picking up a precious tea-bowl he had been given. He said, I enjoy using this bowl because it is already broken. I drink my tea from it every day. I enjoy the shape and texture of it in my hands, and when the light strikes its surface, it shows up its rich colours. But if I should accidentally drop it, or knock it to the floor, it will be smashed into pieces. Yes. Of course. But knowing it to be already broken, I appreciate its presence, the life of it, at every moment. So too with this body. I know it is already dead. So where is fear? I live each moment fully, for itself.

When I'd finished, I expected Buckskin to shout out, or roar his approval. But looking over, I saw he was sitting slumped, his head down.

Jess gave us a nod and Vikki moved to the back of the room, put on the music again, the Stringband this time, I recognised the sweet syncopated chords, the single acoustic guitar, Mike Heron's gallus cheeky voice singing *Can't keep me here.*

The words rang round the room, made everybody laugh and cry as we carried Abe in his bright box out the door.

> *I'm going way over the wide skyline*
> *And I'll sing and be happy*
> *And you can't keep me here no how.*
> *Ah baby, don't cry for me*
> *Hey baby, when the sun comes up*
> *I'll be free.*

Free. Down that road. Going home.

The journey to the crematorium was a procession that turned into a parade, like an old-time funeral, everybody walking behind the hearse. A few people had brought drums and tambourines, somebody played a tin whistle. Two buskers on flute and guitar, playing *There is a mountain*, were caught up, carried along. And so was a group of Hare Krishna devotees in their orange robes, clashing their finger cymbals, chanting their mantra, dancing.

'Abe must be loving this!' said Des. 'It's mental!'

At the crematorium, the ceremony was short.

It turned out Buckskin's name was Steve, and he was Abe's last boyfriend, the one he'd been with the night he died. He'd been in touch with Jess, asked if he could choose the music for this bit. She'd said Fine, no problem, told him to make three tapes and mark them ENTRY, COMMITTAL and EXIT.

Whatever Steve had taken, he was manic one minute, weepy the next. But he'd managed to make the tapes, hurried ahead of us to the chapel so the first song would be playing as we came in.

Entry.

It was the Kinks. *Thank you for the days.*

Made us smile. Bittersweet.

Steve wanted to read something, stood up after Jess had said a few words.

'I'll keep this dead short.' He realised what he'd said, slapped his forehead. 'Sorry, I'll keep this really short. Just a couple of lines from that amazing poem Mick read in the park the other week, cause I know like Abe loved it.'

He took a scrap of paper from the back pocket of his jeans, read.

> *Peace! Peace! He is not dead, he doth not sleep.*
> *He hath awakened from the dream of life.*

He swayed a bit, steadied himself, read one more line, declaimed it.

> *Die, if thou wouldst be with that which thou dost seek!*

I heard the familiar clunk and whirr of machinery, the coffin sliding towards the open curtains. I was aware of Jess making a signal to the attendant at the back, to play the second piece of music.

Committal

A voice came out of the speakers, shouting.

> *I am the god of hellfire and I bring you*

It was a moment of complete disorientation, disbelief, chill down the back of the neck. Abe's coffin moving through as the tape played The Crazy World of Arthur Brown.

> *Fire! I'll teach you to burn!*

Steve was bobbing up and down, headbanging to the music. And after the initial shock, most people seemed to be finding it funny. Des caught my eye, shrugged. Whatever.

When the coffin had gone, we all drifted out to the third track. *Set the controls for the heart of the sun.*

Exit.

'Fire!' said Des, back at the hall. 'Fucking Arthur Brown!' He laughed. 'That was a bit wild, even for me! The thing is, I actually think Abe would have liked it. It was twisted enough for him anyway!'

I looked round the room. 'Never knew he had so many friends.'

Most of them had come back, taken communion of my hash pancakes. Vikki was in charge of the music, had put on some blues guitar.

'Feels like the end of a time,' said Des. 'Like it's over.'

'You mean Abe going?'

'That's part of it,' he said. 'But it's, och, everything. I guess you know it's not really working out with me and Jess.'

'I'd guessed.'

'So I'm thinking about moving on.'

'Back to Scotland?'

'Fuck no! There's a world out there!'

A world.

Way over the wide skyline.

Sounded good.

These stories about Zen masters, knowing when they were to die.

The master who wrote postcards to all his friends on the day of his death.

> *I am leaving this world.*
> *This is my last message.*

He gave the cards to one of his pupils to post. Then he lay down and died.

The master who ordered a coffin to be made for him and a grave to be dug, saying he would die on a particular day. His followers humoured him, thinking he was playing some kind of joke, teaching them some profound lesson on mortality. When the day came, he lay down in the coffin. One of the disciples complained that he had not composed the customary four-line death verse. Very well, he said, sitting up.

> *I came from brilliancy*
> *And return to brilliancy.*
> *What is this?*

And he lay down again.
But master, said the disciple. That is one line short. And the master sat up one last time and roared like a lion at the top of his voice.

> *Kaaa!*

And passed on.

The Zen nun who announced she was to leave the world, and had a funeral pyre built. Then she sat cross-legged in the middle of it, and had it set alight.
As the flames rose, a monk shouted in to her, Is it hot in there?
She shouted back, What a stupid question! And she died. And burned.

4

To keep moving, not settle. Not settle for less. To live. Cheat death. Or at least not settle for death-in-life, the grind. Keep moving. A moving target. What the travelling was about.

A Sufi story I'd read.

A man in Damascus had a magic horse that could gallop faster than the wind. One day a friend came to visit him, very upset.

'What's wrong?' said the man. And his friend said he'd just seen Death in the town, and Death had grimaced at him, as if about to take him there and then.

'No wonder you're upset,' said the man. 'But how can I help?'

'I want to borrow your horse,' said the friend. 'If Death is looking for me here, I shall make my escape to Baghdad.'

'Of course,' said the man. And he brought the horse from its stable, and his friend mounted up and rode off, faster than the wind.

Later in the day, the man himself happened to be in town, and he too saw Death, and said, 'My friend saw you this morning, and you showed him such a dreadful face you drove him away.'

Death thought for a moment, then said, 'Oh no, I wasn't showing him a dreadful face, I was just surprised.'

'Why was that?' said the man.

And Death said, 'I was surprised to see him here in Damascus, when I have an appointment to take him this afternoon, in Baghdad.'

No escape. No getting away from it. Whatever we did was just running to Baghdad. Or somewhere else.

I kept travelling for fifteen weird years. Passed myself off as a cook and learned as I went. Picked up enough to survive and move on. Kept asking the unanswerable, repeating it. My mantra, or koan more like. What happens when you die?

*

A clammy October night in Mexico City. *El Dia de los Muertes*. Day of the Dead. Peyoted out of my skull not knowing what was real what was derangement what was vision. Parade with an out-of-tune mariachi band. Skeletons dancing down the street. Voices calling me from dark alleys, from shop doorways. A male skeleton holding a lit spurting firecracker where his cock should be. A female skeleton hugging me – woman in a black body-stocking with the bones painted on in luminous white. And under the painted bones, the clinging material, was warm flesh I could feel. But under that were the real bones, would one day be all that was left of her. She pulled off her plastic death-mask, laughing, white teeth in a wide brown face. Kissed me warm and moist and alive, but again I was aware of it, the skull beneath the skin, and she pushed me away, laughed again, snapped her mask back in place with elastic, ran off.

I followed the crowd down to a graveyard where the parade had ended up, the band blaring out salsa as people danced among the graves. Tables were set up with food to be shared with the dead, an offering. Every gravestone had been washed clean, fresh flowers placed in front of them, candles lit, hundreds of flames flickering. Made the place dreamlike, magic. Fragrance of incense hung in the air, copal, haze of blue smoke. Children dressed as if for communion played amongst it all, bit into tiny sugar skulls. Somebody handed me one and I popped it whole in my mouth, crunched it, let it dissolve into sweet nothing.

Eat death.

This was the way to deal with it, head on, facing down the fear.

Fireworks scattered and burst across the night sky, rockets flared, exploded in showers of light. I threw back my head, felt I contained it all, it was inside me, galaxies, a universe, sparked into life, the big bang. Skeletons danced in the graveyard, on the roof of hell. Kids shrieked, ate more sweet skulls. I laughed. The band thudded on.

Everywhere I went I picked up stories and poems, charms and prayers, incantations, jokes. Maybe someday I'd compile my own Book of the Dead. Reminders, notes to myself. *Mementi mori*.

Like the story of Lupe Velez. I heard it from some American I met in a bar, before I left Mexico.

Lupe Velez was a Mexican filmstar back in the 40s. Decided to kill herself and planned to do it in best Hollywood style. She swallowed a handful of sleeping pills and lay down on her kingsize bed to die a beautiful death. She'd filled the room with flowers and scented candles, dressed in her finest silver lamé gown. Lay back like Sleeping Beauty. The way she wanted to be remembered.

But during the night, the emetic effect of the pills kicked in. She staggered to the bathroom, tripped and fell. Her maid found the dead body next morning, head down the toilet, bare arse in the air, kneeling in a pool of her own vomit and shit.

Rilke's prayer for the Good Death.

> *O Lord, give each of us his own death*
> *The dying that issues forth out of the life*
> *In which he had love, meaning and despair.*

Vomit and shit.

The first time I saw someone actually die. New York City, a vicious December day when the wind ripped unhindered down endless avenues, whipped the taut dried skin on your face, cut, numbed you with cold, seared your lungs. With the windchill it was fifteen below.

I was on my way to start a shift at the diner where they'd taken me on. Short order chef. Basic stuff, burgers and pancakes, eggs any style. Paid cash out the till. No papers, no questions asked. Illegal alien. If anyone came snooping I was out the door. Understood.

I was two blocks from the diner, head down into that freezing wind. Saw him out the corner of my eye, a figure stepping towards me out of a doorway. First instinct was to step aside, speed up. Hey, this was New York. Head down keep moving

123

don't make eye-contact. Then he made a noise, a gasped-out cry, and I stopped and looked and he stared right at me, right into me.

An old man, grey stubble on a grey face, bulked up in layers of old clothes, an overcoat under a torn anorak under a down vest, rips patched with ducktape. Fingerless gloves on blackened hands. Wool hat pulled down over his ears.

I fumbled in my jacket pocket for change, but he let out that cry again, the sound choked out of him. The look in his eyes was panic, a desperate reaching for help, for human contact. Then he made a gurgling noise, flailed with his hands clutched at his throat. And the eyes fixed on me glazed, and in slow motion he fell away from me, keeled backwards and I couldn't reach couldn't catch him couldn't stop it happening, in slow motion he hit the ground and his head cracked so loud on the pavement. I crouched down and he twitched, gave a last rattle of breath and lay still, slack mouth gaped open, eyes clenched shut. Stink of his shit. He was gone. I'd seen enough bodies to know. But never this transition, so quick. One minute alive and struggling, grappling for life. Fish on a hook whipped out of the water. Next minute cold and rigid on the sidewalk. No life left, no consciousness, nothing. Just this hulk left lying. Nobody home.

For a moment the thought came I might be in trouble. People might think I'd hit the old man, knocked him down. But others were around, had seen it all. A young black girl in baggy jeans, a padded jacket, was down on her knees, cradling the old man's head off the hard ground, pulling the wool hat more snug over his ears, wanting to keep him warm. A young boy ran into a pizza place to call an ambulance. An old woman shook her head, said 'Poor soul', crossed herself. A few others stopped, made sympathetic noises, moved on. Young kid with a ghettoblaster pumping out rap, didn't switch it off, looked down curious, checking it out. Above the traffic noise, a siren wailed, whooped.

'What a way to go,' I said to Arnie who ran the diner. 'Ending up a John Doe at the morgue.'

'Ham,' he said, slapping an order slip beside the griddle. 'Eggs over easy. Homefries.'

'Dropping dead in the street,' I said.

'Happens all the time,' said Arnie. 'Read about a beauty in the paper last week. Guy running along the street. It's a bad neighbourhood, a cop sees him, yells out to him to stop. The guy keeps running. The cop yells again, pulls out his gun. The guy still keeps running. Reaches into his inside pocket. Cop figures he's going for his piece, guns him down. Blam! The guy's dead on the sidewalk. Cop goes over, checks the guy out. No gun in the pocket, the guy's clutching a little wallet full of tokens. He was running for a fucking bus!'

'Jesus Christ!'

'So at least your John Doe died of natural causes.'

'Heart failure brought on by hypothermia.'

'Hey, it was quick.'

'If you don't count the weeks and months he was out there, dying slow.'

Give each of us his own death.

John Doe.

'Shit happens,' said Arnie.

I cracked an egg, set it splattering on the hotplate.

Death from natural causes. Death from old age. Death by misadventure. Death in the afternoon. Death camps. Death squads. Lingering death. Sudden death. Death from famine. Death from plague. Death by malnutrition. Death by chocolate.

Sooner or later.

One way or another.

In between the travelling I came back to London. I'd kept in touch with Des and he said I'd always have a place to stay, there was always a couch or floorspace till I got myself sorted out. He never heard from Vikki or Jess. They'd gone to Amsterdam, or somewhere. Moved on.

Des had travelled with me the first time, as far as San Francisco. Our second week there, he got sick, came down with jaundice. We had no insurance, couldn't afford medical bills. Nothing else for it, he had to go home for treatment.

'Tough shit,' I said.

'Fucking tell me about it.'

I saw him off at the airport, took a bus to Mexico for that Festival of the Dead. He didn't travel after that, decided he was allergic to it. Quoted at me, 'The further you travel, the less you know.' From Abe by George Harrison out of Lao Tsu. Didn't make me believe it. I kept moving. Came across funerals everywhere I went.

On a stopover in Dublin, I saw a coffin draped in the tricolour, a black beret and gloves placed on top of it. The coffin was carried by provos in black balaclavas, only their eyes showing. I followed the procession, couldn't help myself, in spite of the tension that charged the air. Two women, one old, one young, leaned on each other for support, weeping. A wee girl in a white dress, white socks, walked up on her tiptoes as if wanting to skip or dance, run away and play. She looked about her, not understanding, at white faces pinched and drawn into carica-ture by grief and pain, fear and hate.

A piper played a lament. A solitary drumtap kept the slow beat. A single churchbell clanged its low note. At the graveside the drummer hit two sharp beats, then pattered out a long dramatic roll, his sticks a blur. The pallbearers pulled on their black berets, fastened white webbing belts round their waists. At a signal they took out automatic pistols, fired a volley of shots in the air. People flinched, covered their ears. A few men cheered. Smoke drifted. A helicopter hovered over-head.

Grief and pain. Fear and hate.

A sunburst of colour, years later in Bali, another procession.

'A cremation is a joyful occasion,' said Agus. 'Now that we are cremating my father's body, his spirit can be liberated into the heavenly world.'

I'd met Agus when I asked him for directions to a temple. 'You want to see ceremony,' he said. 'You must come to my father's funeral tomorrow. It will be a splendid affair. Most lavish.'

'I'd love to see it,' I said. 'But is that OK?'

'Absolutely,' he said. 'Many westerners come to see our cremations. Next to our sacred dance is the most popular tourist attraction.' He grinned wide, shook my hand. 'This is a done deal!'

Over a glass or three of *tuak*, palm beer, in a bar called Paradise, I found out he was a teacher, married with two children. His father had died two years ago.

'Sorry?'

'Two years.'

'And you're just cremating him now?'

'To let you understand, the cremation is very expensive. It costs me almost three years' wages.'

'Jeez.'

'So we had to wait till we raised the cash.'

'And the body?'

'We buried it. Will dig it up tomorrow. It will be very moving for me to see him again, to handle his skull.'

'Oh. Right.'

'Your own father is alive?'

'You could say that, aye.'

I told him my life story and he laughed. 'So it must be meant that you come here. See a different kind of funeral. A different attitude to death. I believe your funerals at home are rather miserable.'

'That's the word.'

He laughed again and so did I. He was right, this must be meant. He was part of my karass. I pictured Abe with his stoned grin, reminding me. Blondie played on the tapedeck. *Dreaming*. We drank more *tuak* and Agus told me how it would be at his father's funeral.

'First we go to the cemetery, dig up the bones. Clean them. Leave them out to dry. In the meantime we have made a small body, a kind of effigy carved from sandalwood. This goes in a little coffin-box, and on top of it we put the *angenan*.'

'What's that?'

127

'Is a wonderful structure! It's a kind of lampstand with the lamp made of an eggshell. This symbolises the soul. The base is a ripe coconut filled with rice. Represents the heart.'

'*Angenan.*'

'That's it.'

'Heart and soul. Nice.'

'My wife will be carrying it on her head. You will see. Her name is Wayan. She is most beautiful.'

'I'm sure.' I had seen some of the women, early morning, walking in their sarongs, baskets of fruit balanced on their heads. I'd never seen such grace and poise in my life.

'The real remains are placed in a coffin of kapok wood, shaped like a lion.'

'A lion?'

He nodded, waved his hands. 'It's a work of art, like a sculpture. Of course in this place, everyone is supposed to be an artist. They say we have a taste for the baroque.'

'Baroque and roll.'

He laughed, clapped his hands. 'Very good! That just says it all. And the best thing is the procession. That's the real fun. The funeral tower is twenty feet high and carried by forty bearers! The tower is most elaborate. It spans all the worlds. The base is the underworld. Then come the forests and mountains. Then pagodas representing the heavens. That's where I will sit!'

'You'll be carried in it?'

'Along with a gamelan musician. And on top of the whole thing is the lingam of the *Tintiya*, the Supreme Being.'

I held my head. 'It sounds wild.'

'Oh it is!' He laughed. 'It is!'

The woman with the *angenan* balanced on her head, Agus's wife Wayan, was the only still point in the whole birling carnival. In a red and gold sarong, she moved slow and serious with a dancer's grace, reached up at every step to steady the precious load that seemed sure to fall but didn't. Total focus inward in the calm face. Delicate expressiveness in the spread and bent-back fingers. Divine refinement.

The rest was baroque and roll.

A gang of youths, barechested, ran with the lion-coffin carried on their shoulders on bamboo poles. They turned and spun with it, whirled it this way and that. Yelled and laughed, jostled and shoved each other, clowned around, raucous. The funeral tower swayed in the air, up on a bamboo platform carried by the forty bearers. Seated up there, halfway to heaven in one of the pagodas, was Agus, dressed all in white, beaming, waving to the crowd. On the level below sat the musician, clanging his gamelan xylophone, its rhythm insistent, mesmeric. The scent of incense filled the air, sweet intoxicating frangipani.

The cemetery was like a picnic ground, full of families making a day of it, vendors selling food and drink. The tower came swaying in, propelled by the squad of bearers. It looked sure to catch on overhead telegraph wires, but just at the last moment the top section tipped over, hinged, to let it pass through as the crowd cheered and surged. It was set down on a pyre of wood on a grassy mound, the lion coffin beside it bright vermilion with a green mane and bulging green eyes, a long black tongue lolling out between bared fangs.

The musician climbed down from the tower, joined a full gamelan orchestra moving into place. Then Agus climbed down and stood with folded hands as a bundle wrapped in white cloth was passed overhead, hand to hand through the crowd. His father's remains, the dried-out bones and skull. Agus received the bundle, touched it to his forehead. The coffin lid was opened and he placed the bundle inside, folded his hands again, bowed.

A priest in yellow robes and a tall sugarloaf hat stepped up to the platform, began chanting Sanskrit mantras, moving round the coffin, dousing it with water from an earthenware jug. It trickled from the lion's belly, and the priest poured on clear spirits from a smaller flask. Then he stood back and the pyre was set alight. The lion's mane took first, flared, then the whole thing caught and burned, its blackened shape wavering in the flames.

Above the flicker and roar of the burning came the voice of the priest again, high and nasal, chanting Sanskrit. Behind that was a constant wash of background noise, the creak creak of cicadas. Then the gamelan started up, slow at first, jangle and clang of cymbals and gongs, its weird atonality creating a context for the rest. The crackle and spark, the Sanskrit, the cicadas, were all caught up in the patterns of sound, the hammering rhythms, the cycles and spirals of melody, the endless repetitions but every time changed.

I felt it in my gut, pure vital energy, felt an expansiveness in my chest. I breathed in the fragrance of the incense, the heaped flowers, the burning wood. The fire danced. The solid world wavered, was no longer real. There were other worlds, beyond this. For a moment I knew. I had stepped outside myself, was not-me. I looked across at Agus. His smile was serene. His eyes shone.

'Is it just me?' I asked Des, back in London. 'I mean, is it selective perception sort of thing? Do I run into all this stuff about death and funerals because I'm looking for it?'

Des had settled for teaching art, was in a steady relationship, talked about getting married. 'Of course it's you,' he said. 'You're a morbid bastard, a fucking ghoul. Spectre at the fucking feast.'

Cheers.

A video advertised for sale in an underground newspaper in San Francisco: *Elvis – the autopsy*.

The man in black who told me a joke.

It was in Ottawa, in a pizzeria called Pizza the action. Right. I'd worked there for a couple of weeks, learned to flip up the dough, spin it in the air, catch it and slap it down. Looked good.

It was midwinter. The Rideau River had frozen over. If you stepped outside without a hat it made you cry. I'd reckon twenty minutes till brain-death.

The man brought the cold in with him. He was shrouded in it, gave it off in waves. A big man with a black beard, black fur hat, black coat with an astrakhan collar. Looked like he'd walked out of a story by Bashevis Singer. Stamped his feet to shake the snow off his overshoes.

'Goddam weather,' he said, scraping a chair on the floor as he sat down. He kept on his coat and hat, rubbed his hands together with a swishing noise. He was the first customer of the evening, had the place to himself, took it over. Ordered the *contadina*, with extra anchovies, side salad, garlic bread. Pot of coffee.

'Should do the trick,' he said, pouring a cup of the coffee, black. 'You new here?'

'Kind of.'

'And Scottish?'

'That's right.'

'Get this cold over there?'

'Never.'

'Lucky.' He shivered, warmed his hands on the cup.

'You work outside?' I asked. I'd taken him for a lawyer, a businessman.

He laughed. 'Sometimes I have no choice! I'm an undertaker.'

'You're kidding?'

'You look surprised.'

'No, it's just, that's what my father does.'

'There you go. Small world.'

Karass.

'Aye.'

His pizza would be ready. I shovelled it out of the oven, served it up with the salad, the bread. *Bon appetit.*

'So you'll know what I mean,' he said, his mouth full of food. 'About working in this weather.'

'I can imagine.'

'Have to bring in heaters to melt the ice, thaw the ground so we can get the graves dug. Even with the mechanical diggers, it's hard going. I wish to God they'd all just get cremated. Hey, do you know any Robert Service?'

'Can't say I do.'

'Cremation of Sam McGee. It's a great poem.' He swallowed a mouthful. 'It's about this guy and his buddy Sam McGee, crossing the Yukon. And Sam's always complaining that he can't get warm. And eventually he dies, and the guy cremates him, in the wreck of an old boat.'

He cleared his throat, took a swig of water, recited.

'Some planks I tore from the cabin floor and I lit the boiler fire.
Some coal I found that was lying around, and I heaped the fuel
    higher;
The flames just soared, and the furnace roared – such a blaze you
    seldom see;
And I burrowed a hole in the glowing coal, and I stuffed in Sam
    McGee.'

'Good stuff.'

'But that's not the end of it. As Sam's burning, the guy looks
in, and sees him sitting up.'

'I've heard it happens.'

'And there sat Sam, looking cool and calm, in the heat of the
    furnace roar
And he wore a smile you could see a mile, and he said: "Please
    close that door.
It's fine in here, but I greatly fear you'll let in the cold and
    storm
Since I left Plumtree, down in Tennessee, it's the first time I've
    been warm." '

He thumped on the table. 'By God that's good! I think I'll have it
read at my funeral. May as well give everybody a laugh. Hey,
somebody told me a funeral joke today. Want to hear it?'

'Sure.'

'It's a Newfoundland joke. Guess that's a bit like your Irish
jokes. Anyway, this old fellow from Newfoundland died, and
his oldest son, who had moved to the city, wanted an elaborate
funeral, no expense spared, just send all the bills to him and
he'd take care of it.

'So the rest of the family made all the arrangements and the
funeral was a great occasion. The old man was buried in a
beautiful suit, in a solid oak coffin. The church was full of
flowers and the reception afterwards was magnificent. The
guests shifted vast quantities of food and drink and everybody
had a great time. The son was well pleased, and more than
happy to pay all the bills as he'd promised.

'A month went by and the family sent him another bill for twenty-five dollars. No problem, obviously some small item that had been overlooked. He sent off a cheque.

'But the next month he received another bill for the same amount. And the next month. And the month after that.

'So he contacted the family, said, What's the story with these bills? I thought I'd paid everything.

'And the family wrote back, said, It's for the hire of the old man's suit.'

Always the jokes.

To keep moving.

Funeral pyres blazing at dusk on the burning-ghats of the Ganges, the holy city of Varanasi, once Benares. A woman wailing, screaming, being led away by friends. Packs of jackals snuffling around, vultures circling, lazy. A solitary figure cross-legged in meditation, among the ashes, the powdered bone and charred wood. He was naked except for a loincloth, hair long and matted, body smeared with ash. Sat unmoving, unmoved.

I had come at last to India, asking my big question. No more jokes, I wanted to know. The third day I fell ill, first time in years. The water maybe, or something I'd eaten. Started with a headache, nausea. Got worse till my head felt cleaved in two, gripes in the gut that cramped, bent me double. Then the whole shebang, vomiting and diarrhoea. Lupe Velez and the beautiful death. Maybe that was it, I had come here to die, answer my question once and for all.

Three days I lay on my back in the grim room I'd rented, sweating the poisons out of me, only dragging myself along the corridor to the toilet. God help anyone who had to use it after me.

Eventually felt strong enough to go outside. Tentative. One step. Another. Legs unsteady. Like stepping off a boat. Towards evening, the lamps coming on in all the little back-street stalls and shops. Heat of the day lingering but less intense. Waft of smells assailing me, drains and incense, spices popping in thick ghee. I couldn't eat yet. Bought a litre of bottled water from a store, checked the seal wasn't broken. The water was warm but it didn't matter, I'd got dried up, dehydrated, swigged the lot in gulps on my way back down to the river, to the ghats.

Another dusk and more pyres burning down. Woodsmoke and burnt meat smell. I sat, still shaky, on the steps leading down, tried to breathe deep, get my strength back. The nearest pyre was a smouldering glow, embers and ash, smoke. Silhouetted against it, a man with a long pole hammered at what looked like a hipbone, broke it up, ground it to dust.

I looked down at my feet in the beat-up trainers, the skinny legs, khaki shorts, faded blue t-shirt. Looked at my hands, flexed the fingers. Touched my face, the rough stubble. Who was I? And what in God's name was I doing here?

A few yards from the pyre was the *sadhu* I'd seen before, seated in meditation, absorbed. I found myself drawn towards him, cleared a space and sat down. He obviously came here to meditate on death. Maybe if I asked him he would know.

I did my best to sit like him, legs crossed, back straight, hands resting on the knees. His eyes were half open, flickered from time to time. His breathing seemed shallow, almost imperceptible. For over an hour I watched him, tried to sit upright, stay alert, the tiredness and weakness dragging me down. Had to keep shifting position to ease the ache in my back, the tearing pain in ankles and knees. But every time I decided to get up and go, I couldn't. Something kept me sitting there.

It got dark and the scraggy jackals came scavenging. A gust of wind blew dust and ash in my face, left irritating grit in my eyes. And the whole time the man just sat there, didn't move. Then he let out a long slow breath, rolled his eyes back in his head, opened them and stared out at me.

'You are restless.' The voice was dry and cracked, high-pitched.

'I'm sorry, I just . . .'

'What do you want?'

Right this minute, not to be. To disappear, be somewhere else, some*one* else. Earth to open up and swallow me.

'Em,' I said. Pause. 'I want to know. What happens when you die?'

He threw back his head and laughed, bared a row of rotten teeth. 'If you sit here long enough, you will definitely find out.'

'Is that why you sit here?'

He nodded, held up a rough white bowl. 'This is all I own. It is made from the skull of an old friend.' He put it down again. 'Yamaraj is my teacher. The Lord of Death. Here he is my constant companion. And here Mother Kali has showed me her terrible face. Once or twice she has even smiled at me with sweetness and compassion.' He smiled, for a moment childlike. Then his face was hard again, stern.

'So.' He straightened his back, took a deep breath through his nose. 'I can teach you nothing. If you want to learn nothing, you are welcome to stay.'

Middle of the night in this howling no-place of jackals and hungry ghosts, out there the endless dark pressing in on me, no-world without end. Nowhere. Now here. Had to stay awake for fear I'd be engulfed by it, never wake up again, be nothing. Be one more corpse in this place of skulls, bones picked clean, reduced to dust, dispersed.

I kept drifting, jerking awake, lost all sense of myself. Shadows, forms, coalesced, took shape, came at me out the dark. Monkey-demons, birds, wraiths – bad trip cartoon horror. One slouched figure I knew brushed past and stood behind me, chilled and numbed me, froze me right through. The Reaper, the sadhu's Yamaraj, Lord of Death. I tried to turn and face him but couldn't move, blanked.

Grey halflight and the sadhu still sitting. I huddled, arms round my knees, couldn't sit upright. Everything hurt. I curled up among the ashes on the hard ground. A momentary acid flashback, foetus in a cage of bone. Then nothing.

Nothing.

Waking, wrecked. Whatever way I shifted was worse. Felt cramped, knotted, clenched. Mind dulled, eyes gummed shut. Tongue thick and dry in my mouth. Warmth of the sun about me. Temple bells. People gathering. I had to move, get up. Sheer effort of will. Onto the hands and knees and by stages up, off the hunkers onto the hind legs. But too quick, felt lightheaded, had to sit back down again. Rubbed my gritty eyes, opened them, blinked. Pilgrims in the first light, immersing themselves in the river. The holy Ganges, an open sewer, shit-brown, carrying the detritus of puffed-up corpses bleached white. They bobbed against garbage and offerings, orange marigolds and plastic sacks.

The sadhu still there, rocklike.

And just for a moment, by some kind of identification, I saw into the space he inhabited. I entered into it, mind scoured and empty, clear. Reality was stark and bleak, cold, void. Nothing mattered. Or everything. And this hard place was the beginning of compassion. I looked again at the sadhu, saw the faintest half-smile on his weathered face.

Then another figure was approaching us, swish of white cloth. A woman in a sari, coming at me out of the brightness, the morning sun behind her head, dazzling me. Some trick of the light, or a visitation from the sadhu's benign Kali. I shielded my eyes from the glare, saw this real woman standing there, looking at me with such concern. Skin warm gold, eyes big and dark, black sheen of hair plaited back, glint of tiny gold earrings. But these were details only, there was more, something I recognised but couldn't name. It felt as if I knew her and always had.

'Are you all right?' she asked, and the voice sounded English, middleclass London.

I tried to speak, moved the thick slab of tongue in my mouth, unstuck it, butted it sluggish against my teeth, managed a grunt.

'My God,' she said. 'You're parched. You need water.'

I nodded. Water. Yes. God yes.

Over her shoulder she carried a square canvas bag, an aum sign printed in red on the side. She rummaged in it, brought out a small plastic bottle of water, unscrewed the cap, handed it to me. My hand shook as I took it from her, raised it to my lips.

'Try and sip it slow,' she said. 'Don't gulp it all in one go.'

136

I swigged a mouthful, swilled it round my mouth, swallowed. Yes.

'Good,' I said. 'Thanks.'

'You're English?' she said.

'Scottish.'

I heard myself, in this ultimate place, still making distinctions. Like it was important. She caught it too, smiled. Lightness.

'What about him?' She glanced at the sadhu.

'Don't think he's Scottish,' I said.

'No.'

'Mind you, he's grim enough.'

Ah me I gravel am and dust.

'I meant would he like some water?'

Of course.

I moved across, kneeled in front of him. He refocused his gaze, from infinity to this nearpoint, me with the plastic bottle. I pointed at it, felt faintly ridiculous. But he nodded, held out his skull-bowl towards me. I poured water in and he sipped it, held out the bowl for more. I poured the rest, the last of it, tapped the base to shake out the dregs. He drank again, finished it, put down the empty bowl, folded his hands, bowed.

Her name was Lila. I asked her what it meant and she said the divine dance, the cosmic play, and she laughed, sweetly ironic, conscious of herself. Walking beside her was intoxicating. I couldn't stop looking, felt again this familiarity. She walked with me through the same back streets now different, changed because I was with her. I blessed the crowds that jostled us, pushed us together. I breathed in her fragrance, scent of jasmine. Once or twice I stumbled, still weak and faint from the long weird night, and she reached out to steady me, light touch of her hand on my bare arm, a charge of pure energy.

We stopped at a tiny hole-in-the-wall café, an image of Ganesh above the door, potbellied, elephant-headed, a smile in the eyes.

'Tea?' said Lila, and for a moment I felt tearful, overwhelmed by this simple kindness.

'This is good of you,' I said.

'It's nothing.'

What the sadhu said he could teach me. Nothing. Nothing special. Have a cup of tea.

She ordered a pot of masala chai, brewed with milk, sweetened, spiced with cloves and cinnamon, ginger and peppercorn, cardamom. I'd never tasted anything so good. I had woken from one dream into another. Dream within a dream.

Lila.

She was in India for her father's funeral.

'Sorry,' I said.

She shrugged. Tensed, untensed her thin shoulders. 'It was what he wanted, to die here, be cremated, his ashes sprinkled in the Ganges. They say if you die in Varanasi, your soul is freed from the cycle of death and rebirth.'

'You believe that?'

'It sounds too easy. There has to be more to it than where you die.'

'You would think so.'

'But he believed it. That's what matters. We cremated him yesterday. Seems a long time ago. I was taking a last look at the pyre this morning when I saw you.'

'I was amazed at you coming over,' I said. 'I mean, look at the state of me.'

She nodded, smiled. 'I know. I saw the sadhu first, was about to walk on, then I saw you sitting there. Just sitting there. And I don't know, there was something. The sun was shining right in your face and I saw you clear, and you looked, it sounds silly, you looked familiar, like I knew you.'

I wanted to take her face in my hands.

'This is so weird,' I said. 'I had the same thing. Kind of recognition.'

We sat and looked at each other, touched hands, tentative, everything focused down to this.

'I'm going back to London tomorrow.'

'Shit.'

'I know,' she said. 'Couldn't have put it better!'

'I don't know what's going on here,' I said. 'But it's pretty intense.'

She squeezed my hand. 'Shall we walk?'

Her mother had died when Lila was sixteen. She had two older brothers, both here for the funeral. She'd done teacher training, decided not to teach. Did secretarial work. Hated it. Lived in a rented flat in Earl's Court.

'On your own?' I asked.

Subtle.

'I am now,' she said. 'There was somebody, but it's finished.'

'Right.'

'What about you?'

'Nobody.'

We'd come to a little courtyard off the street, remains of a temple, a wayside shrine. It was run down and overgrown, monkeys darting out of the shadows. But a statue of Ganesh still stood, stone weathered and worn, eroded but still recognisable.

'He's following us,' said Lila. 'Or leading us. The café and now here.'

Now here.

'Looking out for us,' I said.

'He's good luck,' she said. 'The remover of obstacles. People pray to him when they're starting out on something new.'

'Maybe that's what we should be doing.'

Someone had even put a few fresh flowers at the feet of the statue. Lila kneeled and rearranged them, picked off the dead leaves. Touched the flowers to her forehead, replaced them.

'I should be getting back,' she said. 'They'll be starting to worry.'

'Your brothers?'

'We're staying with my uncle. My father's brother. I'd like to invite you there, but I don't think he'd thank me for it. Bringing home a stray Scotsman.'

'Maybe not.'

There was a silence, just a beat or two but deep, till the shriek of a monkey broke it.

'So where do we take this from here?' I said.

'If we're meant to meet again, we will.'

'Your phone number in London would help.'

'Of course.' She searched in her shoulder bag, found a scrap of paper, a pen. Scribbled to get the pen working, wrote her name and the number, handed it to me. 'You'll be back in London sometime?'

'Soon,' I said, deciding.

'Good.'

'I guess later today's out of the question? Or tonight?'

'We leave first thing in the morning. Everything's too crazy.'

'So,' I said. 'London.'

She touched my arm. 'London.'

A mantra.

I kissed her cheek, her mouth. Soft warmth. This was actually happening. Here in this dream of India, in a ruined temple full of screeching monkeys, we held each other, swayed together, the old stone Ganesh watching over us.

I flew back to London two weeks later, the earliest I could get out on my cheap ticket through Kathmandu. I'd have to sign on, look for restaurant work. But the first thing was to phone Lila. I tried the whole of the first day back, kept hitting the redial button on Des's phone. But no reply. A few times I keyed in the number again, just to be sure I hadn't dialled it wrong. Still nothing. I'd let half an hour go by without trying, then hit redial every ten seconds. Nobody there. I went out for a walk, tried from a phonebox, callgirls' cards and stickers all over the inside. Nothing. The greasy mouthpiece smelled of aftershave and nicotine. I came back to Des's place, tried again. Again.

'So this is love?' said Des, a cynical edge to the voice, a curl of the lip, amused condescension in the eyes. His long-term relationship had broken up.

'I only met Lila the once,' I said, 'and I can't think about anything else.'

'Not even what happens when you die?'

'That's there all the time,' I said. 'A constant. Bass notes. But this is the melody.'

'Profound!'

'Hey!'

I tried the number again, and this time she answered.

'Hello?'

Her voice!

'Hi, Lila?'

A pause. Intake of breath.

'Is that Neil?'

'Hi!'

She recognised me!

'Are you in London?'

'Got in this morning.'

'God, you must be jetlagged.'

'Some. It's not so bad coming this way. Listen, can we meet?'

'Yes, we must.'

'When?'

'When suits you?'

'How about now?'

'Sounds good,' she said. 'Now.'

Now.

Des laughed as I ran out the door.

I couldn't move quick enough, along the road, down the subway steps. Next train 3 minutes. Fuck. So long. Relativity. Ache of waiting, pacing the platform. Come on. The train at last thundering in. Straphanging, impatient, the stations ticking off endless one by one. And every stop Mind the Gap, Stand Clear of the Doors. Aye OK. OK. Get on. Check the watch, only half an hour since I came off the phone, felt forever. Making good time but. Then an unscheduled slowdown and stop in the last tunnel. Shit. The doldrums. Horse latitudes. That comparative quiet, hearing bits of conversation, bare and isolated, exposed. The thin crackle and hiss, the pattering drumbeat filtered through a young guy's headphones, music you can't quite make out. Then a judder and lurch and moving again, on into the station. Up the stairs two at a time, through the barrier and out.

Running now, past latenight grocers, kebab shops, stopping at a corner to check Lila's directions. Found the street, and the house. Less than an hour, a miracle. Entryphone, her name handwritten third from the top. *Her name!* Pressing the buzzer, then her voice through the intercom.

'Yes?'

Yes!

'It's me, Neil.'

Dull buzz of the door unlocking. Push it open and in.

Flat 3, the second floor. She came down to meet me halfway, on the landing. Shock of recognition. The way I remembered her but changed. Not in a sari but jeans and a white cotton blouse, and that shimmer of black hair loose, hanging straight, framing that face I knew, familiar as my own. We kissed, clung together, laughed at this same old thing new, the wonder and the cliché of it.

'I can't believe this,' she said. 'I'm shaking.'

'Me too.' I pushed back her hair, kissed her neck, her ear, breathed her in.

'This is where we left off in Varanasi,' she said. 'Seems like ages ago.'

'How can a couple of weeks be so long?'

'It's ridiculous,' she said, 'but I've missed you.'

'I've been the same,' I said. 'It's mad.'

She took my hand, led me up the rest of the stairs to the flat.

Inside there was a warmth and brightness. Incense burning, gardenia. A richness of colour but at the same time a simplicity. Walls painted a peach tint, spray of lilies in a plain white vase. Indian cushions on a big soft couch, Japanese prints on the walls. All I could take in before she came to me and her arms were round my neck again, I was falling into her.

Through to the bedroom, a poster of Ganesh on the wall.

'Our man,' I said.

'I bought it last week.'

I stroked her face. 'This is unreal.'

'I know,' she said, 'but it's happening.'

'Listen, I don't have any, you know, protection.'

'It should be OK,' she said. 'I'm pretty regular. I've been working it out and I reckon this is my safe time.'

'We got rhythm!'

'Right!'

142

Got my gal. Who could ask for anything more.

'So you're sure about this?'

'Sure as I can be.' She smiled, ground against me. 'Or if you'd rather, we could just have a cup of tea.'

'Maybe not right now.'

I kissed her throat, unbuttoned the white blouse and slipped it off, and she was tugging at my t-shirt helping me off with it. Then the fumbling with belt-buckles and zips, and the struggling out of the jeans, and the finicky fastening at the back of her bra I couldn't undo and she reached behind with both hands, unclipped it, and I held her breasts, cupped them, felt the nipples stiffen, kissed and sucked them and she leaned back her head, gave a little moan. Pants peeled off, chucked aside, we held each other naked, miraculous, fitting together, touching cock to cunt. Then my hand down feeling her there, wet, and kneeling in front of her, kissing, licking it, tasting her, and on to the bed, her lying back, me finding her clit with my fingers and stroking, stroking, and taking her nipple in my mouth at the same time. Her breath came in shorter and shorter gasps and when I thought she was almost there I climbed on top and slid inside her and she tensed and tensed and finally came, and freed I kept thrusting, exploded into her, ecstatic.

The way it was meant to be.

This.

Waking in the night, this soft warm body wrapped around me, Lila, here now. My face in her hair, hand on the small of her back. Caress. Karass. She woke, looked surprised a moment to see me. Then she smiled, recognition, and we moved together, made love again, easy and slow, replenishing flow of pure energy, complete.

We got married a month later, no reason other than it felt right. Des was the best man, even though he had doubts about the whole thing, didn't understand us rushing into it.

'Still,' he said. 'If you're sure. Good luck to you.'

The ceremony was in a registry office, brisk and functional, a formality. I wore a good suit I'd bought in Oxfam that had cleaned up well, a new silk tie patterned with blue flowers. Lila looked incredible in a red sari bordered with gold. Her two brothers came, signed as witnesses. They were civil enough, polite, but stiff, seemed disapproving. Not really surprising, their wee sister marrying this deadbeat she'd picked up at the ghats in Varanasi.

I'd sent a telegram inviting my father. Took a lot. When he didn't reply, I phoned him, shaky, sick in my stomach. Was ready to put down the receiver when he answered.

His voice. All these years. So much older. Thin and reedy. An old man, strange to me.

'McGraw, funeral directors.'

I could just hang up, forget the whole thing. Didn't.

'Hello, Da.' Voice trembly. 'This is Neil.'

A long, long pause.

'Aye. Well. I got your telegram. Quite a surprise. It's been a long time.'

'I know.'

'A hell of a long time.'

'Aye.'

'There's no way I can make it to this wedding.'

'No.'

'It's during the week. I'm working.'

'Aye.'

'And even if I wasn't. I mean, London.'

'Sure.'

Another long silence. The way it always was with him, so much unspoken. Tension that made your teeth feel like chalk.

'This must be costing you.'

For fuck's sake! We haven't spoken in fifteen years!

I said, 'It's OK.' A mantra to myself. Stay calm. Keep the head.

Made more strained smalltalk. Yes I was working, in a Mexican diner, and Lila had an OK job, and yes she was a nice lassie, beautiful. And he couldn't complain, not getting any younger, but business was fine. A few changes. Auld Jack had died, few years back. Andy still there, doing away. That was about it.

'Right,' I said. 'So.' More charged silence down the line. Costing me. So much I wanted to say, couldn't. My voice, cheerful. 'Expect we'll be up sometime. Lila's never been to Scotland. I'll give you a call. Maybe pay a visit.'

'Fine,' he said. 'Do that.'

'So I'll be seeing you.'

'Aye. And, eh, all the best.'

'Thanks.'

When I'd put down the phone I just sat, numbed, stared at nothing, all light and colour drained from the day.

I got in late one night from work, clothes and hair stinking of onions and garlic, spices. The phone rang and Lila answered it.

'Yes, uh huh. Can I ask who's calling?' She covered the mouthpiece, said, 'Andrew McIlroy?'

Meant nothing. I shrugged and she handed the phone to me, moved out of the way so I could sit down.

'Hello?'

'Hello, is that you Neil?' A voice I thought I knew, couldn't place. An older man, Glasgow. 'This is Andy here, Andy McIlroy.' No. Still didn't register. 'Andy the driver. Work for your old man.'

Use the noddle.

'Andy! How you doing?'

'I'm fine, son.' But his voice sounded flat, subdued. 'Listen, I'm sorry, it's your da. He died the day.'

'Jesus.'

The strangeness of this, the unreality, Lila looking across at me, puzzled and concerned.

The old voice, a monotone, continuing. 'He took a bit of a bad turn last night. Seemed to be OK. You know what he's like. Had a job to do this afternoon, a burial. Was a right cold day. Bitter. He should never have went out. They'd just lowered the coffin into the grave when he collapsed, went right in on top of it.'

So they just covered him up then? Save a lot of bother.

Dear God, this terrible sick urge to laugh. I bit my knuckle, breathed out through my nose.

'So that was it,' said Andy. 'Ambulance came pretty quick but he was gone.'

'End of story.'

'Heart attack they said. He's in the mortuary. I thought you'd be wanting to come up and make the arrangements and that.'

'Aye.'

'It's weird that you just got back in touch with him. After all these years.'

'You're right,' I said. 'It is weird.'

'Almost like it was meant.'

'Isn't it?'

Next day there was another call, from my father's solicitor, Mr Jardine. Offered me his condolences. Said he was dealing with the estate. He'd be putting it in writing, but my father had written his will years ago. He'd left me a tidy sum in the bank, as well as the business and the house, everything.

A woman's only child was bitten by a snake and died. Distraught and anguished, she carried the child's body to the Buddha and placed it at his feet.

Lord, she said, this is my son, my only child, and death has taken him from me. I know you have the power to bring him back to life. I am begging you, Lord, to restore him, to return him to me.

And the Buddha nodded and said, I can do it. I can bring your son back to life. All I need is for you to bring me a few mustard seeds.

The woman was overwhelmed with joy and relief. Mustard seeds! I shall fetch them immediately!

There is only one condition, said the Buddha. These mustard seeds have to come from a house that has not been touched by death.

I will do it, said the woman, and she rushed off on her simple quest.

The first house she came to, the door was opened by a young girl. The woman explained what she wanted, just a few mustard seeds, and the girl said she would get them.

But before you do, said the woman, I have to ask if there has been a death in this household.

The young girl started crying. Only last month, she said, my father died.

I am sorry to have disturbed you, said the woman. And thank you for your trouble, but I cannot accept the seeds from you.

At the next house, an old man answered. He too was ready to fetch a handful of mustard seeds from his kitchen. But he too had suffered bereavement – his wife had died a year ago.

Forgive me, she said, I am sorry for intruding.

And she tried the next house, and the next. She spent the whole day going from door to door, asking at every house in the village. And everywhere the story was the same. A mother had died, or a father. A husband or a wife. A grandparent or a child. Every single household had been touched by death.

It was dark by the time the woman returned to the Buddha, exhausted and empty-handed.

Well? he asked her gently. Did you get the mustard seeds?

Sadly she shook her head. There is no house in the village that has not known death.

All who are born must die, he said. Now do you understand?

Yes, she said. Thank you. And she took away her dead child, to bury him.

5

It was like they always say in books, about going back. Everything was so much smaller than I remembered. Shrunk. Was the yard really always this size? Barely big enough for the hearse and the van parked side by side, as they were now, as Lila and I stepped round them. And the building itself – the workshop downstairs, offices on the ground, the flat up above – three floors but so compact, so wee.

It wasn't so much like stepping into the past, as moving through a version of that past, reduced and scaled down, a stage set, artist's impression.

'This is so weird,' I said.

'Must be,' said Lila.

'It's like seeing an old black-and-white film. An accurate re-creation of the place you grew up. Only it's real.'

I turned the key and pushed open the front door, dragged the scatter of junkmail on the mat. And the smells hit me, stopped me right there and churned my guts, a fusty mix of dust and rot and chemicals, old waxy polish and stale air freshener, sick-sweet.

Lila touched my arm. 'You all right?'

I nodded. 'Sure. Fine.'

The office and reception area were much the same. A coat of paint maybe, sometime in the last ten years, change of wallpaper, but the colours the same brown-fawn-tan-beige, bland no-colour. Framed landscape paintings of Highland glens. This year's calendar with what looked like the same old views of the Trossachs.

I flicked through the mail, bills and circulars, nothing personal. I sat in my father's chair, felt numb.

'Aren't you going to show me round?' asked Lila.

'Of course. Right. Aye.'

The back area had been completely transformed, rebuilt, part of it converted into a small viewing room, soft lighting, a dais fringed with satin where the coffin would rest, chairs round the walls for the bereaved. On a pine shelf stood a blue vase with what had been a fine display of mixed flowers, must be hothouse at this time of year, now wilted and withered, dried out, no water left in the vase. I picked them up, automatically, to ditch them. The blossoms rustled like paper, shed dry petals.

The far back space had been changed into a proper embalming room, tiles on the floor, new stainless steel table, big sinks, fluorescent lights. I flicked the switch and it all shone, bright and harsh.

'Wow!'

Lila shivered. 'Give you the creeps.'

'Ain't seen nothing yet.' And I took her downstairs to the basement. Which was almost exactly the same. Half expected to see Auld Jack, polishing his state of the art casket.

Where me and wee Jeannie, yes, all those years ago.

But Jack and his casket were long gone. Jack in the box. But no bouncing back, down in the ground sunk deep.

That wasn't the person, he said, what got buried was stuff. By that time you were out of it. Offski. He knocked my head. Stuff.

The workshop was cold, smelled damp. A skittering under the floorboards sounded like mice. I remembered, looked for the secret place, prised up the loose board.

'Ha!'

'What?'

'Where I used to stash my sweeties and comics.'

'That is *so* sad.'

'Sherbet fountains and creepy worlds.'

'Anything still there?'

'Nothing. Dust. Mouse-droppings.'

'Oh well.'

Upstairs to the flat. Where I used to live. Again it was the smell that hit me. Familiar staleness that caught at my throat, made me feel sick. Smell of misery.

'I guess your dad lived on his own for a while.'

I nodded. 'Was bad enough with the two of us.'

The kitchen was the way he'd walked out and left it, the day he died. Same clutter of unwashed dishes in the sink, half-rinsed milkbottles on the draining board, full ashtray on the sticky tabletop, brownstained cup with tea dregs in the bottom, burnt spillage on the cooker, congealed lard in the frying pan with bacon bits set in it and a single line of mouse-tracks running across the surface. Detritus. A life. He'd walked out that day not knowing.

His room smelled the worst, window closed, old curtains drawn, dull fug of shut-in fagsmoke, the rank stink of bedding not changed in weeks or months. Dust everywhere.

Lila opened the curtains, pushed up the window. Let in light, air. 'It's a start,' she said.

Going in to my own room was the strangest. The bed was still in the corner, the chair and table still there where I used to do my homework. On the wall there were still patches where the paper was paler, rectangles left where my posters and pictures had been taken down, one tiny ragged triangle of white, up high, where the corner of a poster had stayed put, held there by a strip of yellowed sellotape. Nothing had been taken out or rear-ranged, but things had been piled in on top, cardboard boxes and plastic bags dumped on the floor, the desk, the bed.

'Turned it into a storeroom,' said Lila.

'Rubbish tip more like.' I looked in a box, saw sheaves of old papers, letters. 'Christ. This is going to take some sorting.'

And I suddenly felt claustrophobic, overwhelmed, had to get out.

The pub was noisy and bright and warm and just where I needed to be.

'So you'll have to make the arrangements,' said Lila. 'For the funeral.'

'Who buries the undertaker?' I said. 'Like who shaves the barber?'

'Eh?'

'It's a song. Who shaves the barber? The barber shaves himself.'

'Really?' she said, not impressed.

'Who takes care of the caretaker's daughter when the caretaker's busy taking care?'

'Hm.'

'Who takes under the undertaker?'

'You're drunk.'

'Maybe. Ever so slightly.'

'But you will have to take care of it.'

'I could do it all myself. See him off. I did help him out often enough. Nothing to it.' The drink talking. Ironic but meaning it.

'I think he'd like that,' said Lila.

'I don't imagine he's bothered one way or the other. Not now.'

'You know what I mean.'

'Aye. Sure.' I sipped my pint. 'And you're right. It would probably be a good thing to do. Might even make me feel better about the whole business.'

'I think so.'

'But I'm not embalming him.'

She shook her head, shuddered. 'No.'

'Got to draw the line somewhere. And it's not as if we'll be having a viewing. Just keep it simple. Lay him out, box him, bury him.'

'I don't know how you could do an embalming anyway. But certainly not on your father.'

'Mind you,' I said, 'there were times when he was alive I could happily have gutted him.'

'Neil!' She hit my arm. 'You don't mean that!'

'Don't I? No, I suppose not. He was still the Da, when all's said and done. When all's sad and done. Christ, you're right. I am drunk!' I raised my glass. 'All right, Da. I'll take care of it. Be the last man to let you down.'

I made all the arrangements, booked the crematorium, contacted the minister, did the paperwork, placed the obituary notice.

McGRAW, Alexander William, suddenly on 17th February. Beloved husband of the late Irene McGraw. Much loved father of Neil McGraw.

The standard format, the accepted form of words. *Suddenly* rather than *Peacefully* or *After a Long Illness*.

Beloved. Much Loved. Always the same, no matter what the truth of it. Wouldn't do to write *Much Loathed. Heartily Despised. Feared and Hated.* Had to be the Dear Departed.

And if I placed an In Memoriam notice, or chose a verse for the Book of Remembrance, the sentiment would be the same.

> *Silent thoughts of times together*
> *Hold memories that will last forever.*

Right.

Lila was gutting the flat upstairs, clearing it out, stuffing all the rubbish into plastic bags. I could hear her moving about, knocking the place into shape.

Andy had helped me bring my father from the mortuary, driven the van, helped me carry him in, lift him out of the body bag, lay him out on the steel table.

'It's good that you're doing this,' said Andy.

'Suppose so,' I said.

'It can't be easy when it's your own.'

'No,'

'I know you and him never saw eye to eye. But he wasn't a bad bloke. No better or worse than the rest of us.'

'That's true.'

'Maybe this'll give you a chance to make your peace with him. Before you see him off.'

'You could be right.'

An awkwardness in the face of my lack of response. 'Well, if you need any help, just give me a shout.'

'Will do.'

'And I'll see you in the morning.'

'Quarter to ten.'

'The hearse is immaculate. Spick and span.'

'Thanks, Andy. He'd appreciate that.'

'It's only right. His final journey and that.'

'Aye.'

'So. In the morning then.'

'The morning.'

And he left me here with what had been my father. Mortal

remains. The wee pale body, exposed and cold and vulnerable. Brutal the t-shaped incision in the chest from the post mortem, stitched up rough like a seam on sailcloth. Cardiac blue discolouration. Flesh slack on the skinny frame, the ribs showing through. The mouth slightly open, no teeth, the cheeks clapped in. The way he looked sometimes when he fell asleep drunk, paralytic.

But he wouldn't wake up from this stupor. This time he was out the game for good. I remembered talking to Rab Deans all those years ago when his father died. Ten guitars. The sense of waste, and no more possibility of sorting things out between you. A wish it could have been different.

And looking at those familiar features, I saw them much more like my own than I'd ever realised or admitted. One day this would be me.

Upstairs my wife he had never met was clearing out his things, making space. He had left me the lot. The house and workplace. The vehicles. The tidy sum. The business to take on or sell. With goodwill.

Was that it? Had there been some vestige of good will towards me? His flesh and blood. Or guilt over how he had treated me? The child in question.

I tried to read something into the look on his face, but there was nothing, a blankness, mouth in a final twist of surprise and pain. I shivered, rubbed my hands together and blew on them, my breath clouding in the cold air.

I had filled the electric kettle with water and put it on to boil. The kettle was old and had no cut-off switch. I was sudenly aware of the lid rattling, steam hissing out. I shut it off, poured the water into a plastic basin and cooled it just enough, swishing with my hand. Felt I should be testing it with my elbow, like for bathing a baby. The water warmed my numb fingers. I found a clean cloth and soaked it. Washed my father's body, head to toe. Dabbed gently that scar on the chest, as if it might be sore. Flinched a little at the violence of it, barbaric surgery. Wiped the gaunt face and smoothed the wisps of grey hair. Wet the cloth again and ran it down the arms and legs, eased it round the groin, a bit selfconscious because although this was just a shell, just dead stuff, still it was the old man. But not. Him but not him.

I dried him with a hand towel, moved into functional mode again. Just stuff. Pushed in the wads of cotton wool. Then I dressed him. Clean set of underwear we'd found in his drawer. Clean white shirt Lila had ironed. His good suit, the funeral suit. Seemed appropriate. Put a pair of black socks on him, cover his feet that were blue at the heels. No point really in putting the shoes on, or footering with a tie. He was past being bothered and nobody else was going to see. So leave it like that. Would do fine.

I was suddenly tired. The day had felt a week long, the week a month. The striplights made a faint low buzz, threw their weird cold light on everything, on the dead body lying there. My father. Dead as everybody that had ever died.

Och, Da.

The suit did for me. Like a last attempt at dignity. And the open-neck shirt, the stockinged feet, looked wrong.

I put up his shirt collar, fastened the plain black tie in a simple knot, folded the collar down again and smoothed it flat. Then the polished black shoes, size nines with the hard toecaps. Right first, then left, double-knot the laces. Better. What he'd have wanted, to be properly dressed. I nodded, smiled. Good.

And I wanted to talk to him. But how much I was saying, how much I just thought, God knows.

I guess you know now, what happens. One way or another. Ye ken noo! Know everything or nothing. Is there anybody there! I'm sorry, Da, the way things worked out. I know it can't have been all your fault. Must have been times I was an obnoxious little prick. But by Christ you could be a vicious old bastard. Speak ill of the dead, eh? Sorry, but there it is. Not that it matters a damn of course. Not now. All just dross. Still. Could have been different, that's all.

Andy had helped me bring up the coffin from downstairs, lay it on the trestle alongside. Polished mahogany, one of Auld Jack's creations, just the right size. Could have been made for him, maybe was for all I knew. Coffin they carry you off in.

OK, Da.

I got my right arm under his shoulders, my left behind his knees and I lifted. Heavier than I'd thought but I got him up. The arms flapped, the head lolled back. Pieta. I bundled him into the coffin, stretched him out.

So that's it then.

I took a last look at my father's face. Closed the lid, screwed it down.

A chesting.

When I got upstairs I was shaking.

Lila had cleared out my room, moved all the boxes of books and papers into what had been my father's room. She'd dusted and washed all the surfaces, hoovered the old carpet. She'd even changed the bedding, found clean sheets and blankets on a shelf.

'Miraculous,' I said. 'Looks cleaner than I ever remember it.'

She'd had a bath and she ran one for me, deep and hot, the air dense and steamy. I lay and soaked, in the same old sarcophagus of a bathtub, its surface flaked and peeling even more. And a memory bobbed up of lying there years back and drifting away, and back before that in the coffin, floating up out of myself. Was this really what dying would be like – dissolving, letting go, the drop entering the ocean?

Downstairs in the cold back room, in his good suit, in his mahogany box, my father lay, starting to rot. And I felt his expression on my own face. Surprise and pain. It was there again in the mirror when I'd dried myself off, wiped a clear circle in the steamed-up glass to look at my reflection. Saw his face in mine, found myself twisting my lips to mimic his grimace, saw my own death to come.

Lila was already in bed. She'd switched on the bedside lamp, left the gas fire burning at low to keep the chill from the air.

'You all right?' she asked, her voice sleepy.

'Fine,' I said, climbing in. 'It shook me a bit, that's all.'

'Poor baby,' she said, stroking my hair, the nape of my neck. And I clung to her, alive, flesh against warm flesh as if to merge, in this house where I'd grown up, this house of the dead, in this bed where I'd dreamed myself so many absurd couplings, I breathed her in, her real scents and smells, tasted her actual mouth, neck, ear, breasts. We stroked and held each other, couldn't get enough, felt and touched and licked and sucked, wanting more, and she climbed on top and I slipped in and smiled up at her rocking above me. We made this slow familiar friendly love and when we bucked together, finally came, I died into sweet nothing.

Sweet. Fuck. All.

It was the same old drab cold church I'd been in so many times. The same old hard wooden pews, too narrow and upright for any kind of comfort. The same old smell, like a musty cupboard kept locked for years. The same miserable Godfearing faces.

Not a huge turn-out. My father's two older brothers had died before him, the oldest childless, the second with one son who had emigrated to Australia. So no family, except for me and, if you counted her, Lila. She was wearing a plain white sari, turned a few heads. The only others I knew at all were half a dozen fellow undertakers, a couple of the old man's drinking cronies. The rest were just those faces, strangers to me, members of the congregation, diehard churchgoers.

Same old.

But there was somebody different in charge, a ferocious old thunderer of a minister glorying in the name of McNaught. His grimness made my father look mild and benign. The few words he spoke at the service moved from being a sermon to a rant.

'Alexander McGraw was a man known to many of you. On countless occasions such as this one, he was a quiet, dignified presence. A decent man, by all accounts, and certainly that was my own impression, gathered over the years in my dealings with him, observing him at work in this most necessary and difficult of trades.

'The motto of his family firm is Rest Assured. And that simple message of quiet confidence has brought comfort to bereaved families for generations. Bury your dead, the Bible tells us. And in helping us do just that, Alexander McGraw has been doing the Lord's Work. He has also assisted at a great many cremations, that being in the nature of the job. But I am disappointed that he has chosen this form of disposal for himself. Bury your dead. The Good Book is quite specific. It does not say, Burn your dead. Nor does it say, Scatter their ashes on a football pitch. Which is the kind of thing, lamentably, that has become the fashion.

'In the book of Isaiah it is written,

> *Your dead will live; their bodies will rise.*
> *You who dwell in the dust wake up and shout for joy.*
> *The earth will give birth to her dead.*

'But how will their bodies rise if they have been reduced to ashes and scattered to the four winds? I do not doubt the power of the Almighty to, as it were, reconstitute us from our mortal remains, to give us new and glorious bodies which will not perish but dwell with Him forever. But surely there should be some raw material for Him to work with, some remnant of our physical form, no matter how corrupt or decayed? And why should we make matters more complicated by departing from His injunction? Bury your dead!

'And like so much else in our society, this craze for cremation is primarily a matter of expediency. It is cheap and convenient. Quick disposal. This is the world we live in, and sometimes, regrettably, we have to abide by its mores. Our departed brother, Alexander McGraw, was doing his job, according to the custom of our time. I simply wish that at the last he had chosen to be laid to rest in the earth, in a traditional Christian burial.

'But may his spirit indeed rest assured, at peace in the Lord. For he that believeth in the Lord Jesus Christ shall be saved. And though he die, yet shall he live. And Alexander shall live on in the hearts of his family and friends, those who knew and loved him.

'Our thoughts go at this time to his son Neil and daughter-in law . . .' He dropped his eyes to his notes. ' . . . Lila. In this time of loss, hold fast to your memories of the man, and give thanks for his life. Now, let us be upstanding and sing a song of praise and faith. Will your anchor hold?'

He nodded to the woman sitting at the organ upstairs, and she hit the opening chord, paused, and we belted it out, my father's favourite hymn.

> *Will your anchor hold in the storms of life*
> *When the clouds unfold their wings of strife?*
> *When the strong tides lift and the cables strain*
> *Will your anchor drift or firm remain?*

Then the chorus, soaring.

> *We have an anchor that keeps the soul*
> *Stedfast and sure while the billows roll*
> *Fastened to a rock which cannot move*
> *Grounded firm and deep in the Saviour's love.*

I took the weight of my father's coffin, felt it dig into my right shoulder, Andy beside me, four of the fellow undertakers behind.

'All right?' said Andy.

'Sure.'

Sure. Stedfast.

Will your rancour hold?

We carried the coffin outside, the weight of it biting deeper at every step. The wind whipped up, threw sleet at my face, numbed my fingers, battered against the box as we steadied it, eased it in to the hearse. Andy drove with me alongside him, Lila squeezed in beside me on the seat. The fellow undertakers had brought their own limo, the cronies had piled into a taxi and we set off, a short convoy to the crematorium. We moved slow through these grey streets that were familiar and strange, glimpsed in the clear between the beat and swish of the windscreen wipers.

'Dreich,' I said. 'That's what the old man would call it. Trust him to go out on a day like this. And to get a minister even grimmer than himself.'

'Quite a number,' said Lila.

'Some spiel he came out with,' said Andy.

'I couldn't believe it myself,' I said. 'The earth will give birth to her dead. Sounds like a schlock horror film, all the graves opening up.'

'Nicely dismissive of other cultures,' said Lila. 'But I should be used to that.'

'I mean, surely nobody really believes all that stuff any more. Resurrection of the body.'

'I don't think he does either,' said Andy. 'I think he was having a go at the other undertakers. Hoping he'd get through to them.'

'Ach,' I said. 'It's what the old man deserves, having some old git ranting at his funeral. Serves him right. Hell mend him.'

Lila elbowed me and Andy turned round.

'No a very nice thing to say, wi him lying there in the back.'

'He's past caring,' I said.

The minister had driven on ahead, was waiting to meet us at the crematorium. The wind and rain slashed at us again, the last few steps to the chapel. We laid the coffin down on the bier in the middle of the room, sat in the pews soaked and dripping, listened to Handel's *Largo* on tape as the rain squalled and blurred the windows.

The time allowed at the chapel was short, so McNaught kept his speech brief. A prayer for the departed. Gone beyond the vale of tears. In hope of resurrection and the life to come. Then the tape was playing again. Orpheus Choir. The Lord is my shepherd, I shall not want. And in behind it the faint clank and whirr of machinery, and the coffin was descending out of sight, down below to be conveyed into the furnace and burned.

I stood up and went to the door, shook hands with everyone as they left. The undertakers all wished me well, said to keep in touch, call if I needed any help with the business. I apologised for not having a reception, explained there was no other family to speak of, I wanted to keep it simple. They all said they understood.

Last to leave was the minister. McNaught.

I shook his hand. 'Interesting sermon back there.'

'I believe in speaking my mind.'

'You know, my father was quite definite about wanting

cremated. He'd seen enough of rotting bodies, preferred the thought of getting it over with, quick.'

'I understand that. As I said, this is the age we live in. But I like to speak out when I can for strict adherence to what is written in the Scriptures.'

Another hearse had already drawn up, the next in line.

'Packing them in,' I said.

'Exactly the kind of thing I mean.' He waved a hand in the air, impatient. 'It's getting like an airport, where they have to queue up, taxi round and wait for their slot.'

'It was a bit rushed in there.'

'It's all part of the same mentality. Everything secularised. Expediency rules. Instant disposal. Chuck the body in the fire and be done with it.'

'But cremation is how lots of cultures deal with their dead.'

'Just because something is prevalent among the heathen, that's no reason to adopt it.'

'Heathen?' said Lila, who had stood back, kept quiet.

'No offence intended, Mrs McGraw.' He couldn't help glancing down at her sari.

'Well there's plenty taken, Mr McNaught.'

We all stepped back as the next coffin was carried in.

Outside, rain and sleet were still chucking down from a bruised yellow sky. McNaught snapped up his umbrella. He resumed his conversation with me, as if the exchange with Lila hadn't happened.

'My understanding is you'll be taking on your father's business.'

'Sounds suitably scriptural,' I said. 'But no, your understanding is wrong.'

'In more ways than one,' said Lila.

'Oh well,' he said, again ignoring her. 'If you should change your mind, no doubt our paths will cross again.'

'Unlikely,' I said.

Andy had gone out ahead of us, was waiting in the hearse.

'What a horrible man!' said Lila as we climbed in.

'The thing is,' I said, 'when he talks about heathens, he's including Catholics.'

'The kind of guy that gets religion a bad name,' said Andy. He drove us home, parked the hearse in the yard. 'Aye, well,' he said.

'Listen,' said Lila. 'Why don't we go and have a bite of lunch?'

'Make up for not having a reception.'

'Sounds good,' said Andy.

'If you just give me a minute to change,' she said, heading upstairs. Her white sari had got spattered with mud and the soaking had made it sag, heavy.

I sat in my father's chair, took off the black tie, wrapped it round my hand. 'Can't be bothered getting changed myself. Too tired.'

Andy nodded. 'Just feels like too much of an effort. Takes it out you this stuff. When the wife died, couple of years back, I mind when I got to this stage I just slumped. And I'll tell you, your old man was a great help, seeing me through it. Rock solid, he was. Kept me going.'

'That's good,' I said, shifting in the chair.

'I know you and him never got on. But don't think too badly of him. Not now. I've said it to you before. He was a decent bloke.'

'I'm sure he was.'

'And being on my own showed me what he'd been through.'

'Aye.'

Lila came downstairs, wearing blue trousers and a red jersey, burst of brightness in the dull room. 'Right!' she said. 'Where's it to be?'

'I could murder a curry,' said Andy.

She laughed. 'Where I come from that's a serious crime.'

'Right enough,' he said, a lightness in his eyes for the first time all day.

'Mind you,' I said, 'if I remember rightly, the restaurants up here are liable to do it for you.'

Andy's car was parked in the street. He took us to a place he said was not bad, did a reasonable business lunch. The first mouthful cauterized the tastebuds. Andy had ordered extra hot, happily dabbed the sweat from his forehead, doused the fire in his mouth with ice-cold lager.

164

'Better than a sauna,' he said.

I screwed up my face at him. 'Thanks for that, Andy!'

'So what's the verdict?' he asked Lila.

'Guilty as charged,' she said. 'Murder.'

'Sorry.'

'Don't look so serious,' she said, laughing. 'I'm teasing you. It's fine, really.'

'That bad?' he said.

Over dessert, ice cream for Andy, tinny lychees for me and Lila, he asked again if we'd decided on our plans.

'You could do worse than taking on the business. You could do it, no bother. You know the ropes. You can stomach the work. I just think it would be nice if you kept it in the family. Continuity sort of thing.'

'Och, I don't know,' I said. 'I can't see it.'

'Don't get me wrong,' he said. 'I'm not wanting to keep on with my job. It's definitely time for me to pack it in like. I'm getting too old for the lifting and laying. But there's plenty folk would jump at it. The amount of people that's signing on these days. I mean, nobody's secure. And that's all the more reason for not turning down a chance. Your own business and that. Not to be sniffed at.'

'Unless the body's been lying a while!'

'Neil!' Lila punched me on the arm, not too hard.

'Just as well you've finished your vindaloo,' said Andy. And there was a glimmer of the old Andy I remembered, the one that was always telling me stupid jokes.

He drove us home again. The rain had eased to a smirr, a thin drizzle. Before I got out of the car, he shook my hand, serious.

'Now mind, if you want any help with this lot, setting up or clearing out, just give me a shout.'

'I will, Andy. Thanks.'

As I made to open the door, he touched my elbow. 'Hey.' He half turned, included Lila. 'Heard this one? Woman takes her wee boy for a walk in the cemetery. And he's looking around, reading all the inscriptions on the gravestones. And he's looking more and more confused. And eventually he asks his mother, Where do they bury all the bad guys?'

*

It was still raining next day when I went to collect the ashes. I didn't know why I was doing it. I could have just left them to be scattered in the Garden of Remembrance. What most people did. Simple and direct. No fuss. Nothing special.

But the feeling had got hold of me, a need for something more personal. A sense of things left unfinished, unsaid.

The Director of the crematorium, Mr Sim, met me in person, showed me in to his office. 'Of course I knew Sandy well,' he said. 'Did business with him for years.'

Sandy? I'd never heard my father called Sandy in my life.

The room was overheated, too brightly lit, smelled of carpet. The desktop was uncluttered, mahogany veneer. Perhaps he had cleared it specially. Placed there, between us, was the urn.

An urn for cremated remains should be strong enough to resist breakage in transit. The lid must fit tightly and the fastening should be strong enough to prevent the lid being forced open by distortion through maltreatment in transit.

I remembered that from some leaflet, remembered the language. Distortion through maltreatment.

The urn was basic grey ceramic with the engraved nameplate. What was left of my father. Cremated remains. Cremains. We both sat staring at it.

'A fine man,' said Mr Sim.

I saw myself pick up the urn and smash it against the wall, burst it to shards and smithereens, fill the air with exploded ash.

Instead I nodded. 'Indeed. Yes. Aye.'

'I hear you'll be following in his footsteps.'

'Och, I'm not sure yet.'

'Well, you could do a lot worse.'

What Andy said to me years ago. Always a job.

'Never goes out of fashion,' I said. 'Death.'

'Exactly. And I like to think there's still a place for the small family firm. Always hate to see them go under. If you'll pardon the expression.'

A joke. He smiled, looked at the urn, straightened his face again.

166

'Right,' I said, standing up. 'Thanks.'

He shook my hand. 'If you need any advice, just give me a call.'

He handed the urn to me, the moment bizarre and solemn, like presenting a trophy but with no joy in it, no celebration. I should hold it aloft. *San-dy! San-dy!*

Sandy. The cremains.

I felt the weight of it in my hands.

The cremation of an adult will normally result in cremated remains weighing between 2 and 4 kilograms.

Mr Sim cleared his throat. 'Have you decided what you'll do with the ashes?'

'Not yet.'

'Have you got transport?'

I shook my head. 'Came in a taxi. I thought the hearse would be a bit over the top.'

Driving through the streets with the urn in the back instead of a coffin. Or if I'd brought the van, zipped the urn in a body-bag. Or I could have propped it up in the passenger seat, held in place with the seatbelt. *All right there, Da?* Clunk Click.

'So you'll be wanting a taxi back with it?' Mr Sim picked up the phone. 'Allow me.'

The taxi came in five minutes, sat purring outside. 'Hell of a day,' said the driver as I climbed in.

'It is that.' I gave him my address, sat back cradling the urn in my lap.

The driver clocked it, glancing up at his mirror. 'Somebody you knew? I mean like family or that?'

'The old man,' I said. 'My father.'

He gave a kind of rough throaty chuckle, like hawking spit. 'Well, you hope it is anyway!'

'Excuse me?'

'The stories you hear.'

'Like what?'

'Well, about these people mixing up the ashes, you know? I mean, how can you tell? Ashes is ashes, right?'

'Suppose so.'

'If you ask me, they just rake out the oven at the end of the day and shove it all in these containers.'

'That's not what it says in the literature they give out.'

'Ach! They'll tell you anything. I read this story in the paper, about a woman that got her husband's ashes back, supposed to be. Only her husband had all his own teeth, right? And when she pours out the ashes there's these 29 false teeth in amongst them! She ended up suing the cremators for quite a whack.'

I looked at the urn. 'So this might not be the old man after all?'

'Oh here,' he said. 'I didny want to upset you, cause offence or that.'

'No, of course not.'

'It's just me. I open my mouth and say what I think.'

'Foot in mouth disease.'

'Eh? Oh aye!' He had stopped at the lights, roared off on the amber. 'But the thing is, they're all at it. Recycling coffins is another one. The cremators are in cahoots wi the undertakers. Another lot of rogues by the way.'

'Is that a fact?'

'You're no going to tell me they burn expensive coffins?'

'The ones for cremation are usually that bit cheaper.'

'Even so, they're worth a bob or two. So they whip out the body after the ceremony, burn it in a basic plywood box. The coffin gets taken back and used again, over and over.'

'Amazing.'

'It's a fact. I read it.'

'Oh well then. It must be true.'

'And it makes sense in a way. Waste not want not. Only thing is, folk are getting ripped off.'

'Over here.' I said, indicating where he should pull over, at the entrance to the yard.

He looked at the nameplate. 'Leaving the ashes here? At the undertaker's?'

'For the time being. And I live here. It's the old man's place.'

He worked it out. 'Your da's the undertaker?'

I held up the urn. 'Was.'

'Fuck it,' he said. 'Me and my mouth.'

Next morning Des turned up at the door.

'Hey, I had to come and check this place out for myself, before you sell it.'

'Des!' Lila called out, coming downstairs. She gave him a hug. 'Welcome to Neil's ancestral home.'

'I'm disappointed,' he said. 'I expected the butler to answer the door.'

'I know,' I said. '*You rang?*'

'Or the guy from the Rocky Horror Show.' He sang. '*Let's do the time warp again.*'

'You want the guided tour then?' I asked.

'Sure thing,' he said. 'Lead on McGraw.'

'I'll leave you to it,' said Lila. 'I'm still sorting things out, upstairs.'

I showed him the office, my father's urn on the desk.

'Fucksake,' he said.

I took him through to the back. 'Embalming room.'

'Jeez.' He stared at the table. 'Seriously chilling.'

'The instruments are in that steel cupboard.'

'I'll take your word for it.'

Downstairs in the basement he just gaped, stood staring, amazed.

'You really grew up here? No wonder you turned out such a weird bastard.'

'If you need a place to stay, we can fix you up in one of these.' I tapped the side of a coffin. 'Padded, nice and comfy, just need a sleeping bag.'

'You're sick!' he said.

'Gives a new meaning to the term box bed.'

'You know, you could probably sell that as an idea. Fit a foam mattress cut to shape. Get all these zonked-out Goths buying them. Double up as a bed and blanket-box. Then when they finally o-d or choke on their own vomit, you just slap the lid on and that's it, ready to be carted away.'

'And you think *I'm* sick!'

Upstairs, Lila had made spicy tea. The kitchen was unrecognisable, clean and uncluttered, felt almost spacious.

'So,' she said to Des. 'You're welcome to stay over. We've got plenty room.'

He laughed. 'Thanks but no thanks. I've already seen what's on offer.'

'Sorry?' She pushed a strand of hair back behind her ear.

'I was giving him his choice of those nice quilted boxes in the basement.'

'Right,' he said. 'So I'll stick to my cardboard box in a shop doorway, thanks very much.'

'Good choice,' I said.

'Seriously,' said Lila. 'Have you got somewhere?'

'No problem,' he said. 'Got a couple of old mates sharing a flat up the West End. They've offered me a couch.'

'Psychiatrists are they?'

'Listen to it! Box beds in the crypt. You're the one that needs help!'

'No, but I mean it,' said Lila. 'If you need a place just ask.'

'Thanks,' he said. 'I will.'

'How long you up for?' I asked.

'Tell you the truth, I'm thinking I might move back up here. It doesn't feel half as bad as I remembered it. And London's pissing me off. What about yourselves? Made up your minds about what you'll do?'

'I have to talk to the lawyer,' I said. 'Work out the details.'

'Any chance you might keep the business going?'

'Och, I can't see it. It's just not me.'

'Are you sure?'

'How do you mean?'

'It depends how you approach it. Could be a laugh.'

'Oh right, aye. I wonder why I'd never thought of it that way.'

'Failure of imagination?'

I crooked my hand to my ear. 'Hear that?'

'What?' he said, listening.

'My old man turning in his urn.'

Lila had done a preliminary sorting of the boxes and bags in my father's room, divided it into junk that could definitely be thrown out, and the bulk of the material, stuff I would have to sift through. Again I felt overwhelmed by it, oppressed, kicked into a kind of panic. Everything I touched left a thin film of dust on my fingertips, clogged my sense of touch.

Most of it was to do with the business, bills and invoices, receipts. A breakdown of the costings for a funeral.

Funeral Director's fee (including disbursements)	*£254*
Coffin	*£209*
Hearse	*£56*
Limo	*£50*
Embalming	*£34*
TOTAL	*£603*

There were clippings from newspapers, obituary notices, the odd memorial verse that must have caught his fancy.

> *And with the morn those angel faces smile*
> *Which I have loved long since but lost awhile.*

I picked up an old brown envelope, nothing written on it, shook out the contents. A few smaller envelopes, loose sheets of paper, old letters on thin paper. I started sifting through it all, the bits and pieces, fragments my father had kept.

My parents' marriage certificate. April 13th 1950. A newspaper cutting, yellow and brittle, announcing the wedding. Mr Alexander McGraw and Miss Irene Murray. A wedding photo, mounted on card, the two of them stiff and formal in the way of that generation, not at ease with the camera, but smiling and so young. So young. My mother with her round face and permed dark hair, her cupid-bow lips. And my father, so much of me in the eyes and nose, his wavy hair parted and brilliantined, head slightly to one side. And in spite of his awkwardness, self consciousness, the face radiated a happiness I had never seen in him my whole life.

I looked at the picture a long time, tried to relate it to what he became, the man I had known. In another envelope were more photos, small square snapshots with that faded khaki look. There were three taken at the same spot, a bridge over a river that ran through a park. One shot was of my father, leaning on the parapet with one elbow. He wore a tweed suit that might be lovat or tan, a soft hat angled over the eye. The second was of my mother, leaning in the same way, wearing a neat fitted coat, a handbag tucked under her arm. The third showed the two of them together, perhaps snapped by a passer-by. More relaxed than the wedding photo, the smiles less tense. The young couple, their lives ahead of them. They thought. I turned the picture over. On the back in fluid copperplate, the ink faintly brown, it read *Kelvingrove Park. June 27th 1950.*

There were other pictures, the one I had seen as a child – my mother in wartime uniform, another of my parents dressed up at a night out, startled by the flash as they sat laughing, tipsy, my father with a drink in his right hand, a cigarette in his left.

Fucksake, I heard myself say. I never knew you at all.

And I put everything back in the envelope, took it downstairs and laid it on top of my father's desk, beside the urn.

The doorbell rang, four o'clock in the afternoon, the day already starting to get dark.

'Expecting anybody?' asked Lila.

'Definitely not. Unless it's Des dropping by again.'

She answered it, showed a woman in to the office where I was sitting. The woman looked in her sixties, a feeling of strength about her, endurance, but a tiredness, a sadness in the eyes.

'Mrs Robertson,' said Lila.

'Neil McGraw.'

'Aye,' she said.

A silence.

I motioned to her to sit down. 'What can I do for you?'

'It's my man,' she said. 'Archie. He's took a heart attack and died. Fell down in the street, just like that.'

'I'm sorry to hear that.'

'Aye.'

Another silence.

She looked about the room, seemed to register the place was in disarray, a bit cluttered, in need of being dusted, hoovered. She stared at my father's urn.

'So,' I said, feeling I was caught in a loop. 'How can I help?'

'I need to organise the funeral,' she said. 'I'd like you to do it.'

'The thing is,' I said, 'my father's dead as well.' I gestured towards the urn, the irrefutable proof. I caught myself doing it, felt absurd.

'I know,' she said, looking at it, then back at me. 'Him and Archie were old pals. That's why I came to you.'

'But you don't understand. It was my father's business.'

I was sounding like McNaught, quoting scripture. My father's business.

'But I heard he'd left it to you.'

'Who told you that?'

'One of Archie's pals. Was at your da's funeral.'

'Amazing how word gets out, eh? But I haven't actually taken it on. And I wasn't planning to.'

'Oh.'

This time the silence was long.

'It's just, not what I want to be doing.'

'I see.'

'I'm sorry.'

'So am I. Archie always wanted your da to do it. He trusted him like. Felt safe.'

'Rest assured.'

'That's it.'

She made no move to go, and I had nothing else to say. Lila beckoned me out of the room, through to the back.

'I think you should do it,' she said, keeping her voice to a whisper.

'Eh?'

'You should do the funeral. I mean, you've just done your father's, and that's about as difficult as it gets.'

Our breath clouded in the cold air as we spoke.

'You want me to do this, as a job?'

'All I'm saying is, here's a poor soul that's turning to you for help. And you could do the job standing on your head.'

'That would certainly be different. Maybe I could juggle as well.'

'Idiot! You know what I mean.'

I knew. We went back through to the office where the old woman still sat, patient. 'All right,' I said, sitting down. 'I'll talk you through it all. Then we can work out what you want and I'll give you a quote.'

She nodded, smiled. 'Thanks son.'

I drove the van to the mortuary, to pick up the body.

In behind the familiar stink of formaldehyde was another smell, something meaty I couldn't quite place. But when I pushed open the door to the office, I got the full waft of it. Bacon rolls. The mortuary superintendent was sitting down to a late breakfast.

'The name's Ernie,' he said, through a mouthful. 'But folk call me Ernest.'

'As in Dead?'

'That's it!'

A big man, beefy red face, grey hair cropped short. He swilled down some tea from a chipped tannin-stained mug with a lion rampant on the side. Wiped his hand on his apron and held it out for me to shake.

'Neil McGraw.'

'Thought it must be. I knew your old man. Funny thing is, he ended up in here, laid out like, with it being a sudden death.'

'Right.'

No more to be said on that one.

'Hope you don't mind if I finish my breakfast.'

'Not at all.'

'Been rushed off my feet all morning. Never got a minute to myself.'

'That bad?'

'Three messy ones first thing. A drunk that got hit by a bus. A guy they fished out the river. A woman with her head battered in.'

He took a bite of his second bacon roll, another swig of tea to soften it to mush in his mouth. 'Cup of tea?' He pointed at another mug, with Kermit the frog on it.

'No thanks, I'm fine.'

'You sure? I've got a couple of scones, pot of jam.'

'No, really.' I'd seen them sitting there on the table, the bakery bag, the jam jar. 'An embalmer once put me off strawberry jam for life.'

He laughed. 'I can imagine! Still. It doesn't do to have too vivid an imagination. Not in this business. I mean that's me this morning, I've already filleted three of them, scooped out their innards. Can't go being squeamish about it, know what I mean?'

He savoured the last bite of his roll, chewed, washed it down. Banged the empty cup down on the table. Wiped the grease off his chin. Stretched, belched. Let out a sigh of satisfaction. 'You fit?'

I nodded. 'Ready when you are.'

'Robertson,' he said. 'The old guy you've come to pick up?'

'That's right.'

'Straightforward heart attack. Coronary artery atheroma.' He slapped his gut. 'Probably how I'll go. Too many fags. Too much bevvy. Too many bacon rolls! But what the hell! Here, your man's in the post mortem room.' He stopped at the door, put a hand on my arm. 'I'll show you something. It's the latest thing.'

He showed me in to a square ante-room, not much bigger than a cupboard. Two hard chairs, a TV monitor high up on a shelf in the corner. Ernie switched it on.

'Watch the screen,' he said, and disappeared out of the room.

At first the screen was blank, then after a couple of minutes an image appeared, black and white, a body laid out on a table, covered up to the neck by a sheet. The image wobbled a bit, jerked out of focus, then zoomed in to a close-up of the face, an old man, head turned to the side, mouth a tight line, eyes shut tight, as if he had been caught out, startled by the suddenness of the pain that stopped him. Then the image disappeared, blacked out, switched off, and Ernie was in the doorway behind me.

'What d'you think, eh? Pretty good!'

'I take it that was Mr Robertson.'

'That's your man. Had his wife in the other night to identify him.'

'And she just did it from that?' I pointed up at the screen.

He nodded. 'This is what's so good about it. Saves quite a bit of distress. Especially if there's been damage, or the body's started to go off. Don't have to deal with the smells or any of that.'

'More clinical.'

'That's why it's black and white too. Colour shows up the blemishes, discolourations, all the injuries.'

'A bit too vivid.'

'Right. This way you just see a darker patch, a smudge. And we only go in as close as we have to. The camera's up on the ceiling, just swivels round from one table to the next, zooms in and out. A bit like the Golden Shot!'

'Know the only thing that bothers me?'

'What?'

'I think people need to see the body, touch it even, to really say goodbye, let go.'

Ernie rubbed his face, scratched his stubble. 'I know what you're saying, but usually there's the viewing later on, after things have been tidied up a bit. I mean, what's in there can be pretty brutal.'

'People can't take too much reality? Ach, you're probably right.'

'I'll give you a hand with the body, help you get it into your van.'

'Thanks.'

I followed him in to the PM room, freezing cold with four other bodies laid out on tables covered over with sheets, the huge drawers along one wall, like a filing cabinet. We covered the old man's face, folded the sheets round him and lifted him onto a stretcher. *One, two, three and hup.*

I glanced up at the TV camera. 'Know what else I'm thinking?'

'What?'

'If somebody just looks at that screen, they're not actually seeing the body.'

'Technically, no. But it's closed-circuit. What you see through there is what the camera's pointing at in here. Live TV sort of thing.'

'But folk could be watching a video for all they know.'

He laughed. 'Ever thought of writing detective stories?'

'Maybe I should!'

'Actually, sometimes people do have a problem with the picture on the screen. Like they're not sure.'

'See! There you are.'

'This old guy came in the other week. His wife had died, right, and him and his son came in to identify the body. So I show them in to the wee room, and they look at her face on the screen. And the boy nods and says, Aye, that's her. But the old fella's no sure. He looks, and he looks again, and says, No, it's no. And the boy says, Da, what are you saying? That's my ma. The old guy shakes his head, says, No, it isnae. So they go on like this for a while, and the old guy's getting more and more adamant. It is definitely not her. And he's getting a bit upset by this time, so I says, Come into the office and have a cup of tea. Get him to calm down and that. And I'm thinking the only thing is to take him in to the PM room and let him see the actual body.'

'This proves my point.'

'Aye. But before I can suggest it, the old guy gets an idea. I want to see her feet, he says. Her feet? Aye, he says. Can you move the camera down so I can see them? No problem. I go in and lift back the sheet, adjust the camera so the feet fill the frame, get it in focus and go back through to the wee room. And there's the old guy looking at these feet and saying, Aye, that's her, that's definitely the wife!'

'You couldn't make that up, could you?'

'Makes you wonder right enough.'

We took an end each of Mr Robertson, put him in the back of the van.

Mrs Robertson couldn't decide on a coffin.

'I know it sounds terrible,' she said. 'But Archie wouldn't be seen dead in any of these!'

I laughed. 'Very good!'

'They're all just too heavy, you know, cumbersome.'

'I know what you mean.'

'Oh it's not the cost, you understand.'

'I know that.'

'He just liked things simple. Hated fuss and bother.'

I flicked through the catalogue, showed her the simplest plain pine coffin. 'How about that?'

She squinted at the picture. 'It's nice enough. But it's maybe too much the other way, you know? Like it's kind of unfinished. Needs something else.'

'Maybe we could customise it,' I said. 'Paint a wee design on it. Tasteful but. Nothing too flash.'

Her eyes widened. 'Boats!'

'He liked boats?'

'He loved them. Worked all his days in the yards, till they shut down.'

'There you are then.'

'So you could do that? Paint it on?'

'I think I know somebody that would do a really good job. And I don't think he'd charge too much either.'

'Sounds perfect.'

'Right then. I'll ask him.'

Des liked the idea. 'Like the one I did for Abe, remember?'

'Course I do. That's why I thought of it.'

'Brilliant.'

'Just work out what you'd charge,' I said, 'and we'll build it in to the cost.'

'Magic.'

And so it was, what he came up with.

On the sides of the box he did the two elevations of an ocean-going liner, seen from port and starboard. On the lid he did a plan view, the same liner seen from above. he continued the design round on to the ends of the box, so the prow was at the top, the stern at the bottom.

'It's absolutely beautiful,' said Lila.

'Like a real boat,' said Mrs Robertson.

Des grinned. 'What can I tell you? I'm a genius!'

Back in the same drab kirk the coffin-boat was a triumphant affront. McNaught said that on this occasion, out of deference to the deceased and respect for the widow, he would allow the ceremony to proceed. But he felt it his Christian duty to record his disapproval of this gaudiness, this frivolity being visited on the church. He cut his oration short, moved quickly on to the hymns. Again we sang, Will your anchor hold? And this time the words rang with a new resonance. The painted boat shone in the gloom.

The boat made me see the whole thing fresh. Instead of feeling trapped by the job, I could make it something different, something new.

'I mean, why does it all have to be so fucking dreary?'

'Too right,' said Des. 'Get a bit of imagination into it.'

'Bit of colour,' said Lila. 'Make it beautiful.'

'Go out in style!' said Des.

'Good slogan,' I said.

'Yeah!'

'So you're into it?' I asked him. 'Doing the job?'

'Sure,' he said. 'I've checked some of the boxes downstairs. I can easily keep on making those, no bother. And I'll do the special painted jobs for folk that want them.'

'And the ceremony itself,' I said. 'We can help people do it the way they want.'

Des laughed. 'All singing all dancing funerals!'

'Can't imagine too many of those. Not here. But if that's what they want. Hey!'

'Can just see you in the wee director's chair.'

'Funeral Director!'

'Right!'

'So what do you reckon?' I asked Lila. 'Will we move up here, give it a go?'

'Why not?'

It was starting to feel inevitable. Meant. What I had to do. 'So we're in business.'

Des punched the air. 'Yes!'

He stopped me in the street, a hand on my arm. My first thought was to step back, but he said my name.

'Neil?'

I didn't recognise him. Older than me, thinning hair, stubble. But something familiar in the eyes.

'Rab,' he said. 'Rab Deans.'

'Jesus Christ.' Now I saw, knew him. Not older but looked it. Worn. I shook his hand. 'How you doing?'

'Och, you know.' He shrugged. 'Surviving. Just about.'

'You working?'

The standard opening question where we grew up. Never mind smalltalk about the weather. Get straight to it. Are you working? How do you live?

'Bits and pieces,' he said.

'Still doing your motor mechanic?'

'Garage I was working for shut down. Cutbacks. Right now I'm signing on. Doing the odd homer, fixing folk's cars and that.' He looked round. 'Don't tell the broo!'

'You married?' I asked. 'Family?'

'I got married to Helen,' he said. 'Remember her?'

Rab's wee bird. Sleek black hair and a red dress at a party. Back row of the Vogue. *Premature Burial.*

'Sure,' I said. 'Any kids?'

'Two boys and a lassie. Fucking monsters! How about yourself?'

'Married, no kids.'

'Wise,' he said.

'Travelled a bit. Never really settled.'

'So what you doing back here?'

'My old man died. Left me the business.'

'And you're doing it?' The look on his face was disbelief.

'Why not?'

'You always hated the thought of it, more than anything.'

'Got to earn a living somehow.'

'Tell me about it!'

'And I want to do something a wee bit different.'

'Jazz it up a bit?'

'Kind of.'

'Good luck!' He laughed. 'You an undertaker! It's funny!'

'Thanks!'

'No, you know what I mean.'

'Sure.'

'Don't suppose you need a mechanic?'

I slapped my forehead. 'What the fuck am I thinking about? I need somebody to be a driver-bearer, look after the motors.'

'I could do that! Fucking Yosser, eh?'

I looked him over. 'You'd need to shave, wear a suit and that.'

'No bother,' he said. 'King of the mods me, in my heyday. Remember?'

'Aye.'

'I'll be sharp as fuck.'

'So you're on then. Got yourself a job.'

'It's like *The Magnificent Seven*,' said Des. 'Getting your squad together, everything falling into place.'

'Magnificent Four,' I said. 'You, me, Lila, Rab.'

Lila took on the redecoration, had the walls painted soft blues and greens. The old paintings and calendars were replaced with Chinese landscapes, Japanese brush drawings. Created a sense of space, a feeling of peace.

'What about the desk?' she asked. 'Do you want to keep it?'

'Definitely not. It's too big and old and heavy. We'll ditch it.'

I looked at the urn, still sitting there. I decided.

We drove to Kelvingrove in the van, Lila in the passenger seat holding the urn, Des sliding around in the back, braced against the side to keep his balance.

'This is no joke,' he said. 'Rattling around in the fucking corpsemobile.'

'Would you have preferred the hearse?' I shouted back to him. 'Could have stretched out, waved at passers-by.'

I took a corner too sharply, heard the dull clunk of him banging the side again.

'Seriously man, the first thing you have to invest in is a half-decent car.'

Outside it was cold, dank. Our breath clouded. A grey mistiness hung over the park, damped the bare trees.

'A good day for it,' I said. Checked with Des. 'Have you got the camera?'

'Sure,' he said. 'Just hope it's survived that journey.'

'Black and white film?'

'Yup.'

I knew the bridge, knew the exact spot.

I posed first, leaning on the parapet, holding the urn. Then he took one of Lila, in the same place but without the urn. For the third, he snapped the two of us together, holding the urn between us.

'Right,' I said. 'Let's do the deed.'

I unscrewed the lid from the urn, leaned over the parapet.

'OK, Da. This is the nearest I could figure to what you might have actually wanted, if you'd ever given it any thought.'

The river was slow and sluggish, yellow-brown. I tipped the urn, emptied out the ashes, watched them scatter and drift, always more than you think, seemed a long time trailing down to settle on the water and disappear. And I suddenly felt focused entirely on what I was doing, in the action itself. The feel of the urn. The cold of the day. Myself there in the moment. Watching the drift and flow. No thought and no feeling. Mind empty, heart still.

I was conscious of Des clicking his camera a few more times. As I shook the urn to empty the last of it, the wind changed, threw a sudden handful of ashes into my face. I heard the camera click again.

'Nice one,' said Des.

I blew out through my mouth, tried to brush the powder from my face and hair, rub the grit that had got in my eye.

'Old bugger,' I said. 'Might have known he'd take the chance to get back at me one last time!'

I closed the lid on the urn, took it in both hands and raised it above my head, like taking a throw-in, watched it arc in the air, turning, splash as it hit the surface, bob as the river carried it away downstream.

'Way to go,' said Des.

'Now that *is* a good slogan,' I said.

'Isn't it!'

It was.

Way to go.

The death-verses written by Japanese haiku poets, wandering monks and nuns, looking at things for the last time, with a clear eye.

> a short night
> wakes me from a dream
> that seems so long
>
> let's follow
> the sound of bells
> to the other shore
>
> death poems
> are mere delusion
> death is death

6

Most people still wanted the standard, traditional funeral. Nothing fancy. What my father had offered. And his father. And his. Rest assured.

But word had also got out. We were different.

We produced a brochure, a photo of Mr Robertson's coffin on the front. The stark shape was unmistakable, a universal symbol. But cutting right across that, a subtext, was Des's painted design, the oceangoing liner off on its last voyage. And the way it was done, the simple stylised lines, made it look like a child's toy. It made you smile. Above it was printed WAY TO GO, and beneath it, *Neil McGraw. Creative Funerals.*

I had written the text, with help from Lila.

We all die, sooner or later. It's inevitable. No reprieve. Bottom line, as the Americans say. Comes to us all. Or as Dickens' great character Mrs Gamp puts it, 'It's as certain as being born, except that we can't make our calculations as exact.'

When someone close to you dies, it's a time to grieve, for there's nothing as deep as that pain of loss. But it's also a time to celebrate the person's life, give thanks for having known them, give them a good send-off.

We're here to help with that, whatever way you want. We're an old family business and can still do things the traditional way, if that's what you'd prefer. Our coffins and caskets are handcrafted on the premises, in our own workshop. We also offer a full embalming and cosmetology service, and our peaceful viewing room is available for sitting quietly, paying your respects, saying goodbye.

But if you want a ceremony that's a little out of the ordinary, we'll work on it with you. We can make customised hand-painted coffins (see illustration on front cover). We can help with your choice of music and readings, make the whole event a performance – funeral as theatre.

If you decide on cremation, we can help with suggestions as

187

to what can be done with the ashes, in some cases taking inspiration from the ancient traditions of other cultures.

In keeping with the increasingly multicultural nature of this city, we can organise ceremonies following the observances of Hindu, Buddhist, Taoist, Muslim or Sikh faiths – in fact any religious tradition, or none.

We are also conscious of the spiralling costs of funerals these days, and do our best to keep our prices down. By keeping everything in-house we can make savings which we pass on to you.

Of course, if you want to go for something extravagant, we can provide that too. To quote Dickens again, his undertaker Mr Mould states his aim: 'To provide silver-plated handles of the very best description, ornamented with angels' heads from the most expensive dies. To be perfectly profuse in feathers. In short, sir, to turn out something absolutely gorgeous.'

At the other extreme, we can go for the minimal purity of a simple white pine box with rope handles. We are also interested in the current movement towards 'green' or eco-friendly funerals. Biodegradable body-bags are not out of the question.

So, from drop-dead gorgeous to the bare bones, we can accommodate!

But whatever you choose, we feel strongly that the funeral should not feel like part of an assembly line, perfunctory and impersonal. It is, after all, one of the few great formal, sacred ocasions in our lives. A time to celebrate. A time to grieve.

On the back cover was a photo of a New Orleans funeral procession, a black jazz band leading the way, and underneath was our slogan again. WAY TO GO.

'It's very good,' said Lila, looking it over. 'It reads well. Kind of friendly. Though I'm still not sure about that awful joke.'

'Ach!' said Des. 'You should have gone the whole hog. Right over the top, you know. *Be dead cool! Go out in style!*'

'We'd have all these headbangers at the door,' I said. 'Folk as daft as yourself.'

We did anyway.

*

'I'll be frank with you.'

OK Frank, I'll be Neil.

He was in his forties, thin and nervy, worn down.

'Fire away,' I said.

'I'm scared of premature burial.'

'It's a common fear.'

'Isn't that because it happens all the time? I read this article about it, and sometimes I can't sleep for worrying.'

So you'll be so tired from not sleeping, you'll eventually fall into this deep deep sleep like a coma. And the doctor will be in a hurry, preoccupied, and he'll pronounce you dead, and they'll cart you off to the morgue.

'I'm sure there's nothing to be afraid of,' I said.

'But cases have been documented down through the ages.'

'I know. I've read quite a few.'

'One Victorian book catalogued seven hundred instances.

'The Victorians went in for that sort of thing. There's a limerick.

> *There was a young man from Nunhead*
> *Who awoke in his coffin of lead.*
> *He remarked in a huff,*
> *It was cosy enough*
> *But I wasn't aware I was dead.'*

'I'm glad you can joke about it.' He looked serious.

'Goes with the job,' I said. 'Kind of defence mechanism.'

'But some of the stories are horrible,' he said. 'People waking up on the dissecting table. Or halfway through an embalming.'

'Nasty.'

'And there's people been dug up and they've changed position in the coffin, and their nails and fingertips have been torn away. And sometimes the coffin lid is damaged from the inside, like it's been battered in a frenzy.'

'Other explanations have been given, though.'

'Like what?'

'The body shifting around in transit. In fact one woman who *was* in a coma was jolted awake as they bumped the coffin

189

downstairs. She lived a few more years, and when she died for real, her husband told the bearers to take it easy going down the stairs, be careful not to bump her!'

'That's not exactly a reassuring story.'

'Sorry.'

'OK, that would explain part of it. What about the torn fingers?'

'Rats. There's usually other bite marks as well.'

'Yugh. And the damaged lid?'

'Explosion of putrefying gases in the body.'

'Jesus!' He held his head. 'Is that what happens?'

'So I've heard.'

One last stupendous post mortem fart.

'And you don't believe there's such a thing as premature burial?'

She was placed alive in the tomb.

'Oh, I'm sure it's happened, like you said, down the ages. And at certain times it must have been pretty common, say during a plague epidemic. With the risk of infection, there was probably a bit of a rush to get the bodies into graves. And hey, dead or half-dead, what did it matter?'

'Oh dear.' He was tugging at the slack skin on his throat.

'It's like that Monty Python film. Was it the Holy Grail? They're going round with a cart gathering up the bodies. Bring out your dead! And this old guy's dragged out, and he's saying, But I'm not dead! So they crack him one on the head and chuck him onto the wagon with the rest.'

'You're giving voice to all my worst fears.'

But I couldn't help it. I heard myself keep on talking. An out-of-mouth experience. 'There was a joke that there was one church in France where the priest said *Requiescat in Pace*, and voices came from all the graves, saying *Amen*!'

'You've told me all I need to know.'

'No, but we're talking about centuries past. That kind of thing can't happen now.'

Who am I kidding? State of the health service, it's probably happening more than ever.

'I've made up my mind,' he said. 'I want to leave instructions that before I'm buried, my head should be removed from my body.'

'That would certainly clinch it.'

'Only way to be sure.'

'I suppose the thing to do is talk to your solicitor. Get him to instruct the mortuary.'

'It shouldn't be a problem. They must remove bits all the time, for transplants. Spare parts.'

'This is true.'

'And I'd like you to double-check before I'm buried.'

'Make sure the deed's been done.'

'Exactly.'

'Sometimes,' I said to Des later, 'this job can be fucking gruesome.'

'I don't see why I can't just be chucked on the compost heap. Get the son and daughter to lug me to the bottom of the garden, dump me there and let nature take its course.'

He had long white hair, swept back, a bushy moustache. He was just back from Findhorn.

'I've heard of people's ashes being sprinkled on compost,' I said.

He shook his head, impatient. 'Not the same thing. And besides, I'm not sold on cremation. Not environmentally friendly. Polluting the atmosphere with all those chemicals. Heavy metals, hydrochloric acid, carbon dioxide, sulphur dioxide, the lot. And graveyards are a waste of space.'

'So you reckon composting's the answer.'

'Have you read Joyce?'

'Long time ago.'

He fumbled in his coat pocket, brought out a few sheets of paper, folded. He opened one out, then another. The third was the one he was looking for.

'This is from *Ulysses*,' he said. 'A newspaper advertisement.' And he read it out to me. 'Well preserved fat corpse, gentleman, epicure, invaluable for fruit garden. A bargain. £3-13-6.'

I laughed. 'That's good!'

'Can't beat Joyce,' he said. 'Ould Seamus Joyous.'

'He could do the business right enough.'

'And clearly alert to the possibilities of composting our remains.'

'You're serious then, about wanting dumped at the bottom of the garden?'

He smiled. 'I think my family might be a bit squeamish. And I can't see it going down too well with the neighbours.'

'No.'

'But I have been talking to a friend, who has been thinking along the same lines. And he's come up with a design for a compostorium.' He unfolded another of his sheets of paper. 'These are his notes, and a rough diagram of how it could be built, on site.' He passed it over to me, but the line drawing, the figures, meant nothing.

'Essentially it's a kind of pressure cooker,' he explained. 'The body has to be disembowelled first, of course.'

'Of course.'

'Avoids the danger of harmful pathogens. You put the guts in a methane digester, and the gas creates the heat to keep the whole thing reducing slowly. After about twelve weeks it's ready to be ground down into a kind of slurry. Then you can mush that up with straw and other stuff. Mulch it into your garden and there you go.'

'Prize crop guaranteed.'

'All flesh is grass.'

'Slurry,' said Lila when I told her about it. 'Mulch. It just *sounds* horrible.'

'Compost,' I said.'

'And that quote about using it in your fruit garden.'

'Tough on vegetarians,' said Des. 'Wouldn't know who you were eating!'

'Although in a way,' I said, 'it's like the ultimate vegetarian death. Being eaten by vegetables.'

'Now why don't I find that comforting?' said Lila.

The breakthrough came when Lila brought home a book about African coffins. *Going into Darkness*. A large-format artbook full of colour photos.

'A bit pricey,' she said, handing it to me. 'But I couldn't resist it. It is *so* beautiful.'

The cover picture showed a group of young African men, wearing what looked like football jerseys, all bright stripes. They were carrying above their heads the magnificent figure of a lion, covered in red hide, a shaggy mane of hair round its head. Teeth bared, eyes wide staring, it looked ferociously dignified and comical at the same time.

'It's like one I saw in Bali,' I said.

'Isn't it great?'

'It's wonderful!'

I flicked through the book, amazed at the images, painted wooden coffins shaped like an eagle, an aeroplane, a blue fish, a cocoa pod.

'They're glorious!'

A red pepper, a fishing boat, a trowel, a cow.

'We have to show Des.'

A training shoe, an elephant, a chicken, a Mercedes-Benz.

Des looked at the book and let out a whoop. 'These are incredible!' He turned the pages, eager. 'Did you see the leopard? The pigeon? Oh, man, look at the bus!'

'It reflects what the person did in life,' said Lila. 'The eagle is for a chief or a big shot. The cocoa pod for somebody that made his money growing them. The fish is for a fisherman.'

'Nice,' said Des. 'He spends his life catching fish then this big one swallows him up!'

'The chicken is popular for women with children,' said Lila. 'A brood.'

'And the bus?'

'A bus driver?' I asked.

'A guy that owned a fleet of them,' she said. 'These things don't come cheap.'

'I wondered,' said Des. 'I suppose the Merc is the ultimate status symbol.'

'That's it.'

'So, are there lots of guys making these?'

'Just one or two craftsmen and their apprentices,' she said. 'In Ghana. It's been passed on for a couple of generations.'

'Just a couple? So it's not some ancient traditional thing?'

'Started in the fifties. And this one guy, Kane Kwei, developed it into something amazing.'

Des turned the pages again, laughed in sheer delight. 'They're stupendous! Look, there's a dove here. And a bible. And they were both made for ministers.'

'Had to be something with a sacred connotation,' she said. 'Otherwise it's not allowed in the church. They reckon all these other designs smack of fetishism.'

'Heathen images,' I said. 'The spirit of McNaught is everywhere.'

'God!' said Des. 'Can you imagine his face if we started churning out these!'

I laughed. 'Funny you should say that!'

Des caught what I was saying. 'Aw, man! Do you think we could do it?'

'Make them here?' said Lila.

'Take orders. Whatever people want.'

Des held the top of his head. 'Wow!'

'It's down to you,' I said. 'If you can take it on.'

'I'd love to! Course they'd cost quite a bit. The time involved. But I'd get faster the more I made. Materials would be cheap enough. And if you think what people pay for one of these fancy caskets, you know, some mahogany monstrosity, it might compare quite well.'

'The other thing is the size,' said Lila.

'Overtime for the gravediggers,' I said.

'They are a bit bigger than your regular coffin, said Des. 'But if you look, a lot of the designs are really quite compact. They keep the basic streamlined shape. It's brilliant.' I had never seen him so excited. His eyes shone.

'So,' I said. 'Are you on?'

'Yes,' he said. 'Definitely. Aye. Yes.'

He wouldn't let us in to the workshop, worked late after his regular shift. After a week he had something to show us. He called us downstairs, Lila and me and Rab. The room smelled of gloss paint and glue. The shape was draped with a sheet.

'You have to understand,' he said. 'This is just a prototype.'

'Come on,' said Rab. 'Get on wi it.'

'Aye,' I said. 'Let us see it.'

'Leave him alone,' said Lila. 'He wants to do it with a bit of style, a bit of ceremony.'

'Thank you,' said Des. 'Now.'

And he took the end of the sheet, whipped it off with a flourish, a fanfare. 'Ta-daaa!'

Unveiled a beautiful coffin-sized replica of a fishing boat, a trawler, painted red and blue.

'Ian Hamilton Finlay eat your heart out,' I said.

'The whole top part's the lid,' he said, taking hold of the funnel and lifting up the deck. 'Inside's just an empty box that can be lined and padded.' He replaced the lid, slotted it back in place. 'There's a fitting here that'll take a mast. Could even rig up sails. Run them up for the ceremony or that, fold them down again for the actual burial.' He stood back, pleased. 'So what do you think?'

'Des, man,' I said. 'You're a fucking genius!'

'It's absolutely beautiful,' said Lila.

'Never seen anything like it,' said Rab. 'It's great.'

'I thought the thing to do was make a couple of models on spec, get the hang of it, see how it goes.'

'Sounds good.'

'I'm keen to try an eagle, like the one in the book.'

'Dying to see it,' said Lila.

'Suppose somebody will be,' he said. 'I mean, dying to use it.'

'I wonder if we'll ever run out of these crap jokes,' I said. 'Get fed up with them.'

'Fucking hope so,' said Rab.

'Listen,' I said, 'we have to get some photos of this boat. Got your camera, Des?'

'Just happen to have it right here!'

He took two or three shots of the boat itself, from different angles. Then I took one of him posing, standing behind it. 'There!'

'We should crack a bottle of champagne over it,' he said. 'Launch it.'

'Should open a bottle of something,' I said. 'To celebrate.' I turned to Lila. 'Have we got anything upstairs?'

'Don't think so,' she said. 'Bottle of Irn Bru.'

'That'll do fine!' And I ran up and fetched it, brought it back downstairs with four paper cups. The drink hissed and fizzed, bubbled over when I unscrewed the cap. I poured some into each cup, raised mine in a toast.

'To Des!'

He trickled a little over the bow of the boat. 'May God bless her and whoever sails in her.'

We swigged our drinks, sweet sticky fizz, bubbly. 'Cheers!'

We used a photo of the fishing boat in a reprint of the brochure, added a pitch for the new figurative coffins.

Based on the sculpted handcarved coffins of Ghana, these offer a unique way of making a memorable tribute to a life, a vibrant affirmation of that life and what made it special. Each coffin is a work of art, created by our own master craftsman, Des Kydd. He can work from your drawings, or photographs, or even just an idea. His specialities include boats and cars, animals, birds and fish. But if you can dream it up, he will do his best to realise it, to ensure that you or your loved one go out in style.

'Go out in style!' said Des. 'You used that!'

'Toned it down,' I said. 'No exclamation mark. And I didn't put Be Dead Cool.'

'Ach. Crapper.' He read it over again. 'Master craftsman. I like that.'

'Good, eh?'

'A nice ring to it.'

We distributed the brochure. Des started work on the eagle. Then our first order came in, our first commission.

Not what we'd expected, not somebody cool and hip and ironic. A wee old lady, neatly dressed in a pale blue bouclé coat, grey hair tightpermed. Glasses that blurred her eyes, with bluewinged plastic frames. Handbag clutched, resting on her lap. Mrs Anderson.

'I picked up your leaflet,' she said. 'Can't remember where. Maybe the community centre?'

'Could have been.'

'Anyway, I like the idea of these tailor-made coffins.'

'Did you have something in mind?'

'Tommy, that's my man, just passed away.'

'I'm sorry.'

'The thing is, he used to drive the subways.'

'Is that right? What a great job!'

I remembered the smell of it, something subterranean, earthy and rich with a whiff at the back of it like oil or tar or creosote, coming at you in a warm rush out the tunnel.

'So I wondered,' she said, 'if you could make him a coffin like one of the carriages.'

'I'm sure we could.' And I called in Des to talk to her.

He was keen. 'What a brilliant idea. And dead easy to do.' He heard what he'd said. 'Sorry, I didn't mean . . . Can't seem to help it around here. It goes with the territory.'

'It's all right,' she said.

He hurried on. 'But it would be easy. Basic box shape. Curve to the roof. I take it you mean the old type?'

'Of course,' she said. 'That's the ones he drove. Not these wee modern streamlined ones.'

'Clockwork orange.'

'That's right,' she said. 'They're not the same. I want one of the old fashioned ones, like a proper railway carriage.'

'With the red livery.'

'That's it.'

He was sketching already. 'I'll get photos out the library, plans maybe. I can build the box to scale and paint in the details, the windows and that.'

'Sounds fine.'

He added to his sketch, roughed in a trelliswork sliding door at the back. 'Oh God!' he said, and for a moment she looked startled. 'You know what I could do?'

'What?' She sounded unsure.

'Only if you want it,' he said. 'But have you got a picture of your husband in his uniform?'

'I have, aye.'

'See, I thought I could copy it, paint him like he's driving the train, like you're seeing him through the window.'

She smiled, said quietly, 'That would be really nice.'

'When I was a kid,' he said, 'I had these toy cars, just made of tin. Probably worth a fortune now! But this one I remember, a cop car it was, and everything was just painted on, all the detail. And there were these two cops supposed to be inside. And their faces were painted on the windscreen, and their profiles on the side windows, one on the right, one on the left.'

'And the backs of their heads on the back!' I said, seeing it. 'I remember those!'

'So that's how I could do it,' he said. 'Do a front view and a side view of him.'

She couldn't share his excitement, the vision he had of it, but she trusted him to do a good job. 'Sounds fine,' she said.

He took great care, researched it meticulously, found out when her husband had worked in the job and copied the right model for the period.

The photo Mrs Anderson handed in showed her husband in middle age, somewhere in his forties, sure of himself in his dark uniform, his peaked cap. Des did a fair copy of the face onto the front window, the right and left profiles onto the sides, gave the face a benign, knowing smile, like someone enjoying a quiet, private joke.

Des moved round, looking at it from different angles.

'I used to find it so weird when I was a kid,' he said, 'looking at that cop car. If you turned it round, you could see the front and side of the head at the same time, but separate. I don't know, it just gave me the strangest feeling.'

'Couldn't get your head round it!'

'Right,' he said, flat. 'Made me very uncomfortable.'

'Probably two different parts of your brain working at once,' I said.

'The front and the side?'

I laughed. 'The bit that wants to experience the illusion, and the bit that wants to analyse, take things apart.'

'Whatever it is, I'm getting it again, looking at this.' He put his hands to his head, holding it together.

When the old woman came in to see the coffin, she walked round it, stopped in front of the face on the front, breathed in sharp.

'Oh my,' she said, touching her hand to her own face.

Des was anxious. 'Is it all right?'

'It's great,' she said. 'It's just him to the life.'

'I'm glad,' he said. 'I've got one more suggestion. How about some passengers, at the other windows?'

'I'd like that,' she said. 'And I think he would too.'

Later, when Des was mixing his paints, I reminded him all the seats in the subway carriage faced in. 'So you'll have to paint the backs of their heads.'

'Good point,' he said.

'Like the back window of your wee cop car.'

He held his head again.

When he'd done painting in the passengers, he stepped back to look at it, walked right round it again.

'Just finishes it off beautifully,' I said. 'Gives it a kind of Magritte quality.'

'It does, doesn't it?' he said, laughing. 'Surreal or what?'

'Definitely what!' I said.

On the day, it turned heads. As we drove through the streets to the graveyard, I could see people stop, stare, point. I would see the change. First the sombre look at catching sight of the hearse, part reverence, part discomfort, concealed dread. Then a sudden double take, confusion. This didn't fit, didn't make sense. One or two looked baffled, even annoyed, maybe thought it was some kind of stunt, a bad joke. But mostly people smiled. They had seen something extraordinary, and it brightened their day.

'Made folk smile,' said Mrs Anderson at the graveside. 'That's the thing.'

And it brought a lightness to the ceremony. Hard to be grim gathered round this bright toy train.

'I'm glad it's being buried and not burned,' said Des. 'Seems the right thing.'

'Underground!' I said.

'Instead of a gravestone they should put a subway station sign, with his name on it.'

Mrs Anderson turned again to Des. 'They wee passengers were a lovely idea. Makes it more real.'

'Thanks,' he said.

'And it's like he's got company,' she said. 'On his last journey sort of thing.'

And the way she said it changed it all, made it something else. In the moment, I saw the reality of it for her. I stood with my head bowed as they lowered the toy train, the real coffin, into the ground. Absurd and moving. Surreal and what.

It bumped as it hit bottom, came to rest. The old woman threw the first handful of dirt. Earth to earth. The reality. The sound of it. Hit and scatter. The gravedigger shovelled in more. Thud on wood.

The wind gusted, caught the smell of the dug grave, wet earth. Subterranean, like that other smell that rushed at you out the tunnel. Underground smell. Smell of the subway.

Gradually other orders came in. A tugboat. A Spitfire. A VW Beetle. A double bass. And we had our first visit from the press. One of the Sundays sent their local man round with a photographer.

'The editor thought colour,' said the journalist. 'Photo-feature for the magazine.'

The photographer took a few shots of Des and me, posing in the workshop. 'Suppose I couldn't persuade you to lie in one of the coffins?' he asked.

'That's right,' I said. 'You couldn't.'

'Pity,' he said, and he took a few more from odd angles.

The interview was quick. Pocket tape-recorder on the desk. Leading questions about the business and how I'd got into it. What I was trying to do with it and why. The kind of response we were getting and whether some people found the whole thing offensive.

'I suppose death is still the ultimate taboo in our society,' he said, leaning across to switch off the taperecorder. 'People just aren't comfortable talking about it, or thinking about it.'

'It's true,' I said. 'Though maybe that's changing.'

'And what you're doing is part of that?'

'I hope so.'

'Tell me,' he said. 'Are you afraid of death?'

'I don't think anybody's ever asked me that outright.'

'There you are then. So what's the answer?'

'I suppose I'm afraid of a messy painful death. And most deaths are.'

'I think my favourite quote is that one from Woody Allen,' he said.

'I know the one you mean.'

'I'm not afraid of dying, I just don't want to be there when it happens!'

'That's it.'

'So anyway, thanks for your time. If they're going to use the piece, they should be running it next week.'

'You won't change your mind?' said the photographer. 'About posing in one of the coffins?'

'Right again,' I said.

'I want to bury my wife in the back garden.'

Ah well, sir, we all feel like that sometimes.

Something in the old boy's look, his demeanour. Straight out of an Ealing comedy, the black-and-white fifties. Heavy over-coat buttoned up – a good coat, a Crombie, but old. A muffler at the throat, not a scarf, a muffler, tucked in. And the soft felt hat he'd taken off and now held by the brim. Lugubrious was the word. Straight man in a music-hall routine.

I say I say I say! My wife's gone to the West Indies.

Jamaica?

No, she went of her own accord!

Boom-Boom! Every one a gem.

Buried the wife the other day. Had to – she was dead.

Ha!

'Cancer,' said the old boy, bringing me back to this.

'I'm sorry, when did she pass away?'

'She hasn't. Not yet.'

I say I say I say.

Stop it.

'No, but the doctors reckon she's only got a couple of months at the outside.'

'I see.'

'So we've talked it out, and this is what she wants.'

Fertiliser. Compost. Good for the roses.

'We've built a kind of pagoda. She likes that sort of thing. Taste for the exotic.'

'Yes. Right.'

The Crombie. The muffler. The hat rotated in his hands, its brim passed between his fingers.

'Only thing is, we were wondering if it's allowed.'

'You mean by law?'

'Aye. No legal impediment sort of thing.'

'I'd have to check the bye-laws. But as far as I know it's all right, as long as you're not interfering with a water course.'

'And how would I find that out?'

'Get somebody from the Council to come and check. I could look into it.'

He nodded. 'Thanks.'

'There is just one other thing. Is your property in its own grounds?'

He shook his head. 'Row of bungalows. Semi detached.'

'Have you sounded out your neighbours?'

'Nothing to do with them.'

'Just thought I'd ask.'

'Aye. Well.'

There goes the neighbourhood!

'So, would you like to give me some details?'

Sunday morning I was down at the papershop when it opened at six. Ahead of me in the queue, an all night party animal, dishevelled and hungover, buying his *News the World*, packet of fags, bottle of Irn Bru. He grimaced at me. 'Might as well measure me up now, man, the way I'm feeling.'

I laughed, uncomfortable, bought my paper.

A story my father had told me, about the time a friend had asked him just that – one night in the pub, to measure him up for a laugh. And my father had done it, taken it in good part, had a tape-measure with him, sized him up, head to toe and across the shoulders, told him the size of casket he'd need. A joke. But a week later the friend dropped dead, just like that. My father had to change to a different pub.

Out in the street I flicked through the colour supplement, tried to control the rest of the paper as the wind caught it and leaflets, catalogues, special offers slipped out and fell to the pavement. Fuck it. Pick them up and stuff them in the rubbish bin, carry on looking through the supplement.

And there it was, under the heading *Dead Rite*. A three-page spread. Full colour pictures of Des at his workbench, shaping a wing of the eagle, and me, stood posing in front of the Volkswagen, rictus grin held in place for the camera.

The British funeral is traditionally a sombre affair. But a young Scottish undertaker is setting out to change that.

'Yes!' I punched the air, dived back in to the shop and bought three more copies of the paper, ran back round to the house.

'Its in!' I handed Lila the magazine, open at the page.

'Dead Rite! How could they do that?'

'There's definitely something about death. It sets people punning like crazy.'

She caught sight of my picture, laughed. 'Look at you!'

'It does look a bit dodgy.'

'Would you buy a funeral from this man?'

'Like I'm trying to sell the car.'

'Only one careful owner!'

'The guy that interviewed me thought the coffins should be recycled. All that craftsmanship and they end up buried or burned.'

'But that's the beauty of it. Like those Indian ceremonies where they spend months on this intricate carving of Siva or Ganesh. Then after the puja they float it away on the river, let the water take it.'

'Well that's kind of what I said to him. Maybe not so

eloquently. I told him the transience is the thing. It's what it's all about.'

'Sounds eloquent enough to me. He must have thought so too – look, he's quoted you.'

Transience is the thing, says Neil McGraw, explaining why these exquisite creations are interred or consigned to the flames.

'Mind you,' I said. 'I suppose we could work something out. Use the fancy coffin for the ceremony, maybe with a simple removable box inside. And that's what gets buried or burned.'

Lila looked surprised. 'I can't imagine anyone wanting to be laid out in someone else's coffin. No matter how beautiful.'

I shook my head. 'No, I just meant like families, or groups of friends. They could pay for the coffin between them.'

'Kind of time-share!'

'That's it! And in between times it could be on display. A sculpture in the back garden.'

'Conversation piece in the lounge?'

'Why not?'

She laughed. 'I don't think Scotland's quite ready for that!'

'Maybe not.'

She looked again at the article. 'What else does it say?'

Death has been the McGraw family's business for genera-tions. Their motto – Rest Assured – creates an image of sober restraint. How, then, does Neil think his new slogan, Way To Go, will be received in the dour Presbyterian North?

'The last thing I want is to cause offence,' he says. 'And of course, mourning has its place. But I think funerals can also be celebratory. We can learn a lot from other cultures.'

And jazzy African-style coffins are only part of it. He wants to offer funerals conducted with flair and imagination as well as sensitivity and tact.

'They should be tailored to the individual,' he says. 'The way the funeral business is going is like everything else. It's all being taken over by multinational conglomerates. They talk about economies of scale, and offering consumers more choice. They sell what they call pre-need schemes where you pay everything up front. Pay now die later! I suppose I just hate the jargon, the

*way it's pitched. The American way of death is taking over. I'm
trying to fight that, create something different.'*

*Well and good, but where does it end? Burning ghats on the
banks of the Clyde? Tibetan sky-burial on Arthur's Seat?*

'Hardly,' says Neil. 'You have to draw the line.'

*But just where that line should be drawn is sure to be a
matter of debate. And if in his quieter moments Neil McGraw
hears a faint dry rustling sound, as of old bones and winding-
sheets, it might well be his immediate ancestors turning in
their graves.*

'Why did he have to put that last bit in?' said Lila, re-reading
it.

'Ach. It's journalism. Could have been a lot worse.'

'Worse puns?'

'You betcha. Could have called it Grave Concern.'

'Ouch!'

'Or how about Dead Chuffed?'

'Ow!'

'Anyway, you know what they say. All publicity . . .'

'We'll see.'

The calls started next morning, the Monday, and never stopped
the whole day.

It's about that article in the paper.

How quick can you build these fantastic coffins?

Do they have to be ordered well in advance?

Can you do one like a dragon?

A Mercedes-Benz?

A football boot?

The Starship Enterprise?

About this sky-burial. Where d'you get the vultures?

*Daily Record here. We'd like to do a wee piece on you.
Thought we could call it Dead Brilliant.*

Gradually too, they started coming in off the street, some of
them clutching the article cut from the magazine. *Is this the
right place?*

Des would be working overtime.

*

We bought a plastic construction kit of the USS Enterprise. That gave us the shape, the proportions, exact.

'Simple enough,' said Des. 'The whole top of the fuselage can be the lid. Lay the body out inside the base.'

He started work right away, cutting the plywood sections to shape. 'I take it the guy's a Trekkie?'

'Was,' I said. 'In a big way.'

'Don't tell me. Somebody's going to look in the coffin, then turn to the congregation and go, *He's dead, Jim!*'

I laughed. 'I wouldn't be surprised! They're doing the whole bit, with the costumes and everything, like a Star Trek convention.'

He shook his head. 'Not life as we know it, Jim!' Got back to his job of building a starship.

On the day, it was carried into the hall by a guard of honour in Federation uniforms. In the front row, Spock-eared Vulcans sat next to members of the Klingon high command. The ship was placed on a black dais, facing a large video screen. The minister said a few words about the unusual nature of the ceremony, but said it was no less sanctified for that. The departed, Malcolm Scott, was being given the send-off he had always wanted, by the family and friends who loved him. He had gone beyond the final frontier, and would find it just the beginning, of life eternal in the Lord.

Then a small greyhaired man stood up, in the uniform of a Starfleet Admiral. Straightened himself up, cleared his throat. Said he'd just like to add a few words to what the minister had said.

'Malcolm was always known to us as Scotty. And now it's his turn to beam up. And if I can just echo the words of Spock at the end of *Star Trek 2, The Wrath of Khan* – he was, and always will be, our friend.'

He touched the tailfin of the starship. 'And of course we'll miss you, wee man. But it comes to us all. Time to boldly go. Seek out new life. Full impulse power. Warp factor six. Straight ahead.'

He turned with a TV remote control, pointed it like a phaser at the video screen. 'Energise!'

The screen flickered and came to life. Showed in colours that were lurid and too bright the final scene from *The Wrath of Khan*. Scotty in a kilt, pumping out *Amazing Grace* on the bagpipes as Spock's coffin eased out and was launched into space, traced a perfect arc, a slow parabola, to touch down on a newborn planet in a flare of light.

And in spite of myself I was touched. Something in the sheer absurdity of the whole thing, the incongruity and tackiness. And yet.

Des nailed me about it in the pub. 'Looked like you were quite moved there.'

'Ach. It was all the wee guys standing there in their uniforms. They had a kind of ridiculous dignity.'

'You want to watch out,' he said. 'Let stuff like that get to you and you'll start to lose it.'

'I don't know. It was just the way I saw it. Have you ever read that Flaubert story, *A Simple Heart*?'

He shook his head. 'Can't say I have.'

'It's about this simple peasant woman. Félicité. She works all her life as a servant in a big house, and she winds up looking after this parrot.'

'A parrot?' he said, deadpan.

'I know it sounds weird, but it's a beautiful story. She becomes absolutely devoted to this parrot – it's her whole life. Then right at the end, as she's dying, she has this vision. It's like, she perceives the divine, it comes to her, in the form of a giant parrot. So, hey, a parrot, a starship, who cares? Whatever it takes.'

'Whatever,' said Des.

The old boy in the Crombie came back.

'It's the wife. She's gone.'

Jamaica?

'I'm sorry. Are you still planning to lay her to rest in the back garden?'

'It's what she wanted. And it's what I'll want for myself, when the time comes.'

'Well, let's hope that's a long way off.'

'We'll see.'

Seen it before with old couples, so many times. One goes, the other follows double quick. Suppose they can't face being alone after a lifetime. Fade away. But almost like a conscious decision. Time's up. Pack it in. Had enough.

'Anyway,' I told him, 'I've checked with the Council, and I was right, there's no law against it. I believe they sent somebody round?'

'That's right. Young lad. Looked about twelve.'

'I've got his report and there's no problem with the water flow.'

'Good.'

'So we can go ahead.'

'Fine.'

'The only other thing I did mention was the neighbours.'

'Sod them.'

He would have dug the grave himself, but he hadn't the strength. Might have collapsed into it. And although that might have been fitting, even handy, we brought in Rab to do the job.

The pagoda was built of brick, plastered over and faced with tiles. 'Monstrosity,' said Des when he saw it.

Whatever.

The old boy was inside the house, fiddling with the record player, setting it up so the speakers faced out the open window, would blare across the garden. He had put on a stack of singles, to play one after another.

'Kind of medley of her favourites,' he said. 'She chose them herself. Sort of *Desert Island Discs*.'

He turned the switch, hurried out to the sound of the Bachelors singing *I believe*. Made it to the graveside, out of breath. Somewhere in the darkest night a candle glows.

No family or friends in attendance, no minister. Just myself and the old boy, Des and Rab, heads bowed. No speeches either, just the songs crackling out. Jim Reeves. *The sound of distant drums*. Cliff Richard. *Travelling Light*. Made me smile. *No bags and baggage to slow me down*. Changed the whole meaning. *A whoop and a holler away from Paradise*.

Once or twice I looked up, saw curtains twitch in the house

208

next door. The neighbours. We lowered the coffin into the ground beneath the tiled pagoda as lush Mantovani strings played *Eternally*. Then another gap, a click and hiss, another disc dropping into place. Old wartime musichall number. *Wish me luck as you wave me goodbye.*

'She wanted this one last,' said the old boy, a choke in his voice and finally tearful. He threw down a handful of earth, and Rab shovelled on the rest, smoothed it over. Cheerio. Here I go. On my way.

There was no reception. The old boy shook hands with us, thanked us. We left him to it.

Out in the street the nextdoor neighbour came after us – a man in his fifties, angry and tightlipped. 'You want to be ashamed of yourselves,' he said. 'Encouraging that old fool.'

'You might show a bit of respect,' I said. 'The man's just buried his wife.'

'Don't I know it! Five yards from my back door! I mean, how would you like it?'

'It's perfectly legal,' I said. 'I checked.'

'Oh I'm sure you did. But how d'you think this is going to affect property values? We're already in negative equity as it is. Now this! Bloody graveyard next door! It shouldn't be allowed!'

'But it is.'

He threw a look of pure hate at me. 'You're that bloke that was in the paper, aren't you? Talking about weird coffins and funeral pyres and sky burials and all the rest of it.'

'Just trying to brighten things up a bit.'

'If you ask me, it's sick.'

'I don't think I did ask you. But it's good of you to give me your opinion.'

'Sick!' he said again, and he stamped in to his house, slammed the door.

'Be happy to do him a nice sky burial.' said Des. 'Any time.'

'Mind you, he's got a point. About the grave next door.'

'Negative equity!' said Des, laughing.

Des was holding a football boot, adidas black leather with the three white stripes. A bit scuffed at the toe, the studs worn down.

'Just a young boy,' he said. 'That's always the hardest thing to take.'

The family of the boy had handed in the boots for Des to work from. The boy had been sixteen, died of a brain haemorrhage. One minute he's running up and down, warming up for a training session, the next he's collapsed, holding his head.

'His pals thought he was kidding,' said Des. 'Clowning about.'

He held the boot in his hand, at eye level, squinted at it. Hamlet with the skull. Alas poor Jimmy.

'Died with his boots on,' I said.

'Early bath,' said Des. 'Red card. What a fucking referee.'

He copied the shape of the boot to perfection, scaled it up. Jimmy was laid out in it wearing his Scotland away strip, the actual boots, polished, back on his feet.

'When Mad Max croaked it, me and the boys thought we should just eat him.'

Piltdown was the leader of the local Hell's Angels chapter. He was not joking.

'I don't mean like raw or that. We're no fucking barbarians. I mean we'd have cooked him like. Made him into burgers or something.'

'Maxburgers,' I said.

'Big Max,' said Des.

Piltdown let out a roar of a laugh, slammed his hand down on the desk. 'Aw that's good that! Max would have liked that!' He shook his head. 'Big Max!'

'But you, eh, changed your mind?' I asked him.

'Ach aye. No everybody fancied the idea. Some of them couldnae stomach it. In fact one or two of them's vegetarians. So that put the kibosh on it.'

'Might have been a few legal problems,' I said. 'You read stories, you know, people shipwrecked, surviving a plane crash, that sort of thing. Necessity. But generally I think the law frowns on cannibalism.'

'Fuck the law.'

'But you did change your mind anyway.'

'Aye. So then we thought we'd put him on his Harley, run it off a cliff somewhere, into the sea. But that seemed a waste of a good bike. Specially to the guy he left it to.'

'So.'

'So that's where you guys come in.'

'What did you have in mind?'

It was a new challenge for Des. They didn't want a box, just an actual-size replica of Max's bike, sturdy enough to take his weight. Meatball, who had inherited the original, brought it round to the yard. Des drew up his blueprint, got to work.

'Fucking ace, man!' said Piltdown, walking round the finished model.

'Sound,' said Meatball.

They laughed and slapped Des on the back.

On the day, the model was bolted in place between the original – to be ridden by Meatball – and Piltdown's bike. The model was fixed a little higher than the real bikes, so its wheels didn't quite touch the ground.

I had been working on Max, brought him out of cold storage and did an embalming job on him. Plugged and sealed and wrapped, got him into his stinking old jeans and t-shirt, biking boots and denim waistcoat, Nazi helmet, goggles over the closed eyes.

Meatball was shocked. 'He doesn't look like himself, man.'

'Well he is fucking dead,' said Piltdown.

'Naw, but he looks too healthy, man.'

Complexion by Safranine Pink.

With a bit of effort we managed to heave Max into position astride the bike. The frame shuddered and held. We strapped him in place, upright, against the raised seatback, tied his gloved hands to the handlebars. He was ready.

They drove him out, Piltdown and Meatball on either side of him, leading a procession of forty bikers roaring down the road. We followed behind in the van, Des drumming his hands on the wheel, singing *Born to be Wild*.

Because of Max, the lead bikes had to go slow, take it easy on corners and roundabouts. After half a mile there was a tailback behind us, nobody able to overtake. We could feel the build-up of rage bearing down on us, traffic snarled up, blocked.

Des laughed. 'Bet Max would have loved this!'

'Havoc,' I said.

'Chaos.'

The cortege wound and snaked its way across town, fouled up the traffic flow, rated a mention on radio bulletins. Delays likely. It moved on past run-down schemes and derelict industrial estates, out past the city boundary. Beyond the pale. Out to what they still called greenbelt but was nothing more than wasteland.

Out here a few of the Angels had a piece of land, and this was where Max was to be buried.

'Didn't want to put him in a graveyard,' said Meatball. 'None of that consecrated ground shite. Max was a pure pagan.'

'Probably wouldn't have him anyway,' said Piltdown. 'They'd shove him out in the unconsecrated bit alongside the murderers and suicides.'

'And stillbirths,' said Des.

'Is that right,' said Piltdown. 'I never knew that. Damn shame.'

The ground was fenced off and a wooden shack had been built in the middle of it, a few tents pitched round about. Flags fluttered from some of them – Scottish saltire, Confederate banner, skull and crossbones, swastika. At the perimeter, sheltered by a scrub of bush, the grave had already been dug, deep and wide enough to take Mad Max and the wooden bike. With ropes through the wheels and looped round the handle-bars, a crew led by Piltdown and Meatball managed to ease the bike down into the hole. Tensed and braced to take the strain, they kept the bike upright, dropped it down a foot at a time till it hit bottom. Max's head in its helmet lolled forward one last time and came to rest.

Piltdown wiped his hands on his vest, cleared his throat, spat.

'Suppose it's down to me to say a few words.' He looked down into the grave. 'Ya mad bastard, you've done it this time!'

The crowd laughed, cheered. He ripped open a can of beer, drank half of it, belched, carried on. 'I'm no into all this religion shite, heaven and hell and the rest of it. As far as I'm concerned you get one life and you've got to live it. And by fuck Max lived it!'

Another cheer.

'But I'll tell you this. See if there is a hell, and Max is down there, the devil must be shiting himself!'

A huge roar of laughter.

'To Max!'

And they shouted back. 'Max!'

And Piltdown slugged the rest of his beer, threw the empty can into the grave where it clunked as it glanced off Max's helmet. That set them all laughing more, and as Piltdown threw the first handful of dirt, the booze was brought out, bottles and cans cracked open. A ghettoblaster was switched on, cranked up loud, belting out *Bat out of Hell*.

A squad got down to shovelling the pile of earth into the grave, filling it up, and a few empties were lobbed in. When the earth was packed down, the mound over the grave levelled off, Piltdown stepped forward again.

'I always said I'd do this if Max went first. And the cunt said he'd do the same for me!'

He unzipped his jeans, directed a stream of steaming piss onto the grave. Got the biggest cheer yet, and they started queuing up to do the same.

I caught Des's eye. 'Time for a sharp exit?'

He nodded. 'Be tears before bedtime if you ask me.'

As we got in the van to go, Piltdown came over, shoved a wad of money at me.

'Bread on the night, man. That's the deal.'

'Thanks,' I said, taking it.

'You guys done a good job,' he said 'Yous are welcome to stay for the party. There's loads more folk coming, a band and everything.'

'Thanks all the same,' I said. 'Got to get back.'

'Sure,' said Piltdown. 'Whatever.'

As we drove off we looked back. Piltdown and Meatball

waved at us, gave us a clenched-fist salute. Behind them it looked like a fight had broken out, two of them going at it with boots and fists. There were lights on in the shack, and the sound system was boosted up loud, booming out heavy metal.

Over by the scrub of bush, two men and a woman were dancing on the grave.

'I want it to be like a stookie,' said the wee man. He took off his bunnet, patted the strands of his thin white hair into place, flat on his skull.

'You want to be buried in a plaster cast?' I asked him. 'Like a mummy?'

He shook his head, laughed. 'Naw! I want a box, but just a simple white job. And I want everybody to write on it, wee messages and that, drawings.'

'Like a stookie. Right.'

'I always mind it when I broke my arm. The things people wrote on it! So that's what I want.'

'Easy enough to do.'

'I'm ordering it myself cause I don't trust the family to do it.'

'No problem. One plain white box, matt finish for writing on.'

'And a set of magic markers. Different colours.'

I laughed. 'Nice!'

'This may sound like a strange request,' said the woman.

It felt like the opening to some *film noir*. The beautiful young widow opposite. I should have my feet up on the desk. Sam Spade. Come to think of it, not a bad name for an under-taker.

'Try me,' I said, in best Bogart style.

'Well, you'll probably think it's the ultimate in yuppie nonsense. But the fact is, he wanted buried with his mobile phone.'

'Suppose it symbolised something for him,' I said. 'His achievements. Like the Pharaohs being buried with their wealth.'

'Not exactly,' she said. Was that a faint look of amusement in the eyes, at the corners of the mouth? 'It's just that he was terrified of being buried alive.'

Another one. 'Poe and Vincent Price have a lot to answer for.'

She nodded. 'It reassured him. The thought that if it did happen he could phone out, get help.'

'Funnily enough, there was a fashion for that in the early days of the telephone. Of course it was only the rich that could afford phones. And quite a few of these big family tombs had the phone installed, just in case. So there's a precedent.'

She smiled. 'There you go.'

Scenario for a horror story. The yuppie gets buried with his phone, and it turns out he is still alive. He wakes up, and while he can still breathe, before the air runs out, he phones home – the only number he can find from memory without having to see. And he gets through to the answering machine.

'Sky burial,' the man said, staring at me. I hoped he might mean he wanted his remains transported to Kyle of Lochalsh, over the sea to Skye, buried in the cemetery at Portree. A Skye burial. Nice.

But no. He had read the article in the paper.

'Mentioned sky burial,' he said. 'And I thought, brilliant. See, I've thought about it before. I saw this Chinese film about Tibet. And it showed it, the real thing. Wind blowing across this big empty plain. Body left out to be eaten by vultures. Something really stark about it. Bleak. Elemental. Quick job they made of it too. Neat and clean. And I thought, That's for me.'

'Listen,' I said, 'I don't think . . .'

'And there's places in India where they've built these towers.'

'Towers of Silence.'

'That's right!'

'You saw a film about them as well?'

'Read a book. They're really well designed, you know.'

'I'm sure.'

'They're divided into receptacles, in concentric circles round the tower, with channels running into a central drain.'

'Fascinating.'

'Apparently from a distance the towers look black, like they're covered with a fungus. It's only when you get closer you realise it's a living mass of vultures.' He leaned towards me, spoke quietly. 'It seems once they get a taste for brains they won't eat anything else. Turn up their noses at it.'

'Beaks.'

'Sorry?'

'They don't have noses. They'd turn up their beaks.'

I was losing it here.

'Aye,' he said. 'I suppose you're right. But the thing is, we'd need to make sure we got birds that hadn't been spoiled like that.'

'No gourmet vultures need apply.'

'Otherwise it takes too long, you see.'

'Look,' I said. 'This is not going to happen. The Council are not about to build towers of silence in your local scheme. You won't get away with laying out bodies on the roof of a highrise. And I think you'll find vultures are in short supply around here. Mind you, it's a while since I've been out in Possil. Wouldn't surprise me if the place was swarming with them. Picking off the alkies and junkies, folk that have died waiting for a bus.'

'I thought we could work something out.'

'That'll be the royal we.'

'Eh?'

'Include me out.'

'Why?'

'You think you can just be pegged out in the graveyard? Put up a wee sign saying Do Not Feed The Birds?'

'I was thinking more of out in the country. The far north. The wilds, like in the Tibet film. Somewhere up in the mountains.'

'I'm sorry,' I said. 'It's not on.'

'Too difficult to organise?'

'Something like that, aye. Why don't you go home and think about it? There must be something else that's . . . imaginative, but more sort of . . . manageable.'

'I've got my heart set on this,' he said.

'What can I say?'

'None of the other undertakers would even talk to me about it. Wouldn't entertain me. So thanks for that.'

'It's OK.'

At the door, he turned. 'Am I right in thinking it's all right to have a funeral on your own land?'

'Aye, but . . .'

'That's all I wanted to know. I'll be back in touch.'

The orders kept coming in. A fish for a fisherman. A lion for a Scottish nationalist. Yellow submarine for an old hippy. Assortment of cars – the ones people had driven or had always wanted to drive. A book for a writer. Rugby ball for a scrum half. There were images poetic and beautiful in themselves – an eagle, a dragon, a dove. And there was the bottle of whisky.

I tried to talk the woman out of it, but she wouldn't back down.

'The bastard drunk himself to death,' she said. 'Made my life a misery. So this is bang on.'

'One for the road,' said Des.

'Right!'

Des liked the idea, talked me round. 'It's pure pop art,' he said. 'Warhol would be proud of us.'

'Suppose so.'

'And it's such a statement about this fucking country.'

'I just had a thought,' I said. 'Did you ever call an empty bottle a dead man?'

'Ha!' Des liked it. 'I'll write that on the bottom, in small letters. *Another dead man.*'

The coffin was simpler than most of the ones he'd built. The bottle's distinctive shape was straightforward, triangular in section. He painted the surface the rich gold colour of the liquor, suggested with highlights here and there the reflectiveness of glass. Then meticulously he reproduced the bottle's red and gold label.

'Should get sponsorship for this one!' he said.

'I don't think the company would see the funny side.'

'Maybe not.'

Somebody else didn't appreciate the joke. An outraged

McNaught phoned me up. 'It's disgraceful. It's sacrilegious. It's downright obscene.'

'Don't hold back!'

'If you think we'll allow that abomination to be laid in sanctified ground, you can think again. Have you no respect?'

'Well, to be honest, I did have my doubts. But the widow is pretty definite about what she wants.'

'Oh, so that's all that matters is it? That's your credo? Give the people what they want?'

'Within limits.'

'And what limits are those? The bounds of decency? A modicum of good taste? It doesn't sound like it to me!'

He must have hung up, left me with the dialling tone buzzing in my ear. Even that sounded irritated, like an angry bee.

Next thing the tabloid press were chasing me up, a reporter at the door, photographer lurking behind him. 'Just a minute or two of your time.' He had interviewed me before, down the phone.

'What are you going to call it this time?' I asked him. '*Dead Drunk*?'

'That's good.' He scribbled it down. 'That's *very* good!'

'So what do you want to know?'

'Well, I've already spoken to the wife, the widow. She's given us an exclusive. And I really just wanted your take on the whole thing.'

He asked a few questions. Did I think this sort of thing would catch on? Cigarette-shaped coffins for smokers? Giant syringes for junkies?

I gave guarded answers, non-committal. Could be. Who knows?

Didn't I think the whole thing was disrespectful? In bad taste?

A delicate area. A matter for the individual.

So I didn't mind if some people were shocked?

Not the intention. In fact, it was more likely to raise a smile. Maybe no bad thing in the face of death.

'Great!' he said. 'Thanks! Now, if we could just take a picture of the coffin?'

The article appeared next day. The usual travesty.

Lisa Anderson (49) put up with her husband's hard drinking for 25 years. And when he died, she decided to get her own back and have him buried in a bottle! Not pickled in whisky – she says that's the state he was in anyway! No, she's going to lay him to rest in a specially built coffin, shaped like a bottle of 90 proof. The coffin's to be made by controversial undertaker Neil McGraw whose previous custom-built caskets include replicas of a fish, a football boot and the Starship Enterprise!

But surely this latest effort is in questionable taste?

'Not at all,' says Neil. 'In fact – who knows? – it might catch on. We could have coffins shaped like cigarettes for people who smoke themselves to death. Or giant syringes for junkies who overdose.'

He clearly doesn't mind if he shocks people, but thinks he's more likely to make them laugh. 'And that's no bad thing,' he says.

But one man who is definitely not amused is James McNaught, the minister of Mrs Anderson's local church.

He has point blank refused to conduct the funeral service, refused to allow the coffin in his church, refused to let it be buried in the adjoining graveyard.

'It is an abomination,' said Rev. McNaught. 'It starts with ecumenism. Pandering to Rome. Standards are allowed to slip and the rot sets in. Before you know it this heathenish nonsense is being tolerated.'

But the last word – for the time being – comes from the widow herself. Lisa, speaking last night at her home, said, 'It was booze he lived for, it was booze that killed him, and this way it's booze he'll be remembered for.'

And Lisa has already chosen the music she wants played at the ceremony – Dean Martin's Greatest Hits.

McNaught stood his holy ground, and it spread a kind of unease. Other ministers, council officials, cemetery managers, stalled when I phoned, said they'd get back to me.

'It's not exactly celebratory,' said Lila. 'But then it is a statement by a brutalised woman.'

'Thanks for the feminist subtext,' said Des.

'I'm not trying to justify it,' she said. 'I had reservations about this bottle idea right from the start. And I don't think it's a road we should be going down.'

'It's no more over the top than any of the others I've made,' said Des. 'In fact it's pretty tame.'

'But the point is,' said Lila, 'the others were all designed out of respect, as a tribute. This one's an act of revenge. The motivation's all wrong.'

'Sounds like the guy was a total bastard,' said Des. 'You said it yourself, Lila. The woman was brutalised.'

'I just think it sets a dangerous precedent,' she said.

'There's too much hypocrisy about these things,' said Des. 'I say good luck to her.'

'But we could end up engaged in an act of pure spite,' said Lila. 'Defamation of the dead. We have to draw the line.'

They were both looking at me, waiting.

'Fine,' I said. 'Fine. There's a line to be drawn, I'll draw it.'

But the churches and cemeteries were drawing the line for me, refused to have anything to do with it. Finally Lisa Anderson agreed to cremation. The tabloid ran another story, under the headline *Bottled Out*.

Asked what she would do with her late husband's ashes, Mrs Anderson said she was planning to put them in an egg-timer.

'He never did a hand's turn in his life,' she said. 'So now I'm putting him to work.'

Somehow that put things back in perspective, even made Lila smile. I cut out the article, pasted it in the scrapbook with the rest. And indirectly, the press coverage led to another development, another twist. The phone rang one day, a Mr Samuels anxious to talk to me.

'I read a couple of articles about those coffins you make. I was particularly taken with the whisky bottle. And I loved the other ideas you came up with. The cigarette, the syringe.'

'The thing is.'

'I want to commission three pieces. One of each.'

Pieces!

'Are your friends dying off from various kinds of excess? Or are you trying to scare them back to the straight and narrow?'

Memento mori.

'You don't understand.'

'No, I don't. Are they for yourself? Are you keeping your options open about how to go?

There was a kind of dry chuckle down the phone. 'I want to exhibit them. In my gallery.'

Pieces. Commission.

A cartoon lightbulb flashed on in my brain.

!

Right.

'I suppose it's the aids thing primarily,' said Samuels. 'People dying out of time. Before their time. But given time to look at their own death. Plan it even. And give some thought to their funeral. See it as a statement. A celebration maybe.'

He was about fifty, his grey hair crewcut. His office was tiny, cluttered, the desk buried under stacks of paper. Posters on the wall, a Hockney swimming pool, a Mapplethorpe nude.

'So you think there is such a thing as dying before your time?' I said.

He looked surprised. 'Don't you?'

'I don't know,' I said. 'I really don't know.'

'Surely when somebody dies young?'

'Presupposes we're entitled to a long life. Like it's a right.'

'I guess it's the biblical notion,' he said. 'The allotted span. Three score and ten. Anything else feels like you're being cheated.'

'By fate?'

'Call it what you like.'

'If you call it God, you're saying God's unfair.'

'Feels that way.'

'Could take the long view. Call it karma. Consequences of past actions.'

'You're not saying aids is a kind of divine punishment?'

'On gays and junkies?'

'Not to mention babies born with it. Or the poor sods that got dodgy blood transfusions.'

'Doesn't figure, does it?'

He smiled. 'You had me worried there. Thought you might have been one of these fundamentalist headcases. This is God's justice. A plague visited on sinners and perverts.'

'I don't know that punishment comes into the picture.'

'Thank God for that!' he said. 'So how does this karma business function then?'

'You're asking me?'

'You sound as if you've thought about it.'

I thought about it. 'Seems to me it's cause and effect. Pure and simple. You do something, something else follows, inevitably.'

'And it carries on from life to life?'

'If you believe in reincarnation.'

'And do you?'

'I suppose I've always thought of it as a kind of metaphor. Like it's a beautiful and very lucid way of expressing a particular truth about the universe and the way it evolves. Original sin is another metaphor. DNA is another.'

'Nicely put.'

'And they all catch part of the same truth, some aspect of it.'

'But none of them's the whole picture.'

'Right. And sometimes you come across a story that makes you aware of that. It zaps you between the eyes. Takes your received wisdom and turns it upside down.'

'Such as?'

'Have you read the *Mahabharata*?'

'The odd story.'

'There's one about this king who falls in love with a beautiful woman. I mean, he is besotted with her. Completely loses it. So he pursues her, and she agrees to marry him on one condition.'

'Of course.'

'He mustn't ever question anything she does.'

'Some condition!'

'So he agrees, and they get married, and pretty soon she's expecting a child.'

'It happens.'

'She gives birth to a beautiful baby boy. And the king is delighted. But as soon as the baby's born, the mother takes it out and drowns it in the Ganges.'

'Heavy.'

'Of course the king is distraught. But he's made his promise. He can't question anything she does.'

'Tough call!'

'Time goes by and she has another child, another boy.'

'Don't tell me.'

'The same thing happens. She drowns the child in the river. Again the king can't say a word.'

'His promise.'

'So this goes on, year after year. Altogether she has seven sons. And she drowns every one of them, doesn't even let them live a day.'

'And the king lets it happen.'

'You got it. But he's not a happy man. And when she gets pregnant again, he's really troubled.'

'You could understand him being a mite apprehensive.'

'Apprehensive about the mite! No, he is. He can't face the whole thing happening again. The child is born, another healthy boy.'

'Number eight.'

'And the king finally makes a stand. He tells his wife he won't allow it. This time the child will live. And she says, Yes, this is the way it must be. And now you have broken your promise, I have to leave you. But since you have been good and patient all these years, I will give you an explanation.'

'About time too.'

'So she tells him the whole story. She says these eight sons who were born to her had all been brothers, living in some celestial realm. And they had caused serious offence to a great sage, and he'd cursed them. But here's the switch. He cursed them to take human incarnation, to be born on earth.'

'That was a curse?'

'Apparently. And the eight of them were appalled. A life on earth! The suffering! The pain! It was too much to bear!

Couldn't he mitigate their sentence? But no, he was having none of it. They would have to take human birth.'

'Bummer, eh?'

'But then one of them had a bright idea. They went to the goddess Ganga, who was renowned for her beauty and compassion, and who also gave her name, incidentally, to the River Ganges.'

'Ah ha!'

'They pleaded with her to have mercy on them, and she agreed. She said she would also descend to earth. She would give birth to each of them in turn, and she would make sure their life on earth was as short as possible.'

'By killing them.'

'Returning them to the celestial realm.'

'So the king fouled it up by letting the last one live.'

'Ah, no. And this is the really neat bit. Before she could set all this in motion, the goddess had to go to the sage who had cursed them, get his permission for the whole thing. And he said, Fine, except for one of the eight brothers. He'd been the ringleader you see, and his offence had been more grievous than the rest. So he had to do his time. Serve his sentence. Live out a whole life on earth.'

'And he was the last one, the one that was spared.'

'If you can call it that.'

'Doing time.'

'That's it.'

'Great story.'

'My wife told me it.'

'Did she? I take it you won't be having any children!'

I laughed. 'Actually you're right. Family's not what we wanted.'

'Interesting.'

'But you see what I mean about the story? I love that sense of there being a pattern to it all, only it's happening at some other level we don't understand.'

He was quiet for a bit, away inside his head. Then he looked out at me.

'Let me run this one by you. Young guy I knew. Twenty.

Everything going for him. Set out to fly to the States. Just going for a holiday. First time he'd been. Gets to the airport and his flight's overbooked. So he gets bumped. No problem. They put him on another flight later in the day. Upgrade him to business class. He's happy. So the plane he would have been on crashes. Everybody's killed.'

'Jesus! You read about things like that.'

'Right. But that's not the end of it. He gets to Kennedy, hears the story. Goes to the airport chapel to thank God, or his guardian angel or whatever. I know all this because he phoned me, to let me know he was safe. Then he gets in a taxi to go to Manhattan. A truck goes out of control on the expressway, smashes into the cab. He's killed outright.'

'God almighty.'

Running to Baghdad

'It's like the whole thing was planned. I mean meticulously.'

'Like it's personal.'

'Exactly! So how do you figure that?'

'Karma? God's will? The negation of God's will by hostile forces?'

'Or is it all just nonsense? Shit happens. We die. End of story.'

'I guess that's part of it too. Randomness. Chaos. Another aspect of the truth.'

He smiled. 'For some reason I find that reassuring!'

'Good.'

'I think you'll like the exhibition.'

'I'm sure a lot of people will.'

He nodded. 'It's the right time. Death is hot.'

The exhibition took up the whole gallery space, a huge converted warehouse in the merchant city. Des had worked hard on the three coffins, done a backshift in the workshop at the end of every working day, finished them off in three weeks. They looked impressive, laid out side by side, the bottle, the cigarette, the syringe. Des posed for photographs standing beside them, selfconscious and proud. A caption on the wall behind read *Name Your Poison*, and information panels carried details of his work, a few quotes from me about the business, and notes on Kane Kwei the coffin-maker from Ghana.

Des grinned. 'It's magic. They're treating me like a real artist.'

'Well so you are,' said Lila.

'Aye,' said Rab. 'A piss-artist.'

Lila turned on him, annoyed. 'Now that's uncalled-for.'

'Just a joke,' he said, hands up, innocent.

'But why does everything have to be so reductive?'

'No offence,' said Rab.

'None taken,' said Des. 'Ya bastard!'

'I give up,' said Lila.

Samuels was making his way round the gallery, an entourage following in his wake. 'Everybody happy?' he asked. He was dressed all in black for the occasion, expensive black suit, black shirt, black tie.

'It's great,' said Des. 'Excellent. You've done us proud.'

'He's right,' I said. 'Everything's perfect. The way you've placed them, the lighting, the information. Everything.'

Samuels beamed. 'Why thank you! Have you had a chance to look round, see the rest of the exhibition?'

'Just bits and pieces,' I said. 'It's a bit crowded.'

'Yes indeed. It's quite a turnout, even for this place. It shows we were right. Death is a hot topic.'

'I'll come back sometime when it's quiet and I can take it all in.'

'Best thing to do,' he said, and he gave us all a wave, moved on.

For some reason we all looked at Rab.

'What?' he said. 'What? I never said a word.'

I came back with Lila midweek, during the day when it wasn't too crowded. We could take our time. I bought a catalogue, moved systematically, clockwise round the space. Lila just wandered where the mood took her, went off at tangents and doubled back, followed what caught her eye.

The first exhibit was a kind of *danse macabre*, like a tableau from the Mexican Day of the Dead. Three skeletons stood, hands on hipbones, grinning out. The one on the left wore a man's suit, a shirt and tie, skull and skeletal hands and feet protruding. The one on the right wore a woman's shift dress, green satin. Only the one in the middle was naked. The bare bones. At their feet was the skeleton of a dog. In front of them was a coffin mounted on cheap screw-in legs to make it a coffee-table. Coffin-table. Resting on the lid, suspended in a goldfish bowl, was a three-inch fishbone, and beside that, a set of false teeth in a glass. On a tape loop three mournful voices intoned over and over a mediaeval *memento mori*.

> *As you are so once were we.*
> *And as we are so you shall be.*

The whole exhibit was labelled *The Nuclear Family*.

Next round was a video installation, called *Last Words*, something straight out of Waugh's *The Loved One*. Four TV monitors were set up, each one showing a different video of somebody talking to camera. They were placed just far enough apart so you could concentrate on any one of them and still hear the others as a droning intrusive background. Each talking head delivered a monologue, a valedictory speech, last words from beyond the grave. The voices were all American, and the tapes were the genuine article, the real thing, recordings made by people who knew themselves to be terminally ill, were leaving a final message for posterity, to be shown at their funeral.

Each tape began with scenes from nature, a river flowing into the sea, the wind shaking autumn leaves from a tree, a flight of birds against a sunset sky. The music ranged from *My Way* played by some bar-and-grill synthesizer combo, to an ambient piece of Satie minimalism on piano – *Gymnopedie No. 1*. The Satie was one I genuinely liked, even though I'd heard it used in an ad on TV, selling God knows what, and again in a Japanese soap on American cable, underscoring the images with a sense of melancholy and loss. *Lent et douloureux*. Here it was the backing to an old man propped up in bed, eyes staring out at the camera, spit gathering between his lips as he mouthed his parting litany.

'I guess by the time you see this I'll be gone. Down that long lonesome road. Comes to everybody that ever lived, and I ain't no exception. When your time comes it comes. Fought the good fight. Now it's time to rest. So this is just to say goodbye and God bless.'

The next tape showed an old woman, thin white hair crimped into tight curls, face powdered and made up, pink blusher applied to her cheeks. She looked as if she'd been embalmed, veins pumped full of preservative, eyes glazed in a doped-up morphine haze. The music was *Yesterday*, played on lush strings.

Old still photos faded in, spanned the woman's whole life in a couple of minutes. Baby a shapeless bundle, young girl looking out with a look of pure mischief held in check, posed group shots, the family, the class at school, intense adolescent all awkward angles and gloomy stare, young woman laughing, more sure of herself, then the wedding photos, happy couple, then the babies, the children of her own, two boys and a girl growing up growing up, the pictures changing from black and white to colour, the family groups with suddenly grandchildren, the photos always taken at Christmas with the tree and the presents and everybody gathered round, and one with her husband gone, just herself surrounded by family, the music coming to an end, now I long for yesterday, old woman with the pink face the drugged eyes numbed with painkillers her words slurred.

'Everybody's been so good to me here, the doctors the nurses everybody. Fact it was them that said I should do this, leave a message for you all. Keep me alive in your memories they said. So here I am. Feels funny knowing you'll be watching this maybe after the funeral or maybe again at Christmas when you're all together. I'm sorry I can't be there with you, though if you're watching this I guess I am in a way. But it's not the same is it? Anyway we'll all be together someday. In the sweet bye and bye. So don't be sad, is all.'

On the next screen a much younger man stared out, maybe late thirties, forty, but wasted away to a gaunt death's head, greying hair cropped close to the skull, eyes sunk, cheeks clapped in, had to be cancer or aids.

'Seemed like a good idea to do this, chance to say goodbye to you all while I still can. Leave my ten cents' worth. Star in my own TV show. Fifteen minutes of fame. I'm gonna live forever! No I'm not. But what the heck. So long as men can breathe and eyes can see, so long lives this and this gives life to me. OK I know that should be Thee, but hey! It's my show! Lights camera action. Is it rolling Bob? Have to put *A whiter shade of pale* on the soundtrack. I like the thought of you all sitting round watching this. Big Chill with a vengeance. I hope you're all drunk stoned smashed. Only way to pay your respects. Yo! So what to say? Rosebud or what? I don't know. Love one another. But be careful or you'll end up like me. Hey you're gonna end up like me anyway! But maybe not so soon. And this is too soon. Way too soon. Or who knows? Maybe they'll find a cure for this fucking virus. Eleventh hour. Last minute reprieve. Jimmy Cagney on death row waiting for that phonecall from the governor. Maybe not. It's over. Golden days before they end. I have to say these morphine shots have well and truly mellowed me out. It sure takes the edge off. Means I'm going gentle into that good night. Good night sweet prince. No more burn and rave. Goodnight.'

The frame froze on his sad, tired smile, his right hand raised, with effort, in a peace sign. The tape faded out on *A whiter shade of pale.*

The fourth tape began with a sunrise over mountains, a Chopin nocturne, cut to another old woman smiling at the camera, but only with her mouth, the eyes fixed straight ahead, flickering from time to time in what looked like panic.

'I want to say hello to Robert and Henrietta. And Lucy and Marianne and George. Jacqueline and Greg and little Louise. Chloe and Dave and Dave Junior. Mildred and the twins. Hello. Hello. Jeannie. Charles. Monica. Everybody. Hello. And of course goodbye. Goodbye too. Cause now you're watching this means I've passed on. Spooky, huh? You're listening to a dead person.'

She almost laughed, the eyes a moment manic before settling back to their dead look, the odd flicker. 'I guess Mr Goodman has talked to you all about the will, about dividing everything up. I've tried to be fair, to make sure everybody gets what they need and deserve. If anybody isn't happy well I'm sorry, that's too bad. I did my best. So that's it. I've had a long life and mostly happy. Can't complain. Thanks to all of you for being a part of it.'

She leaned her head back against the pillow, closed her eyes, opened them again, spoke to the side.

'Is that enough? Is that what they want? I'm sick of this. I'm tired.'

The Chopin nocturne again. Sunset over more mountains. Fade.

'Why did they leave that last bit in?' asked Lila, coming up behind me. 'Surely those last few words were meant to be off camera.'

'Out-takes,' I said. 'Who knows? Maybe the person filming had a sense of humour. And it was the most interesting part. I mean it was real.'

'Thinking of offering this as a service?' she asked. 'Film of the dear departed?'

'Might not be a bad idea. This *was* your life.'

Another installation had its title in neon flashing on and off.

THAT STUPID CLUB

A caption explained it was a quote from Kurt Cobain's mother, about how she'd told him not to join that stupid club, rock stars who killed themselves. A video wall showed nonstop footage of Cobain, Jimi Hendrix, Janis Joplin, Jim Morrison, Sid Vicious, Ian Curtis, lines from their songs juxtaposed in quick jump-cuts, the whole sequence repeating, a loop.

Where you going with that gun in your hand break another little piece of my heart love will tear us apart again I hate myself and I want to die I did it my way this is the end.

The next space along was given over to suicide notes, blown up huge. It was called *To whom it may concern*. Sad banality of desolation. To have reached this endpoint. *Nobody understands*. The handwriting, last pathetic flourish of individuality, scrawled or meticulously printed. *Can't go on. No point any more.* And the unbearably mundane detail. *I've cancelled the milk. Jeannie can have my cassettes.* Sometimes bitterness. *Fuck the bastards. Fuck them all. Maybe now they'll see.*

The suicides I'd dealt with. Worst part of the job, the most depressing. Scraping brains and tissue off the ceiling, the businessman who'd shot himself. The old woman fished out of the river, coat pockets filled with stones. Care in the community. The young boy who'd had a fight with his girlfriend, gone to the top of a highrise, twenty-third floor, thrown himself out the window. He'd landed feet first, the shock of impact bursting his brain.

Painted straight on to the gallery wall, grafittied in red, was a slogan.

SEX = DEATH

A taped commentary, the voice electronic, listed statistics about death from aids. It then explained that the process of evolution requires cellular death. Old cells die that new cells are born. Death is inherent in reproduction. However you look at it, said the voice, sex is death.

I held my head. 'This is making my brain nip!'

'Come and see this,' said Lila, taking me by the arm and leading me over to a display of bright appliqué paintings. 'From Panama. The Cuna Indians.'

One painting showed skeletons dancing, integrated into a psychedelic pattern.

'They're cute,' she said, and it was true, that was the word for them, friendly like cartoon characters. I read the caption.

Though they are symbols of death, they are not terrifying. Their basic friendliness is indicated by the little hearts inside their rib cages.

The picture next to it was even brighter, the colours luminous. It showed a bird surrounded by geometric shapes and patterns, flowers with faces, suns and stars, and seated amongst it all a small human figure.

After death the soul becomes a bird and is taken to the sky-world in a funeral boat decorated with colourful flags. Here we see the end of the soul's journey to the heavenly realm.

'I'd say they were heavily into mescalin. Do you know Walt Disney took mescalin? Back in the thirties? Can't remember where I read that. Explains a lot.'

'I just think these are so beautiful,' said Lila, looking at the paintings. 'They make you smile.'

'It's true. Benign death-forces. The soul-bird flying back to its home. Makes it sound not too bad.'

'Takes the fear out of it.'

'Hey, have you ever thought of taking up undertaking?'

'Oh sure,' she said. 'Like I don't do enough of the work as it is!'

But the thought had walloped me. 'No, but it's a great idea. I mean this whole business is such a male domain. It's like the fucking Masons.'

'And you want me to bring a nice light delicate feminine touch.'

'I'm serious,' I said. 'You'd be great.'

'So how many women undertakers do you know?'

'That's what I mean. There's practically none. It's ridiculous.'

'You think it needs a blast of shakti-power.' She pointed to another painting on display. 'Like that!'

The painting was huge – bigger than life size – an image of Kali, dancing. The face was black with wild blazing eyes, a bright red tongue protruding from the mouth. In her four hands she carried an assortment of vicious blades, and round her neck hung a garland of dripping skulls.

'Lovely,' I said. 'Look good on our new brochure.'

Lila laughed, stuck out her tongue.

I was just in the door, first thing in the morning, when the phone rang. A man's voice, Glasgow accent but with the edges rounded off, a bit of cockney thrown in.

'Neil McGraw?'

'Speaking.'

'The name's Howard. I wonder if I could come round and talk to you?'

'Fine. Is it about a funeral?'

He laughed. 'Lots of them. It's what you might call a business proposition.'

Another nutter maybe. Offer I couldn't refuse. Feed me a steady supply of corpses if I gave him a good deal. Group rate. Cheaper in bulk.

'When can you come in?'

'How about now?'

'Eh . . . OK. Why not?' Might as well get it over with.

'Say five minutes then.'

'Five minutes,' I said. I was laughing when I put the phone down.

'What?' said Lila.

'He said, "*Say five minutes*". And I did. Felt like Leslie Nielsen in *Airplane*.'

She put on an American accent. 'Surely you can't be serious?'

'Don't call me Shirley!'

'So who was he?'

'Name of Howard.'

'First name or second name?'

'Never thought of that,' I said. 'Just assumed it was his surname.'

'Like Frankie,' said Des, stirring sugar into a mug of black coffee, his wake-up shot.

'Funny thing happened on the way to the cemetery,' I said, and that set me laughing again, doing Frankie Howerd. 'Ooh you are awful!'

'You better get a grip,' said Des. 'Pull yourself together before this guy comes in.'

I remembered the old man skiting me one. No joke. No laughing matter. A serious business.

'You're right,' I said to Des. 'You are absolutely right.'

I took a deep breath. Composed myself. Straightened my face. Choked another laugh that snorted out my nose.

'What is *wrong* with you? said Lila.

'I don't know,' I said, wiping my eyes. 'I'm losing it. I think it was the phone call. Something about the guy.'

'Mister Howard Howard,' said Des.

'He just seemed to set me off. A reaction.'

'Well you'll have to put a lid on it,' he said.

'A coffin lid?'

Des gave up on me, shook his head. 'Fine.'

I'd managed to calm down by the time Howard came in, though I didn't dare look at Des or Lila. The man looked like the voice on the phone. Fair hair combed back, styled, long at the ears and at the neck. Navy blue cashmere coat. Grey silk tie. Soft leather briefcase with a shoulder strap. His eyes flicked round the place, took it in, a quick scan. He smiled with the mouth only, what would pass for an easy charm. But though the skin crinkled round the eyes, they were cold.

'Jack Howard,' he said, holding out his hand.

'Neil McGraw.' I shook it. Masonic grip with the thumb. The eyes registered that I didn't respond – just a second, a beat, but the information was filed away.

'Pleased to meet you.' And he handed me his card, a tasteful dove-grey with the lettering embossed in dark blue. *J. Howard. Funeral Director.*

'Can we talk?' He glanced at Des and Lila, acknowledged and excluded them. His business was with the boss, in private.

'Sure.' I showed him into my office area, but left the door open so Des and Lila could listen in. If I looked up I could see them through the glass panel.

I sat down facing Howard across my desk. 'So what can I do for you?'

'Put it this way. It's what I can do for you.'

Give me a break.

He made himself as comfortable as the chair would allow, to show me how relaxed he was, at ease, leaning back and crossing his legs, right ankle resting on left knee. 'You'll have clocked from my card we're in the same line of business. And it is a business, first and foremost. Let's not lose sight of that.'

'It's not just a business,' I said.

He smiled, as if from a great height. 'I've read about you and I like your style. Way to Go. I like that. You've got gumption. Bit of pizazz. A few rough edges maybe, but they can be rubbed off.'

'Sorry?'

'We're operating in a service industry, even if it's a service nobody really wants. But they don't have any option, do they? Comes to us all, right? Oh, there's a few crazies out there – you probably get them coming in for advice. Old hippies, new age types, wanting a do-it-yourself job. Hassle-free and dirt cheap.'

'Good slogan,' I said. 'Can I use it?'

He gave a chuckle, humourless. 'Be my guest.' The foot resting on his knee tapped the air. 'No, joking aside, I want to talk to you about improving the service we offer, and particularly about economies of scale. I mean, we've got our overheads to meet, right? Upkeep of premises, vehicle maintenance, staff wages, the list goes on and on. And it all has to be paid whether you're doing one funeral or fifty.'

'This is true.'

'Now.' He spread his hands. 'At an educated guess, I'd say you were doing – what – five or six funerals a week?'

'About that, yeah.' The bastard knew exactly.

'So, no disrespect, but you're running a cottage industry here.'

'We're doing all right.'

This time the look was pitying. 'All right just doesn't cut it. You could be doing a lot more than all right.'

'Like you.'

If he heard any irony in my voice, he ignored it. 'I've been operating down south. Decided it's time to move into the market up here.'

'The death market.'

He shrugged. 'No different from any other market. You have to compete. Increase your turnover.'

'Turnover in the grave.'

Just the slightest impatience, that foot tapping the air again, faster. 'I'm operating nearly two hundred outlets. It's a matter of pooling resources.'

'Taking over smaller firms. Buying them out.'

'Think about it. If you came in with us, you'd be doing five or six funerals a *day*, in no time.'

'After you'd rubbed off our rough edges.'

'There's maybe some of your ideas we could take on board. Like I said, I like your style. But you could be achieving so much more. Have you heard about our pre-need scheme, letting customers pay in advance?'

'Pay now, die later.'

'We call the scheme *Peace and Dignity* . . .'

Right.

'... and you wouldn't believe how much revenue it generates.'

'I'm sure.'

'It beats inflation, you see. Pay up front at today's prices and that's it fixed. Guaranteed.'

'As long as *you're* still in business when they die.'

'Nice,' he said. 'Sharp. I like that.'

'It's just you hear all these horror stories about old folks getting ripped off, paying all their savings to some fly-by-night outfit that goes bust.'

'It happens,' he said, eyes narrowing. 'But this is no fly-by-night outfit. And I've no intention of going bust.' He clicked open his briefcase, brought out a sheaf of papers, a brochure. 'This will give you some idea of the scale of our operation, the kind of service we're offering. I think when you've read it you'll want to join us. Then it would be a case of looking at what you've got here, working out a financial package.'

'Listen,' I said. 'There's no point in wasting your time. I'm not interested. I've no intention of giving up our independence, being taken over by you or anybody else.'

'Read the material anyway.' He gave me another handshake, a reflex, the grip.

'I won't change my mind.'

'I hope you do. Or you may be the one going bust.'

He nodded at Des and Lila on the way out, and when he'd gone, Des let out a hiss of breath.

'What a tosser!'

'We have just seen the future,' I said.

Lila gave a wee shiver. 'Not a nice man.'

'And how about that accent?' said Des.

'Mangled.'

'Talked like Denis Law.'

Use the noddle. What Andy used to tell me. The old man's watery smile, grudging. Rest Assured. Peace and Dignity. Pre-Need. Cash on the coffin-nail. Turnover in the grave.

I picked up Howard's card. Tasteful blue on grey. I tore it in half, dropped it in the bin.

*

236

We saw him a few months later on TV, being interviewed on *The Money Programme*, a special feature called *Dead Rich*. He had made millions by selling up to the big multinational corporation I'd read about. Universal Rest Incorporated. URI. Known in the business as McFunerals. It was Howard's philosophy on a global scale. Think big, cut costs, maximise profits. They bought up hundreds of small family firms, kept the original names but standardised the operation. On the programme, an American spokesman was answering charges that they employed high-pressure sales techniques.

'We demonstrate the highest degree of professionalism,' he said. 'Our primary aim is to assist client families at a pivotal time in their lives, and to offer them greater choice.'

'Expensive or more expensive,' said Lila.

'Even the Co-op are worried about these guys,' I said.

On screen, the spokesman continued. 'In the near future we'll be travelling round the country with our roadshow, taking our message to the people, letting them see what we're about.'

Then an old man from one of the few remaining independent companies was talking. 'They're buying up businesses like there's no tomorrow. As services get privatised they're taking over cemeteries and crematoria. It's scary.'

Cue a grainy image of a gravestone, the hoot of an owl.

Lila decided, yes, she'd take on the job, learned fast what she didn't already know. And she brought something special to it, a subtlety and warmth, real compassion.

The one thing she wouldn't do was embalming.

'I suppose I look,' she said, 'and I still see the person.'

'Makes it hard to go gouging out their innards.'

'Beautifully put.'

'Thank you.'

I came in one day from a cremation, heard her answer the phone, heard her make soothing noises, talk someone through in that way she had.

'It's all right,' she said. 'Just calm down and take your time, take it easy, we'll get there.'

Somehow I knew it was a woman she was talking to, something in the tone of her voice, a kind of sharing, solidarity.

'There,' she was saying, 'we'll sort something out. Maybe the best thing would be if you could come in. You know where we are? Fine, that's great, I'll see you then.'

She put down the phone, looked troubled.

'What's the story?'

'Poor woman,' she said. 'She's really upset.'

'She's lost somebody?'

'Her son. The thing is, I couldn't get much sense out of her. She kept saying, I just want to be with him but they've taken him away.'

'They?'

'The men. I couldn't get any more than that.'

'Think she's a psycho?'

'No I don't!' Annoyance in her voice. 'She's breaking her heart.'

'Sorry. So. She's on her way in?'

'About half an hour.'

'I'll look out for her. If you need any help give me a shout.'

'Sure.'

The woman came in, right on time, went straight to Lila. 'Was it you I spoke to on the phone?' Eyes red, voice shaky, a paper hanky crushed in her hand. She wasn't old, no more than forty, so her son must have been young.

'Sit yourself down,' said Lila, touching her arm. 'Can I get you a cup of tea?'

'Oh God, hen, that would be lovely.'

'Milk and sugar?'

'Please. Two.'

She watched Lila make two mugs of tea, one for herself. Add the milk and sugar, stir. And the simple ordinariness, the human kindness, reached her. She untensed, breathed out, exhausted. Whatever she had been through had completely drained her. She'd been holding it all together by sheer effort of will.

'When you're ready,' said Lila. 'Tell me about it.'

For a moment I thought the woman was going to lose it again, start to cry. But she didn't. She held on.

'My son died yesterday,' she said. 'Nineteen he was. But we knew it was coming. He'd been ill for a long time. And I nursed him at home. Looked after him.'

'That's good,' said Lila. 'Good that you could do that.'

The woman nodded, went on. 'So when he went, I wanted to keep him there. Have the viewing at home like.'

'Of course.'

'So after the doctor had been, I washed the boy and dressed him, combed his hair and that, made him look nice. His face was that peaceful.'

'It's often the way,' said Lila. 'Like the suffering's finally over. No more pain.'

'That's it exactly. So then I phoned the funeral directors. Looked them up in the book.'

'Sorry?' said Lila, puzzled. 'You're saying you phoned another undertaker?'

'That lot down the road. Suppose I picked them because they had the biggest advert.'

Local firm, now owned by URI.

'So what happened?'

'Well the two men came out. And they were as nice as you like, you know, really sympathetic. And they're asking about this and that. And I'm saying I want to keep my boy in the house, and they're saying Fine, no problem. But they still haven't seen the body. So I shows them in and one of them says, Oh he's that young too. And the other one says, What exactly happened? And I says, He had aids.'

'I wondered,' said Lila.

'Well that was it. You could have cut the air with a knife. This guy puts his hands up and says, Oh no, we can't leave him in the house. It's against regulations. And I says, What? And he says, Company policy. Risk of infection. We've got to take him away.'

'That's outrageous,' said Lila.

'I mean, I nursed him for God's sake. And the hospital told me the risks. I took all the precautions. But no, that was it. High risk. Against regulations.'

'It's against regulations all right,' said Lila, her voice rising.

'And I'll tell you who makes the regulations. A bunch of men. I'm damn sure you wouldn't get a woman being so cruel. What right have they got to stop a mother from seeing her son?' She glared across at me, the representative brute male. I held up my hands, innocent. Then she turned to the woman again, stood up. 'Come on. We'll sort this out.'

'Do you want me to come along?' I asked her.

She shook her head. 'I'll take care of it.'

A few hours had gone by when the phone rang. Lila. I recognised the way her voice was, dealing with something by keeping calm about it.

'You have to come down here. You have to see this for yourself.'

When I got there she was sitting at reception, staring straight ahead. Again I could feel it from her, the rage held in.

'Where's the woman?' I asked, looking round.

'I sent her home,' she said, standing up. 'They kept us waiting here all afternoon, then finally agreed to let me go through. Not the mother of course, just me. But thank God for that. There is no way I'd want her to see this.'

She led me through the waiting room and past the viewing area, purposeful, head down. Through a door, along a corridor and down a flight of steps. Through another door and we were outside the building, out in the yard at the back where they parked the vehicles. Across the yard and into the garage.

'There,' she said.

He was in a black body-bag, lying on the stone floor. Written on the bag in red paint was the one word. AIDS.

'In the name of God,' I said.

A man appeared in the doorway, someone from the company. 'I understand you're going to move the remains,' he said.

'He's one of them,' said Lila. 'One of the four that brought him from the house and dumped him down here.'

'You'd think it was the plague,' I said. 'It's like the fucking Middle Ages. Bring out your dead!'

'No need for obscenity.'

'That's the fucking obscenity.' I pointed at the bag, its message, its warning daubed in red.

We came back later, after dark, to pick up the body. We took it out of the bag, laid it on a stretcher with a zip-up plastic cover, loaded it up in the van, drove it to our place.

'I'll phone his mother,' said Lila, 'tell her we've got him here.'

The woman decided to have the viewing at our place, instead of taking the boy home. No embalming, she said, just make him look nice.

She sat with him for three days, sometimes talking to him, sometimes sitting quiet. Word had got out and all the boy's friends came in to see him, all the young dudes, to hang out one last time, and she welcomed them all, received them.

'Like a party in there!' said Lila at one point, as a burst of laughter came from the room.

'You did a good job,' I said.

And at the service in the crematorium, the boy's mother made a speech and thanked us, especially Lila, for not treating her boy like a leper, for giving him some dignity, for helping her give him a decent send-off. I could see Lila was moved.

'Can you imagine?' she said later. 'What kind of world is it when people feel they have to thank you for simple humanity, for treating them like human beings?'

'This is it.'

'And that's why it matters. What we do.'

'Absolutely.'

Absolutely.

The Ghanaian villager in his lion-coffin, carried through the streets to the graveyard. The men chanting a war-song.

'Who wants to fight a lion, without good reason!'

The mourners shouting at the dead man. 'It's dark. Be off!'

7

The Funeral Roadshow rolled into town, a convoy of gleaming hearses, filmed for TV, cruising across the city to the Exhibition and Conference Centre. URI had spent a lot of money. The biggest space was given over to a huge exhibition aimed at drawing in the public. Everything you always wanted to know about death but were afraid to ask.

A young joiner at a workbench built a simple pine coffin from scratch, starting with the panels of wood. A crowd gathered to watch while a video showed a guide to the range of coffins available, from Hollywood silk-lined caskets, with split lids for viewing, half-couch lids, glass panels, to the basic economy model, the pine box.

'You can go even cheaper than that,' said the voice on the commentary. 'Veneered chipboard, plywood, even compacted cardboard, are materials currently favoured by the cost-conscious. But you won't find these at URI. We offer quality workmanship at competitive prices. Of course, cost isn't always a consideration, but if it is, you can be sure that you and your loved ones will get value for money at URI How do we do it? Economies of scale.'

I turned to Lila. 'This is sounding horribly familiar.'

'After all, we are the biggest funeral company in the world. And for those of you who are not constrained by cost, those who can afford that little bit more for yourself or your loved ones, here are some of our more exclusive models.'

'*My Way*', instrumental, tinkled on the soundtrack. Always *My Way*. Same old same old. Done to death. And one of those big American voices, half an octave down, intoning, savouring the names of the caskets shown on screen.

'The Leonardo, with the Last Supper painted on the inside of the lid.

'The Chaparral, with leather-effect finish and cowboy motif.

'The Rameses, and its companion the Nefertiti, with carved sarcophagus detail.'

The joiner looked up at the screen, took a break from his work, laid his plane down on its side, blew away shavings, ran a finger along the edge he'd just smoothed. Nice job. He stepped back, poured himself tea from a flask into a polystyrene cup, stood sipping it. A young woman photographer asked if he'd mind posing for a couple of shots. Only take a minute, she smiled, be in tomorrow's paper.

'No problem,' he said. Put down his tea, wiped the front of his overalls to brush off the sawdust, the paperthin curls of shaved-off pine.

'Actually,' she said, smiling again, 'the tea was good.'

'Sorry?' He looked puzzled, like the tea was OK but not worth mentioning. Nothing special, just tea.

'I mean it would look good in the picture.'

'Oh aye!' He laughed. 'Right!' He picked up his cup again, stood awkward.

'If you could just get behind the head of the coffin there, I just want to get the shape of it. Great, now if you could lean over it, sort of rest your elbows on the sides, right, and raise the cup like you're drinking. Cheers. A wee bit more.'

'Hell of a uncomfortable this. I mean it doesn't feel natural.'

'That's OK. It looks good. Trust me. Now could you lean forward a bit more, over the coffin?'

'Feels even worse.'

'No, no, it's great! Now smile!'

And he did, and she took him, clicked five or six shots in quick succession, rapid fire. 'That's it. Brilliant!'

'Excuse me.' A blacksuit from the Company loomed. Tall and silverhaired, senior. Keeping an eye. 'I take it you're from the press.'

'That's right.' She flashed the smile at him, handed her card.

He read it, nodded. 'Of course we're grateful the press are showing an interest. But I think the pictures you've just taken are inappropriate. They create a wrong impression. Perhaps a photograph of the young man concentrating on his work . . .'

We moved on.

Two zombies in grey suits, red ties, tried to make embalming look user-friendly. Stood unrelaxed on either side of a cold steel table.

'Gilbert and George,' I said.

Lila laughed. 'Could be.'

Beside them, on a worktop, the array of implements looked mediaeval, scalpels and knives, a trocar. Behind them a display labelled *Cosmetology* showed the range of products available for patching and plugging and painting.

The Frigid Chemical Company had its own stand, their slogan across the top. *Get Rigid With Frigid.*

I laughed out loud. 'Can just hear Noel Coward singing that!' The two men stood unsmiling. 'I think it *is* Gilbert and George!'

'Embalming as performance art,' said Lila.

'Site-specific. Coming soon to a mortuary near you.'

She hit me with her rolled-up programme. 'Come on!'

We glanced at the other exhibits on the way round, nothing much that was new to us.

Computerised engraving machines produced nameplates for coffins and urns. *Your loved one's name stylishly scripted.*

An insurance man was on hand. *To guide you through the bewildering array of insurance and investment opportunities.*

DSS officers were there to talk about benefits. *On low income? Facing difficulty in paying for a funeral? We are here to assist.*

An old woman with thin wrinkled hands worked on a huge flower display as a tape played the theme from Elvira Madigan with another American voice-over. 'The gentle beauty of flowers can express deep feelings. Respect for the deceased. Loving comfort for the bereaved. The language of flowers says it all.'

Bloom. Wither. Die.

I found myself picking up the pace, anxious to be on and out.

Book of Remembrance Memorialisation System. Fitting and Dignified Memorials. Bereavement Stationery. (Also a wide range of wedding stationery and office supplies). Monumental Masonry. 10% discount. Free Crematorium Tour. (Chauffeur-driven limo). Ask here for details. Latest additions to our 600-strong fleet of vehicles. 4-door Hearse. Matching 6-door

Limousine. Omega Removal Vehicle. Legal advice from established solicitors. Wills, trusts, tax, executory matters. Special 'free will' offer.

'You believe in free will?' I asked the solicitor. 'What about determinism?'

'Sorry?'

'Obscure philosophical joke,' I said, then switched to a Groucho voice. 'There is no free will.'

'The offer closes at the end of the month,' he said, disinterested, unfazed.

'So you're determined to sell me free will?' I turned to Lila. 'Let's get out of here. I'm feeling claustrophobic.'

'He thought you were mad,' she said, taking my arm.

'Probably. Another nutter roaming the streets. Example of care in the community.'

We passed the young photographer again, sweet-talking an undertaker into posing beside an elaborate casket and pretending to measure up an old man who had wandered past. 'If you could just hold the tape a bit higher, that's it, and smile. Great.'

I swigged a cappuccino from a paper cup in the foyer café, felt the caffeine rush restore a sense of wellbeing, at least for the moment. Enough to get me through the door into the lecture theatre, where the presentation was to take place. Invitation only. Strictly trade. The sales pitch aimed at telling us why we should be bought out, taken over.

First up was a young man in a broadshouldered double-breasted suit. Slick gelled-back hair. Big orthodontic smile. The voice was nasal, ingratiating, with that irritating habit of flicking up at the end of a sentence, like everything was a question?

'What we're after, what we all want, is enhanced consumer satisfaction? I mean, we're dealing with what you might call a reluctant clientele? But what can they do? There's a dead body in the living room, it's a matter of some urgency? Our job is to offer services and merchandise that make people feel better at a tough time in their lives?'

'Pass me the sick-bag,' I said, to Lila, but loud enough so a few others looked round. The speaker continued, dropping the question-marks.

'We're all about offering consumers more choice. And people are choosing to spend more on funerals. Our revenues have grown considerably, and that's because we're giving the public what they desire.'

'Give me a break!'

This time he broke his stride, spoke directly to me. 'You have a problem?'

'Giving the public what they desire. But you're creating that desire, talking them into something they don't need and can't afford.'

'I can assure you sir, that is not our policy. If you read our Code of Practice, our Client Pledge . . .'

'This whole pitch here today is about maximising profits,'

'And what's wrong with that?'

'It shouldn't be above all else. Bigger isn't necessarily better.'

'I take it you're in the trade yourself, otherwise you wouldn't be here.'

'Got it in one.'

Somebody passed him a note. He read it and smiled. 'Mr McGraw?'

'That's right.'

'Way To Go. Nice snappy little title. So you're not above a little marketing yourself.'

'Of course not. I've a business to run. And I want to carry on running it, the way I choose.'

My Way. Fuck it. I felt my voice rising. 'I don't want swallowed up by some monstrous conglomerate. And whatever way you tart it up, maximising profits means squeezing your customers, persuading them to spend more. And I just think it's sick to do that to people when they're vulnerable.'

He smiled, showed those teeth, held up a hand as if calming me. 'Maybe this is something we could discuss at a later date? But for now, I have a presentation to make?'

'Sure,' I said. 'I'll leave you to it.'

Lila and I made our way along the row. A few folk tutted,

irritated, but one or two gave us the thumbs up, pat on the back as we passed.

Quite right. Well said.

As the door closed behind us, I heard the presenter pick up again. Must have made a joke of it, got a laugh from the audience. Somebody had followed us out. I turned and was dazzled by a flash. The same photographer, giving us her smile.

'Great!'

The article appeared in the paper next morning, under the headline *Dead On*. Photos of the young joiner with his cup of tea, the stone-faced embalmers, the old fellow being measured up, and one of Lila and me leaving, captioned *Way to go! Controversial undertakers Neil and Lila McGraw leave the exhibition in protest at the sales pitch. Mr McGraw's designer coffins include caskets shaped like a cigarette, a whisky bottle and a hypodermic syringe.*

'I suppose I should be used to this kind of thing by now,' said Lila. 'But it still annoys me.'

'Och well,' I said. 'It'll annoy URI even more. Get right up their noses!'

The two mafiosi from the Firm chose a good day to come and make me their offer. A few interesting customers had turned up at the same time. The two men were a double act, one thin and intense, the other stocky and jovial.

– *Good afternoon sir, I'm Mr Hardy and this is my partner Mr Laurel, and we'd like to interest you in a little business proposition.*

– *That's right, it's a turnover, a pushover, a takeover.*

I only half heard what they were actually saying, let it wash over me. But it sounded no less strange. They were offering a chance to expand my horizons, become part of a much larger concern.

'And I do mean concern,' said Ollie. 'After all, what we're selling is trust and reassurance.'

'Customer care is the means to self-gratification,' said Stan.

'Kind of statement that could be misunderstood,' I said.

'Excuse me?' Stan looked baffled. I expected him to scratch his head.

'Forget it,' I said.

Slap on a false moustache, cross my eyes and become James Finlayson. Grab a shotgun and chase them from the premises, blast them as they run down the street.

'This is a bad time,' I said.

'Sorry to hear that,' said Ollie in his concerned voice, oozing unctiousness.

'No. I mean right this minute isn't a good time to talk.'

'We'll wait,' he said.

'Or come back when it's more convenient,' said Stan.

'It won't ever be more convenient.'

'Well in that case,' said Ollie, 'we'll definitely wait.'

I looked up at the other people in the waiting room. I glanced at Stan and Ollie. They wanted to wait, fine, let them wait.

We'd rearranged the space, had three areas curtained off, like little cubicles. Lila was dealing with an old couple, gentle looking souls, whitehaired and clear-eyed. The old boy reckoned he hadn't much longer to live, a matter of months. He wanted a cremation, but for some of the bones to be saved, not ground down to powder, rescued and carved into musical instruments.

Des was talking to a nervous young man, agitated and fidgety, whose father had died leaving very precise instructions.

'He wanted buried at sea.'

'It's costly,' said Des. 'And it takes a bit of organising. But we can do it.'

'The thing is, he wanted something a bit special, out the ordinary. Something spectacular.'

'What did he have in mind?'

I had drawn the short straw. Vulture Man, still wanting left out for sky-burial.

'I'm sorry,' I said. 'The authorities just wouldn't wear it.'

'But you said you can be buried on your own land.'

'Buried, aye. Not left lying about.'

'I've bought a bit of land, and it's far enough away not to bother anybody.'

Try another attack, the expediency of the thing.

'Where would you get the vultures? Scotland isn't exactly hotching with them.'

'They've got a pair in the zoo. I thought maybe I could borrow them. Or hire them.'

'Oh right. Sort of carrion escort agency. Excuse me, I'd like to take your birds of prey out to dinner. Only I'll be on the menu.'

Carrion. Carry on.

'You don't think they'd rent them out?'

Ollie was whispering something to Stan, who was making notes.

'What kind of musical instruments?' said Lila.

'The thigh-bone could be drilled to make a flute,' said the old man. 'I like the idea of that. Or you could put strings across the pelvis, turn it into a wee harp.'

Des's customer was explaining his father's plan. 'He read about you people in the paper. That's why I came to you. He wanted one of your coffins shaped like an aeroplane.'

'No problem, but I thought you said he wanted buried at sea.'

'He does. I mean, he did.'

'So he wanted the plane dumped over the side into the sea?'

'Not exactly.'

Vulture Man wouldn't give up. 'Maybe there's other birds we could get.'

'You want eviscerated by a flock of seagulls? Pecked by a bunch of sparrows, mob-handed?'

His eyes shone. 'I thought maybe eagles.'

Lila smiled at the old man. 'I think it's a lovely idea. It would be a case of extracting those bones before they're reduced to ash.'

'So let me get this straight,' said Des. 'You want him put in a coffin shaped like a plane, and dropped from a real plane into the sea?'

'That's right. He wanted to fly one last time then plunge into the waves.'

'Watery grave.'

'That's it. Sunk without trace.'

'I think it's brilliant!' said Des. 'Absolutely mad. Ridiculously expensive. But brilliant.'

I called over to him. 'I think you're right. Take a bit of work, but it would be beautiful.'

The image had caught me, the arc of the plane curving in to the sea to splash down and sink.

Full fathom five.

I turned to Vulture Man. 'Listen, I'm sorry, there is no way this is going to happen.'

'Could always go to Tibet,' said Des, chipping in. 'Bung the local lama. Fix you up when the time comes. No problem.'

'Or become a Parsee,' I said. 'Ask to be laid out on your Towers of Silence.'

'I might do that,' he said. 'Do you know if there's any Parsee communities in Scotland?'

'Can't say I do. But there's definitely Tibetan Buddhists down in the Borders. You could always give them a phone.'

'Thanks,' he said. 'I will.'

He shook my hand and left, his sense of purpose renewed. Des gave me a look and I shrugged. 'I know, I know.'

'The buck stops somewhere else.'

Simultaneously, we both said, 'Whatever.'

Lila was saying she would check the feasibility of the old man's idea, rescuing some of his bones.

'I used to play clappers when I was a boy,' said Des. 'Get them out the butcher's shop. Let them dry out.'

'That's it,' said the old man, smiling. 'That's the kind of thing.'

'Could recycle the lot, turn you into a rhythm section.'

'Now you're talking!'

'A gamelan orchestra,' I said. 'Make a wee drum out the skull.'

The old man laughed. 'A xylophone out the rib cage!'

Lila stayed businesslike, brisk. 'We've all got the general idea. I'll make some enquiries, figure out what can be done.'

'Great!' said the old man. 'Maybe I could be played at a memorial service!'

The old woman smiled, her eyes patient and sad.

Des turned back to the burial at sea, took down the usual details, started sketching the plane, a stylised Spitfire.

I had almost forgotten the two men from the Firm, was surprised to see them sitting there. They stood up, together. Stan looked at his notebook, flipped it shut, put it away in his briefcase.

'Is this a typical day?' he asked.

'Not at all,' I said. 'Sometimes it gets weird.'

'I think you would definitely be well advised to join us,' said Ollie. 'If you don't, you'll be closed in six months.'

'Sounds like a threat,' I said.

'No. It's a prediction. Pure and simple. Six months. A year at the outside.'

I smiled at them. 'We'll see.'

James Finlayson tweaks their noses. Boots the pair of them on the backside, out the door.

The burial at sea was like a military operation organised by Kafka. So much paperwork, so many regulations. There was the hiring of a boat, a retired ferry out of Greenock, and a cargo plane based at Prestwick. The flight path had to be strictly plotted. The drop couldn't take place near fishing grounds or too close to the shore. We had to get a license from the local Inspector of Fisheries, and a coroner's form for offshore burial, and a doctor's certificate of freedom from fever and infection. The body couldn't be embalmed, and it couldn't be dressed, except for a loose cover of cotton or paper. We had to put our phone number – no name or address – on a plastic band round the waist. The coffin had to be solid softwood, with holes drilled in it to let out air pressure, and the joints strengthened with brackets, and two steel bands wrapped round it at right angles to withstand impact, and the whole thing weighted with iron or steel or concrete to a minimum of a hundred kilos.

'Got all that?' said Des.

The inspector came round the night before, a gaunt, thrawn man. Checked everything was in order. Rechecked. Looked faintly disappointed as he ticked each item off his list.

Then he saw the fuselage of the Spitfire, canvas stretched over a plywood frame. It was made in two sections, bottom and top, ready to be clipped round the coffin, fastened with more steel bands. The wings would be slotted in later, bolted in place at the last minute, before take-off. The whole structure was painted green and khaki camouflage, RAF roundels on the wings and sides.

'So it's true,' said the Inspector. 'You're really doing this. It's not just some bad joke.'

'It's what the old fellow wanted,' I said. 'His son was quite definite.'

'The world's gone mad,' he said, and scribbled his signature on our certificate, handed it to me. 'You realise if you're delayed into next week because of bad weather, you have to apply for a new certificate.'

'Go through all this again.'

'Afraid so,' he said, smiling. He clicked his pen, put it away in his pocket. 'So let's hope it keeps fine for you, eh?'

As it was, it rained a little in the morning, cleared up later, a thin smear of sunshine. We'd had to hire a forklift truck and a removal van. Rab trundled the forklift round the yard, enjoying himself. We loaded up the weighted coffin in its camouflage casing, manoeuvered it into the back of the van, put the wings in beside it.

Rab was driving the van to Prestwick and Des was going along to supervise the whole thing, go up in the plane for the drop. As the van revved up, he wound down his window, gave me the thumbs up, said 'Chocks away!' Saluted, pursed his lips and trumpeted the theme from *The Dambusters* as they moved off.

Lila and I drove to Greenock and got on the boat. The old fellow's son, Jack, welcomed us aboard, thanked us.

'Thank us when it's over,' I said.

There were twenty or thirty guests, most of them having a drink in the cabin downstairs. A tape played *Wide Blue Yonder*, as we sailed out past ghost shipyards to the open sea.

At the rendezvous point, Jack made an announcement and everybody piled up on deck, looked up. One or two had binoculars.

Then we heard the low drone, saw the plane in the distance. A few of the guests cheered, waved. The plane drew closer, dropped down low, grey bulk. It banked and curved round, circled. The boat cut its engines, bobbed and drifted. The plane came round again, steadied, levelled out. Its hatch doors opened and the Spitfire dropped out to more cheers, plummeted. The forward momentum gave a brief sense of flight to the descent, the final crash-dive into the sea. It hit belly first, tore in to the water and disappeared. The cargo plane swung round again, headed back.

No cheering now, one or two folk started to clap, stopped. Something solemn at last in the moment. The finality.

'It was that quick,' said Jack. 'All that work, then Boom!'

'This is it,' I said. Profound.

'You expect an action replay. Like if you go to the football nowadays, and somebody scores a goal, you're expecting to see it again.'

'That's right!' I remembered it, the slight shift of focus, disorientation. This was real time, a one-off.

'That's the beauty,' said Lila. 'That things are fleeting. Like this today.'

Jack looked pleased. 'It was some operation,' he said.

She smiled. 'It was.'

'So can I thank you now?'

'Sure thing!' I said.

He shook us by the hand, invited us downstairs to take a drink. The tape was switched on again, played the Dambusters March. The boat's engines roared back to life as it turned about, made for shore.

He's a bit of an anorak,' said Des.

'Which bit?' I said. 'The toggle? The zip?'

'He's got all these ideas for how we could be using computers.'

'Save me.'

'Death on the Net.'

'Sounds like an Agatha Christie.'

'His name's Eric.'

'It fits.'

'He's keen to talk to you.'

'Now?'

'Come on, you're always giving it out that you're open to new stuff, new ideas.'

'It's just all that cyberspeak makes my mind glaze over. My forehead scrunches up and my brain feels like a wee dried pea.'

He laughed. 'Serious technophobe. You should at least talk to the guy.'

'I know, I know. I'm just stalling.'

'Will I send him in then?'

There was no escape. No *Quit File* command to highlight.

'Fine,' I said.

New File. Open.

Eric came in, shook my hand. He looked like Clive Sinclair force-fed on cholesterol, sleeked up to a butterball shape. He gave the impression of a skinny man inflated to fill out his jersey which was fawn, patterned with black horizontal lines and zigzags.

'I've got a few ideas,' he said. His eyes, magnified by his glasses, had a curious kind of manic brilliance, a visionary glint, a shining stare.

'Des was telling me,' I said. 'Something about death on the Net.'

He grinned and crinkled his eyes, nodded very fast. 'That's a kind of shorthand. Name of my website.'

'I see.' I felt the numbness begin.

'Mind you, that's what Timothy Leary wanted to do.'

'What?'

'Die on the Internet.'

'And how would he do that?' I had some image of him downloading his consciousness, his being, into an electronic network, converted into digital signals and sent out.

'I think he wanted to transmit pictures of his final moments. Last words, message for posterity, all that, then finish.'

'Turn off.'

'Right. In the end he settled for the last words.'

'Which were?'

'Why not? Yeah!'

'Deep.'

'But they did do something amazing with his ashes. They launched them into space.'

'I think I read about that. Didn't the Star Trek guy do it as well?'

'Gene Roddenberry, that's right.'

I remembered our wee man Scotty in his starship coffin.

'They put the ashes in a capsule,' Eric explained. 'A hundred and fifty capsules in a satellite. Launched from a rocket.'

'Space funerals,' I said. I liked the sound of it.

'They pass overhead every ninety minutes. They orbit for a few years then re-enter the atmosphere and burn up.'

Ashes to ashes.

'Must cost quite a bit.'

'Three or four thousand quid. I've got mine put by. The interest should cover inflation. I thought maybe you could make the arrangements.'

'It's not, we're not talking imminent here? I mean, you're not ill?'

'No, no,' he said. 'Just planning ahead.'

'Fine. OK. I can do that. But you said you had a few ideas.'

'Interactive wills,' he said.

Humour him. 'Kind of Vulcan mind-meld?'

He looked confused, then worked out what I was saying. 'No! Wills as in Last Will and Testament!'

'Right. Of course.'

'Could design it in such a way that you had to answer a question to move on to the next stage. And what people get left in the will depends on how they answer the questions.'

'Multiple choice.'

'That's right. A test. Go down one road and the whole estate is yours. Go down another and you're disinherited.'

Yes/No. Abort. Retry.

'Mean,' I said.

'Just a safeguard.'

'Can see it in a film. Everybody getting the answers wrong. And the cute kid going straight to the heart of it. But not before the wicked half-brother's hacked in and messed it all up.'

'You should copyright that.'

'OK so your interactive wills might take a trick with some young solicitor. What other ideas have you got?'

'Well, I mentioned death on the Net. It's more like funerals on the Net.'

'So instead of a ceremony you'd have a website.'

'It's the way things are going. In fact I think we'll eventually do away with cemeteries and gardens of remembrance, the whole time/space nexus.'

'Just launch everybody into space.'

'And into cyberspace.'

'Eh?'

'I'm talking about virtual gardens, virtual memorials.'

'Virtual funerals.'

'More or less. You could create your own space. Make it a paradise. Have images of the deceased there so you can talk to them, be with them.'

'Sounds like the holodeck from *Next Generation*.'

'That's exactly what it'll be like.'

'But it's not real.'

'So what's real?' He looked round the office. 'This?' Picked up my brochure from the desk. 'This?' Pointed at himself. 'This?'

'OK, I take your point.' A headshaking response to things where I came from. *It's no real.* 'But it's all the real we know.'

'What I'm saying is we create the world anyway. We're already living in a virtual reality. The world we think we know is just our thoughts, fears, desires, imaginings. We're projecting all the time.'

'But we project onto something.'

He widened his eyes, looked more manic than ever. 'The void, my man. The void!'

And just for a moment I felt it opening up, the nothing in behind it all. Not the whole story, but another part of it, another view.

Save Changes. Yes/No.
Close file.
Shut down.

'Clugger McDuff,' I said.

'Now there's a name to conjure with,' said Des.

'Played centre half for Rangers in the forties.'

'Iron curtain defence. They shall not pass.'

'Got suspended *sine die* for one bone-crunching tackle too many.'

'What about him?'

'He's deid.'

'*Sine die* right enough. So are we burying him? Red, white and blue coffin with a spray of orange lilies on it?'

'Close,' I said. 'Seems he never won the Scottish Cup. So what they've done is get a wee replica of it from some trophy place. And they want to put his ashes in it. Carry them round the pitch before the next Old Firm game. A final lap of honour.'

'And the management are allowing it?'

'They must reckon it's good PR. Sense of history. Tradition. Continuity.'

'Bizarre.'

It was one we both wanted to see, and so did Rab. He drove the car, McDuff's son in the front with the mini-trophy in his lap, red, white and blue ribbons tied to the handles. Des and I sat in the back seat, kept our faces straight as we swept in through the stadium gates.

Before the game the two teams came out to warm up. The noise battered my ears, forty thousand howls of hate. A voice on the PA announced there would be a one minute silence as a mark of respect for McDuff. The Rangers end stood quiet. A bit of whistling, spate of jeering from the Celtic end.

'Could have been worse,' said Des.

'Aye,' said Rab. 'Could have been Aberdeen.'

At the end of the minute, the referee blew his whistle and the ground shook to a great roar of release. Above it the PA voice explained what was happening with the ashes. McDuff Junior carried the cup to the touchline. The two team captains jogged over to him, shook his hand, took the cup between them, a handle each, ran round the track with it.

We stood watching from the tunnel. 'Hope the lid's on tight,' said Des.

'Superglued.'

'Good,' he said. 'I've heard of spilling on to the track, but that would be unfortunate.'

When they'd finished their lap, they handed back the cup to Son of McDuff, sprinted out to the centre circle to the biggest roar yet.

'Will you be sprinkling the ashes on the pitch after the game?' asked Des.

'Not at all,' said the man. 'This is going in the display cabinet with his league medals and his Scotland cap.'

He raised the trophy in the air, towards a section of the crowd. They cheered, and a few of them started chanting, forcing the syllables into the tune of *Juantanamera*.

> *One Clugger McDuff*
> *There's only one Clugger McDuff*

(Someone shouted, *And he's deid!*)

> *One Clugger Maac Duff*
> *There's only one Clugger Maac Duff.*

For a moment I thought the son was going to give in to the emotion, a quiver in the lip. But he didn't, he controlled it, turned to us, said, 'Thanks, for everything.' Headed back up the tunnel, made his way to the directors' box to watch the game.

I caught a glimpse of him later, on the TV coverage, saluting a Rangers goal, kissing the cup, jabbing the air with Clugger's ashes.

A week later we had a letter from the stadium asking about the feasibility of developing a range of coffins in the team colours, to be advertised and marketed through their shops, the club to take a percentage. A merchandising opportunity.

'Why not?' said Des. 'Man United are probably doing it already.'

'Special burial strips. Home and away.'

'One for viewing, one for committal.'

'One for midweek.'

'One for when there's an R in the month.'

'Funny old game.'

Samuels phoned, left a message on the answering machine. He sounded breathless, his voice hoarse and throaty. Bad flu maybe. He wanted to commission another coffin, the regular standard shape, but covered in fake fur.

I called him back, asked if he was organising another exhibition.

'Not exactly,' he said. And he laughed, coughed, harsh and rasping.

'Sounding rough,' I said.

'Cough that carries you off!' He wheezed, catching his breath again. Said he'd explain it all if I could come round to the house. Gave me the address.

An old red sandstone building in the West End, big bay-windowed flats facing south. I was buzzed in, met at the door by a young man in a suit.

'Sam's very tired,' he said. 'But he needs to talk to you.'

He showed me into a bright high-ceilinged room, the sun streaming in at those bay windows. An old comfortable sofa had been pulled across in front of them, and stretched out on it, propped up on cushions, covered by a Mexican blanket, lay Samuels. Sam. And my own breath caught, a sharp gasp at the sight of him. Emaciated, wasted, burned out.

'Fuck,' I said.

'Eloquent, he said. 'Succinct. Says it all really. Fuck, indeed.'

'Sorry,' I said.

'Not at all.' He waved a thin hand. 'An honest and heartfelt reaction to my depleted state. So. Can I get you a cup of tea?'

The answer to everything.

'Em . . .' I was readjusting. Not the visit I'd expected. 'That would be nice, thanks.'

'Earl Grey, Darjeeling, Lapsang Souchong? Or there's herbal.'

'Earl Grey's fine.'

'Jamie,' he said. 'Pot of Earl Grey. Lemon Verbena for me.'

The young man nodded, went out. 'Sweet boy,' said Samuels. 'Now, thanks for coming over.'

'I'd no idea you were so ill.'

'So I look that bad!'

'Bad enough.'

'You know that Stanley Holloway song?'

'Which one?'

'*My word you do look queer*!' Now that's appropriate, isn't it? Anyway, it's about this guy, and he goes out feeling fine, and everybody he meets says the same thing to him. My word you do look queer!'

'And he starts to believe it.'

'That's it. Gets worse and worse till he thinks he's at death's door. Then he meets an old friend who says, *My word you do look well*! And that's it, he's transformed. In the pink. Life in the old dog yet.'

'In that case, you look great!'

'It won't wash. This is for real. I *am* at death's door.'

'I'm sorry.'

'Been HIV positive for some time now.'

'I didn't know.'

'No reason why you should.'

'And now it's worse.'

'Fullblown aids. Just a matter of time.'

Jamie came in with our tea on a tray, set it down on a little table beside the couch, squeezed Sam's hand, backed out.

'I'll be checking in to a hospice soon. For what they call palliative care. Means I won't be checking out again! It's a case of easing the pain, helping me through.'

'That's good,' I said. 'Good that you'll have support.'

'There's a wonderful Ginsberg poem,' he said. 'He wrote it on the death of Kerouac. And the end is amazing.

> *And while I'm here I'll do the work.*
> *And what's the work?*
> *To ease the pain of living.*
> *Everything else drunken dumbshow.*'

'That is beautiful,' I said.

'That *pain of living* bit reminded me of your *Mahabharata*

263

story, about human life being a curse. But it can be a blessing too.'

'Both.'

'God, it can be sweet.' He smiled. 'Now, pour the tea, and let's talk about my funeral!'

We knew time might be short, so Des made the coffin quickly, gave Sam a chance to see it. He'd chosen ocelot, loved the glitziness and kitsch of it. Had the box lined inside and out so it would be comfortable.

'I know that's ridiculous,' he said, stroking the fur. 'But for some reason it matters.'

Jamie had brought him over in a taxi, helped him downstairs to the workshop. The effort it took was immense.

'This may sound macabre,' he said, 'but do you think I could try it out?'

'No problem,' I said.

Best thing was to put the coffin on the floor. Des and I lifted it down. Then I helped Jamie ease Sam down into it, Jamie holding him under the arms, me taking his legs. So light, nothing to him.

He lay back, looking up at us like a child tucked in to bed. Smiled. 'It *is* comfortable. Cosy. Maybe you should just pull the lid over me, let me go to sleep right here, drift away. Be quite convenient really.'

Another spasm of coughing racked, shook him and he sat up sweating, eyes watering. 'No such luck though. Got to go through all this.'

We got him up on his feet again, steadied him as he stepped out.

'Nice job,' he said to Des, shaking his hand. 'Beautiful. Thanks.'

Next time I saw him he was sagging in his hospital bed. I couldn't believe the speed of his deterioration, just in a matter of weeks. Even thinner than he'd been, Belsen thin, stark caricature of himself. The nurses told me he'd fallen the day before, his legs had just buckled under him. He was losing the sight in his right eye, damage to the optic nerve.

'No joke,' he said, his voice watery, bronchial.

I nodded. Nothing I could say.

He'd wanted to talk to me about his choice of music for the funeral.

'First I was going to go for a new Joni song,' he said. 'Sex kills. Then I thought, Maybe not!'

> *And the gas leaks, and the oil spills*
> *And sex sells everything, and sex kills.*

'It's a long way from We are stardust we are golden.'

'Don't want to bring everybody down. So then I thought of the old Blondie number. Die young stay pretty.'

I laughed. 'Should raise a smile or two.'

I sang it, rapped out the reggae rhythm on the bedside table.

> *Die young, stay pretty*
> *Live fast, cause it won't last.*

He tried to join in, couldn't.

> *Deteriorate in your own time.*
> *Deteriorate in your own time.*

'That's good,' he said, getting his breath back, enough to speak. 'Then I thought something classical in the middle. You know Barber's *Adagio*?'

'Nice and sombre,' I said. 'A real weepie.'

'But exultant. The way those final chords just open out. Kronos Quartet do a great version of it.'

'Should mellow things out beautifully. Anything else?'

'The finale has to be Queen,' he said. 'Bohemian Rhapsody.'

'Nothing really matters.'

'That's it. Nice one to end on. Freddie strutting his stuff. And he's been here, been through this. Down this same road.' He looked out at me. His sunk, dark-rimmed eyes burned. 'Can I tell you something?'

'Sure.'

'I had this dream last night. Only that's not what it felt like. Not a dream. It was too vivid. Too real. More real than this.' He looked round the room, then back at me, intense. 'I was standing looking at the sea. And I wanted so much to dive in and swim, but I couldn't. I was afraid. I knew I didn't have the strength. I looked down at my body and it was dried up, covered in lesions and sores. And a voice was saying, Come on. It's time. And I stepped in to the water, felt it wash over my feet. And I waded in and it felt so good, not cold like I'd expected, but warm, friendly. I eased myself in, pushed off, and I was floating free, I'd left this behind.' He held up his bony hands in front of his face. 'I had a new body, not flesh, it was made of light. And I woke up in tears, ecstatic. And that's it, I'm ready now. There's no fear. I know I'm more than this.'

He died the next morning, while the nurses were bathing him.

The funeral went as he'd planned it, the chapel at the crematorium packed with his friends. The music did its work, made them laugh and cry. The furry coffin sat, camp and sad and ridiculous. Jamie read a short poem by Raymond Carver, one of the last he wrote, called simply *Late Fragment*.

> *And did you get what*
> *you wanted from this life, even so?*
> *I did.*
> *And what did you want?*
> *To call myself beloved, to feel myself*
> *beloved on the earth.*

All any of us wanted, God help us.

Lying in bed beside Lila, end of another long day, dealing with grief and pain and loss.
    'It goes so quick,' I said.
    'What does?'
    'A life. You can't grasp it.'
    'That's the point,' she said. 'If you try to grasp it, you lose it.'
    'So you have to let go.'

'Surrender. Be in the moment.'

'Sounds easy.'

'Wish it was.'

'You batter away at it, year in year out. Then you die.'

'What's brought this on?'

I laughed. 'I can't imagine! I mean what could possibly be filling my head with thoughts of mortality?'

She prodded me. 'I meant apart from the usual.'

'I don't know,' I said. 'We're great at talking other people through it, but how will we deal with it ourselves?'

'The way everybody else does. We'll get on with it.'

What I was trying to say. 'One of us will have to take on the other's funeral.'

'If I go first,' she said, 'keep it simple. Basic cremation. Plain coffin with just a touch of colour. Something subtle. Get Des to paint a single flower. And for the ceremony, just a couple of verses from the *Gita*. Maybe a Tagore song. That's all.'

'And the ashes?'

'Nothing special. Just scatter them.'

'Doesn't have to be in the Ganges?'

'The Clyde'll do fine! So what about you?'

'My funeral?' I tried to give it some thought, imagine it. 'Cremation as well, definitely. And for the ceremony, I'd like everybody to have a good laugh.'

'Stand up comedy?'

'Why not? Get Des to do a routine, all these crappy jokes about death!'

'Send them out smiling.'

'You realise more and more, funerals are for the living. I mean the dead don't care. They're out of it. It's the ones left behind that need the ceremonies. To make sense.'

'I know what you mean,' she said. 'At the same time, I like to think part of you is hovering around, watching the proceedings.'

'Nice thought,' I said. 'So if I'm the one left, it's the *Gita* and Tagore. And maybe just one wee joke.'

'And if it's me, I'll send you off with a stream of jokes. And one verse from the *Gita*.'

'Deal!'

We kissed, held each other, warm and alive.

A thigh-bone, a curve of pelvis, a handful of other little bits and shards of bone, odd shapes. Lila wrapped them carefully in a white cloth, took them to an address she'd found in a health-food shop.

Lothlorien. Musical instruments for the New Age. Wind. Strings. Percussion. Made to your specifications.

The old hippy who ran the business, a grizzled old hobbit called Clive, said he'd see what he could do.

He phoned a week later, said he'd bring the stuff round, if that was all right. Lila called the widow, arranged for her to come in at the same time. She arrived early, sat fidgety, nervous. Lila brought her a cup of tea, tried to put her at ease.

'It just feels strange,' said the old woman. 'Doing this. The whole thing with the instruments. I mean, he always used to say it as a bit of a joke, you know. But then he came in and spoke to you about it. And he put it in his will, that this was what he wanted. So I felt I had to see it through.'

Lila put a hand on her arm. 'It was a good thing to do. You'll see.'

'I suppose the thing was, he always wanted to play, but he never learned. So this'll be like he's playing music.'

'Or music's playing him.'

'Right.'

Clive showed up, was just the way Lila had described. Small and chunky in dungarees and donkey jacket. Kind eyes behind wireframed specs. Over his shoulder he carried a big holdall made from patterned carpet. He set it down, opened it up.

'I hope you like these,' he said to the old woman. Brought out first the pelvis, the bone polished to a dull sheen like ivory, the curves carved and shaped, accentuated, four strings stretched across to make a little aeolian harp.

'Oh my,' said the woman as he handed it to her. 'Isn't that nice.'

'Try it,' he said, and she plucked the strings, laughed at the *pling*.

'Sounds Chinese!'

'Doesn't it?' He reached in to the bag again, brought out a set of windchimes, the smaller bits of bone cut into discs and hearts and stars. He shook it and they clacked together, made a noise like dice. The old woman nodded, smiled.

Next out of the bag was a length of bamboo. He turned it upside down and it made a noise like a rush and hiss of water.

'It's a wee rainstick,' he said, upending it, making the same noise. 'It's got all the little scliffs of bone inside, along with some seashells, odds and sods.'

'Lovely and peaceful,' said the old woman, and she took the stick, turned it, made it shoosh.

'Now,' said Clive. 'This last one's the best.' And he brought out the thighbone, transformed into a flute.

'Is that no amazing?' she said, taking it from him, holding it out for us to admire.

'Do you play?' Clive asked her.

'No me,' she said.

'Do you mind if I?'

'Not at all,' she said, handing it back. 'Give us a tune.'

'In fact,' he said. He tightened the strings on the harp, tuned it, passed it to Lila. 'Just pick it, or strum. Any sequence, the tuning fits.' Then he asked me to shake the windchimes, the old woman to keep turning the rainstick, got us all playing together. It made a texture, and over the top of it he played *Amazing Grace* on the bone flute, the sound sharp and breathy like a Japanese shakuhachi. And the whole thing was funny and touching and quite eerily beautiful.

Later I noticed Lila smiling to herself.

'What?' I asked.

'A verse in the *Gita*,' she said. 'Krishna tells Arjuna, *Be Thou a mere instrument*.'

'Maybe the old boy read it. Took it literally.'

'Maybe!'

'It made me think of a Lew Welch poem,' I said. 'He was one of those old Beat poets, pal of Gary Snyder. Wandered off into the wilderness and was never seen again.'

It was from a sequence called *Hermit Poems*.

> *I saw myself*
> *a ring of bone*
> *in the clear stream*
> *of all of it*
>
> *and vowed*
> *always to be open to it*
> *that all of it*
> *might flow through*
>
> *and then heard*
> *'ring of bone' where*
> *ring is what a*
> *bell does.*

Ring of bone.

A Hindu funeral Lila organised.

The temple was an old church hall, painted white inside and out, carpeted blue and gold, bright coloured statues of Siva and Krishna, Kali and Ganesh. The coffin lay open on a raised bier covered with flowers, the dead man wrapped in a simple white cloth, a garland of marigolds round his neck. Each family member passed by, did *pranam*, dipped a finger in a little bowl of scented oil, dabbed a single drop to the dead man's forehead. Then the younger children, six of them, stood round the coffin, each one holding a lighted candle, singsong voices chanting a mantra, as a priest in orange robes clashed finger-cymbals.

The thick musk scent of incense hung in the air, and the fragrance of the flowers, the scented oils. And I felt suddenly intoxicated, lightheaded, drawn in again to this dream of India.

Siva in meditation, a cobra rearing over his head. Blue-skinned Krishna playing his flute. Kali dancing in her necklace of skulls. Ganesh's elephant head, eyes smiling, benign.

The priest chanted, a mantra I knew, had heard before.

> *Asato ma sad gamaya*
> *Tamaso ma jyotir gamaya*
> *Mrittyor ma amritam gamaya.*

Lead me from the unreal to the real. Lead me from darkness to light. Lead me from death to immortality.

At the crematorium, the dead man's oldest son had the privilege of switching on the furnace. Lila had arranged it. 'Traditionally, he'd set the flame to the funeral pyre,' she said. 'This is the equivalent.'

'Just as well they don't still believe in suttee,' I said. Or the old boy's widow would be in there with him.'

Lila gave a shudder. 'Horrible. All those poor women.'

'Burn me, burn my wife.'

'The assumption being that it's better to burn to death than live without a husband.'

'I guess it was also a way of getting rid of burdensome female relatives, not having to support them.'

'And you know the really sick part? They think the whole thing was deliberately introduced by the priests, doctoring a sacred text.'

'Dear God.'

'Misogyny or what?'

Real to the unreal.

I mentioned it to Des and he said we should offer it as a service. Optional suttee.

'URI are probably on the case already,' I said. 'Special pre-need package.'

'Burn two for the price of one.'

'Economies of scale.'

'Offering the customer more choice.'

'You *know* it makes sense.'

'I'm sure the government would be interested,' he said. 'Think what it would save in widows' pensions.'

'Why stop there? Burn the unemployed. The homeless. The old. The sick. Single mothers. Anybody claiming any kind of benefit.'

'Scrap welfare altogether.'

'The word is *modernise*.'

'Modernise or die!'

URI gave up trying to buy us out. We were just too weird to fit in with their corporate image, or to be passed off as a traditional family firm.

We'd heard stories. They hustled mourners at funerals, tried to sell them expensive memorials. They wouldn't allow the use of anything but their own coffins. In the States, they'd sent a body back home in a bag, refused to bury it because the bills hadn't been paid and the family's credit rating was bad.

These were the people who'd decided we were giving the funeral business a bad name. They assumed the increased competition would freeze us out, close us down, a process of attrition. But people kept coming to us, trusting us. We'd been recommended by a friend, or they'd read about us, thought we might still provide the human touch. We survived.

It was Lila who had the idea of a shopfront. She'd read about funeral supermarkets opening in France, a branch in London, thought we could do something similar.

'A deathmart,' said Des. 'Sounds good.'

'But do it in our own way,' she said. 'Make it really beautiful. Let people see what we're about.'

It felt right, the thing to do.

It took us six months to find the premises, an old car showroom, took three more months to fix it up. The space was laid out like a gallery, painted in bright warm colours, friendly. We brought in people we'd worked with over the years – a florist, a stonemason, a sculptor, a potter – let them set up their own areas, incorporated in the overall design. First thing you saw when you came in the door was a mass of flowers, real and artificial, and next to those were vases and urns. In the centre of the space was a fountain that might have been lifted from a Japanese garden, water trickling over a huge rough stone, river through mountains. On either side of that were a few simple headstones and some pieces of sculpture, a marble bird in flight, echoed by a Brancusi-curve of shining steel.

Further in were a few comfortable chairs, a place to browse through leaflets. The usual mundane stuff. Legal advice. Social Security entitlement. Burial or cremation. Facts about embalming.

'Planning to do hands-on demonstrations?' said Des. 'Flower display one week. Evisceration and cosmetology the next.'

'Bring in Gilbert and George,' I said. 'Rigid with Frigid.'

We had a bookstall, with books people might find helpful. *The Natural Death Book*, *Fireside Book of Death*, *How We Die*, *Tibetan Book of the Dead*. Collections of poetry, the odd novel like Waugh's *The Loved One*. Thirty or forty titles, and I realised I'd read them all, every last book on the shelves.

'Told you years ago, said Des. 'You're a morbid bastard.'

'Still seeking,' I said. 'Looking for the big answer.'

Through in the far back, behind shoji screens, were the coffins. A few traditional ones in pine and oak. Cheap eco-friendly cardboard jobs. D-I-Y flatpacks. Body-bags and shrouds. A truly beautiful structure of wicker, woven like a basket. A few curiosities, coffins that doubled as a table, a blanket-box, a bookcase. And two of Des's masterpieces, a tugboat and the bottle from Samuels' gallery. Another of his creations, a magnificent red-plumed bird of paradise, was on display in the front window, caught the eye from the street.

A good crowd had turned up for the opening, along with the press and a TV crew from the teatime news. We were good headline fodder. *Coffin you carry off (in a pack). Tomb it may concern.* Variations on *Shop till you drop.*

Straining.

Old greyhair from Findhorn was there. Years since he'd first come to see me. Amazed he was still alive. He was going ahead and building his compostorium, on a friend's farm in the Borders. He wondered if I'd take a few leaflets, let people know about it. A green option.

Sure. No problem.

Mulch.

Laurel and Hardy had showed up, the men from URI, taking notes. No doubt The Firm were making plans for a megastore on a greenbelt site. A large scale pre-need retail opportunity.

I saw Vulture Man deep in conversation with Eric the Anorak, felt a momentary panic at the thought they might gang up on me, talk me to death. Good copy for the press. Become another hands-on demonstration, laid out maybe in the bird of paradise in the front window. And the camera crew right there. Doing a Tommy Cooper, dying on TV. Just like that.

But no, the two men ignored me, talked on, seriously interactive, opening up worlds of possibility. Virtual sky-burial. Virtual vultures picking virtual entrails. Virtual towers of virtual silence.

I turned away, left them to it, saw Andy coming towards me. An old man now, he'd aged, the way it happens, not gradually but with sudden acceleration. One day you're old. Just like that.

'Still using the noddle, young fella?' He shook my hand, looked round. 'Changed days, eh? Ach aye, you've done well for yourself. And I know this wouldn't have been your old man's style, but I think he'd have been proud.'

Sure.

The TV crew butted in, asked if they could take one last shot of me and Lila outside. We posed and grinned in front of the window, the sign up above, WAY TO GO, shining in blue neon.

Sri Ramakrishna knew that one of his disciples – a young man – was dying. He told the family to send for the best doctors, but he knew the boy would not recover.

Ramakrishna was at the bedside when the boy died. The family wept for their loss, but Ramakrishna laughed aloud. He felt no grief, just stood there and watched. He said it was like seeing a sword being drawn out of its sheath. The sword was still the sword as before, its blade shining. Nothing had happened to it. And the sheath lay there, empty.

This is how a man dies, he said, how the soul leaves the body. And when he saw it, he was overwhelmed with joy. Why should they grieve?

They took the body away and burned it, and Ramakrishna laughed and sang and danced.

But the next day he returned to the house and was overwhelmed by a sense of grief and loss. He experienced the pain of it, what the family had gone through. He said he felt as if a wet towel was being wrung inside his heart.

If I feel so much pain, he asked, what agony must these householders suffer?

Ramakrishna had to understand both sides.

Both true.

8

First sign was so slight I almost didn't notice. Thought nothing of it. Let it pass. Began with stomach pain. Constipation followed by diarrhoea. Something I'd eaten maybe, though Lila was fine. Go and see the doctor, she said, and I didn't. But it went on for a week, two. Got worse. Hurt a bit when I shat. No joke. Managed to make an appointment the following week. Sat half an hour in the waiting room, staring at a fishtank, listening to people cough and hack and sniff, thought if I wasn't sick when I came in, I would be by the time I left.

The doctor was a young man, thirty, give or take. Looked tired and pale, unhealthy. The little things you remember, the details. A nick in front of his ear, a shaving cut clotted. A bit of stubble he'd missed, under the jawline. I stared at a kid's drawing, a house with curly smoke, done in bright felt-tip, as he asked me questions, made notes, how long I'd been experiencing discomfort, any change in the colour of my stools, their smell. This was getting personal.

He prodded, poked, noted where it hurt. Checked something in a book, said '*Hm*.' Tapped his lips with his pen, said he'd like me to see a specialist for tests.

'It might be nothing.'

Drab feeling of tiredness from him. End of the day.

Nothing.

'Or?'

Metastasis. The nature of cancer's malignancy, to spread, migrate, rampage through your system. Vicious streetgang out of control, ripping up the neighbourhood.

What the surgeon found was an advanced carcinoma, necrotic at the centre. Meant rotting. The really bad thing was it had already metastasized into the surrounding tissue, invaded the lymph nodes, the vascular system.

'So it's just a matter of time,' he said, 'before other organs are affected, if they're not already.'

'Not sounding too good then,' I said.

'You could say that.'

'In fact the prognosis is fucking terrible.'

'Afraid so.'

So hard to find the words, to voice the question, because that meant accepting, admitting it.

'So how long?'

'Hard to say. I don't like holding out false hope.'

'So hold out real hope.'

'Even if there isn't any?'

'How long?'

'Three, maybe six months.'

'Fucking hell.'

'I'm afraid some of it may be, yes.'

Lila said no. Kept saying no. Wouldn't believe it. There had to be a way.

Radiation. Chemotherapy. Poison me or nuke me.

What the surgeon said was in twenty-five years, he'd only seen genuine remission in three or four cases like this. And none of them had been as far gone as me. He said the oncologists would advise me to have the treatment, they almost always did. But I had to balance that against the almost certainty I'd die anyway. I had to consider whether I wanted to spend my last few months suffering the side effects of treatment that probably wouldn't work.

'Some choice,' I said to Lila. 'Kill or cure.'

Killer cure.

She kissed the top of my head, held me close.

Rab came in to visit, was awkward, not knowing where to look. He'd brought me some fruit, in a plastic bag, set it down rustling on the bedside table. Stood there uncomfortable, eventually found the words.

'It's a bastard, eh?'

'It is that,' I said. 'Hit the coffin-nail right on the head. Death is a bastard.'

*

'So,' said Des.

'Aye.'

'Fucking bombshell.'

'I'm claimed,' I said. 'The Reaper's asked me outside for a square go. Except it isn't. He's got this big chib.'

'Ach,' said Des. 'Stick the head on him. The old Glasgow kiss. Tell him to fuck off.'

The surgeon was right. The oncologists advised a course of chemotherapy. Three months initially. Three of my precious months. Lila not wanting to give up. The slightest chance. Fuck it. I said yes.

Three months of toxic cocktails, mainly interferon. I had to go back to hospital so the treatment could be monitored, as the drugs, like the cancer itself, tore through me. A gang war, one heavy mob taking on another, my body the wasteground where they fought it out. I'd never known misery like it. Cure worse than the disease. Constant nausea and headache. Vomiting and diarrhoea, leaving me red raw. Deep-rooted pain right inside the bones.

By the end of it I felt ravaged. The original tumour had shrunk a little, but its outreach had spread even further.

When they suggested radiation I said no. I wanted to go home, face this in my own way. Deteriorate in my own time.

Before I checked out of the hospital, a woman came to talk to me. Her name was Molly and she was Irish, I'd guess in her fifties, had an easy relaxed way about her, a warmth. She was some kind of counsellor, a therapist.

'You're used to dealing with death,' she said.

'Not my own.'

'Takes a leap of imagination, doesn't it?'

'And how.'

She smiled. 'It's all about letting go. That's the hard part.'

'You still want to hope,' I said.

'And so you must. It's right.'

'But how does that square with letting go?'

'Letting go is surrender. Acceptance of what happens.'

'What about hope of remission? The miracle cure?'

'That can be good too,' she said. 'But it can get in the way. Stop you seeing clear.'

'A kind of denial.'

'Exactly.'

'So what's to hope for that isn't denial?'

'A good death.'

'And that's it?' I said. 'God, I sound like Woody Allen!'

She laughed. 'Death can be messy. More than likely will be. But the hope is, we can face it. Be ready.'

'Let go.'

'Something that can help is to see your life as a story. And in telling it, you find its pattern, its meaning.'

'You mean write it down?'

'Why not?'

To make this daft life into a story. Write it down, tell it. To see it clear, give it shape. To accept it, and let it go. My own death the end of it. The answer to my big question on the last page.

I borrowed the laptop we used for accounts, started writing, discovered the form as I went along. I wrote it like a novel, changed bits, exaggerated for emphasis. I read out some of the funny bits to Lila, made her laugh.

She hadn't given up that other kind of hope. Cure. Remission. With a single bound the hero was free. She was reading about alternative remedies, aromatherapy, a detox diet, visualisation exercises. She gave me grape juice, massive doses of Vitamin C. She found a mantra for good health, and we chanted it together, selfconscious at first till something came through the words, a power.

> *Tejohasi tejomayi dhehi*
> *Viryamasi viryam mayi dhehi*
> *Valam masi valam mayi dhehi*

A prayer for dynamism, energy, strength.

It might have been the mantra, or the remedies. More likely it was Lila, the sheer force of her will, her love. But I started to feel better than I had in months.

My father came and stood at the end of my bed. Spoke to me in a language I'd never heard and couldn't understand. I woke up crying.

Intense awareness of light. Light all around me, flowing through my whole being. Myself expanding into it, becoming light.

Those near-death experiences you read about, emerging from a tunnel, entering into radiance. A real foretaste of eternity? Or the brain's chemical laboratory going into overdrive *in extremis*, producing a last narcotic high to ease the way to extinction?

That Kurt Vonnegut novel, *Sirens of Titan*. Two images of the hero at the end. Flying in a Tralfmadorian spaceship, meeting old friends he'd thought were dead. Then set down in the street, snow falling, to wait for a bus he doesn't catch, because he freezes to death, an old downandout, stiff and cold on a bench. But at the same time, *at the same time*, he's flying again in the spaceship, heading home. The two realities are simultaneous, juxtaposed.

Princess Diana's funeral on TV, I couldn't believe what I was watching, this enormous outrush of grief, public and orchestrated, but tapping something real and deep, an overwhelming sense of loss.

The strangest part was people clapping as the hearse passed by, bearing the coffin through London.

'What is that all about?' I said, sitting up on the couch. 'What are they clapping for?'

'It's showbiz,' said Des. 'I guess they don't know what else to do.'

'Applauding a coffin!'

'It's like throwing the flowers,' said Lila. 'There's a need to *do* something, be part of the event.'

Des chuckled. 'Just something I read in the paper. About this family that set up a shrine for Diana in their living room, with her picture and flowers and candles, the whole bit. Only the candles must have caught on something, set the shrine on fire. Burned the whole house down!' He laughed again. 'Sorry. I don't know why that's funny.'

But even Des had been touched by actually seeing people going down and placing flowers in George Square.

'OK,' he said, 'in one way they're doing what they see on TV, the whole thing is created by the media. But it really meant something to them. You could see it.'

On screen, the hearse continued on its slow way through the streets as the crowds moved forward, threw more and more flowers.

'It's beautiful,' said Lila. 'Almost devotional. People need to rediscover that, find that part of them that hasn't been numbed and deadened, can still feel. And of course it gets maudlin and over the top. But through all that there's something genuine. People really do want to believe, in beauty and grace, a kind of goodness. She seemed to embody all that, even though her life was a mess. And now it's snuffed out. It's sad.'

I heard the choke in her voice, the tears at the back of it. She took my hand. Des said he had to be going, took off.

'I'm sorry,' she said, and she slumped in on herself, cried. 'It's this.' She pointed at the screen. 'It just brings up everything you try to keep down. That's what's happening to all these people. There's the whole communal thing, the mourning. But it's individualised. It's personal. It makes you grieve for what you've lost, what you'll lose. It brings it home.'

'Ach,' I said, holding her. 'I know.'

Seeing Borges years ago on TV, on the Wogan show of all things. Surreal combination. Borges old and frail, almost translucent, blind. Wogan sleek and smug, doing the twinkly Irish banter.

Not the exact words, but the gist of it.

Well, Jorge, you're old and blind and death can't be far away. How d'you feel about it?

And Borges answering, a lightness still in the voice.

I've had a good life, and I'm ready for death. I'd be happy to die today. No, wait, I've got some friends coming round for dinner tonight. So let's make it tomorrow. Oh. No. Sorry, there's a concert I want to hear tomorrow. So, the day after?

The day after tomorrow.

A good day to die.

Des brought me a newspaper article about the death of the Reverend McNaught.

'You won't believe this!' he said, laughing.

We hadn't seen McNaught for years, not since he'd raged at a family for taking a group photo after a funeral. 'You think this is a happy occasion?' he'd shouted. 'Something to be commemorated? It's a time for mourning and lamentation, not preening and posing for cameras!' And he'd more or less thrown them out of the church.

Now and again we'd read about him in the papers. He'd eventually left the Kirk, set up a church of his own, the True Free Brethren. With a handful of followers, he was forever demonstrating outside galleries and theatres, denouncing ungodly exhibitions and performances. He guaranteed good box office.

He'd also taken to preaching in the city centre, in shopping precincts. The article said his last sermon had been in Argyle Street, the Saturday after Diana's funeral. He'd ranted at the idolatory of the whole thing, of addressing her as if she were to be worshipped. Speaking to the dead as if they were alive, he said, had its roots in Roman Catholicism, in praying to the plethora of saints. This displayed the most abysmal spiritual darkness. It was taken for granted that the Princess had entered Heaven. But what warrant was there for such an assumption? Those who opted for the hollow happiness of the world could not be classed as righteous and godly, no matter what good works they might do.

As well as the funeral itself, he said, the floral tributes, the books of condolence, the entire display of mass hysteria, were all quite deplorable. And as for centre stage being taken by Elton

John, a singer whose immorality was public knowledge, it was offensive in the extreme.

As McNaught had worked himself up in righteous wrath, a crowd had gathered. At first they'd just laughed, heckled a bit. Then they'd started getting angry, shouting abuse, and that had only fired up his rage.

What next? he'd asked. Canonisation? Will it be Saint Diana? Or even Saint Elton? We lived in a dark age, and here was the proof. What they'd witnessed that week was unacceptable to the majesty of Heaven. It was a refusal to accept that the taking of Diana was the providence of the Lord.

As he'd reached full rant, screaming at his hecklers, McNaught had suddenly burst into flame, apparently burned up from within, consumed in a matter of minutes. By the time the police arrived, and an ambulance, and a fire engine, there was nothing much left of him.

At first the police had assumed there was foul play, he'd been firebombed, or doused in petrol and torched. But the inquest had come to the conclusion it was a case of spontaneous combustion.

The newspaper headline was *Holy Smoke*.

'That's the most bizarre thing I've ever read!' I said.

'I told you,' said Des. 'Straight out *The X-files*.'

'You think McNaught was an alien?'

'Would explain a lot! But at least it proves one thing. God's got a sense of humour.'

The Reaper came at me in the night, hacked at my bowels again and again with his vicious blade. Said *Make a fucking joke out of this/this/this*.

I spoke to Des about my funeral, told him he should start stockpiling jokes. He asked me, tentatively, if I'd given any thought to the coffin.

'Good question,' I said. 'What to make for the undertaker? I guess we could be really radical, and do one that looked like a coffin!'

'Only we'd know it was a copy, a replica.'

'We'd be quoting. A nicely ironic piece of postmodernism.'
'No, but seriously,' said Des.
'Seriously.'
'Whatever you want.'

A simple pine box, painted sky-blue with that weathered look, a wash, a natural fade. A brush-drawing on the lid in darker blue, a single stroke, A Zen circle, incomplete.
'That's all?' said Des.
'That's all.'

A dream I had. I was with Lila, though it didn't look like her, somewhere like Manhattan, though it wasn't. We took an elevator to the top of a high building. But I knew I had to go further. She waited and I climbed on, up a ladder through a narrow shaft. Emerged into a beautiful garden that opened into fantastic landscapes, the colours vividly intense. Animals roamed around, some of them dangerous. I glimpsed a tiger, snarling, a snake darting under a rock. I had to go past them to get where I was going, and my fear faded as I walked. I came to a huge white building, a palace. I went inside. In the centre of the palace was a courtyard, and in the centre of the courtyard was a fountain, and beside it were a man and woman on horseback. I realised they were my mother and father, both young. I was overwhelmed with delight at seeing them. My mother said she had a present for me, got off the horse and walked with me to a doorway. You'll come again soon, she said, handing me the gift wrapped in gold paper. I stepped through the doorway into a lift that took me back down to the high building where I'd left Lila. I started to tell her what had happened, where I'd been. But as I spoke, I realised my parents were both dead. And I woke up still tasting the intoxication I'd felt in the garden, but with it the immense sadness of loss.

The symptoms came back again, pain and fever, nausea. I lost weight, was constantly tired. I was more and more selective about what I could read. A handful of books. Japanese death verses. Gospel of Ramakrishna. Ray Carver's late poems. A few others. Books that could still speak to me in this last place.

Ramakrishna died of throat cancer. As he lay on his deathbed, one of his followers begged to be allowed to take some of the suffering from him. Ramakrishna said, 'Where do you think I got it from in the first place?' Taking on their karma, their pain.

One of the Carver poems I wanted to read out to Lila. But I knew I wouldn't get through it. Carver's cancer started in the brain, spread to the lungs. He kept working, kept writing to the end.

The poem was called *No need*. I handed Lila the book, open at the page.

'Says it all.'

> *I see an empty place at the table.*
> *Whose? Who else's? Who am I kidding?*
> *The boat's waiting. No need for oars*
> *or a wind. I've left the key*
> *in the same place. You know where.*
> *Remember me and all we did together.*
> *Now, hold me tight. That's it. Kiss me*
> *hard on the lips. There. Now*
> *let me go, my dearest. Let me go.*
> *We shall not meet again in this life,*
> *so kiss me goodbye now. Here, kiss me again.*
> *Once more. There. That's enough.*
> *Now, my dearest, let me go.*
> *It's time to be on the way.*

When she'd read it, and re-read it, she nodded. Put the book down and held me. We said nothing a long time.

'It's going to come to that,' I said. 'Sometime. You're going to have to let me go.'

'I know,' she said. 'But not yet. Not now. It's too soon.'

Way too soon.

My father came again, stood there looking at me, not speaking in tongues this time. Not speaking at all. Finally said just one thing, smiled a way I'd never seen, with compassion. *You have to learn.*

The Reaper was sitting at the edge of an open grave, his legs dangling over. Beckoned me to sit beside him and I did. He looked like the old sadhu I'd met in Varanasi, and I felt no fear. I wanted to ask him my question. I can answer it, he said, but only in silence.

Listening to music on the radio, through headphones, surfing till I found something I wanted to hear. Sometimes getting that sense of it all as personalised soundtrack, two or three songs in a row speaking right to me. Verve. James. Pulp. The drugs don't work. All roads lead on to Death Row. Stop asking questions that don't matter anyway.

Then some dance track pounding my brains. Switch to Radio 3, catch part of the Mozart *Requiem*, the one he's supposed to have written for himself, all sombre gravitas. Let it carry me, bear me up. Switch off and lie in silence when it's finished.

The decline was faster than I expected. The pain unremitting. Sores on my legs that wouldn't heal. Festering lesions under the arms. Diarrhoea and vomiting. Inability to eat. No other way, I had to go back to the hospital. Lila didn't want me to, but finally agreed. Let me go. Time to be on the way.

Deteriorate in your own time. Child in question. Ring of bone. Intensive care. Jewel in the lotus. A Glasgow kiss. Hell's teeth. Good hope. Shards. Particles. Rain. A policy of isolation. The divided self. Billion-year-old carbon. Continental drift. Black holes. Dancing in the dark. A hill of beans. Silt.

Fed from a drip. Morphine for the pain. I could go any time. Next week. Tomorrow. In five minutes. Now.

What happens when you die?

*

It's as if am watching it all, Tom Sawyer at the back of the church, late for his own funeral. Mr Sim at the crematorium has given us a double slot. Gratitude for all the business over the years, my father before me etcetera.

The blue coffin is carried in, placed on the catafalque, Bach on the tape, Glenn Gould playing the aria that begins the *Goldberg Variations*.

When everyone is settled, the tape switches to Laurie Anderson. *Born, Never Asked.*

> *It was a large room full of people, all kinds.*
> *And they'd all arrived at the same building*
> *at more or less the same time.*
> *And they were all asking the same question.*
> *What*
> *is behind*
> *that curtain!*

As the riff on the synth fades out, Des stands up, comes forward. He puts his notes on the lectern in front of him. Takes a deep breath, starts.

'A horse walks into this bar. The barman says, Hey! Why the long face?'

Delayed response, a burst of surprised laughter, one or two chuckles.

'Neil really liked that joke. No accounting for taste, eh? But also, I think it's what he wanted to say to you today. Why the long face? Life's too short. That's why he asked me to get up here like a wally and tell all these crap jokes. And that's what death is. The ultimate crap joke.

'So here we go.'

He looks about him, nods at the coffin.

'Of course funerals don't come cheap these days. Know what I'm saying? No wonder they talk about the dear departed.

'But you can't take it with you, can you? Like they say, there's no pockets in a shroud.

'There's these three guys, a Scotsman, an Englishman and an Irishman. Of course. And their friend dies. He'd be a Welshman, of course. And he leaves a last request that his friends put a wee bit money in the coffin, to be buried with him. Fine, says the Irishman, and he puts in a fiver. And the Englishman's not to be outdone, he puts in a tenner. Then the Scotsman says, I'll put in fifteen. So he writes a cheque for thirty, and takes back the fifteen as his change.

'Ach aye. Funny old business.

'Old couple came in last week, and they're arguing away, slagging each other off. Eventually the old woman says, When you go, I'll dance on your grave. The old boy says, Fine, I'm going to be buried at sea.

'Boom Boom!

'Another old guy insisted that a bottle of whisky be poured over his grave. His old crony says, No problem, I'll just pass it through my kidneys first.

'Old people are funny about death, aren't they? No offence missis. But take my mother. Please! No, but she's what you might call obsessive. I went to visit her the other week and she's sitting reading the obituaries and going through the phone book, scoring out names.

'For my birthday last year, she bought me a burial plot. Fine. I'd always wanted to own a piece of land. This year she didn't buy me anything. What's up? I said. Why didn't you give me a present? She says, You didn't use the one I gave you last year.

'At my old man's funeral, the minister got as far as Ashes to Ashes, and she says, See! I told you where he'd end up!

'Ah well.

'Sometimes you do get worried all the same. Just last week, I caught the bouquet at a funeral.

'Mortality, eh?

'One thing I don't relish is having to break the news that somebody's died.

'This young soldier's away with his regiment, and word comes through that his mother's died. So the CO calls in the sergeant major, tells him to break the news to the lad. But for God's sake, he says, do it gently.

'So the sergeant major calls the whole squad out to the parade ground. Barks out an order. Right! All of you whose mothers are still alive, dismiss! Johnston! Where do you think you're going?

'Suppose nowadays you could send round a singing telegram.

'Weird.

'Reading a will. What's that about? A roomful of people hearing a statement from somebody dead saying he's of sound mind and body.

'And don't people die some strange deaths? These two guys are on a motorbike, and it's a really freezing windy day. And the guy that's the pillion passenger is getting fed up with his coat ballooning up in the wind. So they stop, and he puts his coat on back to front to stop it happening. Couple of miles down the road, they go off the road, smack into a tree. The driver's killed outright, the guy with the coat's knocked out. Later on, the coroner arrives, asks this young policeman what happened.

'Well, he says, one of them was dead when I got here. And by the time we'd straightened round the other one's head, he was dead too.

'Got to laugh, eh?

'That's all, folks.'

Lila gets up, graceful in her white sari, changes the whole atmosphere just by standing there.

'We had a deal. A kind of trade-off. All these jokes for one passage from the *Gita*. So here it is.

'As a man casts off an old worn-out garment and puts on new clothes, so the embodied soul leaves aside the worn-out body and enters into a new form for manifestation.

'The body is perishable. The soul, the real in us, is deathless, immortal. Beyond birth and death, constant and eternal is the soul.

'Weapons cannot cleave it, fire cannot consume it, water cannot drench it, wind cannot dry it.'

Lila bows with folded hands, sits down.

With that soft whirr and hum, an electric aum, the coffin starts its slide through.

The tape plays again, a lot of hiss because it's a rough copy we made from TV. Allen Ginsberg singing *Father Death Blues*.

Hey Father Death, I'm flying home

There is a brief silence after that. Then Lila gets up, bows again, leads the way out. The last piece of music is the final reprise of the Bach aria, the *da capo* from the end, back to where we started, complexity resolved in simplicity. Yes we are mortal, the music says, this life ends. But in the moment we can know eternity.

Later, the body in its blue coffin is taken from the committal room, slid into the furnace and incinerated. I see this as if watching a film. This body, something I once was, reduced to ash and fragments of bone. When it cools it is raked into a cremulator, pulverised by steel ballbearings, the ash sifted into a ceramic urn. What I asked Lila to do. She takes the cremains to Pyrotech, a company that makes fireworks to order. The ash is mixed with gunpowder, packed into a dozen rockets.

After dark they go down to the river, Lila and Des, Rab and his wife Helen, old Andy, a few others. There's a gap-site that used to be a shipyard and was briefly a festival garden.

It's late autumn, the air sharp with the first real chill. City lights across the water. Stream of traffic on the motorway. Above it all a big round moon, almost full.

Lila has brought the rockets, carries them carefully, wrapped in a white cloth. Des and Rab help her push the sticks into the soft ground, angled, lined up in a row ready for lift-off.

Des hands her a lighter and she flicks and flicks it with her thumb, the wheel grinding. Flicks a third time and it takes. She bends to the first rocket, holds the flame to the touch paper, steps back. It splutters and fizzles, then it catches, flares, swishes into the air trailing smoke. They all cheer and laugh as it explodes, showers sparks. And they take turns, light all the rockets in quick succession, watch them soar, one after another, starburst of colour, momentary mandala, these ashes the last of me scattered into the night.

after the fireworks
cold and still
the moon